WAVES OF LOVE

Lettice stood frozen with fear on the dark deck of the ship. Someone was creeping up behind her. She opened her mouth to scream a warning, but a hand closed over her lips. A knife point pricked her neck while savage indignities were murmured harshly into her ear. In panic, she kicked out, then felt the knife break her skin.

There was a sudden rush of air from above, and Geoffrey landed beside her. Lettice could sense but not see the struggle of the two men. There were blows and grunts of pain. Finally a skull struck the bulkhead with a sickening thud. A body slid to the deck.

She called his name softly. "Geoffrey?"

"I am here," he answered, and his strong and reassuring hand reached hers.

Blindly, they held each other. She still shook with fear and cold. His body warmed hers. "I could tell something was amiss," he said. "Foolish wench. It is an ill task for a lady to play rescuer." His words were tender as he slipped his arms under her soaked mantle to draw her closer. His touch burned into her rain-chilled flesh. He bent to kiss her lips. Startled, Lettice made as though to move away, but he held her fast. Then she met his passion eagerly. A sweet liqueur seemed to spread from his mouth to hers and throughout her body. They clung to each other longer than was safe, forgetful of danger. . . .

Also by Avis Worthington:

Bitter Honey

Love's Willing Servant

Avis Worthington

PINNACLE BOOKS   LOS ANGELES

LOVE'S WILLING SERVANT

An original Pinnacle Books edition, published for the first time anywhere.

First printing, December 1980

ISBN: 0-523-41017-4

Cover illustration by Norm Eastman

Printed in the United States of America

PINNACLE BOOKS, INC.
2029 Century Park East
Los Angeles, California 90067

ACKNOWLEDGEMENTS

To those experienced swordsmen and members of the Society for Creative Anachronism, Nicholas Addison Worthington and Richard Louis Worthington for technical information.

To Cleo Jones for editorial help and moral support.

Love's Willing Servant

I

Fixing her eyes upon the carved oak door of the small parlor, a young woman not yet 20 waited for the sounds of footsteps. Like a confined panther she paced, her silk skirts rustling. She warmed her hands over the fire that burned in a huge fireplace surmounted by a carved-oak chimney piece. Her eyes settled on the family arms painted there— azure with a bend argent, decorated with a silver dagger.

This day seemed to mark the end of her branch of the family—the Cliffords—who had always been a passionate and heedless lot, filled with the same desires she felt.

Outside, unwatched, another spring stirred through England, and the countryside awoke. King Charles was restored to his throne. War-ruined houses were lost in an overgrowth of thorn and ivy; cut forests sprouted. Up in London, Sir Christopher Wren started the work of rebuilding after the Great Fire. By this year of 1675 the worst had been forgotten.

But the worst had only just come to Brookside. Rain misted over the small diamond panes of the little parlor so that the drenched English landscape was reduced to a gray-green blur. The rest of the manor house was even drearier—hangings, old weapons and armor pulled from the walls, only a few pieces of furniture unsold. Brookside was a solid house, built to serve generations, but plainly its present owner was packed to abandon the place.

The lady, Lettice Clifford, sat to watch the door again. She was listening for Molly, the last of her servants, who would soon usher in the visitor her mistress had bid come. Lettice had known Philip Isham since both were in infant dress. All her life she would run to him, laughing without

1

ceremony, to hang about his neck, teasing and joking. But she must not today. It had only been a minute or two since Molly had left, but Lettice sat with clenched fists, her nails digging into her palms. Waiting did not suit her nature.

Two years, Lettice thought, since Philip had been sent by his father to the Inns of Court in London to become familiar with the law as befitted a large landholder.

She glanced about. How would the stripped parlor seem to him? A single ornament remained—a rather severe, heavily framed portrait of her long-gone mama, thin face circled by a lace-trimmed collar, a gleam of white on the dark varnished background. Enormous gold brocade sleeves disguised mama's lifelong frailty. Alas, the portrait painter was at fault. Mama was never severe, only weak and vacillating, lost among the vibrant Cliffords. Mama had educated her daughters herself in the secrets of housewifery and of letters. But Lettice had inherited the character of the Cliffords.

Now mourning her father, too, she must look much like a stark ink blot against the dark paneling. Lettice lifted the looking-glass tied to her girdle to see. A small, white cape over her throat and bosom and her fine white undersleeves were the only relief to the darkness. Black really made her skin look more creamy, but her sunny nature felt confined nonetheless.

She sighed, letting the glass fall. Her low spirits were more likely to turn Philip away than her dress. All their lives they had wildly ridden about the countryside—she often racing with more daring than he. Their games were their secret. He would help her to present a smooth cheek and unruffled exterior to the grownups. She longed to be able to ride out with him again—perhaps with a falcon—and forget all this somberness with a kiss and a caress, with his soft touch upon her tender nipple.

At last she heard sounds, and the door opened. Philip stood there, blond hair long and curled, scarlet ribbons tied at his knees, sword at his side. His short scarlet cape was turned back over his shoulders, showing its gold lining. He had grown more elegant. Perhaps that was why his expression seemed more serious than usual.

What did this serious look mean? She lowered her head for a moment.

"Lettice!" Philip demanded.

She rose to her feet, the rustling of the black silk the only sound in the room. He stretched narrow, strong hands to her.

"Lettice!" Though he spoke her name clearly enough, his tongue seemed somehow twisted as he uttered the rest. "Your eyes are . . . as beautiful . . . and as blue as . . . ever." His lips upon hers felt cold, but they soon blazed up so that she began to relax, clasping him about his green velvet jerkin. Warm tears filled her eyes as they parted. Her voice was husky.

"I was afraid you would not come."

His hand pressed hers. As he raised it to his soft and sensual lips, the old familiar warmth began to spread from their twined and tingling fingers.

"What is happening, Lettice? The house is empty. I am sorry, sweeting, that I had to be gone when your father died."

"It has been very hard." She leaned against him, her free hand toying with a silver button on his jerkin. "And my cousin will arrive presently to take the house. But worst of all, I heard the hardest rumors in the neighborhood. They said you were to wed Mary Wells. I would have laughed, but with Father dead, it was dismal." Giving the button a final twist, she looked up at him, half smiling.

He turned away to stare out through the rain-spotted panes of the casement and into the gathering evening. In the gray light Lettice could see his high cheekbones and long, almost severe nose in profile. She did not like the expression on his face.

"I have married Mary Wells—two weeks ago—in London."

Lettice drew in a painful breath as though he had slapped her. Furiously she fought to control her tears while the enormity of his betrayal choked her.

"Married! You said you would marry me, Philip! Me, and no one else! You promised to resist any pressures they would put upon you. From the days of Cromwell, when we were still lisping babies, you said it—that you would marry Lettice Clifford and no one else!" Biting off her angry words, she stared at Philip's narrow-featured face. Had she ever really seen him? His skin was pale and fine as a maid's, though it was stretched upon a frame undoubtedly

3

masculine. But was there something not quite sound, not quite honest, about this face that she had always loved?

As she shakily sat upon an oak bench, her skirts belling below her waist, Philip went down on one knee before her. His wide, fine Spanish boots creaked only slightly, they were of such fine quality. He touched her smooth cheek with a finger. Light from the fire cast warm highlights upon their clothing.

"Sweeting," he soothed. "We were but children. It was but a baby's game."

She raised her head slowly, meeting his eyes with her own smoldering ones. "Then you did not mean it!" she accused.

Philip's brow wrinkled. "Of course I meant it. I loved you more than life itself—and do so still. But what children cannot understand is that gentlemen do not marry for love, but for property."

Lettice straightened, stretching her slender neck proudly. A deep flush washed pink over her bosom, which was showing plainly beneath the white lace. She drew a breath from the very soles of her feet, feeling her cheeks burn as she spoke. "It is true I have no property. What was not entailed in favor of my cousin went long ago to the King's cause."

Philip's gray eyes sharpened. "And had your father looked to his family affairs after the King was restored instead of spending his days in drink and hunting. . . ."

Lettice's violet eyes flashed. "Pray you stop, Philip! My father is dead."

Philip leaped impatiently to his feet. "I'm sorry, sweeting. But it pains me that he thought so little of his daughter that he did not see to her fortune."

Tears of injured pride filled Lettice's eyes. "What more is there to say? You have your . . . your . . . wife and her fortune. It only remains for you to leave. It seems your own fortune, large as it is, was not enough. You are blessed, Philip. Your father had more political acquaintances than mine and survived the bad times better."

"I dare not ever go against my father," Philip said seriously. "His estates are prospering under His Majesty, and he seeks to make what connections he can for the family."

"I, alas, have no connections. My estate is entailed."

"You have me, my dear." Philip knelt beside her again,

placing a hand over hers. "I will not let you go. My father relent, hearing him speak in that way of his heart.

He kissed her brow with soft affection as she began to relent, hearing him speak in the way of his heart.

"How could Mary compare with you, hmmm?" He nuzzled her neck. His long fingers twined in her hair. "Her brown hair is like worn linen, yours like silk. Her skin has a greenish cast; yours is like white petals blushed with pink." He sighed. "I fear that bedding Mary is but a grim duty. Besides, I doubt the woman ever laughs."

Lettice drew away from his magnetic warmth. The mention of Mary made her uneasy. She clasped her slender hands with their tapering fingers and looked studiously upon the oak floor.

"I would prefer less eloquence and more sound action, Philip. You have often become overblown when the matter required simple thought."

"Sweeting." He laughed as he had always done whenever she had chastised him. "How can I refrain from eloquence when I look at you?"

She turned away, making her voice as steady as she could. "How would you care for me, Philip?"

Seizing her hand, he pulled her about on the bench to face him, smiling eagerly. His face was level with hers. In truth he made a dashing figure, the young cavalier. She had known him as a ragtag boy, running through the fields. Yet the man was the same as the boy.

"There is an empty cottage on our estate," he said. "Big enough for you and your maid. And a garden so that you will not miss the one at home."

Lettice considered. "And you would place me there, returning when you must to your wife?"

"Yes."

Suddenly Lettice flushed with rage. "And you and Mary and your children would live in your father's large house and receive the whole of the countryside and give balls, while I and my children sit by the chimney in a poor cottage?"

Philip looked at her blankly, his long, light curls framing his handsome face. He gestured as though to brush that consideration aside. "I had not thought of children." Then he smiled impishly. "Sweeting, do not worry. We will provide something. Something will be done."

5

"Oh, Philip," she began sadly. "You are trying to make me your second choice—an outcast." She rose and began to pace tensely, speaking nervously with scorn, her silk petticoats hissing.

"Philip, you would ruin me. I have waited too long for you as it is. Many a daughter is married years before my age, though my sister was married late and to an ill-tempered man who dragged her half across the world. But you are right, Philip. We Clifford daughters could have bargained better if we had been left fortunes."

Philip sprang to her side, seizing her wrist and raising it to his lips. "You are having one of your rages. As I recall, I am the only one who has ever been able to make you angry," he said with self-satisfaction. Opening her fist, he gently kissed her palm. "Please be soothed, my love. And think, after all, what other choice have you? Do you expect to wander the roads and hedgerows? Or find some genteel household willing to take you in to perform menial tasks? If you belonged to the old Church, you might go into a convent."

Laughing at her foolishness, he drew her into his arms. His hands spread over her black mourning garments as he murmured into her silky hair, "I could never let you go. How sweet you smell! Ever since I was a lad, no matter what woman I was with, I have thought only of you, Lettice."

For an instant she started to melt, but his words were wrong. They jarred. Her arms slackened from about him as she realized with surprise that at the back of her mind some shadow of caution about Philip had always lurked. He seemed almost—dare she admit it?—laughable. A clown in his red and gold cloak. "I cannot do what you ask."

His fingers tightened on her arm. "Oh, can you not?" his voice mocked. "Though you are above eighteen or nineteen years old now, my pretty, you do not know the ways of a man with a maid. All the sweet tussling we did in this corner and that as gangling children is only the beginning. There is much more to be learned, and nineteen is riper than sixteen."

"And do you know so much, then, Philip?" she cried. "You were always the braggart, I think. Have you practised with many ladies?"

6

"Oh, yes, my dear. And most often not with ladies. I have much to show you." His gray eyes were steady with purpose as he pressed his body down upon hers, awkwardly, upon the oak bench. It was too small for them to lie upon full-length. Kissing her deeply, he felt the insides of her lips with his tongue. Then he straightened to look into her eyes, judging his effect.

Feeling a honeyed weakness flow through her body, the familiar love desire he had always known how to evoke, she turned her face aside, gasping. But this hard persuasion, this manipulation, was not what she had dreamed of all those lonely nights in the last two years. "I will not be your toy, Philip. I care not a fig for all that you have learned from your whores."

He grasped her chin to make her face him, then forced his tongue between her lips. Pushing aside the lacy cape impatiently, his long slender hand reached into her bosom.

His assurance pricked her. In a blaze of red, Mary's pale and anxious face appeared. Then icy fury swept Lettice as she realized the enormity and finality of his crime—not only to her, but to Mary as well. As he bent to kiss her again, she shook her head abruptly and sank her teeth into his lower lip, tasting blood. With a startled, low cry, he fell back upon his heels. "Vixen!"

Angrily she pushed him back so that he struggled to keep from falling backward. Her voice shook with rage. "Marry, will you! You promised me your name, and now all you do is half break my back upon a hard bench! If this is the kind of lover you will prove to be, if this is the future you offer, I want none of it! We shall just see, Master Philip! Now there is nothing to keep me from marrying someone else as well!"

Philip unbent his long legs and stood, wiping his mouth with the back of his hand while she sprang to her feet, smoothing her skirts. Wildly she walked from one end of the parlor to the other. "By God, Philip, I do not take betrayal lightly."

His mouth tightened, but he stood well out of her reach, pressing a thumb to the swollen place on his lip. His usual look of cavalier arrogance was gone, and the sullen look of a thwarted child took its place. "And so will you stay here alone in this empty house until your cousin arrives? Do you think to persuade that miser to keep you?"

Regarding him thoughtfully, she shook her head, her hair shimmering. But her heart was troubled, though she would never let him see it. Her cousin was not a kind man. "No, Philip. I am packed and ready to leave. I will be gone when my cousin arrives."

"Gone? You must come with me. Say you will. I know that under that demure look a devil dwells. And I know you love me still."

"Love you?" The corner of her mouth turned down with scorn, but he was too self-absorbed to notice. "Why, certainly. Who, after all, could resist such a charming cavalier? Pray call my maid for me."

He opened the door and called out, his voice booming through the empty halls. His confidence returned, and he placed a reassuring arm about her slender shoulders. "Learning to make love will do you good, sweeting. And I will show you very well. I would have taught you sooner were not your father, with all his low ways, a dragon about your chastity."

"We shall see who shall teach whom," she said, shaking him off.

A ruffled cap appeared about the door. "Yes, sir? Yes, mistress?" The small figure came hesitantly into the room and bobbed a curtsy.

"Are we packed up and ready to go?"

"Yes, mistress."

"And do you have men from the village who are ready to aid us?"

"Yes, mistress." The little maid's brow wrinkled, and her light-blue eyes took on an apprehensive look. She smoothed her palms on her apron.

"Then we will leave tomorrow."

Philip glanced from one to the other of them, puzzled. "And where will you go?"

Lettice smiled into his eyes as though she would love him and give in to his every whim. Then the corners of her mouth quirked down bitterly, and she stamped away. "To my sister's house. To Virginny to hunt for a rich planter who will marry me, fortune or no! And I hope I will find much gold in his bed."

Philip's gray eyes grew dark and hard. Furiously he turned on the heel of his Spanish boot, hesitated, then

8

swung back. "And do your sister and that sour husband of hers know you are coming?"

Lettice spoke without faltering, though he struck a sensitive spot. "Not yet. It is hard to send word from here. And then I did not yet know that you were married."

"Then I think you might delay until you know what your welcome will be." He spoke coldly; his short, pert cape hung like a flag at half-mast.

"No, Philip," she said wearily. "I will not delay. Molly, show Master Isham to the door."

The little maid fixed bright eyes upon her mistress, then curtsied and stood back to let Philip go before her. Philip's eyes burned, then he turned, his cape flaring, and bolted through the door.

Molly closed it gently behind him.

As soon as the door closed and the two were gone, Lettice burst into torrents of weeping, choking back sobs until she judged Philip to be well out of hearing. She had hoped somehow that all their childhood promises would be fulfilled. Yet in the back of her mind there was a strange feeling of relief. She sighed. Now there was indeed nothing to do but to proceed to Virginia with the small amount of money and belongings she still possessed. Her brave words about seeking a rich husband seemed less impressive now that she was left alone. Virginia was far away—a strange and savage place. She had seen little of the world beyond Brookside.

The massive oak door opened, and Molly's diminutive figure came to her side. Great ladies might envy Molly's golden curls and daintiness of face and limb.

Lettice, in contrast, was taller than Molly, the contours of her face smoother, her complexion creamy. Thick, dark lashes framed her deep-blue eyes. Fine straight brows made her seem more serene than she was. Her long ash-brown hair was not of an extraordinary color, but it shone like the rarest silk. The attraction so obviously offered men by Molly often irritated Lettice, but in truth it was the maid's daisy to the mistress's rose.

"There, there, mistress." Molly stroked Lettice's bowed head. "Don't take on so. It be only a man after all. If he was one among many you had known, you would not grieve so."

9

"Oh, Molly, be quiet." Lettice's words dripped ice. "You know perfectly well that Philip is the only man I ever wanted."

"It do seem an awful waste, mistress." As Molly reflected aloud, her voice was as small and light as her body, but it often rose to shrillness. "Ladies has their good names to look to, more's the pity. And you be growing old, mistress, for one who has never known a man."

Lettice bit her lip. Suppose her maid were right and she would never nestle in a man's arms, baring her small but full breasts, the smooth skin of her hips and the firm gentle curve of her belly indented by a most elegant naval. Perhaps her love of Philip had been nothing but a waste of time.

"And he be fair aroused. I thought from the look of you that he had tried to force you. It do surprise me he gave it up so easily."

Lettice straightened in surprise and stared at her maid as though that small person had thrown a basin of cold water upon her. "He did try. It was quite . . . quite difficult to stop him."

Lettice became so irritated she forgot for a moment her grief. "Did you not see the great gash I have him upon his lip?" Once again she thought the sauciness of her maid could anger a saint. "Just because you drag your petticoats through every cottage in the village, Molly, you needn't think you can gossip about Master Philip and me."

"Well, I be glad I have had some pleasure, surely, if I be dragged all the way to Virginny." Molly showed no fear of her mistress's disfavor. She had been Lettice's personal maid and confidante for several years, though the maid was a year or two younger. Lettice knew it was a mistress's duty to correct her maid. But often their relationship became relaxed, and they giggled together. There were few young gentlewomen in the neighborhood.

"It will be very well for you to give the young men in the village a rest," Lettice said severely.

"I am," Molly said enigmatically.

Lettice suspected she had lost her heart to someone in the village. It was only under pressure and for lack of alternatives that her maid had agreed to go to Virginia. The village was less than flourishing of late. And then up until the last moment the two of them had expected a reprieve by way of Philip. Well, it was hard to deny her maid her pleasure when she herself desired it so.

Molly stood drooping near the fire. "I did hear about the countryside he was to wed, mistress."

"And so he has," Lettice said wearily.

Molly fixed a knowing look upon her. "You well know, mistress, that you could stay if you've a mind to."

Lettice flushed. "I see you have been listening at the door again. Well, I tell you I will not be kept in a cottage like a common whore. Besides, Philip lied to me. To the likes of you it may seem well enough to live so, but I will not."

Molly was unaffected by her mistress's harsh words. There had been many such words exchanged between them over the years. The maid's pert features became dreamy. "I have heard, mind you, that the streets in Virginny be lined with gold."

"Not gold. Merely tobacco, but that seems gold enough. My sister, Dorothy, and her husband prosper exceedingly well."

"Tobacco, eh? And can a poor man do well there?"

"Yes. And there should be many fine men for you to marry—perhaps even someone with a parcel of land."

Molly thought about that. Then her face brightened, and her voice rose joyously.

"Well, then, there'll surely be many men for you to marry, mistress."

"Exactly." Lettice's face took on a calculating expression. "Someone with acres of tobacco, I pray. Someone dying for female companionship, which I shall supply. Hopefully someone more handsome than ugly." Lettice paced restlessly in the small parlor that had seemed so warm and inviting back before all the furnishings were stripped from it. The neglected fire had gone out, and even her strong emotions could not keep out the chill.

"Fancy, Philip was married in London while I have been stuck all my life in the country. It is unfair! Oh, were my fortune bigger, I would go to London, seek to make myself known at court. My family is gentle enough. But I must do the second-best thing and search for my planter while keeping my sister company." Lettice's smooth round forehead creased as she contemplated her future.

"Now, mistress. You need a bit of rest, I think. And if

11

Master Philip be the man I think, he may well be back at the dark of night."

Lettice's near-violet eyes took on a look that was hard to read. It was almost as though Molly's words pleased her. Then she sobered. "I am resolved, Molly. Philip cannot think he can have me by a snap of his finger. Go tell the carter to fetch us in the morning to some place where we can arrange for a coach or some tented-over wagon."

The two walked about the empty house, their heels clicking upon the bare oak floors. The rooms had grown shadowy, almost dark. The manor was cold without the colorful hangings or weapons used by this or that ancestor in this or that battle. Some of these she had piled in a corner for her cousin, the rest had been sold off.

"We have little for our journey," Lettice sighed. "The pewter was next to worthless, and all our plate was sold years ago for the King's cause."

" 'Tis best to look after yerself and not worry about kings." As usual, Molly's golden curls were bursting from under her cap. But then her spirit was equally difficult to subdue.

"It's little you know about it," Lettice snapped. But she leaned on Molly all the same, for the maid was her chief support, and Lettice would be lost without her. After all, one did not expect servants to be as concerned with the King as were the gentry.

At least a warm fire burned in the house's grate. Molly added more wood. The solid bedstead would be left, though the bed hangings had been removed. There were only a few old bed covers for her to wrap in. Lettice looked at the satiny oak wall panelling sadly. How would she find a house this comfortable in Virginia?

Molly watched as her mistress donned her nightcap and slipped into a pink silk nightgown trimmed with ribbons. Then the maid carefully folded and hung her mistress's clothes and put out clean linen for the morning.

"Get a good rest, mistress. Traveling in carts and coaches can fair break your back. And the oceans, they say, be terrible to go over." She went to latch the diamond-paned window carefully, standing on tiptoe, she was so short.

After the little maid left her, Lettice opened the casement again and leaned out to see the gentle English countryside just budding into spring. But it was so dark all she could see were the black, awkward shapes of rooks roosting in the tree outside. Alas, there was no sign of Philip. She closed out the chill damp air and lay down on a comfortless bed.

For all her anger and resolve she remembered the feel of Philip's arms about her. It was hard, very hard, to lose him. Tears seeped from beneath her lashes.

Still, she did not regret her angry words. He deserved much worse punishment. He deserved to lose her.

Molly lay in the arms of her beloved in a corner of a cow shed. Her lover had escaped from his mother's cottage for this tryst. They ignored the scratchiness of the hay and the smell of cow dung. It all seemed like heaven to them. It was pitch black, but a touch of hand or lips or thigh told them each about the other.

"Your arms be sweet," she said as she shifted in the hay. "I wish mistress would know how sweet it be. Master Philip ain't the man for her—he be nothing but promise. He turns her sour, and then she snaps at me."

"Hush, now," her lover told her. "That's no way to talk about your mistress. And we may have her to thank if our plans go well."

"Ah, you be the most sober-sided man I've known," she sighed, stretching to kiss the top of his light-blond hair, which smelled of sunlight even in this midnight dark. Her bodice was cut so low it barely contained her full breasts as she pressed against him. Her petticoats were drawn up to her waist, and she wore no underclothes.

"Maybe it's good you knew all those others before me," he said gruffly, running his hand over her belly. "Maybe it'll keep you from straying for curiosity."

"And you . . . you be so old compared to me. Twenty-six, is it? Be your curiosity all gone by now?"

"Hush," he said, covering her mouth with his. Then he kissed her cheek gently and spoke seriously. "Is the carter coming early in the morning?"

"Yes. I hope mistress be ready to travel, though I'd not be surprised to find fine Master Philip returned to spoil her sleep. He does have a passion for her, and that whey-faced Mary Wells will never satisfy him. And mistress saying no has turned him all aflame."

13

Her lover grunted, reaching for his breeches. He had never taken off his shirt. "You'd best look to her."

Molly sighed. "It seems safe here, somehow. And we are to go half the world away." She shook her petticoat free of chaff and made sure her bosom was somewhat covered.

He picked a straw out of her wild curls, then bent his tall body to kiss her forehead. Hand in hand they walked out into the night. The clouds had parted, and the spring flowers in Lettice's formal garden looked unearthly in the strange light.

"Mistress'll be sorry to leave all this. I wonder if there's snowdrops and primroses in Virginny." Molly's unusually shrill voice sounded dreamy.

Suddenly there was a harsh cawing as the rooks left their perches, their dark shapes black against the moon.

"Hush." He placed a hand over her pouting lips and spoke in a low whisper. "Here be something strange."

Molly looked up at the square brick house. It was not large, and though it was no older than Queen Elizabeth's day, it had grown quite shabby. A figure was scaling the ivied wall. "Well, look at the gallant cavalier!" she giggled when her lover removed his hand.

"Hush," he whispered once more, then he seized the ivy near him and began to scale it to the roof, using the frame of lattice beneath it for footholds. She stood below in the shadows, knuckle to her mouth, watching. At the top there was no lattice, only ivy alone, clinging to the spaces between the bricks. She thought she heard one tendril snap away. Then he heaved himself onto the roof. He walked around the corner on the slates, avoiding chimney pots that led from the various fireplaces. Finally he stood directly above Philip Isham, for it was he. Philip had paused and gazed through the small panes to the casement that opened into Lettice's bedchamber. The window was opened a crack. He was startled as Molly's lover lowered himself foothold by foothold until the two men were facing.

"What's this?" the young cavalier said half-aloud.

The poorer man seized Philip by his lace-trimmed sleeve and continued his descent. Philip clung desperately to the ivy-covered lattice. He gave way inch by inch until the two fell the last few feet together.

"What's this?" Philip demanded, groping for his sword, which seemed to be stuck in its scabbard.

As the two rose together, the other studied Philip carefully, then swung with a workman's fist and knocked the gentleman down. Philip's half-drawn sword clattered uselessly to the ground. Molly's lover bent to examine his victim. "Brained him," he breathed.

"Is he all right?" Molly asked, coming to his side.

"I expect his head will hurt in the morning."

"Why ever did you do that?" In the luminous blue light she saw her lover's eyes gleam with satisfaction.

"We have plans of our own, my love. And this gentleman will have no part of them."

"So that's what it is," she murmured half to herself.

"Look to your mistress," he ordered, "while I tie this pretty one to his horse and head him in the direction of home. But I'll have to hold my nose; the smell of his perfume is so strong."

"We'd best leave early before he comes back," she laughed.

"So we must," he said.

She looked up at him and said in her high voice, "You be an adventurer, my dear."

He reached to clasp her small, fine hands. "Aye. Better to adventure than to nurse our love here on the thin, trickling milk of cold poverty."

Philip came to his senses without knowing where he was. Then he realized he was at Woodbine, his father's large and substantial house. Clad in his shirt alone, Philip lay behind the purple curtains of his own bed. Strange shadows filled the room. A candle flickered on a table and another in a wall sconce. His wife had hold of his hand and was stroking it. He looked down at her big-knuckled hand and drew his own free, pulling the plum-silk coverlet up to his chin.

"Oh, my dear," Mary said when she saw he was awake. "We were so worried."

A deep frown line cleaved her brow, and her complexion looked even more sallow and greenish in the candlelight. The entire effect of her green bodice and mustard-yellow undersleeves was unfortunate. Mary was a vulnerable soul who tried hard and was easily wounded.

15

Philip half sat, gazing wildly about the room. "What hour is it? Have I been asleep long?"

"It is some seven or eight o'clock." She pushed gently on his shoulder so he would lie back again. "When the servants cut you loose from your horse this morning, your mother had you brought here and gave you a sleeping draft. You have slept the entire day." Mary was too good a wife to ask immediately what had happened, and her husband did not volunteer the information.

Philip fixed irritated eyes upon her. Her dull hair hung limply, her dark eyes were pained with concern that made him feel guilty. "So I have lost a day," he muttered, yielding to her pressure and giving himself up to his bed. He could hear rain beating against the casement and wondered if Lettice had left and where she might be. As the effects of the sleeping draft wore away, he felt only a faint pain lingering from his attack. Otherwise he was as good as ever—except that it seemed he had lost Lettice.

Could Lettice really be bound for Virginia, or was she merely trying to provoke him? Women played these tricks, always fighting to keep men at their beck and call. They would control any fool weak enough to succumb to their wiles.

Philip was no fool. Let her set out if she dared. Though they had romped as children and played other games when grown, he had never known her body as he would. And he had half a mind to make her pay for his humiliation.

His wife was discarding her sleeves and her petticoat and donning her nightcap. Good God, the woman meant to lie beside him, and he only had thoughts of Lettice! "Put on your nightgown, woman," he ordered, "and send Daniel to me for a private talk. I shan't want you here until we are through."

She nodded and quickly slipped on a silken nightgown. Clasping her chapped hands together, she looked at him with entreaty. "Is it about your accident? Who bound you, my dear? We were so worried, but we thought to wait until you had recovered to call a magistrate to hear your story." Then seeing his expression of wrath, she bit her thin lip.

"I shall see no magistrate," Philip said. "Send Daniel."

When Philip's trusty servant came, bowing and clutching his cap, Philip explained to him that his master must know

16

the whereabouts of Lettice Clifford and her maid, Molly, and that Daniel should get word to his master as soon as they were discovered. They would probably be headed' for London. Whatever happened, however, he was to keep Lettice from setting sail.

Daniel bowed again and smiled a gap-toothed smile. He would in fact have gone to the ends of the earth for his master, though his master beat him often. But Philip was a god to him. Daniel trembled to do his bidding.

The business with Daniel arranged, Philip lay back grimly to await his wife. This night, he thought, would be a good one to make a child upon her. Then whatever relation he and Lettice might have, the creation of an heir would be started.

There were hesitant footsteps outside his door. Then it opened slowly. "My dear?" his wife questioned, poised upon the threshold. There were deep shadows upon her face.

"Come in," he ordered.

She entered timidly.

"Take off your clothes," he said. Faugh, how would he manage upon such a scrawny, yellowish body. She cast down her fearful and modest eyes. "Lie back," he ordered, yanking the purple curtains closed.

Behind his eyelids he conjured up Lettice's long silken hair and gentle curves.

II

It was gray and raining when Lettice Clifford and her maid settled into a hired coach that went lumbering off on broad wheels in the direction of London. Wrapped in a sodden cloak, black hat pulled low upon his brow, the coachman sat above with another man who had appeared at the inn. Lettice thought she had detected the stranger slipping her driver a coin. But she did not mind an extra man riding along in the countryside. The coach was awkward and defenseless in an area where horse-riding was the more common mode of travel.

Imitating her mistress when traveling, Molly wore her golden curls free and flowing as ladies had since King Charles had been placed on the throne. But with the wet weather both young women wore riding hoods, Molly's russet and Lettice's still black. Lettice also wore her mantle for extra warmth.

Lettice sighed. On the second day on the road the hired coach was scarcely more comfortable than the farmer's wagon in which they had ridden to the inn—and it had had no canvas covering. Threatening clouds had gathered throughout that first day, waiting to spill over like the tears back of Lettice's eyes.

The night before her departure from Brookside she had slept poorly, wakening several times. Half expecting Philip's return, hearing strange sounds in the darkness that made her heart lurch, she had tossed and turned. He had not come back. She burned now with desire, now with anger, that he had been so easily discouraged.

Perhaps she would die an old maid, selflessly aiding her sister with her children in a faraway land. No, she was determined to find her rich planter. All else mattered little, provided this as yet unknown gentleman had enough money. She knew that younger sons of some of the first families of England had gone out to Virginia to make their fortunes larger. There was land to be had, and there was money to be made in tobacco.

"I had not one wink of sleep in that dirty inn last night," Molly grumbled to her mistress. "I shall sicken for home before we even see the ship."

"It was a miserable place," Lettice agreed. Then her spirits lifted as she thought that at least she would see London, and the wide oceans and a new land! She had never before traveled so far from Brookside, never even seen the sea. In London she might discover the latest fashions. She promised herself she would buy some pretty things to take with her to Virginia.

"I am tired of this dreary black dress," Lettice complained.

"If you put on your scarlet sleeves in London, no one there will know you are in mourning," Molly said. "The old master was lighthearted enough and will likely never know nor care from wherever he may be."

"But I would know the difference." Lettice gave her maid a look of reproof. But as soon as proper she would don gayer attire, the better to catch a gentleman's eye.

Rain drummed steadily on the roof. A good deal of it oozed in past the windows in an unabated trickle. The leather-covered seats were damp and musty.

Lettice heard the baying of hounds, each bugling his own note up and down the scale. She pulled aside the leather curtains to look out upon the countryside. Two gentlemen rode with a pack over the ploughed brown fields in pursuit of unknown quarry. The coach was going through an area of much open country with patches of brushwood and tall trees. They passed several cut-over tracts; the living forest had no doubt been sacrificed by gentlemen who were striving to maintain themselves while supporting the King's cause.

Now that Cromwell and the Protectorate were gone, and Charles II was on the throne, many of these loyal Cavaliers were still possessed of reduced fortunes. In these days of religious and political faction the King had trouble enough keeping his footing—though his head seemed more secure than did that of Charles I. But England was more stable than she had been since the days of the good Queen Elizabeth. Pray God the King would keep it so. Lettice could still remember her terror as a tiny child when bands of men, now Cavalier, now Roundhead, would sweep the countryside. And the Cavaliers were almost as hard on their friends as the Roundheads were on their enemies.

A cow shed, timbered and thatched, came into view as they lumbered awkwardly around a corner on the rutted road. It was the only building in sight, though a clump of trees indicated the presence of a secluded farmhouse. Lettice let the curtains drop. Her maid dozed in a corner, her feet resting upon boxes and bundles on the floor. Lettice grew hungry. She had had nothing but some bread and cheese, which she'd snatched hastily that morning. The journey was expensive. She would have little money when she landed in Virginia.

The coach slowed and came to a halt. Lettice was startled. Only a fool or a highwayman would stop on a road so deserted—unless something were wrong.

Once more Lettice pulled back the curtains. The driving rain had lightened somewhat, and she saw some men standing about, looking uncertain. It was obvious that they were not highwaymen. While the slanting rain beat down on them, they discussed with Lettice's coachman how to right a substantial coach that had gone over in a ditch. It was now lying at an angle so she could see its mud-encrusted, red-painted wheels.

The men strained without success until Lettice's coachman went to gather up a large branch that had blown across the road in the bad weather. He and the other man who rode above began to pry the coach out of the mud with the branch. The three from the overturned coach pushed until it was freed and suddenly righted. The door flew open from the jolt.

Lettice drew in a quick breath as her eyes met those of a man inside. The change of position had thrown him so that now his shoulder was against the door's edge. A further shock would have sent him through the door and into the mud of the road, unable to help himself.

He was bound and gagged.

Lettice felt herself flush as the two of them gazed at each other. His eyes were dark and angry, his hair dressed plainly. He wore leather clothing, though she knew him to be a gentleman and not a Roundhead or Presbyterian either. He was less slender than Philip, but more muscular.

Their eyes held. Lettice's face burned, but she could not look away. How could a man tied so tightly fix upon her eyes so frankly sexual? She could not see the expression of his mouth since he was biting upon a gag—but she was almost certain that his blazing look softened to one of near amusement. How extraordinary!

Her little maid stirred and leaned over to peer past her mistress. "Bless me," she said, startled out of her grogginess.

Just then one of the men noticed the open door and slammed it shut, throwing a nervous look toward the two young women. Lettice withdrew her hand from the curtains, which fell into place. The incident had startled her and made her conscious of how alone and defenseless she and Molly were on the deserted road.

"Bless me," Molly said once more. "He must be a rogue to be tied so."

"He has always been known as a wild-enough gentleman," her mistress said thoughtfully. "But I am surprised to see him in this state." She pulled aside the heavy curtain again, but the second coach had fallen far behind as theirs had gotten under way now and was proceeding briskly.

"You know him, missus?" Molly bristled with curiosity.

"He is one of the wild Finch brothers—a pair of twins some four or five years older than myself." Lettice recalled that she had last seen the two of them galloping away from a fair, a peasant tradesman shaking his fist after them. They were ever up to pranks.

"Old Sir Giles's sons?"

"Yes. Philip often hunted with them, though the twins considered me a baby." She remembered how crushed she had been once when her father had actually condescended to take his seven-year-old daughter to a fair, only to have young Giles call her "the old man's baby." Giles had laughed nastily, but then his twin, Geoffrey, smiled at her to ease the hurt he saw on her face.

"I've always heard Sir Giles were a wealthy man—but if this be his son, he's not dressed fine for a gentleman."

"Maybe his trouble has reduced him."

"Which one is he, then? Young Giles or Geoffrey?"

"There's no way of knowing, they look so alike. But Giles usually stays close to home, since he is the heir." Besides, she was almost sure this one was Geoffrey, since something in their expressions was different. Once she had wandered about in a nearby wood all alone, as she often was, looking for strawberries. Giles had sprung from behind a tree and tossed a frog on her. She had collapsed in childish tears, which angered her and made her cry all the harder. Then Geoffrey ambled up and gave the smirking Giles a shove. Geoffrey helped her up with her basket of spilled berries and looked about for those that were lost. When she tried to thank him, he only shrugged.

"I wonder what this one did to cause them to bind and gag him so. He must be a bad one, indeed."

"Yes." Lettice paused as the coach swayed. "At least I hope so and that in fact we have not abandoned him in the hands of wicked men."

"Oh, mistress, what a thought!" Molly's eyes grew sharp with concern. Reaching up to tuck a straggling curl under her hood, she added quickly, "But there be little we can do about it."

"Indeed." Lettice drew her mantle more closely about her to keep out the chill. Her first recognition of Geoffrey Finch had shocked her into pity and fear for him. She had restrained herself. She was emotionally overwrought and too susceptible after Philip's betrayal. Geoffrey doubtless deserved his present condition. Yet. . . .

Lettice knocked on the ceiling to attract the driver's attention. He halted and came around to open the door.

"Mistress?" His leather coat and buckskin breeches were quite soaked from the rain, though the afternoon sky was clearing at last. He had discarded his dripping cloak. On the horizon Lettice saw grayish clouds becoming tinged with yellow. Here and there blue patches appeared.

"Tell me," she addressed the coachman. "Tell me, did you see the man bound in the other coach? Did they say why he was bound?"

"I only had a quick look at him, missus, though I know murderers are bound so."

"Murderers? Indeed?" She considered uneasily for a moment. "It is so deserted here," she said after awhile. "Do you think we will come upon a farmhouse or inn soon so we may dine?"

"There's some building ahead," he answered. "It may well be an inn, it's so close to the road." He touched his forelock and clambered back onto the coach.

The horses started up and strained to pull the heavily laden vehicle up the slope. At the top of the hill sat a plain stone building that was indeed an inn.

As they stood in the courtyard, they saw the coach they had helped earlier pass by. It was slowed by some damage from the accident. With a wrinkled brow, Lettice looked after the departing vehicle. It did not stop but continued to drive slowly in the direction of London, revealing no further view of its bound passenger.

Lettice and her party were glad to be inside. The dining room was surprisingly crowded for such an isolated spot. There were few women, and these looked to be of low character. Half of the countymen who were there must have come for some cheer and company on this rainy day.

Lettice's coachman and his companion went to dry themselves by the fire. The flames sputtered as they shook themselves like drenched dogs that had just come inside. The two women walked through the heavily beamed room and sat themselves at the table. A tallow candle sputtered, giving little light in the smokey dimness.

The hostess served up portions of a collar of boar and cabbage and warmed some ale, for though it was spring, they were chilled. Lettice found that all the emotions of leaving home and of traveling had killed her appetite. She could only toy with the heavy food. The room was small and stuffy. She prayed they would find better fare in London.

The maid and her mistress looked up as they heard the clatter of hooves in the courtyard. A rider entered with haste and shouldered his way past the table toward the two men at the fire. He seemed to be speaking to them. The man's rough but sturdy clothes indicated he was a retainer or messenger for some of the gentry. Lettice looked quickly down again at her trencher. For a moment she'd had a foolish hope. It was not the elegant Philip, after all, though something in his awkward walk seemed familiar. Molly continued to gawk—the goose. She always had an eye for the men.

Out of the corner of her eye, Lettice saw the messenger walk away through the dark-paneled dining room and demand a drink of the landlord. The men at the fire had evidently not helped him. Lettice then noticed her coachman's companion sit up from his seat by the chimney. This tall, muscular man with his shock of blond hair came to stand beside Molly and herself, giving a hint of a bow as though he were unused to such courtesies. He moved so as to block her view of the rest of the room.

"Missus," he said. "Yon driver says you be bound for Virginny."

Lettice hesitated, then saw no reason not to answer. "I am."

"I be a poor man, but bound there myself," he said. "I'm headed for London town to find myself a ship and sell my services."

Lettice looked at him blankly and nodded.

"But a lady traveling without protection be fair game for rogues o' the road. I be offering my services, mistress, for the journey to London."

Lettice studied him. "How do I know you're not a rogue of the road yourself?"

"Mistress!" Molly protested. "He don't look like a rogue to me."

"I've heard the best ones don't." Lettice did not want to be taken for a fool, nevertheless she hesitated. It would be a blessing to have a reliable man along to help with their boxes and bundles and find them a ship. Indeed, Lettice had no idea how one found ships or knew when they were sailing. Anxiety gnawed at her as she thought of her rapidly diminishing fortune. Perhaps this man could bargain for their fare.

"Very well," she said. "But I can pay you but little."

"I ask little."

"And what is your name, then?"

"John Martin, missus."

"Very good, John." Lettice handed him money for the landlord and dismissed him.

He seemed reluctant to leave, then said in an urgent low-pitched voice, "Let us go hastily, mistress." He bounded away toward the landlord to pay him for their meal.

Wondering at his alarm, she looked about the room and over toward the rider who had so recently entered. There was a clear view of him, since the crowd had thinned. He

25

stood drinking with his back to the diners, then turned for a moment to look toward the fire. When he opened his mouth, she saw the gap between his teeth.

Lettice stiffened. No wonder he had looked familiar! He was Daniel, Philip's man. He must have been asking for her and most likely had already questioned her newly hired escort. Quickly she donned her hood, drawing it forward. She gestured to her maid to do the same, blessing her new manservant's caution. In their hoods it was difficult to distinguish them from the local women.

"Well, missus?" Molly said when they were outside.

"It was Philip's man, Daniel. Search my boxes for my mask." Like many ladies, Lettice had a mask to protect her face from the sun or severe weather.

" 'Twill only delay us, mistress."

"Well, then let us make haste."

Molly looked up at her mistress, an expression of doubt on her clear-skinned face.

"I knew him right away and wondered, mistress, if you would greet him and stay, or run."

"Run, of course," Lettice snapped.

"And if Master Philip had come himself?"

"The same," Lettice insisted. "And besides, you see, he does not come." But as she settled herself stiffly into the coach, she wondered if she lied. If Philip cared as much for her as for his wife and estate, why did he not come himself instead of sending a servant? No, it was but a sign of the low station to which he would assign her—a woman without honor, bearing bastard children.

She closed her eyes, feigning sleep, so that her maid would not notice her agitation. She would not have Philip, she vowed. Yet, as the coach departed once again for London, she longed for him. And with half her attention she listened for the sounds of hoofbeats behind them.

They swore there could not be a pebble on the road they had not painfully felt. Travel by farm wagon could scarce have proved more uncomfortable. No wonder coaches had come into fashion so slowly. Lettice stared at the nail-studded leather door with dislike. But she was exhausted enough from her days on the road to drift into sleep with Molly sleeping by her side.

When Lettice awoke, she was conscious that the coach

was at rest and someone was tapping lightly on the door. Molly's heavy eyes opened. Lettice pulled the curtains aside to find the coachman tugging at his forelock.

"We've come in sight of London, Mistress."

"Oh, mistress," Molly breathed in Lettice's ear. "Let us get out for a look!"

Lettice needed no urging. The two women and the men stood on the marshy Southwark bank and looked across the wide river. Before them a panorama of the city followed the curve of the river from the tower to Fleet Ditch. St. Paul's, the principal church of London, was missing from the horizon. It lay a heap of picked-over rubble, victim to the Great Fire of ten years earlier in which so much of ancient London had been destroyed. Other towers stood in ruins. Fresh red brick marked the many new buildings, though patches of charred rubble here and there showed properties not yet restored.

"Oh, mistress, I never seen so many houses in my life afore. Be they not grand?"

Lettice nodded, smiling. The bustle of the city raised her spirits. The Thames was aswarm with craft of all kinds, a brisk wind filling their sails. Barges were stacked high with barrels and bales and loads of vegetables for the city's markets; there were piles of hay and straw that were destined for the stables of inns; watermen ferried passengers from one landing stair to another.

Lettice and her party drove onto London Bridge and could see the river water hurl itself in whorls against the stone piers—Molly counted 18 of them. Lettice stared out of her coach window while they passed the many houses and shops built on the bridge.

"My," said Molly, "this be a grand bridge to have its own houses on it."

After consultation with the coachman, the party settled at the Fountain Inn in the Strand.

In the morning Lettice and Molly and John walked about the Strand, examining the goods in the market. Though John was eager to be off to find a ship, he feared the women might fall prey to pickpockets or footpads. Finally Lettice persuaded him to leave; so while Lettice and Molly continued on their little shopping jaunt, John went in search of the docks.

Inside a dark shop Lettice fingered a piece of deep-blue

27

silk, examining it as close to the candle on the counter as she dared without risking scorching it. She heard a sound and turned to see a sedan chair set down before the door. The attendants opened the narrow chair door and helped a very tall lady emerge. She wore a plumed hat, and as she entered, Lettice quickly examined her clothes with the eye of a practiced seamstress. They were exquisite. She admired the way ladies in London were pulling their overgowns up and back to reveal rich petticoats of contrasting colors. This lady's petticoat was olive-green silk tabby with its watery gloss. Her overgown was pale pink with rose ribbons.

Lettice thought she could rework her own plum silk to a more fashionable style, and from this deep-blue silk that she had just found, she could sew a superb petticoat. She felt amongst the sovereigns, crowns and pennies in her pocket, considering.

The shopkeeper's wife came forward. Eagerly, she greeted the elegant blond lady, dipping a knee. "Milady," she said.

The lady fingered the beautiful materials as though they were coarse woolens. Her oval nails picked at a piece of lace. Lettice drew in a deep breath of wonder. It was the loveliest lace she had ever seen—a glistening silver wrought with great delicacy. It must be fearfully expensive, she thought. How beautiful it would look upon a deep-blue petticoat—argent and azure—the Clifford colors. But surprisingly, the lady discarded it. Lettice reached out to grasp it. Oh, it would bedazzle any Virginia gentleman! She must have it, whatever the price!

The lady looked up and saw her with the lace. "Let me see that once more," she said.

"I'm sorry," Lettice answered. "I intend to buy it."

"But I have not finished looking at it." The lady's voice turned hard and shrill. The corners of her perfect mouth drew down.

Lettice turned stubborn. "I *have* finished. And I have made up my mind to buy it."

"Give it to me!" The woman's elegant fingers seized the lace, her sharp nails scraping Lettice's knuckle.

Lettice grew still more stubborn. She would not give in even if they tore the lace to shreds.

The merchant's wife squeezed her plump hands together

in agitation. "Ladies! Ladies!" Then she turned her full attention upon Lettice. "Please let the Lady Isobel look at it, mistress. She is one of my best customers."

Lettice's sense of fairness was outraged. She stuck out her firm, round jaw. "I have decided to buy it." She gave a sudden great tug.

The lady's fingers slipped loose, catching and breaking a nail in the process. Her silky skin blazed. She stretched her swanlike neck angrily. The gesture raised her full, round breasts so that they almost showed her nipples above the low-cut bodice. "Very well," she said. "I shall shop elsewhere." With a swish of her petticoats she went out the door and stepped into her sedan chair.

The merchant's wife fixed enraged, beady eyes upon Lettice. Still flushed, Lettice looked down at the lace. It was so well made it had not suffered during the struggle.

"I shall have the silk and the lace." Lettice turned a deeper red, wondering if she ought to go to such great expense. But she could not back down now. "And I will have some yards of scarlet ribbon for my maid." She decided to show she could be generous even if the Lady Isobel could not.

"Oh, mistress!" Molly breathed.

But the shopkeeper's eyes were cold as Lettice placed her coins on the woman's open palm.

When they walked out again onto the cobbles, Molly said, "That blond lady be a witch!"

"Thank heavens there will be an ocean between us," Lettice said. "I never want to see the elegant Lady Isobel again."

As she returned to the inn to dine, Lettice considered the fact that she had not thought of Philip since she had first sighted London. If only she might return here some day as a planter's wife.

Daniel, Philip's man, hurried toward the docks, once again, praying that he had not failed his master. Oh, but it was black as pitch down by the water, and full of dangerous characters too. There were strange sidlings and sounds of murmurings and splashings.

He wandered the riverside for days, searching for information of ships bound for Virginia and of ladies bound there too. And only late last night had he finally been able to learn of the ship that had among its passengers two country women bound for Virginia. He now hoped he could find the vessel before she set sail.

The riverside was full of taverns, and they were full of verminous wretches—sailors with their prostitutes, barefoot and diseased children, greasy fish dames, the very dregs of the city. Round and about all snapped mangy, half-starved dogs. Daniel ducked into one of these taverns in the hopes of obtaining some information.

Seated before a pint of ale in the tavern was a tallow-faced man with black and sinister eyes who now slowly edged closer and closer to Daniel and offered to buy him a drink. But a sailor on the other side dug an elbow into Daniel, whispering, "Beware, mate. 'Ees a crimp. 'Ee'll lock you in a hole, and when you come to again, ye'll find yerself in Virginny, bound as a servant."

Daniel paid hastily and left. Once outside, he asked the first sailor he met about the *Anne and Mary*. The sailor was quick to point out into the harbor. And there she stood at anchor.

Oh, why had his horse lost a shoe and he, Daniel, eaten a bad venison pastry at a moth-eaten roadside inn? He had spent two days spewing his guts out, which had delayed him until it appeared as if he were almost too late. But his pain would not matter to his master. He would but follow it with blows should he discover Daniel's failures.

Out on the water a man raised a torch as cargo was being loaded from a boat onto the ship. Daniel could see the *Anne and Mary* plainly, her three masts naked of sail.

Mistress Clifford must already be aboard. And surely they would set sail tomorrow! He must accost one of these dockside ruffians and ask how he might reach the ship. But how would he return the mistress to the shore? Doubtless a plan would occur to him.

Through the gloom he saw approaching a tall fellow who seemed vaguely familiar to him—a fellow with a shock of light hair. Daniel saluted him, "What, ho!" Then he confided, "I'm seeking to go out to the *Anne and Mary*."

"Are you, now?" the other murmured.

And then Daniel saw a fist coming toward him that blotted out the torchlight and the night itself.

* * *

30

Around and about the ship as it was loaded, the rough and dirty crew busied itself. Throughout the day barges and lighters had plied back and forth between the ship and the quay, taking in cargo for Virginia. It was quite late now. They would sail with dawn.

Hidden by the rigging on the bow of the *Anne and Mary*, Lettice stood alone on the quarter-deck, gazing toward shore. No one had observed her leave her cabin. The countless twinkling candlelights of London would be among her last memories of England. To her right loomed the shadow of the tower, and behind it part of the old wall. Lettice felt a great yearning . . . for Philip with his strong arms about her? For a quiet hearth and loving children? For some great adventure to befall her in the plantation of Virginia? All she knew was that she wanted something.

The ship rocked gently, creaking with the motion of the river. She was about to go to her cabin when she heard splashing and dimly saw a boat manned by two loud-voiced women ferrying a sailor and his bundle to the ship. In a moment the sailor had reached the deck. He was carrying a heavy load over his shoulder, which cast a strange shadow. A chill of fear went through Lettice. Surely it was a human body.

She told herself it was only her imagination fired by the view of the bound man she'd seen in the coach on the way to Plymouth. Indeed, even in the dim light it looked like the same man—Geoffrey, or perhaps Giles Finch. It was possible, she supposed. That coach had come along the same road as hers.

She heard a groan from the body. The sailor threw the man down with a callous thump behind one of the boats on the main deck. Lettice winced. She leaned past the rigging. The sailor, busy about his task, took no notice of her.

Surely it was Geoffrey!

Then two other burly seamen, with lantern light flickering upon their backs, seized the trussed body and carried it below like ordinary cargo. She wondered where they were taking him, but was too many yards away from the hatch to judge clearly. The captain must know of this! A gentleman trussed up like poultry could not be borne.

She looked about for John Martin, who had aided her in this journey and who now had paid for his passage by binding out his services to the captain. John was nowhere

31

in sight. She clenched and unclenched her hands. She must go to the captain herself, she decided. She stepped forward to the main deck to attract the attention of a sailor. In the feeble light from the lanterns on the quarter-deck she could dimly see his begrimed and unshaven face and his roughly mended canvas clothes. He looked at her with surprise as though he had never before been so close to such a fine lady. He spoke a dialect so strange and primitive that she could not distinguish one word from the other, though she thought he was English.

He gestured roughly in the direction of the captain's cabin, which was just above hers.

Hastily gathering up her skirts, Lettice sped to where the man pointed. Gazing at the solid door of the captain's cabin, she held her breath for a moment before she could muster the courage to knock. There was no answer. Summoning all her resolution, she knocked again with force. At last the door opened.

The captain had removed his coat and boots and stood barefoot in the doorway. An open bottle of sack rested on his table. "Eeagh?" he questioned with open mouth, revealing a moist tongue.

Staring up into his ugly, reddened face, she addressed him as boldly as she was able. "Captain Quince, I must inform you that a bound man has been brought aboard."

Reaching out a meaty hand to close about her arm, he drew her closer to his circle of candlelight. His surprisingly white teeth appeared in a broad smile. He spoke in a voice roughened and deepened by years of hurling commands to unruly men against the gale. "So pretty to be worrit about some trussed-up scoundrel." He pinched the fleshy part of her arm as he spoke.

"This scoundrel happens to be a gentleman of my acquaintance," Lettice said indignantly.

As swiftly as a full moon is blotted out by storm clouds, the captain's smile disappeared. His bloodshot eyes narrowed. He squeezed the flesh of her arm painfully between his thumb and forefinger, no longer playful. Leaning his face into hers, he breathed windily his foul sack breath. "Ladies must keep their noses out of my business. I am the law—the only law—on this ship." He snatched up a knife from off the table and touched the tip to the underside of her chin, forcing her head back.

"I beg you, sir!" Lettice cried.

"Beg away. If you pray for mercy, I might not slit your throat."

Lettice pulled her arm free, though she could feel herself shake inside. But the captain did not lower the blade.

"I merely look for an answer to this riddle." Lettice thought to placate him, then with a sudden daring, added, "If I don't find why the gentleman is treated so, I must then ask my brother-in-law, Charles Albright, of Virginia, to investigate for me."

The captain's expression changed again—became more calculating. He stood wheezing and unmoving, studying her. Thoughtfully he tested his knife against his thumb, then threw it into the table so that it stuck.

"Charles Albright, eh? I've done a bit of business with the gentleman, though I think he was not so gentle nor of so high account in England. But if Albright sends for his sister-in-law from England, the old skinflint must be seeking profit of his own." With a coarse laugh, he reached to pinch her arm again.

Lettice stepped back in retreat, staring at him wide-eyed. She dare not tell him Charles had no idea she was coming.

Laughing hoarsely, the captain raised his stoneware bottle of sack and drank, leaving a moist smear near his mouth. "Yes," he wheezed. "A pretty profit." Walking unsteadily, he pulled her to him with a rough hand.

"I beg you, sir," Lettice said with indignation.

There was a sharp rap on the half-opened door. Looking back over her shoulder, Lettice saw the light-blond hair of John Martin. The Captain's grip loosened only slightly. John was his property. He had signed an indenture to pay for his passage, and thereby signed away three years of his life. The captain would make more profit by selling this paper in Virginia.

"Captain, sir," John said with more humility than Lettice was used to hearing from him. "I would speak to you privately."

"Can't you see I am busy?"

"It be a matter of profit," John said softly.

The captain narrowed his eyes as he released Lettice. "Profit once more. Come in."

Scarcely looking at John, who had not acknowledged her, Lettice picked up her petticoats and fled once more to

33

the deck. She half-sensed that John had deliberately tried to divert the captain, understanding her danger. Could she demand that the captain return her money and let her take her maid back to the inn?

But however helpless and fearful she might feel, her condition was not as perilous, it seemed, as Geoffrey Finch's. She would somehow discover if he deserved this imprisonment. No, it were best she stayed aboard to do this work, but she must avoid the captain.

She knew not how long she stood there, half-hidden behind the rigging. There were fewer lights on shore now— only those up late with illness or all-night taverns or whorehouses still burned a candle.

It was with a sense that she was dreaming that she saw a sailor come on board, once more carrying a heavy load that proved to be a bound man. As he came upon the deck, John Martin walked forward from the shadows. When his eyes met those of the sailor, Martin nodded slowly, then he rapidly faded into the darkness and disappeared.

This second body, too, was flung upon the deck. Light from the lantern shone down upon it. Lettice stared with shocked surprise. It was Daniel, Philip's man!

Pressing her hand over her lips, she ran to the ladder that hung over the side. Desperately she wondered if there was someone to take her, along with Molly, back to shore. But a ship's officer blocked her way.

"Please." Lettice heard her voice rise in breathless entreaty. "I want to go back to London."

His solid form loomed above her, the river a blackness behind him. "No one is to leave the ship, captain says, since we sail at dawn. We want no light-fingered wenches carrying cargo or tales off the ship. The riverside is full of theives."

"But I've changed my mind."

"It is too late, my lady," he said in a low and ominous voice.

No use appealing to the captain, Lettice was sure. Of course he would let no one ashore now. She and Molly were probably the only legitimate passengers. She shivered. She had spent almost all her money to pay for the voyage. And they were prisoners almost as much as Daniel or Geoffrey Finch.

34

III

No longer did the ship rock gently, but it creaked and groaned, sails snapping in the wind and rain. Out on the deck, in the darkness, the sailing master of the *Anne and Mary* considered taking in sail. His orders were to wake the captain if the wind changed.

Inside Lettice's cabin a candle flame wavered. The window panes looked like black holes into the night. Molly lay feverish on a shadowed pallet, her fine skin red and blotchy. Lettice knelt close by, sponging her with brackish water. Molly was only one of many sickened as the weeks of the voyage dragged on. Lettice thanked God she herself had seen scarce a day's illness in her life.

A hesitant knock startled her. Unfastening the door, Lettice strained to keep the wind from forcing it wide. John Martin stood outside, his blond hair rain-plastered to his skull. Large red hands and wrists hung below his soaked sleeves. Lettice nodded quickly so he might enter, leaving a pool of water just inside the door.

His eyes begged anxiously—a far cry from his usual confident look that ignored differences in rank. In a surprisingly gentle voice he asked, "Does the little one sleep?"

At this, the eyes of Lettice's patient fluttered open, her face betraying no feeling, her breathing labored. Lettice straightened the blanket over her.

John's long black shadow shifted on the cabin wall. His blue eyes, large and painful, sought Lettice's. "What can I do, mistress?"

Another man bewitched by her maid, Lettice thought.

"What can any of us do? Sickness is in the hands of the Lord," she told him.

John's expression grew bleak. He shuffled and wiped his cold nose with the back of one rain-chapped hand. Then he cleared his throat and gave Lettice an odd look, his words tumbling out awkwardly. "Mayhap you'd like a chance to take some air upon the deck, mistress."

"On the deck in the rain?" What a weak ruse this was! What could she do with this lovelorn fool? Lettice sighed with irritation, yet she admitted to herself it was good to look upon any other face besides Molly's, they had been confined together so long.

"There seems to be too *much* air out there," she said with a frown. "Besides, I do not want to find myself cornered by Captain Quince."

"He be asleep in his cabin. And he be sober today, which makes some difference." John clasped his big hands together awkwardly.

Lettice wondered mightily about this man who had appeared out of nowhere, it seemed, to aid them. Truthfully, she longed to escape the four walls of her cabin. Her entire day had been spent nursing Molly so that now she choked on the smell of sour, closed-in sickness. The pestilence surely would strike her next should she remain long confined. But she told herself she could not abandon her patient. Then John dipped the cloth into the basin and gently wiped the little maid's brow, smoothing a tendril of fever-moist golden hair.

Seeing this, Lettice nodded, "Yes, I shall go out." At home she had liked to take long walks in the rain, and scarcely a day passed that she did not ride out upon her horse. This indoor idleness was unnatural to her. She opened her chest and drew out her mantle, fastening the hood over her so that she was two-layered against the rain. With relief, she stepped forth.

Wind howling through the rigging greeted her, the great masts swaying like reeds before it. She heard a sailor cry out somewhere in darkness. Bending against the gale, she made her way to stand near the rigging as she had the first night. Wind tugged at her mantle, twisting it this way and that, drenching her petticoat. She clung to the rail as the ship dipped, then heaved up at an angle in the grip of a giant wave. The rolling of the ship affected her stomach not one whit, though it had distressed Molly. But the air seemed wonderful and clean after the sickroom.

Looking up over her shoulder, she saw a dim light flickering in the captain's cabin, she spotted no sign of movement. She had steered clear of him, taking her meals in her cabin since her fright the night before sailing. Bad weather made this easier, since it kept him occupied.

Lettice had glimpsed the Finch man several times; he'd been let out at nights to walk the deck, guarded by a ship's officer. But where was he now? For several days she'd had no sight of him. He might be ill. Or so many of the crew might be sickened that the rest simply failed to attend to him. She had no idea of Daniel's fate, and she felt some concern for him. ˙

A gust blew a torrent of water into her eyes. Wiping them with a chilled hand, she was just in time to see a man come from below. Slashes of rain blurred his outline, yet she was sure it was the same officer who guarded Geoffrey at night. He walked purposefully away without noticing her.

Now was her chance—the best she would ever have—to speak to Geoffrey. Would she dare? The driving rain smote the ship, and the candles in the deck lanterns bent wildly despite their protective glass. She would only be one more indistinct, dark figure if her cloaked woman's outline did not betray her.

The main deck now deserted, she stumbled to make her way down the companionway to the main deck, past a hatch and around a boat. Then she pushed on a hatch door and stepped over the high threshold that damned the floods. She went down five or six steps, biting her lip as she realized the risk she was taking. In the pitch black below, an overwhelming smell of tar, rope and slops enveloped her. She reached forth a tentative hand, and to her right felt a door. Behind it coarse snorings and mutterings sounded as though several men were groaning in uneasy sleep. For a moment she was unable to move—her stomach clenched in fear. It would be dangerous to enter a place so obviously occupied by so many. Summoning up her courage she pushed past the door, feeling her way under the massive timbers of the ship's deck. Scurrying sounds showed that vermin had braved their way up through the hold. She gave a low cry as something ran over her foot.

Then, seeing a slight gleam ahead, her tentative steps halted. Her eyes strained to see an opening, a door ajar.

37

Peering around a corner, she saw an unattended candle burning low on a table. Her eyes darted about, then hesitantly she stepped inside. Startled, she jumped as a low sigh, almost a moan, greeted her. In the gloom it took her a moment to find him—for it was he—lying on a bunk with his back to her, still dressed in the same leather clothing.

Quietly, she lay a hand on his shoulder. With a mighty twitch he rolled onto his back, fixing fierce eyes upon her. Lettice drew back in fright. She moistened her dried lips and spoke. "You are Geoffrey Finch, are you not?"

The dark eyes that met hers softened, taking on a look of amusement. Of course he could not speak! He was still gagged. Awkwardly, with stiff, chilled fingers, she reached behind his dark head to work on the stubborn knot of cloth that silenced him. It seemed like embarrassingly intimate contact, bringing her face and bosom close to him. She noticed that Geoffrey had several flesh wounds from being bound, and yet he still looked vigorous and muscular. He had always been fond of hunting, she recollected. Or was that Giles?

At last the stubborn knots gave way, and Geoffrey gasped and shook his head like a horse freed of reins. "Some water," he said hoarsely.

"Of course." Lettice went to the water bucket and poured some into a leather tankard, splashing a little onto the table in her haste.

"Careful, now," Geoffrey said.

She held the tankard to his lips. Despite its staleness, he drank with indecent haste, his chest rising and falling with deep breaths. When he had downed it, she reached behind her to replace the tankard. He looked at her directly, the corners of his eyes crinkling as though the situation were a comedy acted upon the stage. There were only some few inches between them; so she could clearly see every expression despite the meager light. She was not sure his confinement was a laughing matter. Then he nodded as though her presence suited his purpose.

"An angel has come to deliver me," he said with a near-wicked smile. "And now if you would free me from my bonds, I might live to see another day."

Lettice started back, wondering if, after all, he might be some condemned criminal. "What do you mean?"

38

"Only that I am somewhat stiff," he answered wryly.

"Of course." Lettice set to work at once, but the ropes proved even harder and more difficult than the gag. He rolled over with his back to her; so she could not see his face. His hands rested just above his buttocks.

Once she had loosened the last knot at his wrist, he lay for a moment, flexing his hands and rubbing the rope-chafed skin. Then he quickly bent to untie his ankles. This done, he raised himself, but swayed with dizziness. He must have been lying in one position for some time. He braced himself against the pitch of the ship, his dark head down.

"You are Geoffrey Finch, are you not?" Lettice asked.

He steadied himself and turned to look at her through eyes that shone black in the candlelight. "No, Mistress Clifford, I am Henry Cooper."

"You most certainly are not." Lettice regarded the man she had rescued with indignation. "You are Geoffrey Finch—unless you are Giles, though I have not seen either of you for some years. And if you are not one of them, how do you know my name?"

"You are quite clever, my dear, to have discovered that I am not Giles. But, nevertheless, I am known here as Henry Cooper. And I do recognize you, though you are somewhat bigger than when I saw you last, and even soaking wet, you are somewhat prettier."

"You are very mysterious." Lettice shook her damp head. Her wet hood fell free to her shoulders. "And how did you come to be here?"

"By the same road as yourself, I think, if you will remember."

Lettice flushed. He had remembered their first encounter. "I mean, for what reason?"

"No reason but madness. The spirits have got me and sold me and are about to sell me again."

Lettice stepped back from him. Was he mad for a fact?

He smiled at her look. "Not the spirits that lurk in damp castles or about graveyards, but those who hide about the docks to spirit men away into indentured servitude in faraway lands. Man spirits, they call them. Their work is spiriting rather than spiritual."

Lettice had never heard of these men, and she wondered

whether to trust Geoffrey's words. "But you were captured far from the sea," she objected.

"So I was." He frowned.

"I do not understand."

"Nor do I, my sweet. Nor do I fully understand whether they wished to capture Henry Cooper or Geoffrey Finch." He was silent for a moment, then spoke in a voice Lettice could barely hear. "Though my brother Giles may know. Or the Lady Isobel."

"Then it is a mystery," Lettice said. She vaguely wondered if this could be the same Lady Isobel she had found so unpleasant in London. It was unlikely. There were many Isobels in England.

Geoffrey nodded, his eyes cold and serious.

"But you have committed no crime?" Lettice asked him.

"No crime save being brother to my brother and a servant to love." And again he spoke in such a low voice that Lettice could barely distinguish the words. Then slowly he straightened and stood. "Come here, my lady, so that I may lean upon you and learn to walk again. No one will buy a servant who does not walk."

She did as he bid her, though she shrank a bit from his touch. He was unshaven and unwashed, and his weakness appalled her. His hair had been hacked off jaggedly. The smell of him was not too pretty when compared with the fastidious Philip. They began to slowly circle the confined quarters.

"Though not your most perfumed and stylish cavalier, I do not usually greet ladies in such sad condition." He gave her a strained smile.

"Your state is shocking, sir. This must not be allowed to continue." But the captain was law, Lettice was quick to remember.

"And you would save me with your petticoats? No, my dear, the captain is a dangerous man. I advise you to keep clear of him. I pray we may reach land soon, though I fear the storm has driven us badly off course."

Lettice, too, longed to reach Jamestown. She wished never to see the ship nor the captain again.

"I think I will sit now," Geoffrey said. "If you will hand me that bottle of wine my cabin mate left behind, I will try to restore myself somewhat." He lowered himself to his bunk. Lettice sat on a stool near the table.

"You are sharing an officer's cabin?"

"It would seem I am of some importance." He drank slowly of the bottle.

"Have you food?"

"Yes. They bring it to me. And you, my pretty, why are you upon this hell ship?"

"I go to my sister in Virginny."

"It were better you had stayed at home."

Lettice hesitated, then said, "there was no place for me. My father is dead."

"And what will you do in Virginny?"

Lettice flushed. "Find me a rich husband." She turned her face half away, proudly, so that her sodden hair caught on her shoulder and stuck to her cheek.

"And if he is rich but odious?"

Lettice did not answer. She did not want to think about that.

Geoffrey got to his feet once more and resumed his pacing. As Lettice sat silently watching, his steps grew firmer and more sure. The water from Lettice's mantle ran steadily upon the floor. Somewhat wearily she wondered what would happen if the officer returned.

"So Squire Clifford is dead," Geoffrey said at last. "He was a good man in the saddle—and a lusty one with a tavern wench, but—"

"He was a good father," Lettice cut in, remembering Philip's hateful words.

"To be sure." Geoffrey stretched his arms, then dropped them again. "Damn, but I think I shall live another day or two." Then he came to put an arm about her shoulders to raise her to her feet. "Come, my pretty, let us take a stroll about the ship. It's none too safe for you here, and I'd like to let the rain beat on my stinking hide." He reached up to a knife that was stuck into the wall and slid it under his belt.

Lettice looked at him with alarm. What would he try?

"I had thought to let you bind me up again, but now is the time—while they are tried and weakened—for me to challenge their game. Come, let us not tarry." He swept her out the door and into the darkened passage before she could consider. She prayed God he was not a murderer after all.

They crept past the first door Lettice had seen. Again

41

she heard low groans and rustlings. Geoffrey paused and freed his arm from about her neck. "What have we here? What other game does the captain play?"

Lettice stood apprehensively while he felt for the latch. As soon as he located it, he lifted it and kicked the door in with his booted foot. It was pitch-dark inside, and the choking smell of vomit and slops rushed out at them.

"Who's there? What is it?" a voice cried from inside in terror.

"Is it you, Daniel?" she called.

"Mistress Lettice." His voice quavered. "I have found you too late—and now you can do nothing for us. And there is a dead man here."

A pang of fear overtook Lettice, but Geoffrey had left her side and returned with a candle newly lit from the old. The little gleam revealed a scene that made her gasp. Five men lay about the tiny room on dirty blankets, hands bound, though their feet were free, and they wore no gags as Geoffrey had. One of them burned with fever, but the most awful of the men lay back, slack-jawed, his color gray and dead. One leg dangled over the side of his bunk.

"You see what work the spirits do," Geoffrey said grimly. Quickly he cut free the hands of the living men. Immediately they rose and went to the water bucket, pushing and shoving to be the first to drink. The feverish man staggered last.

"Easy now," Geoffrey cautioned them. He dipped candle wax upon the table to fasten the candle there.

"Oh, Mistress Lettice." Daniel stood bathed in brown shadows, his hands clasped together, head bowed. "My master's orders were to find you, but man spirits got me on the docks, and now you see me here." He stepped into the circle of orange-colored light, his face tragic.

Geoffrey turned to look at her, frowning. "What's he speaking of?" he asked.

"It is nothing." Lettice flushed. She must try to put the matter of Philip behind her. And she would certainly not tell Geoffrey about it. She placed a hand upon Daniel's rough brown sleeve. "I am sorry for your trouble, Daniel, but you see Master Finch here has suffered the same. I can do nothing but ask my brother-in-law about it when we reach Jamestown."

"If we are so lucky that we reach Jamestown," Geoffrey

said in a very low voice. Then he took command, saying, "Sit tight, you men. It would seem the captain needs hands. Two sailors have already gone over the side, and others are sickened. Anything is better than lying here, breeding fever. I will go on deck to have this quiet one removed and offer our services in exchange for freedom about the ship. Do you agree?"

Two nodded, though the sick man huddled on his pallet. But Geoffrey's words seemed to have little meaning for Daniel. His head wavered with bewilderment and terror. He reached toward Lettice with beseeching hands. "Oh, mistress, please have them take this dead fellow away."

"Hush," Lettice said, somewhat impatient. "We will do what we can, but there is great risk."

"Stay here," Geoffrey told him. "I will bargain with the captain."

Lettice freed herself of Daniel's hands, thinking to offer some assistance to the feverish man.

"Come, Mistress Clifford," Geoffrey said. "It is time for us to take our chances above."

"I must do something for this poor fellow," she answered.

"You shall not," Geoffrey said, taking her by the shoulder to turn her about. "There is no time for you to nurse, and it is not safe for you here."

"I cannot leave the man here to die," she said sharply.

"Mistress Clifford," Geoffrey sighed. "I beg you to understand that we are all in danger upon this ship. You must leave the nursing of this man to his fellows. I thank you for rescuing me, but in fact you may have placed all of us in worse danger than if you had continued to play lady in your cabin upon the deck. Law upon this ship is not like anything you would have known in your sheltered life at home."

"I have already discovered that, but still I think. . . ."

"My dear, I do not have time to argue. Come now, or I shall be forced to carry you."

She bit her lip, but she followed Geoffrey anyway as he felt his way to the end of the pitch-dark passage. He slipped up to look through the hatch, his movements sure and strong again.

"We will stay hidden here until the way is clear," he called quietly to her.

From the black at the bottom of the stairs she could not see his features, nor he hers. Nor in fact could she see anything at all. She heard the sounds of rasping breath, and she wondered if the sudden exertion had made him ill. Then she froze as she realized the sounds came from behind her. She opened her mouth to scream a warning. A hand closed over it. A knife point pricked her neck. Close to her ear, barely uttered speech gurgled. Her mind conjured up the picture of the canvas-clad sailor speaking in some savage and obscure dialect. Her body turned to ice. What did the brutish sailor want? To turn her in to the captain?

No. She began to understand the words he uttered. They were obscenities, indignities that he would perform upon her body. No, she told herself with panic. "No," she said behind the stifling hand. She kicked out, then felt the knife break her skin.

There was a sudden rush of air from above—a crash— and Geoffrey landed beside her. The sailor loosened his grip, and she screamed. Blindly, Geoffrey's arms flailed about until they came in contact with the flesh of the sailor. Lettice could sense but not see their struggle. Something clattered as it fell. There were blows and grunts of pain. Finally a skull struck the bulkhead with a sickening thud. A body slid to the deck.

"Geoffrey?" Lettice whispered tentatively, feeling her way. "Geoffrey?" she called again.

"I am here," he answered, and his strong and reassuring hand reached hers.

Blindly, they held each other. She still shook with fear and cold. His body warmed hers.

"He was there so suddenly. I wanted to warn you."

"I could tell something was amiss. Foolish wench. It is an ill task for a lady to play rescuer." His words were tender as he slipped his arms under her soaked mantle to draw her closer. His touch burned into her rain-chilled flesh. He bent to kiss her lips. Startled, Lettice made as though to move away, but he held her fast. Then she met his passion eagerly. A sweet liqueur seemed to spread from his mouth to hers and throughout her body. They clung to each other longer than was safe.

He released her, running his hands over her sodden hair. "Ah, if only there were more time," he said, his voice long-

44

ing, his fingers tender. He touched the cut place on her neck, and she winced.

"What? Are you hurt?"

"It is only grazed, thank God. He had a knife."

Geoffrey swore beneath his breath. "I did not know. I am sorry I did not cut his filthy throat. Were we not so lucky, he might have cut yours." He drew her quickly to him again and kissed her cheek. "We must be very careful from now on. Life is of little account upon this ship. Lock your door upon the captain and the rest of these villains." He climbed again to the hatch, reaching down to grasp both her elbows and pull her after him.

"Will you be safe?" she asked anxiously.

"It is a gamble. I was fond of gambling once. One quick kiss then, mistress, and make your way carefully to your cabin. Once I see you are safe, I will toss my dice and follow." His lips touched hers, briefly, then he seized her shoulders and thrust her out upon the deck.

Rain struck her face like a blow. But it formed a veil to hide her from whomever might be about. Huddling near the rail, she inched slowly; the deck was flooded and treacherous underfoot. Her wet clothing dragged her down so that she gasped rather than breathed, which made her realize how afraid she was. She must creep up the companionway to her deck. Holding her breath, she took the plunge upward. There was her cabin. Only a few steps. They might believe she had merely come out for air. She saw the gleam from the captain's window. And then, momentarily, it was blotted out as someone passed before the window.

She turned to look back the way she had come, through the storm and darkness. Was that white blur at the hatch Geoffrey's face? A shadow bounded out upon the deck. It was some time before she could clearly make him out, half-crouched, moving toward her on the way to the captain's cabin.

Then the rain slackened, and the clouds parted before a moon that was full that night. And all at once, Geoffrey was plain to see. Seconds later, Lettice noticed another man. The officer who was Geoffrey's keeper tensed and dropped into a defensive position. Geoffrey raised his knife, extending the tip toward him. Geoffrey's voice, filled with the pleasure of danger, came back to her on the wind. "I say, where's the captain?"

Still crouched, hands raised as though to push outward, the officer backed toward the rail.

"Stand where you are!" Geoffrey shouted.

Two others ran from the shadows to rush Geoffrey, but he retreated slowly, pointing his knife now toward one, now another of them. A blaze of lightning illuminated his fencing gestures and his flashing grin. His full light sleeves ran with water; his dark hair separated into dripping strands. But he seemed mad with joy to be free.

"Now, my friends," he cried apologetically, "I really do not want to trouble you. I will give up this knife quite easily. I ask little. I only wish to bargain away my bonds so that the captain may put my hands to better use. Mine and those of the other men below. A good idea, eh?"

His three attackers looked at one another, considering. "I'll speak to the captain. Watch him." So shouting, the officer fled to Quince's cabin, his feet pounding past Lettice.

There was another crack of lightning, and the sky split. Water swept over the deck just as the sky darkened again, with only a glimmering of the moon and the lanterns showing. Lettice retreated farther toward her door, huddled, hoping not to be noticed. She saw that Geoffrey and the two sailors were frozen like statues. As she watched them, she drew a deep breath of surprise. One of the men was reaching slowly toward his waist where a knife was concealed. Before she could scream, Geoffrey saw him. Lunging, he flicked the knife out of the fellow's grasp with the point of his own. The sailor's weapon clattered to the deck. Deliberately, Geoffrey placed his foot upon it. The three were frozen once more in the half darkness.

A jet of light blazed out as the captain's door opened. She could just see his back as he leaned to gaze upon the main deck. Though one hand held a pistol, he still wore his nightcap. But he had taken the time to pull on his boots. The light glinted on Geoffrey's knife momentarily.

"Throw down your knife," the captain boomed, "or I'll blow your head off!"

"It's not mutiny I'm after, Captain," Geoffrey called, "but work. I will trade my bonds for work. We cannot betray you—I and the other men—so far from shore."

The captain hesitated, his gaze raking the ship.

"Throw down your knife," he ordered again.

Geoffrey did not waver. "Not until I have your word that I will be bound no more."

The captain's harsh laughter rang out. "My word, you coxcomb! I'm master here! I give my word to no one!" His head moved slowly as he rested his eyes on each man in turn that they might understand his power. His heavy body swelled with menace. The cabin light shining on his night-clothes made him neither soft nor ridiculous. There would be no snickers at the figure he cut.

Lettice clenched her hands into fists, forgetting that she was hiding. The drama below absorbed all her attention.

"Mr. Johnson!" the captain called.

His officer, halfway down to the main deck again, looked up for orders.

"How short-handed are we tonight?"

"We could use five or six men."

The captain nodded heavily several times before he spoke. "Let him free for now."

Geoffrey's tenseness did not slacken as he looked from the captain to the men. The officer approached him. Geoffrey heaved a mighty sigh and let the knife drop from his hand. One of the men sprang forward to pick it up. Geoffrey stood alert, watching.

"There's a dead man below who needs removing!" he shouted over the wind.

Lettice saw the officer look up to receive a signal from the captain. The officer nodded, then the three on deck closed on Geoffrey. Two grabbed his arms as the officer struck him, once in the face and twice in the belly. Geoffrey doubled over and fell to the deck. Step by step, Lettice retreated to her door, helpless in her fear for him.

The captain still hung over the railing. His white attire was fluttering in the wind. "Stand up!" he ordered.

Slowly Geoffrey got to his feet. Lettice breathed easier at seeing that he was able to stand.

"You will do your share, or more, of the work," the captain ordered. "And you will learn that I am master here and that you, with all your gentleman's ways, are at the very bottom. If you survive the voyage, it will only be because you have learned how to serve without question."

Geoffrey stood quietly, unresisting, not challenging the

captain's words. The captain contemptuously slammed his door behind him. One of the men gave Geoffrey a shove as the four of them went below to free the others to work and to heave the poor dead wretch's body into the sea.

All was quiet save for the sound of the pounding sea. The candles flickered weakly behind their glass; the deck was empty. Lettice drew in a long and shuddering sigh. It had all been more perilous even than she expected. Her life, she supposed, had been very sheltered. She prayed that she had not exposed Geoffrey and the others to more danger at the hands of the captain than had they remained prisoners. But she sensed that Geoffrey was glad to be free, no matter the risk.

Sighing again, she opened her door. Inside the dim cabin John Martin moved suddenly as though surprised. Then he beat a hasty retreat, running out without speaking. After lighting a new candle to the old, which was almost out, Lettice looked down at her little maid. Molly did look better, indeed, strangely satisfied. But what role was John Martin playing in all this?

Sighing, Lettice shed her drenched mantle. She felt again the power of Geoffrey's arms upon her and the burning of his lips.

Why was the maid ever-satisfied and the mistress yearning?

As soon as Lettice had closed the cabin door to walk out upon the deck, John Martin had bent to plant a kiss upon the burning forehead of his beloved. "Well, my girl, what ails ye?"

"Ye'll catch the fever, John. And you be dripping on me."

"It seems measlie, and I've already been spotted with that." John took a corner of the blanket to wipe his face and hair.

"Oh, John, it feels better just to see you. But I am as weak as a bald baby. Why did you not tell me Virginny was so great a way away?"

"I did not know myself. I've been told it was only a day or two by sea, but maybe they lied to get men to go there."

"You should not listen to liars, John. We will never get there, I think, but drop off, instead, at the end of the waters." Her light-blue eyes were strained with worry.

"That's foolishness. The world be not like that." John wiped her burning forehead once again.

"Be it not? But since we thought Virginny closer, mayhap we was wrong in other ways. Wrong to come."

"Look." John reached into a pouch at his belt. "You see this coin? See the words upon it?"

"Oh, John," his beloved said. "Even were I well, I could not read it, for you know I never learned."

"Nor I, but the one that give it to me told me what it says. See," he pointed with his finger. " 'In England land scarce and labor plenty. In Virginia land free and labor scarce.' "

Molly ran her finger over the coin, turning it over and studying it. "It looks to be an old coin, John. How do you know it's true still?"

"It is true," he insisted. "You take my word for it. And there was nothing for us at home. My mother and I wandered after my father and Cromwell's armies for years, stopping here and there. When the Lord Protector and father both died, we came back to our home. But there was little left for mother there, and nothing for me."

"But I'm no Puritan, John."

"I know that well, my lass," he laughed. "Nor am I these days. I only have faith in myself."

Molly gestured for a drink of water, and held the noggin to her lips. Then she lay back again, looking somewhat revived.

"But I'm afeared, John. What if we be separated? You signed that paper for the captain to sell your time for three years. If only you had more money, you could have signed for less."

He squeezed her hand, his face full of love. "We'll not be separated, I promise you. But if somehow we are, it must be faced. There's no way we could make a life in the old country. Here, with some luck, we will have land and money of our own."

"Oh, I'm afeared," she wailed once more. "You shouldn't have had the captain bring Daniel aboard."

He grunted, "I seen that lacky riding about the countryside with the sweet-smelling cavalier. We did your mistress a favor to hide her from that lazy lover. Besides, I made a coin or two for pointing out Daniel to the captain."

"Master Philip may come after her, and then where will I be?"

"He be too lazy, I vow. All will be well, I promise you." He lay down at her side and spoke into her fever-damp hair.

She sighed once more. "Oh, John, will there be savages in Virginny? I've heard they paint their faces and kill Englishmen with hatchets."

"No, no," John reassured her. "They can't stand against stout Englishmen. No, little one, the only savage will be me. I'm fair savage for want of you."

She reached out from under her covers to grasp his fingers.

"Molly," he whispered hoarsely. "Are you too weak?"

"Well, John." She fixed a reddened but flirtatious eye upon him. "If I was to die, I'd want to die happy."

And smiling down into her eyes, he enfolded her in his arms.

IV

Geoffrey had been sent aloft to reef the sails—work that he did none too well, for he was not used to it. And all was doubly hard since he was pained by his beating and still somewhat weak. He could hear the canvas whipping overhead. He did not mind the rain beating down upon him, for it was the first time since his kidnapping that he had felt clean. He owned no cloak to keep off bad weather, but his boots were still good and would last some time.

With a cruel smile, the sailing master had sent him up, daring him to climb in the wind and survive. It was a test they gave all newcomers. Those who hurtled to the deck were unfit to be seamen.

Geoffrey had every intention of surviving. Throwing his head back, he savored the cloudy night. His body was responding to his commands; his strength was returning; he might yet master the humiliating situation into which he had fallen. Geoffrey had been at sea some few times before in his travels. A voyage always made him feel free and unfettered by ordinary cares. Now, just released from bondage, the same feeling swept over him with overwhelming intensity.

From his perch he looked out upon the waters. The waves were indistinguishable in the darkness. How many miles separated them from England by now? The English Channel was a mere trickle compared to the vastness of the ocean.

The thought of England sobered him. Though his hands busied themselves with the lines, his mind raced. He knew his trials were not over, that he had been sold—and sold to the worst of villains.

* * *

"If you sign the indenture, we might not kill you," the captain had said, laughing hoarsely. "Your hide seems too valuable to throw into the sea." And the captain roared with grating laughter, then he took another pull on his bottle, sack running down the black stubble on his chin.

Geoffrey had not doubted the captain's threat and so had signed away seven years of his life on each of two sections of a paper. Half went to him, half to the captain, who could then sell his half and Geoffrey along with it.

Geoffrey was still alive however.

Why am I here?" Geoffrey had asked himself over and over again.

Giles. All his thoughts led back to Giles. Dear brother. They had shadowed and mirrored each other since they had crept from the womb but a few minutes apart, Giles unfortunately emerging first.

"The darlings," their lady mother had always said. "Even I can scarce tell one from the other." She was especially tender with them, for three baby daughters had died one after the other.

Giles was always conscious that though he was indeed first, his brother was close upon his heels. Therefore, Giles was always racing—run faster, ride more furiously, drink more, wench without ceasing and be the harsher with the folk of the estate. Sir Giles, their father, encouraged their rivalry as a way of counteracting their mother's tenderness.

But Giles—the first-born, the favored son—would inherit all the family holdings at Finch's Ford, as well as the title of baronet. The family was not one of the great families of England, but the holdings were substantial indeed.

Second sons, no matter what slender filament of time divided them from the first, were not to be coddled at home to threaten the heir's supremacy. So Geoffrey had been destined for the Church, though a poor psalm-singer he would have made. They had sent him up to Oxford to study, expecting that at the finish he would acquire a substantial living, rising perhaps from prebend to deacon to dean and mayhap even bishop. It was not that any of the Finch family were religious, but that was the way things were done. How else could Geoffrey ever hope to marry and keep a family?

As was the custom among squires and lesser gentry, both Finch boys had attended the village school together, and then gone on to grammar school at the neighboring market town. Geoffrey went on alone to Oxford, relishing his freedom at 15. He had not been sorry to leave home, and Giles as well, behind.

At Oxford, Geoffrey attained a liberal education— beginning with drinking bouts in all the ale houses and taverns of the surrounding area, joining the other young men of his class. They shed their student gowns on any possible occasion and dressed in more fashionable attire, swords at their sides. Drink was popularly thought to fight the damp, musty climate and the unhealthful mists that pervaded Oxford.

Seated among his fellows, quaffing ale in a crowded tavern, Geoffrey learned, like them, to reach under a swinging barmaid's skirt to feel a smooth ankle, or with darting hand dive between the hanging globes of a wench whose arms were too laden to resist. These coltish pranks only whetted his appetite. Fairer and more satisfying game was to be found farther afield.

Between these entertainments he strengthened his countryman's body by walking in the fields, bathing in the river, jumping and running, playing at soccer with the best of companions, who would fall into deadly combat if the results of an athletic contest did not suit them. When they did not fight each other, the young men grew riotous— gown against town—and harried the merchants and folk of Oxford, retreating to shelter among the spires and warm fires of the university.

But there was more to Oxford than all that. Geoffrey somehow learned a smattering of Greek and a good deal of Latin. He read pagan literature, which made him look at the world about him with different and less-pious eyes.

Disappointed in a mistress or two, he became part of a clique that wrote English verse. For a time the idea of becoming a poet—perhaps at court—fired him, until a companion pointed out that his verses were in fact not very good.

All his friends enjoyed life at Oxford in the same way. They were good king's men. England had been gloomy and constrained enough under Cromwell and the Puritans. Everyone knew that King Charles enjoyed his mistress more than his wife, the queen. With Charles, the young gentlemen of Oxford knew, debauchery was loyalty, gravity rebellion.

Geoffrey avoided the more serious scholars, especially those enamored of the Church. He was vaguely aware that there was still another level at Oxford of dedicated, though impoverished, young men who planned to become teachers or members of the lesser clergy. These sons of yeomen, tradesmen and farmers had fewer hours to carouse than their betters. They often drudged as servitors to their fellow students. Geoffrey would come upon them making up beds, or sweeping out chambers, or fetching water, and wonder why it was so important to them to keep at their studies this way. In time he came to understand.

One day Geoffrey received word that Old Sir Giles, his father, fell ill. Geoffrey had some suspicion that it might be the result of the French pox or some similar disease, for even after he married, Sir Giles had been a scourge of the female population of a goodly part of the county.

Whatever the cause, not only his body but his mind became enfeebled. Geoffrey had returned home once, briefly, and had been shocked by his father's condition. The middle-aged man's mind wandered so that it was some time before he recognized his son, and then called him Giles.

Giles strode about the place as though he were already master, and his face wore a habitually complacent smirk. It was with a good deal of unease that Geoffrey returned to Oxford.

Then one night after his return to school, staggering home to his room, somewhat the worse for drink, he found a servant of his father's, who was carrying a message. Word of Geoffrey's bad behavior had reached his father's ears, the missive read. He would be cut off from his allowance until he learned to behave better.

Geoffrey blanched. He would be without any but the small amount of silver he had on hand until his lady mother died and he inherited some property from her. He could not wish his own mother dead, yet cold panic gripped him. Perhaps he should write to her to ask her to intercede.

But the color soon returned to his sun-browned face as he flushed with anger. It was some gross treachery of

Gile's. How dare they—his father and Giles—accuse him of recklessness when they drank and wenched their way unceasingly across the countryside.

Geoffrey remembered a time when he had come across his father one day when he had a frightened young maiden backed up against a tree. Her skirts were tucked up, for she had been working in the fields along with all the people of the neighborhood. Bits of hay and hayseed were caught in the folds of her clothing. Her eyes showed pure terror, for how dare she complain of an attack on her by Sir Giles, the master of the lands upon which her father lived? Though Geoffrey was no saint himself, the scene was too much for him, and he distracted and discouraged his father as best he could.

It might be that his father was angered because his younger son was taking so long to finish at Oxford. In truth, Geoffrey was in no hurry to leave, dreading the next stage of his life. In his heart he knew that he would never be content in the Church. He would much rather be a squire like his brother now was with Sir Giles enfeebled. Would that there were room for two of them. Though Geoffrey loved the theater and the other pleasures of the town, life on the land suited him best of all. Someday he would come into his inheritance—a more modest one than Giles's, it was true. But it might be enough to buy a small manor in the country upon the death of his parents. Still, there was no reason he might not have some in advance if his father would only be reasonable.

No, he decided. He would not beg from his father. His mother was helpless. It would only make her worry. His father was ill, his mind disordered, and Giles would use every resource at hand to poison Old Sir Giles against Geoffrey. The thought of going on his knees to his father made him sick with disgust.

What, then, must he do? If he hastened, perhaps he could take his master's degree. And if he lived soberly, maybe he could continue without joining the ranks of the bed-makers.

Toward the end, however, he found himself reduced to menial tasks, waiting upon those who had formerly been his peers. He would look down upon the floor, his face blazing with shame, as former friends walked by.

He often thought now of traveling to Europe to become

a mercenary, but he had not even the means to take himself there. Without the political backing of his family or his friends in the Church, it would be difficult to get a living had he any taste for the life. No, he thought, he would best become a soldier. Finally he steeled himself to ask a friend for aid.

"My God, Geoffrey, I had no idea you were in such trouble," James told him. He came from one of the first families of the realm, and he had many connections in high places. "But it's no good your trying for the Church. You've offended several of the masters and have shown no real interest whatever. You could go on to the Inns of Court for law, but I somehow feel that's not for you either. Am I to understand that you no longer have any allowance at all?"

Geoffrey nodded, tight-lipped. Charity was galling to him. He could never be a courtier, since seeking favors from even so inoffensive a friend as James proved offensive to him.

"I think some kin of mine have a son about to marry and take the grand tour. They might take you on as a tutor. They are staying not far from your home, but you will leave almost immediately for Europe; so it should not matter.

Geoffrey reflected. "It might save my life, and at least I'd see a bit of the world. But I'd have to change my name. I want no one to know me as a Finch."

"What shall I call you, then?"

Geoffrey cast about in his mind for an unassuming name—a name suited to a tutor. "Henry Cooper," he said after a bit.

"Very good. I will write you a letter calling you Henry Cooper."

Young Robert Ashley was married that very month. Robert actually wanted to go to Oxford, but his father thought him already too bookish for a son and heir. He was 15 years old; so it was deemed best that he take the grand tour of Europe with a tutor before settling down with his tall though fragile-looking blond wife. Isobel, Robert's lady, was already 20 years of age and in possession of a large estate. Young Robert met his bride just before the ceremony and found her an awesome beauty and terribly frightening.

Geoffrey, called Henry now, found her to be a common flirt and was greatly relieved when he and his charge set out, leaving her behind.

They had traveled on the continent for well over two years. Geoffrey taught his charge what he could and learned much of the world himself. In France he would wait impatiently some nights until Robert was settled, and then proceed to partake of what he could from his lowly station of the spectacular court life of Louis XIV. Journeying to Fontainebleau, Geoffrey stood in the background to watch ballets and entertainment by the court playwright, Molière. In Paris the doors of French society were freely opened to young Englishmen, and he often assumed an identity superior to that of Henry Cooper, though he did not admit himself to be Geoffrey Finch.

With the aid of a married lady who found him tender and amusing, he acquired some polish and cynicism. He regretted briefly that he must in time leave France.

"It is a pity you must go," the lady told him in broken English. "I would scheme to keep you here."

He smiled sadly. "And so my choice must be either to become a pet ape for a lady, or a nursemaid to a boy." And they reclined together on the tumbled but luxurious sheets. The lady's scent intoxicated him.

"I can see that neither really suits you, *mon cher*," the lady replied. She leaned so that her ringlets fell forward onto her breast. Propped on one dimpled elbow, she regarded him with tear-drenched eyes, for she was truly fond of him. It was a wrench for him to free himself of her soft clinging. Her life would be drab, indeed, tied to an elderly husband.

"My darling," he whispered to her, his eyes studying every inch of her enchanting features and coming to rest on the beauty patch on her fragile cheekbone. "If only you could come to Venice with me."

She sat up and looked away from him. Tendrils of hair were hiding her face. "I have my duty. This is what it means to be a great aristocrat in France." Then she met his eyes, flushing deeply. "Perhaps . . . perhaps," she began shyly. She moistened her full rosy lips, unable for a moment to go on. Then she leaned toward him and spoke all in a rush. "Perhaps you will give me a child to remember you by. My husband has tried in vain for many years. If he should die. . . ." She lifted her firm, round chin and looked at him less softly. "Please do not think me too wicked, but if he should die, I will have very little protection without an heir. Besides, I am very lonely." She pressed soft, full lips upon his without embracing him. He stiffened, then pressed his hard body upon her ripe curves until she lay beneath him on the tumbled sheets.

But it could not last forever.

When he left her chamber and walked out into the early morning toward the rooms he and Robert had taken, he heard with a chill steady footsteps behind him. He looked back to discover a thin and aging man.

The count! he thought with fear and shame. Thunderstruck, he remained rooted to the pavement as the man's footsteps echoed closer. Then Geoffrey realized that it could hardly be the count, for though the man walked with aristocratic dignity, he wore livery.

The footsteps halted beside Geoffrey. *"Monsieur?"* the thin, reedy voice said.

"Oui?" Geoffrey responded. He added, "My tongue stumbles badly in French."

The retainer continued in halting English. "My master the count requests of *monsieur* that he not visit the countess again."

Geoffrey swallowed, then uttered with difficulty, "Tell your master that I shall not." He stood in the deserted street and watched the ghostly figure retreat into the mist without further words.

Geoffrey left France in ill humor. He never heard afterward whether or not the countess had produced a child.

From Paris, Geoffrey and the boy traveled on horseback with two servants into Switzerland and then to Italy to look at the monuments of classic antiquity. Robert was enthralled by them, but Geoffrey longed for a more active kind of life. In Venice the cosmopolitan society distracted them, and Robert bought a Renaissance painting, which Geoffrey suspected had really been finished some weeks before.

In Venice, Robert fell in love with a 17-year-old English girl. For some weeks he mooned about, wanting to touch her, or at least approach her more closely. Finally, Geoffrey became aware that the youth had gone into her private chamber at the *palazzo* where they were staying. Standing below their room, in the courtyard, Geoffrey held his breath, only to hear, shortly, a door slam. His charge, red-faced, rapidly descended the stone stairs and saw Geoffrey. He would not speak to his tutor for some time.

Soon after that incident Geoffrey and Robert began a leisurely trip home to England. Shepherding a boy throughout Europe, Geoffrey had become a man—a dissatisfied man. He did not wish to spend his life in dependent obscurity.

The Ashley estate was a good day's ride from the Finch holdings. The two families were unacquainted, since the principal estate was some miles away. The lovely Ashley house with its fish ponds and orchards had been presented to young Robert. Soon after reaching Robert's home, Geoffrey sent off a notice to his mother, informing her that he was still alive, but saying little else. He inquired about and soon discovered that his father still lived and that Giles had been married for a year. Then Geoffrey wondered what on earth he should do next, and once more considered becoming a mercenary. He must leave Robert to his lady wife.

"Henry," Robert said hesitantly as they rode out with a falcon early one morning. "I really have to tell someone. I don't know what to do." His thin, sallow, generally unemotional face showed real distress.

"What is it, Robert?" Geoffrey asked genially, for by this time he'd grown quite fond of the boy.

"It's Isobel," Robert blurted after a moment's silence. "I know that she is my wife and that I should bed her, but in her chamber she looks down upon me, for she is some inches taller than I. And her eyes are so cold, and she wears a wicked smile upon her face. She is so beautiful, so finely made, yet she looks down upon me and mocks me." Robert was truly upset. "And so though I want to bed her, I find that I cannot."

"Have you bedded anyone?" Geoffrey asked gently.

His charge shook his head, his fair cheeks flaming. "My father will be angry if I don't produce an heir."

"I see that I have neglected your education." Geoffrey was concerned. He refrained from reaching to pat the boy on his head. Geoffrey often suspected that Lady Isobel had

59

a cruel nature, for he himself had often felt her harsh eyes upon him. Fortunately the house was so enormous that their paths seldom crossed.

Upon returning to the manor house, they encountered the lady herself dressed for riding. She was sampling the cheeses and bread and ale laid out on the sideboard. A fire burned on the grate; the chimney piece was graced with a painting of the smooth-cheeked Bathsheba tempting King David to adultery. Lady Isobel ate standing, her sharp teeth tearing at the bits of bread. She regarded the two males with a somewhat malicious eye. Robert slunk off to his chamber.

"Out so early, Master Cooper?" she inquired, coming to Geoffrey's side and toying with a little whip she carried.

Geoffrey grunted in reply.

She placed a slender hand on his arm. "And will you not ride out again with me today?" Her voice was low and throaty. She leaned toward him so that her breast pressed against him. There was a delicious smell about her.

Geoffrey felt lust rise within him. He was a young man, after all, and though he had sampled the charms of Venice, he'd had no satisfying love since Paris. "As you see, I have just returned," he grumbled, edging away from her. The effect she had on his senses was dangerous. She was in truth a great beauty.

"Riding," she looked at him flirtatiously, "is a supreme pleasure." She moistened her pink lips with her tongue. Her voice descended to a lower, more trembling note. "Surely one ride will not exhaust you so that you cannot pleasure yourself again."

Geoffrey drew in a great breath, feeling himself weaken. Venice was so long ago. He turned and walked unsteadily toward the door and headed in the direction of the stables, not looking back. She was close on his heels, laughing gaily. He gritted his teeth.

Once in the saddle they spoke not a word to each other. She led the way until they came to a garden house that was smothered beneath shrubbery. They dismounted and stood regarding each other and panting in short gasps that had little to do with the exertion of riding. Standing before classic pillars surmounted by cherubs and garlands in stone, she raised her arms to remove her plumed riding hat. She tossed it onto the ground, then began to stroke Geoffrey's thigh with her whip. Licking her lips, she laughed silently. For all her perfect beauty she had a wolfish smile.

His hand lashed out to knock the whip to the ground. He gripped her shoulders, pulling her to him, and ground his hips against hers. Her pale-blue riding dress impeded him. Throwing her head back with a dazzling smile, Lady Isobel freed herself then gestured toward the double door of the garden house. He lifted the latch, and she swept in past him. She turned to look at him and lifted her upper lip in a half-sneer as she began to disrobe. Why did women wear so much clothing? he wondered with irritation as she discarded each elegant article. But when she stood smooth and naked in the mellow light of the little room, he held his breath. She was beautiful and she knew it.

In her arrogance she did not draw the curtains, and she seemed impervious to the chill of the unused room. Angrily he jerked at the dusty material until they were safe from view. Had he seen someone move outside? But his desire for her now was like a pain. Clenching his teeth, he ripped off his shirt and breeches so that his skin might touch hers.

Only a low couch and chairs furnished the garden house. Lady Isobel lay back on the couch, her narrow feet resting on the floor, her nipples facing the ceiling. In a moment he was upon her, his hand reaching for her breast, his hips reaching for hers.

Though her boy husband had had no success, Lady Isobel was not a virgin, as Geoffrey discovered. This eased his conscience somewhat. Just as her mind and nature were at once hard and cold, her body was all silk and fire. His body moved with a will of its own, seeking relief in her delicious, long, smooth curves. He thought for a while that she tried to control her emotion—but she could not. Her lips parted. A low moan escaped. She gasped, then moaned again. Her nails dug into his buttocks. She cried out, shuddered. Then he shuddered as she arched her back, and they climaxed into sensuous relief.

As they lay spent, Geoffrey thought for a moment that he heard a noise at the window. He prayed God they had not been observed. The day was clouding over, his passion dissipated, and he was already regretting what had just happened. He would never be able to make it up to Robert. He must leave Robert's service—and soon.

"Tell me, Master Cooper," she whispered throatily. "You are very mysterious. I would know more of you."

"There is nothing to say."

"Such a handsome face. Yet it seems I have seen you somewhere before. But there could not be two such men in England."

Geoffrey felt a pang of danger. Was the Lady Isobel playing more than one game with him? She pressed her hips against his once more, then with a sensuous movement she drew away. "Well, I think now you may deliver me back to the boy," she said as she stood up.

"He is your husband," Geoffrey said severely.

"And so he is." She raised her arms to detach a leaf from her flowing, pale-yellow hair. "But when he comes to my chamber with that child's look, I can only laugh at him; he is all hands and feet and awkwardness."

"You might teach him my lady." He decided that he really did not like her very much.

"I prefer a man already taught." She turned a profile to him that was perfect and replete with self-satisfaction.

"I would put on my clothes were I you, my lady," he said wryly. "Else the chill will put you to bed in a less interesting way."

She dressed slowly, sensuously. Then she walked out to her mount. Geoffrey pulled on his breeches, then helped her into the saddle.

Loving, Geoffrey reflected, was the only art at which he excelled. It was ironic. He wanted to become a man among men, but this seemed denied him. The look he fixed upon the lady riding beside him was thunderous indeed.

On the way to his chamber he encountered Robert. One look at the boy's face convinced Geoffrey that all was known.

"You have had her before me!" Robert accused.

Geoffrey froze in his tracks while a wave of shame overcame him. "I did but think to prepare your way," he stuttered inadequately. Oh, God, how could he have been so stupid! The Lady Isobel would only learn what she herself desired.

In answer, the sallow, clear-eyed boy swung and struck his tutor in the face. Then he sprang away and ran down the hall, leaving Geoffrey looking helplessly after him.

"Robert!" Geoffrey called. How would he ever make

things right for the boy? Geoffrey cursed the Lady Isobel and her wantonness. Once more he went to the stables where his mount was still saddled. Furious, Geoffrey urged it over a hedge and into the woods. Trees and bushes slapped his face as he sped until he reached the road. His life was intolerable to him. If only he could always be as free as he was now, riding across the countryside. Angrily he urged his tired horse on so forcefully that he did not hear the hoofbeats behind him. He was grabbed and captured before he realized what was happening.

At first he thought that Robert ordered it, yet the boy scarcely had time to make the arrangements. Would the lady have done it? Not likely. She would merely laugh to herself in her chamber. Once more his thoughts turned to Giles.

This reviewing of his condition dampened Geoffrey's spirits. Though weary from his unaccustomed work after his long confinement, he had done what was required of him. He began his descent from high up in the rigging. The rain had slackened, and soon it would be time for him to return to his cabin, if indeed he was still to stay in that place. He suspected that the captain, glad enough for some extra hands, would not be eager to have Geoffrey tell his tale to his shipmates.

Yet what could he say? Many of the men were impressed sailors—themselves seized near the docks. And he had no proof that his brother Giles had so arranged his fate as to come near destroying him. But in his heart he knew it. The rage he had felt toward Giles burned away, and cold purpose replaced it.

He would recapture his life somehow. He would become not a clergyman—clearly he was unsuited to that state— but a free man! Somehow he would gain his inheritance. Then he wondered as he had many times what, after all, Giles had to gain? Did he hate Geoffrey that much? Did he begrudge him the small inheritance when he had, by far, the larger share? Geoffrey was of too free and generous a nature to be very good at hating. Yet his whole being was filled with a desire to revenge himself on Giles, to set these matters straight.

God knew what would happen to him in Virginia. He had promised to serve some master seven years—a promise he had no intention of keeping if it could be avoided. Perhaps the little Clifford wench could help him in some way. She had connections in Virginia. A pretty woman she was, with fine eyes, though no great beauty. He had spied her walking upon the deck occasionally. There was a freshness to her silken brown hair and creamy bright complexion. But he must be careful. Women had done him little good so far. He looked away toward her cabin where he could still see the light of a flickering candle.

The end of the watch was rung. Geoffrey thought to tap upon Lettice's door, but he saw a burly sailor come toward him; the knife Geoffrey had discarded was in his hand. Geoffrey tensed.

"Captain's orders," the sailor said.

Another came forward with a length of rope. "Just your hands, mate," he explained. "Then back below."

Geoffrey's spirits sank. It had been too much to hope. Pray God they would untie him again tomorrow.

"And one more thing," the sailor said. Geoffrey looked at him expectantly. "The captain said you was to meet Swope here." He gestured toward the shadow where a skeleton-thin figure emerged with a blob of white face and pits for eyes. The figure stood in such a strange and silent way that Geoffrey felt a chill about his heart.

"One look at Swope be usually enough to bring a man to order," the sailor chuckled. "And if it be not—we turn Swope loose upon him. He be very good at punishment."

V

Lettice saw the captain's face . . . floating above her . . . red and bloated . . . swelling . . . his eyes fiery. Like a bubble upon the water, it burst.

She awoke, burning and painful. Would she ever reach Virginia, or would she be dropped over the side like those others? The storm had driven the ship far off course. Now they sailed in what seemed an endless ocean with all land fallen off the edge of the world. Rations were short. Lettice's gingerbread and oranges and other provisions were long gone.

Hearing her own shallow breathing, she prayed she would remain conscious at least until her maid returned. Now that Molly was strong, she was ever flitting her petticoats in some distant part of the ship—distant, that is, from wherever her mistress might be. Lettice was lost without her.

What light came in the small window stabbed Lettice's eyes, and the cabin swam. Her fingers traced circles over her body. Were these spots like Molly's? Her blemishes had looked like measles rather than a more dread and scarring pox, but any of these fevers might prove fatal.

Lettice, with great effort, marshaled her thoughts. For measles, a live sheep laid on the bed. That was it. Sheep were easily infected and would draw out the poison from the human body. Unfortunately there were no sheep on board. Lettice could recall no other cures.

She awoke. A cool, strong hand rested on her forehead. She was not frightened, for the hand was gentle and reassuring. Geoffrey's warm, brown eyes looked down at her. His shirt was frayed at the cuffs, and his leather jerkin pulled apart at the seams. But he had managed to shave, and now he was smiling and handsome.

Her lips moved, but no sound came forth. Geoffrey's dark eyes showed concern. "How's this, lady?"

"Water."

He bent toward her. Her voice must have been too faint to hear. She said it again. Obediently, he fetched some, supporting her so she might drink.

"It is my turn to rescue you, it seems." He had not held a woman in such a state of undress since his unfortunate embrace of Lady Isobel. His fingers rested lightly on Lettice's shoulders, and he felt the silkiness of her creamy skin, though fever burned her. He rested his lips briefly on her hot temple.

Lying weak and helpless in her fine, white shift, she revealed a lovely, graceful-limbed body and fruity breasts. He spied one pink nipple nestling beneath the lace trim. Geoffrey felt a foolish languor creep into his brain. He longed to slip his hands into her bosom. But he drew back from her, realizing her poor state. "Where is your maid, lady?"

Lettice shook her head feebly, her heavy lids closing. Incredibly thick, dark lashes rested against her cheek, though she had lost her lovely bloom with her illness. Her pretty lips parted with a gentle sigh.

"You should not lie alone here in the shadows. I will find your maid." Again he rested his lips on her forehead, but he manfully kept his hands from the rest of her. Yet he was touched by her. He remembered her as a little girl, delicate, yet plucky. She would have ridden with Giles and he had they let her. Then he had lost sight of her as she grew. He had never expected her to open such chords of sympathy and desire in him. But this was not the place to think of that.

He stepped out upon the bright deck. He was free and unbound that day. After he had finished his watch, no one had come to tie him again. The ship was short-handed, even with bound servants, both voluntary and forced, pressed into service. Several more corpses had gone over the side as bad food and fever took their toll.

Geoffrey relished his freedom. But it were best to keep clear of Captain Quince. Geoffrey learned how to serve and obey as he never had in his life before. Though his naturally good spirits often burst forth, he knew he must be cautious.

But where had the little maid gone? He had seen her often enough with the tall, blond servant, their heads bent together as though plotting. Once in the shadows below deck he had surprised them in an embrace of desperate passion. The man had flushed to his almost-whitish hair; the maid had shuddered with the intensity of her emotion. The ship offered little comfort to lovers.

Geoffrey saw the maid's greenish skirts coming his way across the deck as she dodged coils of rope, kegs and rigging. Canvas-clad sailors eyed her as she passed. He went forward to take her by the arm. "Your mistress is very weak," he said coldly as she avoided a sailor who was seated upon the deck, mending sail.

"Oh, I know, sir." The girl's expression was genuinely contrite. "I been about the ship, trying to get some decent food for her. They only give me the smallest bit of salt herring—and a poor bit at that. I can scarce eat it myself." Molly showed him the unappetizing bit of food curled in a wooden basin. He was fond enough of herring, but besides wormy biscuit, it was all they had had for the last several days. Some of the men suffered swollen gums.

Frowning, he followed Molly inside the cabin and watched Lettice wrinkle her fine nose and turn her head away. Her lips were dry and cracked. He knelt to feel her forehead again with his browned and newly callused hand.

"I am no pretty nurse," he said. "What would you have, lady?"

"Water," Lettice cried faintly.

After a sip, she dropped her head again. "It tastes so bad." But then she seemed to revive a bit and took another sip.

The water Geoffrey had had that morning was wormy. They needed to clean and replenish the barrels.

Lettice's eyes had shut, but she opened them again and whispered, half smiling, hesitating now and again as weakness swept over her. "I dreamed . . . I walked through a meadow. A clear brook bubbled there . . . and buttercups grew . . . and wild strawberries hid among the grasses. Oh, but they tasted sweet to me. But then I awoke." Her eyes closed again.

"Oh, mistress!" Molly's eyes teared over. She pulled at

Geoffrey's sleeve. "I never seen her so weak. Oh, what'll happen to me, sir, if she dies?"

Geoffrey was startled. Could Lettice be that weak? Poor lady. Her fine, long hair spread about her on the pillow. She had no proper food, but craved the strawberries of some past English summer.

Geoffrey knew the captain did not suffer hunger. His cabin was well-stocked with his personal preserves. At the beginning of the voyage he guarded his private coop of chickens, sharing them only with his officers. There were still provisions bound for Jamestown, but the captain would never allow them to be broken open. He also doubtless had his private barrel of apples.

Without a word to the two women, Geoffrey went out once more to contemplate the captain's oak door. The wind blowing across the deck carried the captain's booming, but muffled, voice from some other region of the ship. Now was the moment for a little theft. Geoffrey smiled to himself; he was at once taken back to some of the pranks of his Oxford days. But this might be more serious, for the captain at sea held the power of life and death over all of them.

If it was his destiny to hang or be thrown overboard, let it be aiding a lady, Geoffrey thought. He lifted the latch and walked into the captain's cabin, leaving the door slightly ajar for safety.

The apples were gone. Biting at the inside of his cheek with his teeth, Geoffrey looked about. There was a small keg in the corner. Quickly he reached inside, only to grasp the rotten portion of an apple on the top. Faugh! But the next one he felt was fairly firm though wrinkled. Quickly he drew out three and slipped them into his shirt sleeve. Then he turned toward the door.

Captain Isaac Quince was there before him! Geoffrey had not heard his step. The captain's shaggy dark brows drew together as he reddened and seemed to swell. He said nothing. Instead, he dragged a loaded pistol from his belt. Raising it with both hands, he aimed directly at Geoffrey. Geoffrey blinked with surprise.

"I could kill you now," Captain Quince said in an unusually soft voice, "even though your hide is valuable to me. Twice you've defied me." One bloodshot eye closed as he made sure of his target.

Geoffrey turned cold. He swallowed carefully. He believed the captain. He had come to know him.

"My hide is surely worth more than three apples, sir." He shook them apologetically from his shirt sleeve so that they rolled onto the planks of the cabin floor. He struggled to remain calm. "I assure you, Captain, apples are all I seek."

"I've killed for less," the captain told him, unmoved. "I must keep law upon my ship."

Geoffrey's mouth grew dry. He saw the captain's desire for absolute discipline war with his greed for profit. He prayed that greed was the stronger emotion.

"It is only for the lady, Mistress Clifford. She is grievous ill."

"What matters that to me?" Quince's powerful hands holding the pistol shook from the effects of drink, but his will was steady enough. "She has already paid her passage."

Geoffrey's face grew hot. He stared at the black hairs on the back of the captain's knuckles. Were he only a little more foolish, he would rush forward and throttle the man until his red face turned purple.

Instead the captain moved his bulky body to the door, kicking it wide, bawling for his men. A vein throbbed in his neck. Slowly he turned back to Geoffrey. His red-rimmed eyes were glowing like a furnace. "You tread very close to death, Master Cooper." The hoarse, almost whispered, words filled the room like tides upon the sands.

Geoffrey swallowed. He was caught. With luck he could seize the captain's pistol. But there were the men. And the sea.

Two seamen appeared at the door. One was Swope. The captain nodded toward Geoffrey. Each man seized an arm. Swope's cold and skeletal hand dug into Geoffrey's muscle like a rake. Geoffrey's head jerked back as he was hit in the face. Blood trickled from his nose and from a cut in his lip. He prayed his nose was not broken.

The captain turned to the death's-head. "Swope, get some rope about this man. It has been awhile since I have given you a bad one to work on. I give you this one."

Geoffrey's heart sank, and he cursed his foolishness. In his present state there was no room for gallant gestures to ladies. But at least the captain had not shot him—yet.

But once he was bound, the blows began. The bloodless one called Swope struck again and again, his dark eyes expressionless in his white mask. Geoffrey lashed out with his knee. Terrified more by the awful face than with the pain, he struggled. The other seaman jerked the bonds while Swope beat him harder. They did not hit his face again, only his body, until he sagged under their hands, near fainting.

"Enough," the captain ordered at last. "We must save some of him to sell in Jamestown."

At this, Geoffrey raised his heavy head and looked directly into Quince's eyes. "Have you not been paid for me once already?"

Quince gave Swope a quick sideways nod. A bony fist plunged into Geoffrey's belly.

"If we do not sell you," the captain said very softly, "it is over the side with you. But Swope will have you first. Remember."

Geoffrey had to be supported when they took him below. From dreams of pain he awakened to see Swope looking down at him. The gaunt, dead face had a strange expression, as though beating Geoffrey had pleasured him and he would do it again if he could, as though he would feel and tear at Geoffrey's manhood.

The captain regarded the closed door thoughtfully. He had no intention of killing the man he called Henry Cooper at sea as he had originally promised the Judas who had betrayed the young man to him. It was a waste when they were bound so far from England and men servants brought good prices. Besides, a good half of all servants died within a few months of their landing; they never seemed to recover from the long ocean voyage. If that happened, it would be no loss to the captain. It was best, though, to get the money before Cooper's death. Though the man's skills were not those in demand, he was young and muscular. Someone must buy him. They must, because the captain could not transport him back to England. That was impossible. And he would not set him free. The one who had paid to have him thrown into the sea might prove dangerous.

But young Cooper must be kept away from the Clifford wench. The captain was well acquainted with the girl's

70

brother-in-law, Charles Albright. Albright was an old skin-flint if ever one lived. Captain Isaac Quince thought Albright would stop at little himself where money was concerned. Yet the man was a member of the Virginia Assembly and might tattle to some burgess who was more fastidious about the source of his profit. Of course the girl might well die before they reached Jamestown, but should she live. . . .

Mumbling to himself and bending with great strain, the captain picked up the three apples from the floor, then walked down the steps to Lettice's door. He let himself in without knocking.

The girl looked poorly and drawn. He gestured to the maid, who dragged a stool to Lettice's bedside.

"Well, mistress," he said, seating himself.

Lettice forced her eyes open and regarded him with fear. He loomed over her just as in her dream, though not so large. The captain reached into his belt for a long, well-sharpened knife. Lettice could hear Molly behind her gasp with fright, but the captain only picked up one of the apples from its resting place on his knee. He quartered it and began to peel it. Then he placed a piece delicately between Lettice's lips. She was too astounded to resist. He fed her the entire apple without speaking more. Then he lay the other two on the table, piling the peels and core neatly beside them.

"I'm sorry to see you so sickly, mistress," he said at last, wheezing as he spoke. "In your weakness you're in some danger from the rogues of the ship. Beware of them for they're a bad lot. Convicts, many of them, both seamen and servants bound for Virginny. Have to keep them tied up."

His bloodshot eyes narrowed, and he reached out with a callused, dirty hand to pat Lettice's fine soft one. "That dark-haired rogue, if you know the one I mean. The one you spoke to me about before we left England. He goes by Henry Cooper. Watch him well, lady. Keep clear of him. He's murdered his share of men in his day, and a lady like you would seem as easy to him as pluckin' a chicken."

Lettice's eyes widened. She remembered Geoffrey's arms about her and the responding honeyed weakness of her body.

"He'll spin you a soft tale otherwise," the captain continued. "Those kind do. But I tell you he was delivered up to me because he killed so many it was not safe to keep him longer in England."

"Why did they not hang him?" Lettice whispered.

"The ways of the law be strange, but here he is, as you see." The captain let go of Lettice's hand and rubbed his stubbly chin, making a sound as rough as his gravelly voice.

Lettice nodded. Perhaps she had been a fool to free Geoffrey. Somehow she had had an unreasoned trust of him with no real ground to support it. The captain's words were logical after all.

Seeming satisfied with his warning, the captain rose to his feet, smiling to himself. As he neared the door, he looked down at the little maid—a succulent bitch. He reached with a fat thumb to pinch her on the underside of her breast. Ah, a ripe one, she. Too bad there was so little time for the plucking.

The *Anne and Mary* rested at anchor, swaying gently with the motion of the water. With a lump in her throat, Lettice Clifford surveyed the shore of the green and misty alien land. England seemed very dear and beautiful by comparison. Lettice suffered the heat in her heavy black clothes, for the Virginia June morning was already hot and sticky with moisture.

Perhaps it was only her weakness that lowered her spirits so. She was barely recovered from her illness. But why had Englishmen chosen to build a town—a mere village really—in a location so low and marshy? On the north and east, Jamestown was embraced by swamp; the wide and muddy James circled it on the south and west, the expanse of water reflecting the blue sky overhead. Gulls soared before the white clouds. From here the river flowed down into the sea.

Her sister had written of brick houses and of balls and receptions at the governor's house at Green Spring. But all that could be seen over the top of log fortifications were the square church tower and a few tile roofs. It was plain that beyond the marshes and the dark sentinel pines the country stood vast and empty.

A low voice beside her cut into her thoughts. "An empty and friendless land."

She turned to spy Geoffrey Finch near the rail. He, too, was studying the shore. The expression on his darkly handsome face was thoughtful and grave.

Lettice flushed, remembering their closeness. But she must not let him deceive her again. He had not come near her since she had recovered, though she had seen him working aloft.

She picked up her petticoats and prepared to return to her cabin, then hesitated. Close by Geoffrey stood another figure—tall, bony, gaunt. But it was the face that chilled Lettice. It was a skull-like face with burning dark eyes that were sunk into deep holes. The man never took his eyes off Geoffrey. Lettice suddenly felt afraid for him, but she turned resolutely away. Philip had taught her to reverse her mother's teachings and look after herself before all else. It had been a hard lesson the way Philip had delivered it. Yet there seemed to be a sad smile in Geoffrey's dark eyes. For a moment she wished that things had been otherwise.

Inside the cabin Molly was closing the rest of their boxes, looking disheveled but pretty. For the first time Lettice wondered how the young maid would fare in this raw land. Up to now Lettice had taken it for granted that it was a maid's duty to follow her mistress to the ends of the earth if necessary. Lettice sighed. She had been quite protected in her life until her father died, and she now wondered if she would be equal to the challenges ahead.

Molly seemed not to be herself, for she dropped the clothing she had been folding without noticing.

"Has John returned, mistress?" she asked.

"No." Lettice picked up her comb and began smoothing her long hair and taking the wind snarls out of it. "I hope he will be honest and do as he was told. It was very difficult for me to get the captain to agree to send him out into the town before his indenture was sold."

"I never thought of that."

"Well, it seems my brother-in-law's name has some meaning. I told Captain Quince that Charles would go surety for John, though I can't imagine John taking to his heels through the swamps and wild forest alone."

"Nor I," Molly said, half under her breath, fumbling uncertainly with the packing. "I do hope he will be well and nearby us, mistress."

Lettice looked more closely at her maid. There was obviously something between the pair, but Lettice could not forget John's betrayal of Daniel, whom she hadn't seen on the ship in some time. If they were separated, the maid would soon enough find someone else. She set down her comb and peered into her looking glass, wondering if the arrival in a new land was occasion enough for her to wear a beauty patch.

"Of course I am not sure Charles *would* go surety for John." She decided it was, and took a silk patch shaped like a star out of her patch box. She placed it high on her cheekbone under her eye.

"Have you seen him, mistress?" Molly smoothed her hands over her dull-green petticoat. Her bright eyes were pained with worry.

"Charles? Once or twice at Brookside and then at the wedding. I must say he does seem a rather, well, hard man." Hard was only part of it. Charles was exceeding close with his coin.

"Oh."

Lettice saw her maid place one glove in her mistress's box and the other in her own bundle. Gently Lettice retrieved it and placed it with its mate. Molly was uncommonly scatterbrained today.

"But my sister is a dear," Lettice continued. "Another mother to me, though she always did try in vain to turn my mind to more serious thoughts. I unfortunately always followed the Clifford side."

"Oh, mistress." Molly finally abandoned the packing and stood straight, with tears in her eyes and her cap askew. "I do fear this new country. I might never see anyone I care about ever again. Oh, I will die here all alone, I know."

"Nonsense," Lettice began, then bit her lip very hard. But tears would not be stopped. "Oh, Molly, I'm afraid too," she admitted. The two of them looked at each other with dismay, then collapsed in each other's arms, sobbing uncontrollably. They were, after all, two very young women many miles from home. Lettice in an instant forgave her maid all her reckless ways, for were they not quite alike, after all? Except that Molly had had so many lovers.

They did not hear the knock on the stout cabin door, nor did they see John when he entered.

"What a terrible noise women make," he shouted to make himself heard. A beam of light coming through the narrow window made his fine, whitish hair a halo in the shadowy cabin.

"John." Molly's hand stole out to grasp his. "Oh, it do look dismal on shore." Her face prepared to crumple again.

"Dismal?" John boomed. "Why it's a paradise just waitin' for men to farm it. There be work for all and land for every free man. These tears are shameful. Excuse me, mistress."

Lettice was daubing her eyes with a linen handkerchief and blowing her nose. "Did you find how to reach my brother-in-law?"

"I did. And since he needed a cooper and a sawyer and I've done somewhat of barrel-making and sawing, he's talking to the captain now to buy my indenture."

"Oh!" Molly clasped her hands together joyously. Then she reached out to touch his arm. "Oh, John!" The tears sliding down her fair cheeks dried, but she could find nothing else to say.

"Oh!" Lettice stopped crying and straightened her black-silk gown. Really, she would get out of mourning as soon as possible.

"He's here on important business—for the governor—mistress. And his lady, your sister, be here too. She waits upon the deck."

"My sister!" Lettice looked at him with amazement. "Here? Why did you not tell me at once?" She flung open the door and raced to the deck, forgetting all appearances. It was her last remaining kin, her dearest sister. In her heart she rejoiced that she might speak to Dorothy before encountering Charles.

"Dorothy!"

The thin drooping figure standing near the great mast straightened.

"Oh, Lettice, is it really you? Is Father really gone? Oh, my dear!" The frail arms enfolded Lettice, and once more Lettice wept. This time she was joined by the sister who had mopped away so many of her tears when she was little.

When they parted, Lettice stepped back to study her sister. She did not like what she saw. Dorothy had grown very frail, her complexion yellowish. Her russet bodice and brown petticoat were tugged and whipped by the river wind. They did not suit her. A white wife's cap sat upon her head. Lines cut deep between her brows; dark shadows ringed her eyes. Her expression was as gentle as ever, but it had grown careworn and sorrowful. Lettice thought she must discover why her sister had altered so unfavorably.

"My darling, I never thought to see you again in this life!" Dorothy said. "And you have grown into a beauty! All the gentlemen of the colony will vie for you."

"I hope so," Lettice said, honest and blunt as always in the face of Dorothy's self-effacing kindness.

Dorothy tucked her sister's arm through hers and clasped her hand.

"But I had prayed you and Philip might marry, you were so thick as children."

Lettice gritted her teeth. Dorothy's memory was too long. "Impossible. I have no fortune. He has married some-one else."

"My poor love," Dorothy soothed. "We must make it up to you. We do, after all, know the best people here."

Lettice looked about cynically. "Are they hid behind the palisades?"

Before Dorothy could answer, the captain's door opened, and a narrow, bent man recognizable as Charles Albright, Lettice's brother-in-law, stepped out. He, too, looked older and thinner. The frown line across his fore-head was a deep trench. His piercing blue eyes were red-rimmed and watery as though he suffered from some per-petual cold. One eye seemed to turn in a bit more than the other. His worsted stockings did not disguise the boniness of his legs.

"I have bargained well," he said with satisfaction. "A cooper, a farm hand, and a black servant who I suspect the captain stole from somewhere. A very good bargain, the African. He will be indentured for life. Most profitable. A few more such bargains and our fortune will be made." Then he turned to look at Lettice and at Molly, who by now was bobbing nervously behind him.

"Sister," he said coldly. "Why did you not send word?"

"There was no time." Lettice's voice faltered; her heart sank. From the corner of her eye she could see Geoffrey approach slowly. She prayed he would not witness her dis-comfiture.

"You will have to help my wife," Charles said sternly. "Virginia is no place for idleness. We must struggle constantly to maintain the colony in this savage place."

"Of course I will help Dorothy." Lettice noticed Dorothy's almost-transparent fingers close into tight fists, the skin white over her knuckles.

Charles turned to regard Molly as though she were a verminous puppy just creeping over the threshold instead of a pretty young woman. "I see you have brought an abigail. That was most unwise. Most unwise. She'll have to work in the fields when needed."

"I never done that at home." Molly cast an indignant look in the direction of her mistress.

"Well, it can't be helped," Lettice said unsteadily. She saw John purse his lips and shake his head at Molly.

"Those are my terms if I'm to keep her at all." Charles looked about sternly, tightening his thin lips, then turned back to the captain's cabin to complete his business.

Dorothy squeezed Lettice's hand and whispered lowly, "I will do my best to smooth your way."

Smooth her way? Was the way to prove such that it must be smoothed? She was aware that Geoffrey was walking toward her. She was about to turn her back on him when her sister spoke, "Is that not Giles or Geoffrey Finch?"

"No, mistress," Geoffrey said. "My name is Henry Cooper."

Lettice turned to look at him fully. His face was very pale. There was a look of strain about his brown eyes. Following him, like a phantom, was the gaunt sailor. There was something dreadfully wrong with the way he looked at Geoffrey, something that smelled of sickness—cruelty—and a particularly twisted cold lust. The women did not interest him. He did not even glance their way.

"How strange," Dorothy was saying. "You look enough like the Finch brothers to be another twin."

Geoffrey smiled sadly.

"But then," Dorothy continued, "it is so long that I am from home, and I may have forgotten."

Geoffrey stood with his hands clasped behind his back. When he spoke, the words were wrung from him. "Is there any chance, lady, that your husband may buy my indenture? I am the last wretch unsold."

77

"Why is that, I wonder? What is your trade? Charles will want to know that." It was plain Dorothy was attempting to be businesslike.

"I am a tutor," Geoffrey said boldly, but the muscles of his arms and shoulders stood out as he gripped his hands behind him.

"Oh, I would dearly love a tutor for my son, but he is very young and tender still. I don't believe my husband would agree to it. He is so eager to find workers on the land, you see."

Geoffrey leaned back upon the rail. The river was all flashes and sparkles of sunlight behind him, and the many masts of the boats that were moored on the James rose and fell.

"Well, I pray God I may find a master soon, else I fear the captain will heave me overboard like excess cargo on the return voyage." His tone was light and humorous, but a muscle twitched at the side of his jaw. His stiff smile did not reach his eyes. Once again she remarked his pallor.

The death's head grew closer. Why did her stomach tighten so at the sight of the unhuman face? Lettice gasped. Suddenly she realized that Geoffrey's feeble jest was the simple truth. There was an ugly purple bruise below his eye, and the bridge of his nose seemed swollen. It did no good to remind herself of the captain's warning—or that Geoffrey had likely changed his name to hide some crime.

"The others were snatched up quickly, but there seems to be little market here for an Oxford man," Geoffrey said with false cheerfulness.

Dorothy, who was oblivious to the air of tension, said, "A pity. I would hope my son might one day see Oxford, or perhaps Cambridge."

Charles and John were approaching.

"Charles," his wife called timidly. "Here is a man whose time we could buy. He is a tutor. It would be a very fine thing for William."

"Gad, woman, a tutor?" Charles almost stamped his stoutly shod feet in disgust. His pale eyes were irritable. "When I have tobacco in the fields and a poor barn and few barrels to my name? You must think I have a brain of feathers."

Dorothy nervously worked her hands together. "You did say you would like William prepared for a university."

"When we have prospered," Charles said waspishly.

Why did they bicker so? Could they not see the expression of despair on Geoffrey's face. Didn't they notice how his muscles tightened and his eyes darted about, seeking escape? Two muscular seamen guarded the shore side.

Words she had not expected rushed to Lettice's lips. "He can do other work when he is not tutoring. The captain will tell you how well he worked on the ship." She hoped he would say that and not blacken Geoffrey's character.

John turned back to look around the large bundle on his shoulder, his strong teeth flashing in a smile. "If barrels be hard to come by, Master Albright, I can teach 'im to make 'em well enough. We can work together easily."

Charles's eyes grew calculating.

The captain was almost upon them. Quince had shaved for the occasion, and he looked almost respectable. He had donned an elegant black coat with brass buttons. When he saw the group of them standing together, a strange expression crossed his face.

"No one has offered for this man, Captain," Charles said. "I might consider him—but only for my own price."

Quince's eyes narrowed. He glanced from Geoffrey to Lettice. "Absolutely not," he said. "I will not sell."

They all stood, thunderstruck with surprise.

"Come, now, Captain," Charles said. "Do not think to force up the price."

"Your price is. always very shrewdly come by, Master Albright. But this man is valuable to me. Very valuable, indeed." His forefinger came to rest on the butt of the pistol that was tucked in his crimson sash. He ran his finger over it while he thought.

"They are all worth their weight in gold when *you* bargain," Charles said almost genially.

"There's value and value." The captain spoke slowly, almost regretfully. "I will not sell."

A bony hand was placed upon Geoffrey's shoulder, and the deep-set eyes in the white face glowed. Lettice drew in a jagged breath, searching about for some way to help Geoffrey.

"I am disappointed in you, Captain," Charles said, then signaled to John to finsh carrying their belongings down onto the small sloop he had waiting alongside the ship.

"Come, my dear," Dorothy said, taking Lettice by the hand. Sadly, Lettice looked back at Geoffrey. He watched them, his tanned face drained of color.

"We must do something!" Lettice said.

"But my dear," Dorothy soothed. "The captain will not sell."

I will look for a magistrate, Lettice told herself as the sloop headed out into midstream. I will demand that someone discover the captain's intentions. She glanced back, then straightened with surprise. Geoffrey pushed aside his awful shadow and sprang to the rail. For a moment he stood poised, then plunged headfirst into the waters. He came up struggling, dragged down by his boots. There was a pistol shot. A ball struck the water. It was the captain with his pistol leveled. As he paused to reload, the deathshead pulled himself up onto the rail. His canvas clothing flapped about the skeletal form. The captain's face reddened and swelled with irritation as he fumbled with his pistol.

"Squire Albright," he called across the water. "If you pick up that man, I will bargain with you for him."

"The price has fallen somewhat," Charles said sourly. "He seems a wild sort of fellow."

"We shall see," Captain Quince said as the sloop changed course to drag Geoffrey from the water. Geoffrey gave them a drenched but flashing grin as they picked him up. Then they returned to let Charles board the *Anne and Mary* again to do a little bargaining.

Dorothy smiled a thin smile, as though she did not know what to think of all this. "Well, I believe it is done," she said. "Charles bargains well."

Geoffrey shook his soaking head as though freed of bonds once more. He took Lettice's hand in his cold wet ones and looked directly into her eyes. "Thank you, Mistress Clifford, for your words to your brother-in-law. I admit freely that I have never been so worried in all my life."

"It seems of little account," Lettice said stiffly, retrieving her hand to smooth her windblown hair. Yet in her heart she had sensed his fear and knew it did not come easily to him. "But who was that awful man who guarded you?"

Geoffrey glanced up at the death's-head, who was now watching from behind the rail.

"A very important man." Geoffrey leaned closer to her

80

with a wry smile. Her flying hair whipped his face. "He is Captain Quince's torturer and executioner."

"Surely not!" Lettice protested.

"I do not want to try him," Geoffrey assured her.

High upon the deck Quince's door cracked open. Then there was a call, and the master's meaty hand beckoned to Geoffrey to come sign the papers.

"Are you sure," Dorothy asked, watching him climb to the ship and cross the deck with newly lightened step, "that he is not one of the Finch brothers?"

"I am not sure of anything where he is concerned," Lettice said. She prayed God she had not brought a murderer into her sister's house to teach her little son.

Daniel felt thankful that he had landed at Jamestown and had obtained a master there. Though the town was small, there was much commerce from England, and many ships anchored in the James. His new master owned a house that served also as an inn, as many of the houses did. Here, travelers from inland met to talk with seamen and merchants as the colony began to take hold.

Daniel found his duties no harder than those he had performed for Master Philip. But Daniel was a plain and loyal man. He well knew he had not carried out Philip's last orders. Perhaps if he succeeded in getting word to Philip, his master might yet come to find Mistress Lettice and redeem his servant as well.

In the inn the week before he had met a drunken one-eyed seaman who was to return shortly to England. This man had claimed to be able to read and write. When Daniel had come upon him sober, he admitted that he lied. He was as illiterate as any other rogue or servant.

No matter. Daniel pressed upon him the last hidden coin his real master had given him. Philip would pay him again four times over upon receipt of the message, he promised. Then they sat down together and repeated the lesson over and over again until the man had it by heart.

Lettice Clifford, he was to tell Philip Isham, was landed in Virginia and had gone with her maid to her sister's house. Daniel knew not where the plantation lay, knew not the name of Mistress Clifford's brother-in-law. But one Henry Cooper, known at home as Geoffrey Finch, had gone with them to the same place. Geoffrey's brother,

Giles, might help direct Master Philip to the house where both Mistress Clifford and Master Finch stayed.

The man repeated Daniel's message over and over again so he would be sure not to forget the words. His ship was to go out with the next tide. Daniel only prayed that the seaman had the story right.

VI

The very heat of Charles's plantation, Albright's Point, seemed ominous to Lettice. The silence weighed. In June at home church bells would be ringing, children would be laughing, village girls would all be chattering as they strolled down the streets, minstrels would be wandering the roads with pipe and fiddle.

Here there was nothing but the hot, soft wind through the trees and tobacco fields. Only an occasional low voice of one of the workers broke the silence. Sometimes Lettice felt eyes watching her from the forest. Did Indians yet linger? She had so far seen only an abandoned dugout log canoe.

"They say the omens be bad this year, mistress," Molly told Lettice. Molly did not like Albright's Point, nor Virginia.

"Nonsense," Lettice said. But she felt uncertain and strange in this empty land. And Molly's description of the omens made her feel very little better.

First, Molly had told her, there appeared a large comet every evening for a week or more, streaming like a horse-tail westward to the horizon. Then the sky was filled with flights of pigeons so vast that no end was visible. At night they roosted, their great weight rending huge limbs from trees. Hunters shot an abundance to eat.

"The old settlers be afeared, mistress," Molly said. "Old Fred told me. He works with John. Last time there was all these pigeons were 30 years ago. Indians killed everyone then."

"And then," she concluded, her bright eyes sparkling with the horror of it, "swarms of flies thick as the top of a man's little finger rose up out of spigot holes in the earth. A month later they was all gone—no one knows where. They be uglier than any vermin in England, they say. Some says it be the end of the world. Old Fred does."

"Nonsense," Lettice said again. The mistress was shaken nonetheless. Molly was set to work in the fields, and she returned with still another story to relate at the top of her shrill voice.

"That overseer be the cruelest man I ever seen, mistress. He works me till I'm ready to drop. And I think he will kill Henry—or whatever you call him. He hates him for being a college man. Wat, the overseer, would beat it out of him."

Lettice bit her lip. She had seen Geoffrey only from a distance, but she'd been able to see that his head was bowed, his feet shuffled, and his muscular body moved as though it were weighted with lead. She had wondered if he were ill. One servant had brought fever from the *Anne and Mary*. Yet she thought it was something else with Geoffrey. He looked beaten and injured. Molly's words confirmed her suspicions. "I will see if there is something I can do," she told the maid.

Lettice had first seen Wat, the overseer, when they had tied up to Charles's wharf. A giant of a man with florid face and thinning hair, he had a layering of fat that seemed to have worked its way to cling about his hips and stomach. But it was his perpetually narrow blue eyes that chilled Lettice. She shivered at the way he looked at the new servants one by one: John, Ajax the black, a poor wretch shivering with fever—and Geoffrey. His look rested longest there, his lips puckered and tightened.

The other servants skittered away fearfully when Wat appeared. And they did not speak much with the newcomers, excepting for old Fred, who had been Charles's first servant.

The year 1675 seemed to offer very little to those so recently come to Virginia. It was a raw land, and the English colony had failed several times before taking root. Yet Charles flourished. He would be a very wealthy man before he were much older. Despite his closeness with money, Charles wished his peers to think of him as a man of substance. His solid brick house had tile floors laid in a herringbone pattern. Upstairs, Lettice had a room of her own. Molly slept on a trundle bed that was pushed under her mistress's great curtained bed in the daytime. Out in back lay the separate kitchen. Chloe, wife to a black servant, usually worked there.

Downstairs in the main house were two big rooms with high, beamed ceilings and furnishings that had been shipped from England. The parlor had good inlaid chairs, though the curtains at the window were only linsey-woolsey. But the floor boasted a green carpet—a luxury even at home.

The great hall where the family generally lived and sat at their ease had more ordinary leather-covered furniture. Lettice and Dorothy sat there sewing, wilted by the warm Virginia weather. The room was full of homey objects: Two red linen chests were shoved against one wall; a cutlass, two pistols, and a powder horn hung on the chimney. A spinning wheel sat in one corner.

Dorothy blotted her brow with a handkerchief. She had dug out a black waistcoat to mourn her father, but she wore a brown petticoat. It scarce mattered what they wore on the isolated plantation, and Lettice longed for color and gaity. They would go to Jamestown soon, or to the governor's plantation at Green Spring. Dorothy had told her many stories of the high life there. So far, Lettice had not even been allowed to set foot in Jamestown. Charles had transferred them immediately from the ship to his own sloop for the journey to Albright's Point. At that time, Lettice's only thought was to see the last of the *Anne and Mary*. On board the smaller sailing vessel Geoffrey had come once to touch her hand. That was the last time she had seen him looking well.

Lettice had asked permission to take a Holland under-petticoat of her own to cut up into a shirt for Geoffrey. He had no extra clothes, and the Albrights were required to furnish him while he was their servant. She thought she could judge his size well enough. She was willing to sacrifice her petticoat, since otherwise they must send all the way to England—cloth was so scarce in this new land.

As she finished the last few stitches, she wondered at her own concern. She did not as yet know the truth of Geoffrey's recent history. She held the shirt toward the light of the window so that the diamond panes left their pattern upon it with a slightly green light from the color of the glass. Smiling to herself, she acknowledged that the shirt was quite prettily done for such an ordinary article of clothing. "Perhaps I'll take it to him," she announced tentatively to her sister as they sat sewing in the great hall. She could see for once and all how he fared.

"Uhm." Her sister, nodding agreement with a pin in her mouth, had a speculative look in her eye. Lettice flushed.

Later, as she walked past the first of the tobacco fields, Lettice saw Molly bending tiredly to pull weeds from among the tender young plants. The little maid straightened for a moment, then lifted a dirty hand to shade her eyes. Damp tendrils of fair hair clung to her red, burnt cheeks. Lettice waved to her sadly, and Molly responded without energy. I must make her a better cap, Lettice thought.

Near some crude log outbuildings Lettice came upon John, Geoffrey and the black slave, Ajax. To her eyes Geoffrey was weakened and thin, yet he looked somewhat better that day than he had before. His hand rested upon a hogshead obviously just completed. Wiping his hands on his smock, John smiled at the workmanship. "Looks like a gentleman done it," he said.

"Come, now, John," Ajax said. " 'Tis better than the one he made yesterday." His ebony sheen was startling next to the fair-skinned, almost white-haired, Englishman.

Hearing her step, the three looked up. Geoffrey's eyes kindled when he saw her. She had vowed to greet him cooly, but she halted in her tracks with astonishment. About one of his eyes was a green, discolored stain—as though someone had struck him some days before.

Under her eyes, his face reddened. He leaned a shoulder back against the rough log wall and looked down at her lazily. "Mistress Clifford. How good of you to visit us, though our table is bare and our furnishings crude."

Lettice was discomfited by his mockery. "I did not come to be entertained."

"We celebrate," Geoffrey still mocked. With concern she noticed that his hands shook slightly. "Wat, our overseer, is dying—or so we pray. We hope he dies in great pain."

Sensing her awkwardness, John explained, "If fever had not struck him, one of us would. He be so cruel. So far, with his illness upon him, his lackeys have let us alone. He has one or two big fellows do his bidding, and the rest be

86

cowed with fear." John, too, did not look well. He had dark circles about his eyes. "But I be feared he will be goading us as much as ever when the fever leaves him. And he be determined to beat Oxford and gentleman out of Henry."

Geoffrey's lips tightened. "Enough. The lady need hear no more," he said.

Lettice looked from one to another of them. "But does my brother-in-law allow this cruelty?"

"Squire Albright sees nothing but his fortune," John said bitterly. "He will kill the little maid with work too, I think."

Lettice flushed with guilt. If only she could do more for all of them.

Touching his tow forelock briefly in salute, John left, followed by Ajax.

"It seems you have friends," Lettice said when they were out of earshot.

Geoffrey's dark eyes twinkled. "This is not England, as you will learn. My fellows are more valuable to the colony than I. Ajax was a seaman and has acquired some education in his travels. It was an ill day for him that he ran into the master of the *Anne and Mary*."

"And for you," Lettice reminded.

"Indeed. Today is my first happy day in Virginia."

Lettice did not know what to say. She still did not quite know how Geoffrey had come into Captain Quince's tender care. Nor would she ask.

"And what brings you to the apprentice barrel-maker, lady?"

"Oh." Reminded of her reason for coming, Lettice unfolded the shirt and displayed it. "We are required to clothe you, after all."

Geoffrey closed his fingers over hers, holding the shirt. "And which of 'we' has made all of these fine stitches?"

Lettice flushed. She added awkwardly, "And if you have time to work with William, it would be helpful."

He bowed slightly. "Upon your command. I have only just finished this hogshead and am not quite ready to continue learning to make barrels properly. You see, your hogshead is a straight up-and-down thing, all very well to ship tobacco. But a barrel must be properly curved and well-enough crafted to hold water."

"I think you have grown very skilled." Lettice laughed.

"Let us hope your brother-in-law agrees." They both became serious at once, for Charles's moods cast a pall over the entire plantation.

"But let us steal a moment—before Wat recovers—though I see his eyes everywhere. I have something to show you." He took the shirt from her, and then he took hold of her hand. Down where the edge of the meadow met the woods she could hear the rippling of a little stream, and she could smell honeysuckle.

"If you will excuse me, my lady." Before her astonished eyes Geoffrey dodged into the trees, stripped off his tattered, soiled shirt and stood bare-chested. He bent to splash crystal water over his face and body. Lastly he braced himself upon the ferny bank and lowered his head, emerging with his hair so soaking wet it looked black. He took up his old shirt to dry himself. Lettice saw that his shoulders were very brown as though he often worked shirtless.

"You have a raw place on your back," she said.

"I'm sorry if it offends you. The overseer struck me with his whip."

"And your ribs are showing."

"The overseer would have me fast. Do you wish to inspect more?"

She blushed, thankful that the thicket screened them from the house. "You were going to show me. . . ."

"This!" He bent to push aside a dark-green leaf growing among the grasses. Underneath hung tender miniature globes of red.

"Wild strawberries!" Lettice recalled her dream and how she had told it. Eagerly, she bent to pick, and just as eagerly to eat. He sampled them, then lay back in the deep grass, folding his arms up behind his head to watch her. "Oh, Geoffrey, they're wonderful!"

"Be careful what name you call me."

"Does it matter so?"

"I don't know." A shadow crossed his tanned face. "Of late I have been punished for things that seemed as natural as breathing at home. But this is not the time to think of it."

Lettice continued to pick in a silence broken only by bird calls. When she had a handful, she sat upon the grass, smoothing her petticoats under her.

Seeing her thus, Geoffrey moved over to lay his still-damp head in her lap.

"Geoffrey," Lettice objected very lazily, a strawberry between her lips. Her words were cut off as she stifled a yawn. "It is not seemly for a barrel-maker to behave so. Nor a gentleman either."

Shifting his tousled head, he looked up into her eyes. His murmur was drowsy and humming like the insects swarming in the heat of the day. "Why not? 'Tis comfortable so."

The blood rose within her. She looked away, yawning, thinking to get up. But he was right. It was comfortable. She continued to eat.

Geoffrey stretched, then he began to recite toward the birds overhead: "When Love with unconfined wings/ Hovers within my gates,/ And my divine Althea brings/ To whisper at the grates;/ When I lie tangled in her hair/ And fettered to her eye,/ The birds that wanton in the air/ Know no such liberty.' "

"That's very pretty," Lettice said as she licked a finger. "Is it Lovelace?"

He nodded. "But it's the end that suits me best. 'Stone walls do not a prison make,/ Nor iron bars a cage./ Minds innocent and quiet take/ That for a hermitage./ If I have freedom in my love,/ And in my soul am free,/ Angels alone, that soar above,/ Enjoy such liberty.' "

His mocking smile returned when he finished this verse.

"I am the one usually confined," she said, "inside the stone walls. You at least have the fields and this stream and the company of other men."

"Wat keeps me on short tether. I dream of nothing but running away. But where does one run to in Virginia? I have thought even of beseeching the savages to take me among them."

"Can you not get word back to England?" She was truly curious about this.

"It is not safe. But if Wat, by some miracle, recovers, I will fly from here even if I am killed."

"Then I, too, must hope he dies," she admitted.

"You will not betray these thoughts of mine?"

"No." Lettice sighed. "My brother-in-law is keeper of us both. I am his prisoner until I marry. I have no fortune of my own, only the tiniest dower." She dropped another berry into her mouth. When the last one was gone, she rubbed her palms together to remove the pink stains. But she was very conscious that Geoffrey lay there, for a curious warmth was creeping through her body. When she looked down, she saw his dark eyes fixed upon her face.

"Ah, my pretty." He raised himself on one elbow. "Come bend to me." Throwing his free arm about her neck, he drew her awkwardly down before she could object. Their mouths came together with a jolt so hard, it pushed their lips back upon their teeth. Lettice could not help laughing.

More businesslike, he changed his position so that he sat beside her. "More softly this time, love."

She parted her lips to protest, but his face was against hers, his lips seeking. She closed her eyes drowsly. His hands moved upon the back of her lace-trimmed bodice; hers reached about him. She traced around the place where he was hurt. Breathing deep on the honeysuckle while birds fluttered in the branches overhead, she drifted into realms of feeling she had never known.

The muscles in Geoffrey's arms tightened. One hand sought her bosom, the hard pink nipple. His touch was as rain to a thirsty plant. It was as though she had been born to have him caress her. Her muscles grew languid and slack as she opened to him.

He grew more ardent. He slipped one hand beneath her petticoats to feel her sensitive inner thigh. Tense with longing, nothing else mattered—only this. Lettice felt she was standing on some precipice and that if she stepped past the edge, she would drift into sensual paradise.

A man's voice called from the distance, the words indistinct, unrecognizable. Half-dazed, Lettice sat up. She felt a quiver of fear. "Charles! What if he should discover us? Oh, it will go badly with both of us! You have been punished enough."

Geoffrey lay back, spread-eagled on the grassy bank. "Charles!" he groaned. "How I wish I could forget Charles!" He fell silent, gazing into the treetops while Lettice sprang to her feet and straightened her clothing.

"But you are right," he said finally with reluctance. "All this sweet tousing leads only to more serious matters. I shall avoid you, mistress, in the future. You are too dangerous."

Lettice looked down upon him with a pang. What could she say?

"At any rate, you might come tutor William."

"When I have collected myself."

Biting her bruised lip, Lettice stepped from the shelter-ing trees and slowly headed toward the large square house. She did not look back. Her limbs seemed to have turned to jelly. As she walked, the afternoon darkened, and a cloud passed before the hot Virginia sun. Her lazy good spirits left her. Her situation showed very little promise. When she considered Geoffrey, coldly, there was no way he could help her. And even were this not true, there was still Cap-tain Quince's story to be considered. There was no society, it seemed, about Albright's Point. She must try to go to Jamestown. That way she might meet some gentleman panting for a wife. But it was hard to think so when she could still feel Geoffrey's arms upon her.

Molly stayed out of the fields the next day to help the women make a barrel of soft soap—a task more disagreea-ble than any Lettice had performed in England where, even in the leanest years, they had sent to London for it. It was well into the afternoon when, tired and reeking of cooking fat, the women poured the cooled soap into an empty barrel from their large, iron wash pot. Chloe had prepared a dinner of beef and quince pie. They would eat it cold as soon as Charles returned.

Five-year-old William played about underfoot, scuffling his square-toed buff-leather shoes. He soiled his smock by rolling about on the ground. He was very proud to be wearing breeches, having finally discarded his petticoats not too long ago.

Dorothy sent him off to see if Geoffrey could come up to give him some lessons. Lettice felt the color seep into her already flushed cheeks. Would Geoffrey come, or was he still about his business of learning cooperage?

"William's restlessness wearies me," Dorothy admitted. She sent Molly to the kitchen to pour some ale to refresh them. Dorothy and Lettice went to sit in the parlor, think-ing it might be cooler, but though the casements were thrown open, not a breath of air stirred.

Lettice looked with affection upon her sister. That good woman had already drawn some sewing from the pocket she wore at her waist, and she was busy at work.

Lettice fanned herself with her handkerchief. She

91

thought she must be some pretty sight after the morning's work. The discomforts of Virginia included not only heat, but horrid mosquitoes that followed even into the house. No wonder Englishmen were loathe to come here to settle. At least the savage wars seemed ended.

"Are there still Indian troubles?" she asked her sister.

"Not for some years, praise God. Time was when we slept not long in our beds. That's why we built the hidey hole."

"Hidey hole?"

Dorothy nodded. "Beside the chimney, behind the paneling."

"Oh, I see. Like priest's holes in England." Lettice knew several houses with hiding places built during the religious troubles. She rose from her seat on the heavy bench and went to discover more of this curious secret. She searched the paneling near the portraits of her parents, which she had brought with her from England. "The wall looks quite sound. How is it opened?"

"There is a spring in a corner of the molding near the chimney." Dorothy continued her stitching without looking up.

Lettice felt carefully until she found it cunningly hidden. A low door sprang open. Inside was a small room without windows, which smelled somewhat dank. "I should hate to be closed up in there too long," Lettice said.

"Fortunately we have never had to use it. You see, if you look carefully, there is a spy hole cut very small in the other corner. But the whole design is really quite useless, since Indians would, in all likelihood, burn the house."

Lettice looked at her with alarm.

"Don't worry, my dear." As she bit off a thread, Dorothy raised serious blue eyes to her sister. "There has been no trouble for many years. We hope never to see war with the Indians again."

Lettice thought that she, too, should resume sewing, but she had left hers in her room. She heard William's scampering feet at the door, but there seemed to be no sign of Geoffrey. "I wonder what is keeping Molly?" Lettice rose to her feet. "I'll see what delays her while I fetch my sewing."

As she went out the back door and neared the kitchen, Lettice thought she heard low and masculine tones combined with the high, birdlike ones of her maid. She stopped and looked about the door frame, not wanting to interrupt Molly's flirtation with John.

But it was not John; it was Geoffrey. His arm was about the little maid's waist, his head bent seriously toward her. Molly still held the pitcher of ale in her two hands.

Flushing hotly, Lettice whirled about and sped blindly up the narrow stairs to her tiny room. Oh, but Captain Quince had been right to warn her! Geoffrey would woo any maiden who crossed his path, be she mistress or maid! Oh, what a fool she had been to let him melt her heart!

And Molly! Had she not enough men by now? It was a wonder she did not swell in the belly. Lettice felt hot tears come to her eyes. "It cannot be that I love him," she whispered. "I cannot be such a fool."

After a while, pressing her lips together, she went downstairs. She stood for a moment in the doorway of the parlor. All was peaceful. Geoffrey and William sat at the carpet-covered oak table, learning letters. William held a little slate, and a hornbook lay nearby. Dorothy was sipping a tankard of ale. Molly gave Lettice a strained smile and poured a tankard for her. Lettice reached for it with her free hand, and then she sat on one of the upholstered chairs. "Henry tells me Wat, the overseer, recovers," Dorothy said.

"Oh?" Despite herself, Lettice's eyes sought Geoffrey's. She could not read the expression in their dark depths.

They all looked toward the door at the same time, for heavy footsteps were heard. Charles entered first, and his cold blue eyes searched the room. Another bulkier figure trod at his heels—a neighboring plantation owner who had adopted the title of Squire Mathew Gower. Lettice had detested Gower the first time she saw his massive, wheezy bulk, his mean pig's eyes set in a florid face, and his buckskin breeches straining over his large stomach.

She had not time to study him further now, for her brother-in-law began to speak. His voice was icy and cutting. "A pretty sight. While I labor to bring my fortune out of this wilderness, they sport, drink ale and enjoy themselves in the parlor.

Dorothy blanched. "We have labored all day till now, my dear. We have a barrel of new soap. And I sent for

93

Henry Cooper to calm William by giving him some studies."

"My dear wife," Charles said, coming to stand over the quailing Dorothy. "William has years to learn, but for now it must be tobacco, tobacco, tobacco! There is no other way we can grow truly wealthy. All labor must be directed to that first. And I see the abigail here. There is no time for such style. If need be, pray ask your sister to wait upon you. Foolish women and college-educated men. Do I deserve no better?"

Squire Gower's bulk filled the doorway, his amusement and wheezing growing in intensity so that it seemed he would swell to fill the opening, sticking like a cork.

"But surely we are rich enough for . . . ," Dorothy began

"Gower prospers," Charles whined. "He does not allow this softness. What will he think of us? And he has come here on a special mission—to offer his hand to our sister."

Lettice dropped her sewing. Her eyes darted from her head! Marriage with this pig? Was this the way she would escape her brother-in-law's house? How Geoffrey must be laughing. But when she looked at him, his tanned face was startled and concerned.

"Well, mistress, what have you to say?" Charles demanded.

Lettice clasped her hands about her tankard, looking down with blazing cheeks. She would with pleasure have heaved it, ale and all, at Charles's head.

"I . . . I . . . cannot." Her voice was faint.

Charles turned to Squire Mathew. "Ah, you know what women are. Give me leave to speak to her, Gower, to bring her to her senses."

Appalled, Lettice looked to her sister for aid. Instead, she found Dorothy white-knuckled, clutching her sewing.

"I will leave it to you," Gower wheezed. They could hear his heavy tread as he retreated. They heard his coarse command, and his black slave brought his horse. Through the watery glass Lettice could see the panting fat man being heaved into the saddle. Then the servant sprang up behind his master. Gower turned his horse's head toward home.

There was silence in the parlor. Surprisingly, it was Dorothy who spoke first, summoning all her courage. Her brow creased, her sewing dropped on her knee as her hands worked convulsively. "We cannot have her marry him, Charles." Her voice was soft, but steady enough.

Still on his feet, Charles drank thirstily. Then he parted his thin lips from his tankard. "And why not, pray? Because he is no beauty, eh? Gower is a rich man. And how much land and silver will beauty bring?"

"That remains to be seen, Charles. Lettice has met no one yet in Virginia. Perhaps if we took her to Jamestown. . . ."

"Must you talk about me as though I am cattle?" Lettice broke out furiously. She would die rather than have Geoffrey hear their awful words. She glanced at him. Still seated at the table, he was white about the lips, his mouth compressed, a muscle in his cheek twitching.

"If Gower cannot have you, he seeks the little maid to wait on him," Charles said.

"The maid?" Lettice sprang to her feet with rage. "You see, all he wants is a servant. Well, he shall not have Molly. She is mine!"

"Then I will not feed her!" Charles set his tankard down and came stamping across the room. His thin body shook with rage.

"Miser!" Lettice shouted.

"He shall have neither." Geoffrey's voice cut in like a steel blade. He rose, resting both hands on the dark-red pattern of the table cover. "It is well known hereabouts that Mathew Gower has beaten a servant to death."

Lettice's stomach lurched. Could it be true, or was it some dramatic fancy of Geoffrey's?

Charles stiffened. He turned to fix a cold eye upon his servant. "And no doubt he deserved it well. I should have let Captain Quince drown you, you ungrateful wretch. Well, Wat will teach you manners. Manners you never learned at Oxford."

Geoffrey's eyes blazed, and the muscles of his arms tightened. "Wat lies near death."

Charles's thin frame shuddered, his hands shook. "What will recover. And I have others to do my bidding. If Gower has beaten a servant to death, doubtless he deserved it."

Geoffrey looked angrily about. His eyes came to rest on Lettice. She paled.

"I need no help from you, Master Cooper." Her voice

95

sounded cold to her ears. "Please go. You are only making everything worse."

He seemed about to say something, then thought better of it and wheeled to bolt out of the door. Lettice was sorry if she had angered him, but she breathed a sigh of relief that he would not suffer a beating because of her. She returned to the matter at hand. "You cannot dispose of my servant," she continued. "She is a free woman. I have brought her from England at my own expense."

"Eh? Who will feed her, sister?" Charles demanded.

"I will," Lettice insisted. "I will pay with what is left of my meager inheritance."

"Then who will feed you, eh? Eh?" Charles stabbed a forefinger between her breasts.

"Must I marry him before you will bend?" Lettice cried in despair.

Dorothy dropped her sewing again, her face contorted. "William, leave the room," she ordered. Obediently the child scampered away. Then she turned to Charles.

"Husband, must you do this?" she pleaded, her face turned even more yellowish than usual. Her twisting fingers showed her tortured state.

Charles was unmoved.

"I cannot give her into his hands," Lettice said hoarsely, conscious of the maid's terrified eyes upon her, yet once again she saw the little maid's fair head close to Geoffrey's dark one.

"Dear sister." Dorothy took her arm. "Come upstairs, and we will discuss it in quiet where you can rest."

Charles stood back to let them pass, a forbidding frown on his face. Upstairs, Lettice sat down stonily on her bed. Dorothy began to massage her temples.

"Stop, Dorothy," Lettice said finally with impatience. She would not let these ministrations distract her. "How can I let her go? I have brought her all the way from England."

Dorothy's cool fingers found a tight knot at the base of Lettice's skull. She persisted, rubbing it until her sister began to relax.

"You must," she said. "The time will not be long. Charles will trade her for the unserved time of a man who knows shoemaking. We have many cattle and unused hides that could prove profitable."

"I see you have been discussing it without me."

Her shoulders hunched, Dorothy sat upon the bed beside her sister, then she threw an arm across Lettice's back.

"What would you have me do, Lettice? Charles is my husband, my lord and master. Have you any idea how lonely it was before you came? I cannot have you sent away."

Lettice sighed. Why was it easier to fight anyone than Dorothy? Perhaps because her sister reminded her so much of Mama.

"But someday I may marry, Dorothy."

"But not that man. They are right. He is a brute."

"Then how will he treat little Molly?"

"It is only for a year or two," Dorothy reassured her. She bent to kiss Lettice's forehead. "We must have you see some more people, my dear. I promise I will take you to Jamestown and to meet the governor's lady. She is very highly connected in England. Surely you will find a fine gentleman to marry. He will perhaps buy back Molly's time." She patted Lettice's drooping shoulders. "And may I tell Charles that you agree?"

Lettice said nothing. Dorothy's brown skirts rustled as she rose. As Dorothy closed the door behind her, Lettice prayed God that she had not given her silent agreement because of Geoffrey.

She awoke later in darkness to hear a rattling at her casement. She went unsteadily to the window to look out. Below in the moonlight Geoffrey bent to pluck gravel from the ground to fling it once more upon her window. There were bluish shadows upon his dark hair and light shirt. He looked up and saw her. "And so, mistress," he called softly. "Which of you will go to Squire Gower?"

Lettice's voice faltered as she called in a low voice, "It is to be Molly."

Geoffrey came back too loud and angry. "I see I should have taken my beating. And there is nothing I can do now, since I am leaving tonight."

"You are leaving?" Lettice looked about to make sure no one had heard. Back among the trees a horse stamped and snorted. Since Wat had recovered, did Geoffrey plan to run away, stealing one of Charles's horses?

"Wait!" She snatched up her silken nightgown and tied it over her shift, barely taking time to slip her feet into shoes. All the way down the dark narrow stairs she stumbled and prayed Charles would not hear her. As she burst through the door and onto the moonlit lawn, Geoffrey came forward to put an arm about her shoulders.

"Sweetheart, why this haste? Can it be that you will miss me? Give us a kiss, eh?"

Cursing her headlong rush, she gave him an impatient shove, tossing her hair over her shoulder. Her ankles were wet from the dewy grass.

"I came out to hear your story. You said nothing of dalliance to me."

"Did I not? My mind grows absent here in Virginia. But it is wicked of me to tease you." He took her hand. "There is much news. First it is certain that Wat is too much the devil to die."

"Then you will run away," she said with a pang.

"I am spared. Charles is sending me to war."

"War!" Lettice said with bewilderment. "What war?"

"Colonel John Washington and another militia officer rode by to tell Charles he must send some men to fight an Indian outbreak. Charles, with his habitual generosity, promised one man—his Oxford man, myself, the most useless man on the place and one who displeased him mightily today. But he acknowledged that I fire a musket tolerably well."

Though the air was sweet with the smell of phlox from the flower beds, Lettice felt the beautiful night grow cold. She clasped her hands together over her silk-covered breasts. "The Indians threaten us? But the news seems to please you. I hope my sister and myself and the child will not all be killed in our beds."

He reached for her hand again and began to play idly with her fingers, his head bent, his dark eyes thoughtful. Lit only by the moon, his face looked very brown.

"It is still far away—in Maryland. I always did intend to go to the Dutch Wars, or some such as a mercenary. But now that Wat recovers, war comes like an angel of mercy to me. It has been long since I have been armed in the face of my troubles."

"Well, perhaps you will not find me so dangerous now."

"No. You are dangerous as ever, but this moonlight has made me mad. And soldiers are always heedless."

"Indeed," she said with mock haughtiness.

He tightened his grasp on her hand and they walked, dappled with patches of moonlight, into the trees surrounding the plantation. Down past the house the river glistened. She could not but feel the magic of the night.

Ask him about Molly, she told herself. Do not let him toy with you. But she stumbled as her foot encountered a root. He steadied her, his hands warm and firm. She could not bring herself to utter the words. Through his body she could feel his excitement, and she knew he relished this war.

"Were there time, I would ask you to sew me fine shirts to travel to the wars." He draped one arm loosely about her while he played with the hand he held.

"I am sure Charles will outfit you as best he can—being what he is," she said throatily, her eyelids drooping and her body growing languid near his.

"A miser, do you say?"

"You have said it." With one finger she felt the place where his jerkin was unsewn, wishing she had mended it. It seemed very little protection against Indian arrows.

By then they had reached the spot where the swaybacked mare stood. Charles must have lent it reluctantly. Geoffrey's blanket was rolled up behind the saddle, and some utensils and his musket were tied on too.

"And you go tonight?" Lettice asked. All of a sudden she felt a wave of sadness.

"I must catch up to Colonel Washington." He turned to look down at her. "Though it will break my heart to leave you, my lady, the thought of engaging in some battle overjoys me."

Was that all he would say to her? Merely joke about his heart breaking? Would he whisper the same to Molly?

"Soldiering is not such good work as barrel-making, I think," she said.

"But more suited to a gentleman. I am resolved to make my fortune as well as your brother-in-law, and I do not intend to do it upon this spot making barrels."

Lettice's interest was piqued. "And how will you do that?"

"I don't quite know, but this war may be the first step. Ripeness is all, as Shakespeare has said."

She could feel his body become still as he considered. "So Charles will spare you to fight," she said slowly.

"Quite happily. And what do you think—can I be spared?"

"If Charles says so." Lettice tried to keep her voice cool. But in the strange light a curious sense of unreality swept over her. She felt they could float slowly like thistledown in the soft air up to the huge moon above.

"Would you care, sweetheart?" Geoffrey's voice filled with laughter as he teased. He nuzzled her hair with his lips.

"Sweetheart!" she protested through lips that were swelled with a desire to kiss. "Have you forgotten how dangerous I am?"

"Ah, you are danger indeed to any poor servant who raises his eyes from his work to behold you. I have shivered many a night, lying alone, contemplating how dangerous you are to my body and my soul." He pulled her up roughly so he might kiss her cheek with an ungentlemanly smack. "But your danger pales in the face of battle. Come, now, will you not give me one kiss upon the lips before I ride off? That is, if Charles will spare me his horse."

Feeling he mocked her, Lettice stood back from him, but in his high spirits he only laughed. "Would you have me killed, then, with nothing to look back upon?"

"No. I would not." Horrified, she heard her voice break. How could she betray herself so? She turned and ran toward the house.

"Lettice!" He was upon her with one bound, grasping her shoulders to turn her about. They stood in full moonlight, careless of observers from the house. "Do not let such a fool as I cause you tears."

"I will not cry. I do not care what happens to you," she said angrily.

"I would like to think one person would care if I did not return." He was not laughing now.

"I cannot deny it," she said unsteadily.

"Then let us not deny it," he said. "Not this once as I begin a new adventure." He drew her to him and kissed her until honey flowed through her body to her heart. She shivered, though the night was warm, and held him closer. He released her after another long kiss.

"Ah, but you are dangerous indeed. I shall have to think about you, and that is grave trouble to someone in so wretched a state in life as I." He sighed a great sigh.

100

"You'd best to your bed, lady. Charles should lock you up, for I have a terrible desire to have you."

She stood without moving. Her gown was flaring in the gentle wind. "Geoffrey." She hesitated to speak the rest of her thought. "Geoffrey," she began again. "I would not have Charles lock me up."

"Eh, sweetheart?" In the moonlight she saw an unbelieving smile upon his strong features. He grasped her about the shoulders. "Are you saying . . . that you will open yourself to me?"

"I do not want to say it, you fool."

"Then tell me with a kiss."

She hesitated.

"So, Lettice?" he questioned.

"So, Geoffrey," she sighed as their lips came together. His arms tightened, and he kissed her harder, more brutally, until both were weak.

"Oh, Lettice," he said huskily. "You could not stop me from having you even if now you were to kill me."

"I do not want to kill you, Geoffrey," she said.

He led her by the hand to where his old nag waited, then he lifted her to sit at the front of the saddle. He sat behind her, holding her about the waist with one hand. They ambled to the bank of the brook where they had kissed and toused before. The night was silent save for the sound of insects and the moon-silvered water running over the pebbles. The old horse's hooves grated upon the stream bed as they crossed to the other side.

Silently, almost ritualistically, they dismounted. Lettice's silken nightgown shone eerily in the half-darkness. The horse bent to drink. Moving languidly, Geoffrey untied his blanket from back of the saddle and spread it upon the ground. Then slowly, as in a dream, he came to take her hand. Their bodies flowed together through their lips. She began to unfasten the ribbons of her nightgown. Gravely, he took it from her and lay it aside. She drew her shift over her head. He felt her smooth waist and hip. Then he drew her down onto the blankets and took off his own clothes, then pulling her fine curves to him. His body soon warmed her.

"No one has had me before, Geoffrey," she said.

"I will be gentle." He kissed her forehead. Then he ran his hand along her thigh to open her.

But he was not gentle—nor was she. She found as she slipped past the precipice that the passions that gripped them were wild and dark indeed. The brief pain that freed her of her maidenhead was forgotten in an instant. Her body shook with her need for him. Her clenched hands could not draw him close enough. She heard herself moan and felt herself begin to flame. She moaned again. She must not be parted from him. Frantically, she raised herself to meet him once again as he descended upon her. Then, gasping, they shuddered together and finally lay still.

"Geoffrey," she said after awhile as they lay tangled in languor. "If only you would not go."

"I must." His hands stretched out to her, and he took her again. This time they savored each other's sweetness. She traced the muscles of his back as though she would learn all of him by heart. He stroked her silky thigh. Slowly they climbed together to a honeyed peak of passion that melted their limbs to weakness.

"Lettice," he whispered painfully. "I will kill that pig Gower if he lays a hand on you. Come running if he should dare try. Better we two should lie on the ground by a campfire."

"Perhaps I should don men's clothes and search for you through the forest," Lettice said. "Why is it that men adventure and women are left behind?"

"Because I would die if anything happened to you," he said, kissing her again.

It was just before daylight when they parted reluctantly and began to dress. Something occurred to him. He reached out to touch her arm as they walked toward the waiting horse. "Lettice, look to your little maid if you can. She may suffer more than you know."

Lettice felt a flash of jealousy that jarred the sweet perfection of the night. "She will miss you, I am sure. She is not in the habit of whispering in corners with me as she does you, and Gower will not allow it."

"Whisper in corners?" His laughter rang out through the night. "Oh, I see. The beast of jealousy gnaws at you. You need have no fear in that direction. Molly's trouble is something else. Foolish woman. Do not let your imaginings mar this night."

"I will not, Geoffrey," she whispered, ashamed.

102

Then he kissed her on her forehead and mounted the old nag.

"Take care, Geoffrey," she called to him.

She watched until he rode out of sight. The desire for him was still strong within her. Then she turned to walk back to the house.

She hoped he would be safe—or was she destined to lose any man she ever loved? As dawn broke upon Albright's Point, she knew that she would not rest easy until she saw him safe returned. As she crossed the dewy lawn before the house, she raised her hem up above the grass. Her slippers and ankles were soaked. At the door something made her turn back. With a chill she saw a figure waiting under the trees—wavering as though with weakness.

Unmistakably it was Wat, the overseer.

VII

Trouble came to His Majesty's colony in Virginia with little warning. Years of peace with the treaty Indians had allowed the English to forget the massacre of some 40 years earlier. But on an August Sabbath morning in 1675 worshipers on their way to church in Northumberland County spied one Robert Hen, a herdsman, lying athwart his threshold. Nearby lay an Indian. Both bore gaping and bloody hatchet wounds. Hen lived long enough to gasp, "Doegs, Doegs," when asked who had dealt him his mortal wounds. Then he had died in the arms of his rescuers. A boy had crawled out from under a bed to say that Indians had attacked at break of day in revenge for the earlier killings by the settlers.

Fear chilled the Sabbath churchgoers. Somewhere, unseen, tribes were shifting. Once the smell of blood was in the air, the killing contagion could spread until the hard-won treaties lay useless—as dead and mutilated as the body of Hen.

And then the fragile peace broke again as friendly Susquehannocks were shot by militiamen who had mistaken them for members of the Doeg tribe. Word of danger spread from plantation to plantation, finally reaching Albright's Point. Charles was incensed at the news.

"The governor must do something!" he shouted, his nose growing redder than usual. "How can they expect a man to raise tobacco till the country is rid of this vermin? By God, the king should hear how his governor shirks his duty!"

Dorothy cautioned William to play only in the dooryard, though he begged and whined to be allowed farther. Squire Gower sold Charles an extra musket, and John went about his work armed. Another man took a musket into the fields.

Lettice was truly frightened by the thought that hostile savages lurked in the forest. The place where she and Geoffrey had loved might never be safe again. At least Molly would be out of the fields at Gower's. Then Lettice dismissed the little maid from her thoughts. There was trouble enough at Albright's Point. She thanked God that Geoffrey was gone. Day after day she saw John and Ajax work to the point of exhaustion. Yet Wat did not hate them as he did Geoffrey. And Wat's sore and burning eyes were often upon Lettice, though he had little traffic with the house.

Would that he had none at all. One morning she burst from the door of the kitchen so rapidly that she brushed against his shoulder. He clamped his strong fingers about her wrist.

"So he entered you, did he, mistress?" he muttered through moist lips half to himself. "The silk-and-satin man. But we will bring him down before he enters you again."

Lettice fixed startled eyes upon him. Her heart sank. Her wrist pained as the giant grasped her more tightly. She tried to free herself, afraid to make an outcry with Dorothy close by. She felt her throat tighten as the red face came closer, the half-open mouth but a few inches away. Patches of his thinning hair had fallen out from fever. With one hand he gathered up the brown locks at the back of her head as he bent to force a thick and foul-tasting tongue between her teeth.

Then Dorothy's step was heard, and he released Lettice and slipped into the house. Drained of all color, Lettice leaned, shaking, against the bricks of the wall. She could find nothing to say to Dorothy.

"Why, Lettice, are you ill?" Dorothy's high forehead creased as she saw her sister's face. Lettice did indeed feel sick. Her body crawled as she wondered how long Wat had spied upon their love-making. It would be better if Geoffrey never returned to serve under Wat.

Molly huddled in a corner of the well-stocked kitchen at Gower's Corner, listening to cries of pain as her master beat his black slave. A puffy, purple bruise already discolored her cheekbone—the result of a blow she had received

106

from Gower. She prayed God that the child in her womb would be protected.

So far she had resisted all Gower's advances. She tied her apron higher so that it seemed he had not discovered her condition. But it could not go on forever like this.

Molly raised her small hand to her mouth and bit a knuckle. Would the screams never stop? Castor still bore stripes on his back from his last beating. The master had told Molly that her hide was too pretty to be marred by the whip, but that his patience was growing short with her.

The day he had struck her, he had ripped her bodice, revealing breasts that in a month or two would be full of milk. All her will had been concentrated on protecting the place where her baby lay. What mattered a bruise on her face?

She turned with a jerk as she heard a step behind her. It was her man, John, large and strong. He closed her in his arms.

"Oh, John, you left your work to walk all this way? What will Wat say?"

"Never mind him. I'm just in time to hear the pretty singing. What be it?"

"Castor dropped master's favorite pipe and broke it."

"Old ale-sodden Gower loves his pleasure, the bastard. And you, love? How do you fare?" He felt her belly and nodded when the babe moved beneath his hand. Then he studied the face beneath her tousled curls. "What be this? That fat pig's laid a hand on you."

"It be nothing, John," she whispered, afraid his wrath would betray them.

His face was blank and expressionless—a sign that he was truly angry. "Bundle your things together, girl," he ordered. "You'll not stay here."

"But where will we go?" The little maid clutched her brown apron in distress.

"You come with me," John said, his fair skin red beneath his shock of pale hair. The skin on his nose was perpetually peeling from work in the sun.

"Oh, no, John," Molly said. "Not yet. There's no telling what they'll do to us. Once the baby's come, it will be too late for them. Surely they can't punish me then."

John folded her in his arms. "Oh, sweet," he breathed

into her golden hair. "I never meant to have you treated so. I only wanted a good life for us."

"We will, John," she said steadily. "I can bide here for a while yet. So far I've kept Gower at bay."

John groaned, drawing a great breath. "How much longer be it?"

"Some weeks, I think."

"Can you send someone to me?"

"The red-headed boy will go," she said with more assurance then she felt.

"If I can take you away before, I'll come."

She looked at him, large-eyed, wanting this dream to come true. If only the two of them could disappear into the forest, build their own cottage, grow their own corn. What good was a rich, well-stocked house like her master's when everyone suffered so much unhappiness here?

They both froze into silence, for the cries of pain and the sound of the whip had ceased.

"Hurry away, John," she whispered. "It will go hard with me if you be found."

He fixed stricken light eyes upon her, then he nodded and quickly ducked out the door.

Looking after him, Molly placed her hands about the roundness of her belly.

Geoffrey awoke, burning with desire. A phantom Lettice had walked toward him through the moonlit strawberry glade. Her silken nightgown shone ghostly like some fairy maiden beckoning him to the hollow hills. When she had drawn close enough for him to touch, she had parted her lips as though to offer a kiss, the honeyed sweetness of which was unknown to mortal man. But when he reached forth his hand, she had disappeared.

He lay wrapped in an old blanket upon the ground, drenched with sweat. It was a warm fall afternoon on the Maryland shore.

Careful, old man, he told himself as he rubbed sleep from his eyes and remembered the shadowy form of his dream. He had always played with fire when he played with love—and this time more than ever. Ah, but Lettice. . . . He shook his head. That kind of dreaming would get him nowhere. She was a luxury he could not afford.

Half-dazed in the drowsy sun, insects humming and

crawling through the grass, he looked about. The English colonial troops had disposed themselves before an old abandoned fort. The Susquehannocks had moved into it after being forced from their original lands when the more powerful Seneca moved down upon them. Three days ago the Virginians had greeted 250 Maryland horse and dragoons that had come to join them. There were now about 1,000 English colonials. Inside the fort, some guessed, were not more than 100 braves, along with their women, children and old men. It should be an easy fight.

But the fort was strong, Geoffrey thought. Earthen banks formed a ditch all around. A palisade of tall trees with their tops tied together surmounted it. Still, they should be home soon.

Geoffrey struggled to his feet. He wore no sword since he was no longer a gentleman. Yet he was possessed of his old nag and an equally old musket belonging to his master, Charles Albright. Geoffrey picked up his bandoleer with its many little packets, each containing a single musket charge of powder. He also carried two powder horns and a bullet bag.

He smiled to himself. Here at this rustic fort he would perhaps fight his first battle. He was a sorry-looking soldier. Some men wore breastplates, others helmets and odd bits of armor. Officers wore steel gorgets over ordinary clothes, but many like himself, who had recently been brought out to fight, wore only leather clothing that was scuffed to roughness with wear and disintegrating about the edges.

Geoffrey was too much of a realist to imagine that war would be as romantic as the tales and dramas he loved as a youth, yet some bit of strategy on his part, or some moment of glory, might raise him in the eyes of his officers, lifting him from his present low condition.

Geoffrey moved closer to the fire where Jud, a grizzled old former servant, now a small landowner, was cooking corn cake on a hot flat rock. No matter how warm the day, Jud always wore a moth-eaten fur cap. The day before, he had instructed Geoffrey in the art of cooking out of doors by burying the rock in the fire until it was hot enough to put the corn upon it.

Jud lifted his cap off his balding head in salutation and scraped his food off the rock with his knife. A drummer boy huddled near by, nibbling bits of corn. The smell of turkey stew rose from an iron pot. They fished out pieces of meat with the ends of their knives. Then a sudden wind change sent the three of them coughing and choking to stand on the other side of the fire, eyes streaming tears. As Jud absently ate, his eyes lighted upon Major Thomas Truman, commander of the Maryland troops, riding through the dry brush surrounding the camp.

The major bore a white flag. His glance fell upon Geoffrey. "You, there!" he demanded coldly. "Fire your musket into the air. Make haste!" He rode on to a cleared place directly before the fort gates before turning back. "Quickly, you clumsy fool!"

Geoffrey clenched his jaw. He had retrieved his heavy musket against a tree and then lit his long match at the fire. But it had fizzled out before he could touch it to his musket. He lit it again and fired toward some idly floating clouds overhead.

The major nodded curtly, dismissing him. But all were conscious of the silence hanging over the fort. No one responded to the shots, and the major's white flag drooped idly in the calm air.

Major Truman raised his chin arrogantly.

Silence.

Jud drew his knife from his belt and fingered the tip of it to test its edge. "They'd be mad to come out," he growled near Geoffrey's ear.

"Indians be mad anyway," the drummer boy nearby commented. "Otherwise they'd be Christians instead of heathen savages."

"Do you know much of Indians, Jud?" Geoffrey wiped his smoke and tear-drenched face on his sleeve.

"Some," Jud grunted.

"What are they like?"

"I been in Virginny many years now, and as I see it, the Indians be a deal more honorable than most Englishmen I've seen or bargained with."

"Nay, Jud. Indians be not honorable," the boy said fiercely.

"Ah, boy, an Englishman will buy you or sell you or murder you as easily with his book and his cross as a heathen savage with his feathers and beads. All men are much the same in most ways."

Major Truman gestured roughly to the boy, who picked up his drum and carried it to the clear space before the fort. The boy raised his sticks, then struck a cadence.

"Parley!" Truman called, dismounting and shifting his feet with irritated impatience.

After what seemed an endless time the gate opened a crack; the crack widened until four men stepped forth unarmed. Two were of middle years, the others aged, with dark, bronze skin furrowed with countless wrinkles. The old men's hair was gray as iron with still-paler white streaks. All were dressed in a mixture of European and native dress. Geoffrey was surprised to see strings of pearls and blue beads about their necks.

Two Virginia colonels, John Washington and Isaac Allerton, rode up. Both wore ordinary hunting clothes of leather with flashing steel gorgets over. They dismounted and left their horses grazing behind them. Truman tensely strode over to take Washington's arm, speaking anxiously as though to impress this middle-aged man from Virginia. The major gestured toward the savages.

"Colonel Washington, here are four cacarouses—we would call them Four Great Men—of the Susquehannocks."

The very oldest raised glittering black eyes; then he came stolidly forward until he was directly facing Truman. Pierced with a gaze so reproachful, Truman looked away for a moment and flushed.

"Truman," the old chief said. "Why do you come with so many men and so many muskets?"

Truman indignantly sought to recover his composure. "You know well why we come—to demand satisfaction for outrages committed in both Maryland and Virginia. I cannot be hoodwinked by your savage flummery. I know it is the Susquehannocks as well as the Doegs who make trouble."

One of the younger cacarouses, muscular and exotic with his topknot and beads, raised his hands and spoke in a thickly accented gutteral voice. His face was tight with fear. "No . . . kill . . . English. Seneca. Seneca."

The oldest chief turned dismayed eyes that were lost in deep wrinkles from one to another of the English. "No kill! Peace! See!" He held forth a small object—a silver medal. "English Great Chief give. He say peace forever." The old man gestured wide. "He protect Susquehannocks for as long as sun burn."

Truman turned a cold-chiseled profile away. "I do not understand you," he said, half in his throat.

"Send for an interpreter," Washington snapped as he turned on the heel of his boot. "Show them the bodies of the men killed in Virginia if they keep protesting their innocence."

The old one shook his head, whispering, "Seneca!"

Four pikemen stepped forward to lead the chiefs away.

Jud tugged at his unkempt beard, his eyes flicking from the officers to the uneasy peace commissioners. Geoffrey gave him a questioning look, and the older man exhaled explosively. "Poor devils—caught between English greed and Seneca greed. It's all land hunger, naught else, though the colonels talk of order and honor. But I think these colonels will make trouble for us poorer folk."

The sun slanted low, and one by one the men took up their blankets to lie down. War, Geoffrey thought as he wrapped himself in his own blanket, might not be as interesting as he had been told.

Suddenly, unearthly cries broke the silence—the screams of men in their death throes. Militiamen sat up rigid in their blankets. They could hear the sounds of moans and struggles and sickening blows. Then there was silence. Then a crashing in the brush and a snapping of twigs. A grizzled old man's greenish face appeared from the bushes. He looked about wildly at the pale faces and poised weapons in the flickering firelight. For a moment he panted—without words—then cried, "We killed them all—all the chiefs—beat them with rocks until they were a bloody pulp! The old one's brains. . . ." At this the hardened man leaned forward to vomit upon the ground. Then he wiped his mouth with his sleeve. "It was poor work. They were defenseless against so many of us—our prisoners—carried a white flag. They hardly put up a struggle. 'Twill bring no honor to Englishmen."

All looked toward the palisade. A face appeared, but no one had the heart to fire at it. The dark face stared fixedly at something the men could not see through the undergrowth. Then the place where the Indian had stood was empty.

Anguished cries and wails from unseen mourners inside

the fort filled the reddened dusk—cries that made Geoffrey's skin crawl.

Jud's face showed shock. His eyes met Geoffrey's.

"Why?" Geoffrey uttered the word in a kind of croak. He stared at Jud, confused.

"No one will be safe now," Jud muttered. "There's Sally, my wife, alone in our little house. Any Susquehannock who lives will want revenge. And it will spread." After a time he added, "The bastards." He did not look toward the enemy as he spoke.

Geoffrey felt his body grow cold and clammy as the wails continued. Suddenly there was silence. He was deafened by his own deep breaths and those of the two beside him. No one moved.

Jud broke the spell. He sat down heavily on his blanket, his face ruddy in the strange, bloody light. "How I'd like to be home now with Sally. A good girl, that. A solid wench—some would call her fat." His voice was soft and loving. Then his mood changed, and he spat into the dust. "Oh, but it's cleaner there. This is a dirty business."

As night settled in, the three of them sat tense. Finally Jud arose and stretched. "Like as not they'll stay where they are tonight. But they'll come out when they're hungry enough." He shook his head, then settled himself down for the night.

Geoffrey picked up his matchlock and checked it in the darkness—the heavy stock, the four-foot-long barrel. Carefully he packed in powder and shot. His long match lay close by.

Geoffrey looked up at the stars above him. Jud and the boy were both limp in their blankets and snoring. After a time Geoffrey's head, too, drooped, and he dozed where he sat. Then he waked again. The image of the old Indian man mixed in his mind with the image of the ancient retainer who had followed him that night in Paris to speak for still another old man Geoffrey had never seen. What was it that had tied them together in his dreams? Oh, yes, he thought as he drifted into sleep. It was betrayal. He also saw Robert's face.

The next days were occupied with nothing more than waiting for the savages to show themselves. The nights were interrupted by some brave's attempt to capture horses for food. Geoffrey had lost his aged horse that way. Dimly he had seen the old nag disappear inside the fort.

"If your master's the miser you say, he'll make Colonel Washington and Governor Berkeley pay," Jud chuckled. "But it must mean they're getting hungry. They'll be missing the taste of deer meat."

Geoffrey hoped his poor mount would not suffer unduly and that the savages would break a tooth on her tough old meat. Then he thought of the long journey home on foot and the explanations he must make to his master. That is, if he decided to return at all.

Often it was not only the horses, but men who were killed amidst horrible shrieking in the dead of night. No one knew how the Indians crept forth. But when the English demanded again and again for commencement of peace talks, the savages only answered, "Where are our four cacarouses? Where are our Four Great Men?"

A permanent look of irritation settled upon the faces of the English officers. They cursed the lax ways of their men. And then the men began to quarrel. Some walked off into the woods to hunt. Some few never returned; it was thought that they drifted back to their lands instead.

Geoffrey was bored and irritated. His officers treated him in the same contemptuous manner as his master. He cooked up fantastic plans of flight that ended with a dream of him bending a knee before the King, who would right all wrongs and restore him to his heritage. He was tempted to fade into the forest like some of the other men. For several days now all was still and quiet under the blue sky of the Maryland autumn.

"How long can they keep this up?" Geoffrey asked Jud, nodding toward the fort. The two of them were cooking about the evening fire along with the drummer boy.

Jud gave a bitter laugh while he stirred a batch of Indian corn mush. "Until they all die of hunger or we kill ourselves squabbling." The older man looked off into the forest, then his eyes found Geoffrey's. "Have you ever loved a woman?" he asked in a low voice, unlike his own.

"Yes." Geoffrey felt his face go red. He struggled not to think of Lettice. But what would Jud understand of his life?

"I'm not askin' if you've ever tumbled a woman—but if you've loved her." He paused for a moment, then said, "Like my Sal. It takes a good grasp of my arms to reach

114

around her, and when I do, I know I'm holding a woman. She don't like me to go off with the militia. But I leave her there with an extra musket. She does what she must. And when I come back—oh, there ain't no lovers in the world has what we have in our little house."

Geoffrey smiled at him, honored by this confidence. What could he tell Jud in return? Of the married lady in France? Of Lady Isobel and her little whip?

Leaning back he stared into the tree branches and the orange-tinged evening sky. It was not these earlier loves who dogged his thoughts. He smiled, thinking of Lettice and of her untying him on the *Anne and Mary*, of her sitting upon the ferny bank, eating strawberries near the gurgling stream. There was a kind of simplicity to her, uncluttered by the devices of other ladies. But it was true that she was dangerously out of his reach, unless his condition changed, unless something happened, unless this war did something for him. In the meantime it was probably best to avoid her. Let her become safely married to someone who could care for her. Geoffrey swallowed. Were he able to claim his own inheritance, he might woo her himself.

They would expect him back after this battle, back at Albright's Point to cringe under Wat and lick Charles's boots—unless he turned the other way and headed into the forest. Why stand in the shadow of Charles's house, yearning for the love of a woman he could not have?

"I wish I was home," the drummer boy said into the gathering dusk. "Don't you, Henry?"

"Ah, what home?" He was some months now a servant in Virginia, and he had done nothing to change his fate. He'd simply been grateful at first that he was still alive. He must at all times away from his home plantation carry his master's letter. Geoffrey knew that both incoming and outgoing ships were searched. He feared to contact his family. Giles had probably had him captured. Young Robert in England would never want to hear of him again, though by now he must wonder what had happened to him.

The puzzle seemed to offer no solution. Then a thought struck him. He sat up with excitement. James! Perhaps he could get word to James. He had helped him once before by getting him the post of tutor to Robert. James had gone on to learn the law and had access to the circles around the king. If anyone could help him, it would be James. But how could he get away from this wilderness battlefield?

Jud stirred and looked over at him. "Still awake, are you? What worries you?"

"I would not be a servant all my life."

" 'Tis a common feeling of common men."

"But I was not born a common man."

Jud scratched his head. "I was. Common as dirt. Yet serving was bitter to me."

"Well, I fear I will be uncommon dead if my overseer has his way," Geoffrey admitted ruefully. "He hates gentlemen beneath him. My back still pains me these many weeks later."

"Each man has a duty to save his life, I think," Jud said. "And to my way of thinking, he owes little to the gentlemen above him. 'Tis hard to run away in Virginia—but it can be done. Some have gone to the Indians and lived and bred among them. Some hide to the west, but it is a hard choice. It would be especially hard for someone like you who had lived among grand folks in England."

"If only there were somewhere I could go while I sent letters to England. There is someone there who might help me. I was impressed, you see."

"As were many others who were never helped. But it might be possible for you to hide for a time among poorer men like myself."

Geoffrey sat up, freeing himself from his blankets. "Would you, my friend? I have learned something of work here, and I would help you."

"If you like. But it's best to rest now, for this war is not over yet." Jud rolled over again so that all that could be seen was his fur cap.

Geoffrey felt his spirits rise. He had said it! He would hide him! Given the time, there must be some way he could make his way back to England. And even if he failed in this, he would be freed of Wat's brutality. Lying down again, Geoffrey occupied himself with many thoughts until he finally slept.

Hideous shrieks awoke him. He sprang to his feet. A cold sweat instantly drenched him. He peered carefully through the screen of undergrowth. The fire's embers gleamed upon the eyes and hair knots of two Susquehannock braves. Their arms rose and fell at all angles of rage above the bodies of the soldiers, who were lying near the fire.

Geoffrey's hand stole toward his loaded musket. He took up his match. Then, gritting his teeth with rage, he ran to the fire. Careless with anger, he lit the long match to the coals, touched it to the musket and fired. One of the savages jerked—and fell. The other started, then slipped away into the night.

Geoffrey scrambled almost into the coals to see what damage was done. He came upon the boy first. Lurid firelight showed the young body, raw and bloody. Turning him, Geoffrey leaned to listen for breath. The slim form was lifeless, dead. Geoffrey let the body fall.

He moved on to Jud. The Indian lay over him. Geoffrey's single bullet had struck the savage's head. A dark pool of blood could have come from either of them. Swearing, with stiff and desperate fingers, Geoffrey tore at the Indian to pull Jud free.

He heard other men hurrying his way. Someone lit a pine branch and stood over the Indian. The dead man's expression was mild and serene—as though he had touched God's hand as his spirit left him. Geoffrey dropped him with a grunt. Falling to his knees beside Jud, Geoffrey drew in his breath with shock. His friend's face was half-torn away and ran blood. His left eye was reduced to a pulp. Yet, incredibly, he still breathed. His good eye flickered open; his browned lips parted. He uttered a terrible groan of pain. Then he raised a trembling hand to feel where his face had been.

"Ahhh," he groaned. "I'm a dead man. Thank God the pain will end." His bloody hand groped toward Geoffrey until he clasped his arm. "Sal . . . ," he said. Then he lapsed into unconsciousness.

But not dead yet, poor fellow, Geoffrey thought. Now to bandage him. Or would it be kinder to let him bleed fast and die?

"What's happening here?" a commanding voice called as Major Allerton stepped into the circle of light cast by the fire, which the men had built up.

No one answered. He looked about, drawing his own conclusions. "Are our sentries asleep again tonight?" he asked bitterly. "These Virginia men will never make soldiers." His booted feet stepped over the dead boy. "You give them an order, and they run in four directions at once. Discipline is beyond them."

"Have you a surgeon, sir?" Geoffrey forced the words through stiff lips.

"A surgeon? This is not England, you know. From your speech I'd judge you know not the harder side of life. Well, you see it here." The officer strode away angrily.

Good God, he was left to nurse! Geoffrey tore a strip from the shirt Lettice had sewn him to press upon the wound. The cloth was soaked in no time. He increased the pressure—wondering if he should remove the destroyed eye. But he had no stomach for it.

From the distance he could hear Major Allerton shout toward the Indian-occupied fort: "Parley! Parley! Come out to talk peace!"

There was a silence until a single, heavily accented voice called in reply, "Where are our Four Great Men?"

Shadows appeared about Geoffrey as some of Jud's fellow soldier, from his hometown came through the encampment to carry him away to be nursed or buried among familiar surroundings. Geoffrey silently picked the old fur cap from off the ground and handed it to them. Their faces were grim and still; and so he did not have the heart to ask if he might go with them.

Several nights later the moon was full over the Maryland shore. The English guards slept, lulled by the knowledge of their great numbers. The troops had learned that 75 Indians, with their women and children, had left the fort by tunneling under the palisades. Only three or four of those too weak to travel had remained behind.

When the Indians were at a safe distance, they had screamed and fired toward the sleepy English, who made no return fire. Then the Indians melted into the forest. There was no English pursuit.

Geoffrey's boots were growing worn. His clothes bore bloodstains from both Jud and the Indian. His officers had already forgotten him as they dismissed the men to return to their homes. "So this is war," he thought. Where would the hidden and fleeing Susquehannocks strike next?

He began the long walk back to Albright's Point. The forest he passed through was ablaze with autumn colors. He

118

thought of going somewhere, anywhere, else. But, as he decided at last, he would go on to Jamestown. It would be easier to send a message to his friend James from there. All his hopes hung on that.

Lettice, too, brought Geoffrey back. He tried to deny it—to tell himself that he would only look upon her face once more and then forget her. Yet his body told him otherwise so that he laughed at his own ruse.

But he could not forget that Wat, too, would be at Albright's Point.

Three miles separated Jamestown from Green Spring, the enormous estate of Governor William Berkeley. There, that august person sat before a writing desk, a periwig upon his head. He bent to go over some papers.

Sir William sighed to himself. As he gazed through his casement out over the snow-sprinkled countryside, he foresaw nothing but trouble for the colony. He no longer had the patience for governance of His Majesty's lands in Virginia that he had shown in his earlier years. Sir William was now almost 70 years old, and he was experienced in both the civil and Indian wars. Though so many leagues from his country, Sir William dressed formally as befitted a minister of the king and the brother of a lord. Today he wore a light-blue coat trimmed with many buttons. Its deep cuffs were of the same yellow as his waistcoat.

Just then, a liveried black servant entered. "Sir Henry Chicheley," he announced softly.

The governor nodded, his heavy, long, curled wig sliding slightly askew. Impatiently he straightened it.

The governor spent some half-hour with Chicheley, informing him of an Indian raid near the falls of the Rappahanock and Potomac Rivers. Thirty-six settlers had been cruelly murdered, he informed Chicheley with indignation. Some had been tortured—their nails withdrawn while they still lived.

"I have been told that the Susquehannocks are responsible," Sir William said. "I want you to raise a force to pursue the Indians to the west. London will be wondering at our neglect if we do not follow."

After Chicheley had left, the governor sat for some time in thought. Then stiffly he rose to his feet, breathing somewhat heavily. He sought out Lady Frances, his wife, who sat sewing by the fire in the main hall.

Lady Frances arched her eyebrows. "Well, my dear?" They had been wed only a few years, and she, who was known throughout the colony as a graceful beauty, was half his age. Firelight glistened on her rose-silk dress and dark hair.

Lady Frances's husband grunted slightly, stroking one side of his long, thin mustache. She glanced at him once more, studying his mood. Then she resumed her sewing in silence, her lively eyes sparkling with unexpressed thoughts.

After a time they both raised their heads when hoofbeats were heard. There was little activity upon the plantation at this time, for winter weather now lay over the land.

In a few moments the black servant again appeared, saying that a stranger had come who refused to give his name.

The governor rose stiffly and peered about the room with his pouchy eyes. "In the parlor," he said wearily.

"I do hope he will not keep you long," Lady Berkeley said.

The stranger who was ushered into Sir William's presence wore English leather clothes, though he walked across the carpet in Indian moccasins. His face was deeply tanned so that he was almost as dark as the savages. Something in his expression was also Indianlike.

"Your name?" the governor asked, leaning back in his Russian leather chair.

"I am a translator for the Susquehannocks. My name does not matter."

The governor straightened; his face grew red. He placed the fingers of one hand against those of the other, and rested them lightly on top of the writing desk.

"And the thirty-six settlers killed?"

His visitor paused, narrowing his eyes as though wondering how best to frame his answer. "They consider that work done." The translator paused. His eyes roamed about the comfortable room as though it were a foreign setting. When he met the governor's eyes, his revealed no consciousness of difference in rank between them. "The Susquehannocks regard you as their father."

Once more the governor's face reddened. "What sons would torture and kill thirty-six of their father's children—their brothers?"

120

"Ah, who is innocent?" the other sighed. "Four Great Men of the Susquehannocks sued the English officers for peace in Maryland. And in answer, each was killed—each undefended."

Sir William's head jerked up. "Is this true?"

With his weather-beaten face expressionless, the translator nodded. "For this, the Susquehannocks have deemed it right to take ten English lives for each of their murdered chiefs. The difference in number is due to rank. Will the governor allow his men to commit such crimes against wise men and do nothing? they ask."

"I have not known of this," the governor said in a low voice. "I hear only of the Indians' barbarous slaughters."

The translator's eyes tightened and deadened. "The Susquehannocks would know why the English, formerly their friends, are now such enemies that they pursue them into the province of Maryland."

The governor raised tired eyes. "I have tried to be their friend, tried to maintain stability, tried to reassure the Indians and restrain the settlers. Peace is good for Virginia, and therefore for His Majesty."

The visitor spoke in a soft and world-weary tone, as though expecting little. "Susquehannocks will renew their ancient league of friendship—upon conditions." He leaned forward and placed the folded parchment of Susquehannock demands upon the governor's desk.

With cold and aching joints, the governor arose and walked to the heavy door to call for his servant. "Show this man to the kitchen that he may eat and drink."

The stranger paused in the doorway. "And your answer?"

"I will think about it." The eyes of the two men met. Both were cynics; neither believed that much could be expected of their fellow men. But there was respect between them.

When the translator was gone, Sir William returned to his heavy chair near the dying fire and lost himself in solitary thought. His servant returned to build up the fire, and Sir William asked him to have a message sent to Sir Henry Chicheley to disband any troops he had raised to pursue the Susquehannocks. Then the governor brooded. He foresaw that much of the work he had accomplished during his life in Virginia was about to be undone. Forces were shaping for trouble. He must constantly restrain the settlers. Many had only contempt for their dark-skinned neighbors. The more settlers arrived, the more the land greed grew. And the land they sought was the Indian's by treaty.

In England they did not understand the governor's problems—problems that issued from the fact that here every man was armed. How could one aging man control all this? And there was another problem still, closer to home—his cousin, young Nathaniel Bacon. Just recently come from Suffolk, he was the most unruly colonist of all.

Yes, fires blazed within young Nate that could only mean trouble. Already he had taken the law into his own hands and had punished some Indians for supposedly stealing corn. There was a burning ambition in this young Bacon cousin. And he hated Indians.

The governor sighed. Young Nathaniel could be the spark to the tinder that would blaze into fatal war.

VIII

Sir Philip Isham gazed into the fire, basking contentedly in the warmth. His hounds and those of his friend circled about their masters. They settled upon the hearth, soon rising to sit upon the gentlemen's boots. Outside, the weather was brisk, and the hall, at any distance from the fire, was just as cold. Philip and his dark-haired hunting companion held tankards of mulled ale.

Upstairs Philip's lusty new son slept. Philip thanked God the boy was sturdy of limb and of constitution, though the mother faded and whitened by the day. She grew more listless hourly. But she had done her work well enough. Philip's father was but newly in the graveyard. All that the old man had labored throughout his lifetime to build was now Philip's, and it would belong to Philip's son ever afterward, as would the title of baronet and the child's mother's portion.

Philip's satisfying train of thought was interrupted by a servant who came to the door. "It is a very poor-looking fellow." The servant hesitated. "I would have set the dogs upon him, but—"

"Yes?" Philip lounged negligently in his chair, his fine light hair one of the few bright spots in the darkly paneled room.

"But he said he had word, Sir Philip, from Daniel."

"Daniel!" Philip sat bolt upright in his leather chair.

The old servant worked his hands together, mumbling and stuttering until he nerved himself to ask. "Shall I send him in?"

Speechless, Philip nodded, and the old man shuffled away.

His companion looked at Philip with curiosity, but said nothing. He merely extended his boots closer to the fire, disturbing one of the dogs.

Both men looked up expectantly as a dirty-visaged, unkempt man with an eye patch was ushered in. He gave a crooked nod, tugging at a forelock. His much-mended canvas clothing indicated that he was a sailor, and he shivered from the cold as though he'd caught the ague. The sailor fearfully glanced about into all the deeply shadowed corners of the room.

"Well," Philip said sharply. "Has Daniel sent you?"

"Wal, sor," the sailor said. "A man did indeed send me to you. His name he swore wor Daniel. And he said your honor would pay me for what he told me."

"Did he, indeed?" Philip replied. "No doubt he was right."

"I pray God he was," the sailor said. "For I been some weeks in London until I could get me a horse at some great cost, mind you. And I come out through the chill weather. It's been a great expense and a trial to me, sor."

"No doubt."

The sailor looked at Philip to see if he needed more prompting, then began again. "Daniel did say it was most important, sor."

Philip sighed. He set down his pewter tankard and rose to his feet to pluck a small casket off the chimney piece. He opened this and fished out two coins, which he handed to the sailor. The sailor studied them carefully, bending so that his good eye was only a few inches from the silver. "It wor an awful long ride, sor," he said reproachfully. "And put me to much expense."

Philip drew out two more coins and tossed them to him. The man glanced at them quickly, pocketing them before he spoke. "Well, sor, 'tis little when you think how I—"

"Enough!" Philip's gray eyes grew steely in his handsome face. "You shall have the rest when your tale is done."

"Very well, sor." The sailor moved closer to the fire and held his large, blunt hands toward the flames. His battered and somewhat misshapen face took on an expression of extreme concentration. "Let's see, now, what wor it?"

"Where did you see Daniel?" Philip interrupted.

124

"Why, in a village inn." The man looked surprised, as though Philip should have known this.

"An inn?" Philip uttered with exasperation. "Why then has he not returned home?"

"He could not very well swim so far, sor."

"Swim?"

"Yes, sor. It wor an inn in Jamestown."

From the shadows came a chuckle. The gentleman's boots and one lean hand were firelit, but his face was obscured.

"Jamestown? In Virginny?" Philip continued.

The sailor looked bewildered. He peered into the shadows at Philip's companion, then back at Philip. "I don't know any other Jamestown, sor."

The dark-haired man's laughter rang out.

"In God's name, how did he get there?" Philip exploded, his high cheekbones standing out even more than usual as he ground his teeth.

"I don't know, sor. That wasn't part of the message," the man said innocently. "But I expect on a ship."

"You faltering idiot! What *was* the message?!"

"Oh, yes, sor. The message." Once more, the man screwed his face with concentration. "I was to tell Master Philip Isham that Lettice Clifford . . . was landed in Virginia . . . and, and . . . what was it now—"

"In Heaven's name. . . ." Philip began.

"Ah, yes. She'd gone with someone, yes, her maid, sor." The one-eyed man stopped completely. His face was growing red.

Philip sprang to his feet. "Good God, man, do I have to throttle you to get it out?

"Oh, no, sor. It was that she had gone . . . with her maid, mind you . . . to her sister's house."

"And where was that?"

"Daniel knew not."

"He knew not? My God, what was the name of that man Dorothy married?"

"Daniel knew not. But there is more, sor."

"Well, out with it!" Philip exploded.

"Daniel said one Henry Cooper, known at home as Geoffrey Finch, went with the lady to the same place. He said Geoffrey's brother, Giles, might know where he was."

Philip's expression grew truly surprised, and he looked

toward his shadowed guest, who had sat up suddenly in his chair so that his face was fully lit by the flickering fire. "Well, Giles, what do you know of this?" Philip asked.

"Nothing," the lean, dark man answered. "But send this fellow away, and we will think on it."

The sailor extended his hand. "Thank you, sor—and if I might have the rest of my money?"

"Your money, you fool! You are lucky we don't knock you down and take the rest back, you tell a story so badly." Philip lounged back in his chair while the man looked at him with dismay. He continued to hold his hand out for some time while the gentlemen sat unmoving. Finally, his face crumpling, the sailor withdrew.

Philip turned to his friend. "I thought your brother was dead."

"It seems he bobs up like a cork," Giles drawled. "And it seems your heart is roving, though what my brother may have to do with Mistress Clifford I cannot understand."

"Nothing, I hope," Philip said thoughtfully.

Giles arose and stretched his muscular body. "We will talk more of these matters. The news is most interesting to me, and I must think upon it. It could come as a shock to my lady mother, who is not well. In the morning I ride out to see someone who waits for me." He clapped his friend upon his shoulder. "But the news is most interesting, and we will talk of it again."

Giles Finch's thoughts were busy the next morning as he rode through the wood toward a secluded hunting lodge where a lady waited for him. He burst in through the door to find the lady still half-dressed, her gold-silk petticoat uncovered by an overgown, though she stood in her riding boots. Her fair hair hung down her back. She laughed with pleasure to see him.

"Why, Giles, what's this?"

"Things are all awry," he said without ceremony. "My brother is alive—and in Virginia."

She laughed again, as though it was but a joke. Then she came forward to press her swelling lips upon his. She looked directly into his eyes, which were on a level with his, she was so tall. "And so you are distressed, my sweet."

"You have to tell me. . . ." He seized her shoulders.

"What, my sweet? What is it you must know?" she teased in her throaty voice.

"Who it is that knows my secret," he choked out.

In reply, the lady merely laughed again. She pushed his hands aside and slipped her bodice fetchingly lower over her bosom and shoulders. She looked even more peachy and glowing than usual, outlined against the rustic wood of the hunting lodge.

Giles dug his fingers into her soft flesh. "Answer me, by God!"

"Stop it," she hissed, her elegant face distorted. "You think I am a fool? I know you well, Giles. We are much alike. It would be dangerous to tell you too much."

His fingers loosened, and he turned from her. "It must have been a servant. If I could think but who. . . ."

"Stop it. . . ," she said once more. "I will tell you in good time. But this latest news does but make the game more interesting. And see how fast you fly to me?" She reached a slim arm about his neck and thrust her bosom against his chest. "It is so nice to love someone so well-matched in size," she said as his arms closed about her.

"What?" he asked with a smile. "Is your husband still not grown big enough, Lady Isobel?"

She smiled at him. Her perfect beauty was marred somewhat, for there were slight spaces between her teeth that gave her a rapacious look. She slipped her fingers down into his breeches, feeling about between his buttocks, then around to the front.

"I would make you big enough," she whispered. "Eh, Giles?"

He responded immediately to her wish, grumbling, "You make but a plaything of me, Isobel."

"Aye—and what play." She led him to the rumpled bed that she had just left. "Take off my boots, Giles," she ordered, leaning back upon her elbows with one leg bent, one raised toward him.

Giles did as he was bid, watching her eyes to make sure her mockery did not go too far. She laughed a little, and he raised a hand as though to strike her. Instead, he tore off his own clothing and hers as well. He shoved her back and entered her.

"How interesting that you are a twin, Giles," she

drawled, then drew in a hissing breath as she felt the pleasure of him. "One half of a whole—and equally big."

He gripped her shoulders fiercely. "But I have given you more pleasure, have I not?"

She spoke with difficulty, since passion swept over her. "I think . . . heat comes quicker to him . . . yes," she sighed, raising her hips. "But he does not love me as you do."

"Aye," Giles exhaled and drew her buttocks more closely to him. "And neither he nor I have made an heir yet. . . ."

After that they were unable to speak more until both were spent. He looked down upon her, fingering her fine yellow hair as she lay in the feather bed.

"Isobel—you must tell me who has told you this secret."

"I shall not," she murmured drowsily, turning her face into the pillow.

"But they told you for a fact that Geoffrey emerged first from our mother?"

"Why, Giles, have I not said so—by a good half-hour."

"And he lives."

"So far."

"Captain Quince must be removed."

She turned to face him, laying a smooth hand on his arm. "Not yet, Giles. We may yet find a use for him."

Lettice walked slowly away through the soggy, chill morning toward the spring house where she had some butter laid away. Looking away across the still-barren fields toward the tobacco-drying barn, she saw a figure disappear around a corner. Was it Wat? She took care never to be alone when he was near. Then she saw the figure veer back around and head toward the house. He seemed to be coming in a way so as to avoid her.

She was sure it was Geoffrey! Although he had been back for some time, he had not come to her nor spoken to her since his return. Angrily, she thought that in the face of his unconcern she would restore her maidenhead if she could. Yet her heart was heavy, and she bit her lip so that tears would not fall. Then she shook her head angrily. A little dalliance must not upset her plans. She would still marry.

Suddenly she stopped, as sounds from within the rough

log springhouse raised her hair on end. She looked about wildly. "Indians," she whispered, biting her lip.

But it was not. The grossly distorted cries were a woman's. Could some tortured soul have been left by the savages to die?

There was no one close. Lettice held her breath and crept closer to look within. Behind the usual churns and utensils she caught a glimpse of light hair and homespun petticoats. "Molly!" Lettice cried, coming to kneel at the maid's side.

A strangled groan answered her.

"Molly, what ails you?" But soon enough she saw Molly's great belly as the girl lay on her side. A cloak was spread underneath her over the dirt floor. Her worn apron and petticoats were all disheveled. A wave of panic swept over Lettice. Pushing the disorderly curls off the maid's face, she saw a great bruise on a temple and another on the fair shoulder where her bodice had slipped.

"Who has struck you?" Lettice whispered.

The maid's dry lips opened slowly. "Gower. He . . . he . . . found out."

Lettice grasped the small work-hardened hand. "You walked all this long way alone—and in your condition?"

"Yes. I feared . . . feared he would kill me, he was so angered."

"Oh, Molly, why did you not tell me? Surely I could. . . ." Lettice looked about the small enclosure in despair. The dampness of the spring made its cold biting.

The little maid's lips moved again—without a sound. Lettice leaned nearer.

"Burn. Don't let him burn me," came the whisper.

"What on earth are you talking about?

Molly whimpered, "They burn them—runaways—burn the letter for runaway into their cheek."

"Brand them?" Lettice grasped Molly's hand tighter. Into what trouble had she led the little abigail? "They shall not brand you, whatever happens."

Molly only grimaced with pain and fear. It must reassure her little that Lettice had failed to protect her thus far.

"Thank God that Charles and John went to Gowers for the day," Lettice said.

"They will find me gone," Molly said sorrowfully.

"We will only have to worry about Wat."

Then Molly's grip tightened as a spasm of pain engulfed her. Lettice thought that a year ago she would have chastised Molly upon discovering her pregnant. All was different now. "I must bring help. I promise you, Molly, that I will protect you."

So saying, Lettice loosened herself from Molly's clutching fingers. The maid's lips were blue with cold. Lettice took off her cloak to cover her, then raced toward the house, her petticoats billowing, her cheeks flushed with emotion. She did not feel the chill of the morning that was just now promising spring. Gasping for breath, she held her paining side as she stumbled into the kitchen. Dorothy was just putting a joint of venison on the spit.

"Why, Lettice, what is it?"

"You must come at once and bring clean linens and warm water. . . ." Lettice leaned on the door frame, catching her breath.

"What on earth?" Dorothy's eyebrows arched high in her narrow forehead.

"My little maid is giving birth in the springhouse!"

Dorothy grew ghastly pale as all the implications rushed upon her. She wiped her hands on her apron and began to wring them.

"Don't grow faint-hearted now, sister," Lettice begged. "There is work to be done, and I know nothing of childbirth."

Dorothy straightened. "Yes, of course. I will go to her at once. Charles . . . Charles will be gone for some time. Find all the clean linen you can, and warm some water— and heat some bricks." Dorothy barely took time to go into the great hall where her kerchief and mantle were lying near William's study table before she sped off.

Lettice breathed a sigh of relief; Dorothy had risen to the occasion. Lettice poured water from a bucket into the large kettle that was hanging over the fire. She was about to go on to the great hall when Geoffrey appeared with young William, whose hair was all awry from tugging at it as he concentrated on his studies.

"What is it?" Geoffrey asked. "Dorothy's face would say an Indian attack." He looked somewhat ragged. He was wearing the same clothes he'd worn to the Indian battle.

Lettice paused to order William back to his studies. He dragged his feet until he made sure they would really have him go. Lettice shook a finger at him, and he disappeared at last. It would not do to have him bearing tales to his father. She turned to Geoffrey. "Molly is giving birth in the springhouse."

Geoffrey gave her a look of embarrassed shock.

"If you knew, you should have spoken," she said. "Though God knows what I could have done. I would have died, however, rather than send her to a brute who would beat her."

The muscles of Geoffrey's jaw tightened. "Has he? Poor girl. The child will go hard against her under the law."

Seeing the expression of concern on his face, she wished she could say more to him, but there was no time.

"Oh, my God!" Lettice stopped, hand on her breast. "Where on earth will we put her? There's Wat—and Charles!" She exhaled with exasperation. "Pray bring the kettle for me, and then—oh, my God, what are we to do?"

Geoffrey smiled at her. "Steady, my sweet. We will win out."

Molly was delivered of a healthy boy in the springhouse. Dorothy was delighted with the child. But then Geoffrey's footsteps approached.

"Charles is come," he called in a low voice. "He has been bawling about the house that everyone is gone and the meat burned in the kitchen, though he blamed poor Chloe, who lies ill. Then he told William and me that he had a headache, and he went up to bed, turning back only to tell me to go make barrels."

Dorthy raised a trembling hand to her lips. "Whatever will we do?"

"Molly must have time to rest," Lettice replied. "We must keep her from Gower as long as possible." And she gave her sister a direct look. "Did you not see the lurid marks that brute left upon her?"

Lettice cast about in her mind for a solution. "We must put her in the hidey hole," she decided. "When he goes out tomorrow, we will move her to my room and pray the infant will be a contented and silent one."

Charles confounded them all by not rising early the next morning to ride about the plantation as was his usual habit. Instead he lay in bed complaining of a migraine. About noon, approaching hoofbeats were heard. Squire Mathew Gower appeared with an expression that was thunderous indeed.

Hearing the commotion of his entrance from her place behind the paneling, Lettice ceased spooning warm broth between her maid's lips. By the light of a candle, she could see that the infant slept like an angel, though the little room was so confining, airless and dark. And soon Molly, too, slipped back into exhausted sleep; so there was no need to warn her.

Lettice crouched to peer through the eyehole. Charles staggered down the stairs with a cloth about his head just before Squire Gower's heavy tread reached the door of the parlor.

"Charles," a rasping voice said, "you have given me a damn-poor bargain, and I mean to have satisfaction."

Charles's face seemed to be turning a horrid green. He reached a thin and shaking hand toward his head. "I know of no bad bargain, Gower," he said querulously.

Gower walked heavily into the room, his face of so red a hue it seemed tinged with purple. "Well, I say 'tis a bad bargain." Gower lowered his broad behind onto a fine chair so that his large belly hung down between his fat legs. "The maid you sent is not only with child, but has run off."

Charles clawed at his head, then tore the rag away with such impatience his wisps of hair stood on end. "The devil, you say, Gower. I must find Wat. Wat will know what to do."

At that, the two men left. Geoffrey, who had been hovering near the house in case the women wanted him, came into the hall to knock upon the panel. Then he pressed the spring.

"Let's move her upstairs," Lettice whispered. "He will not think her there since he has only just come down."

Geoffrey bent to pick up the little maid, who was pale and listless this second day of her motherhood.

"If I could just rest some, mistress, I'd be good as ever," Molly said, looking very small and blond in his arms.

"Hardly, with a child clinging to your petticoats," Lettice answered. "But we will protect you and that child as best we can." Lettice carried the warm, soft bundle that held the child. She could not harden her heart against the mother of so sweet a mite, though she did wonder if she shirked her duty. After they had settled mother and baby, Lettice returned to the parlor while Dorothy bustled about, playing nurse upstairs.

Geoffrey followed Lettice and seized her wrist. "She must not go back to Gower," he said.

Lettice sighed. "But what can we do? She has signed the indenture."

"Under threat. The way I signed mine. I am no excessive coward, yet I will sign much if my life is at stake."

"I wonder if the governor would relieve you of your bondage—if what you say is true."

"If he freed all the unwilling servants, half of those in all the colony would walk away from their masters. There is no proof but the indenture." Geoffrey let go her wrist and leaned wearily against the wall. "John still does not know of this—must not know until I can warn him carefully. He can be hotheaded."

They both raised their heads suddenly as they heard the sounds of the two masters on their way back to the house. The panel stood open, and Lettice instinctively ducked inside. Geoffrey followed and pulled it closed. Sitting on the floor, they bent their heads close to listen.

"She must be about somewhere," Squire Gower said, "unless she was et by a bear."

"We will scour the woods hereabout," Charles said. "My overseer is very clever with runaways." Lettice peered through the hole. Her brother-in-law took a brandy bottle off the table and poured his neighbor a drink. "You are a good and influential fellow, Gower. I will see you stand no loss." His hand raised to his brow as though his head still pained him.

Gower drank deliberately. "We will let the court settle the matter when the girl is found. No doubt we will come out ahead in the long run. For bastardy the fine is some six hundred pounds of tobacco—"

"Which she cannot pay. . . ."

"Well, then, six months of extra service, plus the time lost in giving birth. The father, when you find him, is required to pay three pounds or serve six months extra with nine months more for the keep of the child."

"But if he is one of my servants. . . ." Charles continued.

"Then you may have the extra six months, and I shall have the nine."

"I suppose. . . ," Charles said doubtfully.

During this conversation Geoffrey had leaned for a closer look, and Lettice had moved aside. She could feel his body tense, and she reached for his hand so he would not forget all caution while the two men exited.

Geoffrey was very silent, then he said, "You see what happens to foolish maids who love too well—and too often."

In the dark hiding place it was impossible to read the expression on his face. Lettice turned away from him. "I do not know what to think of love," she said in a low voice.

"It is best not to think of it at all." He reached to grasp her arm and spoke as though to answer questions she had never asked. "I thought it would be easier for me if I did not look upon you, though I want you so that I can hardly tell you. The Indian War was something of a disappointment. I have over six years left as a servant, and no land or fortune. It were better, I think, if I did not look upon any lovely lady."

Lettice swallowed. She knew he was right, yet it pained her to hear his words. "How is it with Wat?" she said finally. "You are not quite so thin or so beaten as you were."

"He watches me. Even hidden here, though I know he is in the far field, I feel his eyes."

She wished she could see his face to read what had become of him since last they had embraced and he had ridden away. She thought he had grown quieter. "He watches me too," Lettice told him.

"I know. And I do not like what he thinks."

It was on the tip of her tongue to tell him that Wat had watched them make love. But she dared not, not knowing what effect it might have on him and how he would risk himself. "Geoffrey, sometimes I am very much afraid," she finally admitted.

He rested his temple against hers. "And I," he said lowly. "For both of us." He felt for her hand and twined his fingers among hers, and for a while they sat in bitter silence. Then he kissed her cheek and said, "Tell me, what do you think of all day, here inside the house?"

"Sometimes . . . sometimes I think of you," she whispered.

"You should not." Abruptly he released her hand and made as though he would rise and leave her. But instead of pushing her away, he drew her to him, smothering his face in her hair.

"Oh, my sweet, you should get yourself a husband better than Gower who can protect you. I cannot. Once I had grand ideas of the place I wanted in the world, but now I would be content with something less if only I could have some kind of freedom. I think that if I might have even so small a space as this to be alone with you without Wat's eyes always upon me, I would be content."

For a while they savored their closeness, then Geoffrey whispered, "And yet it is so sweet to hold you that I would brave almost any penalty."

"And I am supposed to be free." She wound her arms about him. "But who is less a prisoner than I?"

Slowly he brought his head down to kiss between her breasts. She could feel him shake with desire, as she did. She stood to slip off her petticoats. Geoffrey wrapped his arms about her thighs and kissed her, probing with his tongue until she half moaned and sank to her knees. Then they loved as though there were no other moment but this.

They heard a great commotion as firm footsteps raced through the great hall and on up the stairs. A fist beat upon the oak door to Lettice's room, and a voice cried, "Where is she?! What are you doing to her?!"

Lettice and Geoffrey hastily dressed and exited, closing the panel behind them. They were just in time to see Dorothy open the door and then a flash of blond hair as John entered the room upstairs.

Molly, who had been sleeping on her pallet, opened her eyes and spoke softly, "John. I been missing you so."

"My angel." He fell to his knees beside her trundle bed and bent to kiss her passionately upon her neck.

It was this scene that met Charles's eyes as he walked into the crowded room. He put his bony hand to his forehead, exclaiming, "Before heaven, 'tis no wonder I am pained, with a house full of rogues and foolish women. But even at that I did not think my wife would betray me." He staggered slightly to lean against the door frame. Then he

135

looked down at Molly, sternly. "Do you know what the penalties are, wench, for what you have done? And for the man who has aided you?"

"No, sir," Molly whispered. Her eyes filled with fear as she raised them to the severe, awkward form towering above her.

"Bastardy . . . bastardy. . . ," Charles began, shaking a finger. "The father will suffer."

"Well, sir, you don't have to look far, for I must confess that it was me. . . ."

Lettice gasped, for it was Geoffrey who spoke. Her thoughts whirled in confusion. Was it not John? And would Geoffrey lose another year of his life by this?

Stiffly John rose to his feet. "No, Henry," he said. "No one takes the blame for me. And there be no blame, after all, for Molly and I was married in England afore we come."

IX

Moonlight probed through every crack of the crude cabin. Geoffrey rose restlessly, unable to sleep. He could vaguely see John's bundle of blankets in the corner. The door creaked on its leather hinges as Geoffrey pushed it open and walked into the moonlit night. Savoring the quiet and the freedom, he made his way to stand below Lettice's window. He must speak to her, he thought, yet he hesitated to wake her. It was a foolish act. He should stay miles away from the danger of her attraction.

A twig snapped behind him, and a dread voice came softly on the night air. "The silk-and-satin man—howlin' at the moon, are ye? Like a beast in heat."

Geoffrey turned swiftly. Wat was half hidden in the undergrowth. Geoffrey swallowed. The giant walked softly, powerful, full of suppressed hatred. His voice was oily with menace. "How does the silk-and-satin lady like it that you must grub in the dirt like the rest of us? But perhaps this excites her, eh?"

Geoffrey clenched his jaw. His hands closed into fists. He did not want to fight Wat now. He had other plans.

Wat placed one foot steadily in front of the other, his tread crushing twigs and leaves underfoot, his shape ungainly. Close he stood, his narrowed eyes were looking down upon Geoffrey; his breath was foul and tinged with rum. He laughed low in his throat. "We will bring you down, mister silk-and-satin man—and the silk-and-satin lady too. She will spread herself open to all who come. . . ."

Geoffrey drew back his right arm. It seemed an eternity before it connected with the rocklike jaw of the bigger man. Wat staggered back a few paces. Then he pulled himself up to great height, raising both fists above his head, poised to pound Geoffrey down into the ground.

"Have you forgot the lessons I taught you? I'll squash you like a worm."

Geoffrey crouched back, fists raised, swordsman's instincts alert. He had been in many a rough-and-tumble battle as a student. "Try," he said. "We are alone here—just us two. There are none of your slaveys to help you."

Wat lowered his huge fists, but Geoffrey jumped aside. Before Wat had recovered, Geoffrey's fist struck him at the base of his skull, stunning him somewhat. Wat gave a gurgling roar from deep in his throat. Geoffrey stood aside and watched the giant with some alarm. Striking Wat was like striking a mountain. A huge fist came flying toward Geoffrey. He dodged, but one of Wat's knuckles caught him on the mouth, cutting his lip. Geoffrey circled warily, his tongue testing the injury, tasting blood. Wat swung again. And again. Geoffrey dodged.

It went on and on for a half-hour or more. Both were breathing heavily. Finally they staggered, moving slower and slower, wavering like men far gone with drink. Geoffrey's aim was surer, but Wat seemed impervious to pain and injury. Once again, Geoffrey evaded a blow, though his step faltered. Wat lunged and embraced his adversary in a bear hug. Geoffrey drew in a fast breath of shock. This was what he had feared all along. He was no match for this. Quickly he raised his knee, striking Wat in the groin. Wat loosened his grip for an instant, grunting with pain. Geoffrey bent his knees, then shot upward. His skull connected with the giant's jaw. Wat grunted again, then staggered. Geoffrey whirled, his fist seeking a precise target at the base of the massive head. Wat sagged. Then he slumped to the ground.

Geoffrey smiled down at him, his chest heaving like a bellows. It was a secret between Wat and himself. Now they both knew the giant could be beaten. Never again would the larger man attack the smaller—unless he was well backed up. But Geoffrey did not intend to give him that chance. He started to walk toward the house, but his legs gave way under him.

* * *

Lettice awoke in an instant when she heard the gravel upon her casement. Molly was asleep in the other bed. Pray God he would not awake the whole house. She was still tying on her bed gown by the time she reached the door. Geoffrey stepped from the shadows to greet her, placing a finger over her lips to caution her to silence.

"I am going with Charles to Jamestown in the morning," he whispered. "It were best to part, my love. Less dangerous, if you will. And I will find a way there to send some word to England. Someone there may yet aid me."

"I pray that it happens," she said, wanting to hold him in some way, but knowing she could not.

He bent to kiss her lips, but Lettice drew back from the taste of him. "Geoffrey, you are bleeding!"

He laughed low in his throat—the laugh of an unbeaten man. She tipped back her head to look up at him in the darkness. "And you are burning-hot and covered with sweat while I freeze here in the cold night air."

"I burn with victory. I have taught Wat a lesson."

"You have risked your life, I think," she said, her voice sharp with fear. "He will not forget it."

"Nor will I." He seized her wrist to bring her closer. "And while I am gone, I pray you avoid him."

She tried to shake herself free, crying, "Geoffrey, this is serious business!"

"It is. And while he is lost in dreams, I would love you, mistress, uninterrupted—though I swore I would not again. Unless you would wait for a more pretty, perfumed lover."

"Oh, Geoffrey, why do you take these risks?" she sighed. She felt the pull of his body and knew it was not to be resisted. "Would you freeze me in this cold night?"

"No," he laughed. "I would hide with you behind the panel." He ran his bruised hands along her back and hips. "Eh, lady, is that not a good idea?"

"You will make a wanton of me," she said.

There were still some blankets upon the floor of the hidey hole, and there they rested. Their bodies were grown more familiar with each other, but their need was stronger than ever. How could she live without his embrace? Without him inside her? After they came together, he made as though to rise, then inhaled sharply through his teeth with

139

renewed desire. Closing her still more fiercely in his arms, he took her again.

"It's best I go to Jamestown where you will not tempt me so," he whispered at last, pulling on his boots. I shall not see you for a while, my love. Keep well—and never turn your back on Wat." He let himself out, silent as a cat.

Lettice felt herself dissolve into tears. She hated the weakness he inspired in her. Still, the tears slipped down her cheeks, some into her open and silently weeping mouth. She climbed the stairs to her room. Suddenly she began to gag and choke. Her stomach began to heave. She dragged herself to her pewter wash basin and vomited into it.

"Oh, my God!" She glanced toward the sleeping Molly. Now she knew what the abigail had suffered.

The wounded man sat in the April sun, cursing his weakness. He had always made his own way in the world. This draining away of his strength sapped his confidence. Gently he touched his toughened fingertips to the rag tied over the left side of his face. He felt the scarred mass of healing flesh underneath. He tugged at the old fur cap he wore winter and summer.

His left eye was gone forever. Many a day, while roaming about the forest, the quickness of his good eyes had saved him. Now he must squint carefully with one. Despite his weakness, he and Sal did all the plowing and half the planting. Sal would do the rest, God bless her. Then she would go to the neighbors for safety.

Here at Jordan's Point the drum beat, calling out volunteers to fight. It was a lawless gathering. The governor had forbidden the raising of forces without his consent. So far the mass of men milled about uselessly, wanting leadership.

But Jud's fellow small farmers smoldered with rage at the Indians. Underlying all was a mistrust of the big planters. The rights of smaller men had eroded steadily as the king had gained power in England.

Jud sighed. He must see this slaughter started so they could go home again. The blundering in Maryland had touched off a powder keg.

That evening Nathaniel Bacon, the governor's cousin, rode up to the campfire. Only one man sat there. The rest slept in the tents or had gone home to prepare. Coldly, Bacon eyed Jud's rag and his disfigurement. Jud calmly carved upon a stick while the flickering firelight made his scar lurid.

Bacon rode closer to him. "You, there," he demanded. "You have met the Indian before, old man."

Jud nodded, scarce looking up.

Bacon chewed upon his lip for a moment, then said, "Then no doubt you are ready for vengeance."

Jud shook his head. "Vengeance is for fools."

Bacon's face stiffened. "I have many grudges against old men—here and in England—that I would repay. Old men threw me out of Cambridge, my father disinherited me, my father-in-law disowned my wife for marrying me. And here, where the savages owe me much for killing my overseer, an old man has forbidden me to kill them. I will seek vengeance, even if the Lord is against it."

"I fight for other reasons," Jud said softly. "And I am not so old."

"Good," Bacon said. "I may have a use for you that is better and more restful than soldiering."

Jud stopped his carving. He studied Bacon with real curiosity.

"We will have messages for the governor. Your face, old man, carries its own message. He cannot ignore what we say when he looks at you. And while you are in Jamestown and about, you can discover who is for us and what the governor will do. Can you act the spy?"

"If need be."

"You will be a lesson to Jamestown." Without further words Bacon dug his spurs into his horse and rode looking for Captain Crews, one of his henchmen.

As soon as his leader's back was to him, Jud spat upon the ground. "Dirtier and dirtier," he muttered. Jud would fight to restore enough order that he and Sal would be safe in their little house. He was indifferent to any feud between Bacon and Sir William, his cousin. But Jud cherished the vague hope that if these poorer men who were encamped at Jordan's Point banded together, they might begin a force that would limit the privileges of the rich and lordly planters—men like Bacon himself.

That is, if this fool Bacon did not manage to kill them all. It seemed young Bacon's feet were set in some preordained path—as though he walked through a dream that was his alone.

Once more, Jud spat upon the earth and wondered if men were ever better.

Studying the mutilated man before him, Governor Berkeley clearly understood why his cousin had sent him as messenger. The governor offered the poorer man brandy, since his weakness from travel was evident. The news from his cousin filled Sir William with foreboding. He had never felt so old. His periwig was too heavy and warm for the Virginia spring, and he wished he might retire to take it off.

The man seated on the other side of the table from him raised his one expressive eye and gave the governor a look of pity. Sir William cleared his throat. He was not accustomed to receiving pity—especially from one so crippled and low in station.

The governor cleared his throat and then surprisingly he confided in his bored, yet stumbling manner. "I wrote to a friend in England today, saying how miserable is that man who governs a people where six parts of seven at least are poor, indebted, discontented and armed. But they do not understand in England now that the memory of Cromwell is fading."

Jud was moved somehow to reassure him. " 'Tis not like England, sir."

Sir William looked at him for a moment, and then spoke slowly, "You may tell my cousin that I deny him his commission and declare him a rebel. We will not have Cromwell all over again."

"No, sir," Jud agreed.

The governor called for his clerk to make ready the necessary papers. When the clerk handed the papers to Jud, the former left; he was on his way to Bacon to tell him of his outlaw status.

In May, Bacon turned his forces upon the friendly Occaneechee and refused to sue his cousin for pardon. Instead he again demanded a commission.

Governor Berkeley proclaimed him a rebel once more and sent word to England of the rebellion. Then he placed his wife upon a ship for home and begged the authorities to petition His Majesty to send a more vigorous and youthful governor to Virginia.

With one ear alert for sounds from the baby, Molly prepared a turkey soup. The infant lay in a cradle made for him by John. There was much to do in Gower's house and kitchen. The master demanded huge meals, and there were always iron pots to scour and water to fetch and endless cleaning and scrubbing. Often she had to leave the baby unattended.

Well, it was best not to think too much on trouble. She would just hope that things would get better in time. Tomorrow she would fire up the oven to make enough wheat bread to last the squire for a week. And now when the soup was simmering would be a good time to scrub the bricks of the floor. She poured some hot water from a kettle into a bucket of cold water, seizing it by its wooden handles. She dragged it to a corner and tucked up her petticoats. She had just got down upon her knees and begun to scrub when she heard the master's heavy tread behind her.

Fearfully she froze. She could not look up at him. Finally curiosity overcame her. Though larded with fat, he was tall and powerful. He stood silent, red-faced, his eyes bulging, belly swelling. Below his belly was a growing lump as his male organ became engorged with blood and lust.

Molly turned to stone—a small animal facing a viper. Nothing was heard but Gower's increasingly heavy breaths. Gathering her nerve, Molly sprang to her feet, but she slipped on the wet floor so that she sank down upon one knee again.

Gower seized her wrist and raised her to her feet. She looked at him in fear. His fat face seemed huge, framed by wisps of graying hair. He was almost a foot taller than she.

"No, no, master!" she whispered.

In answer he twisted both her arms behind her back and pushed her from the kitchen to the main house. He half dragged her upstairs to his great red-curtained bed.

"No, master," she pleaded as she heard the first cries of the waking baby through the open window.

Gower threw her down full-length onto the bed covers. Then his bulk exploded from his confining clothes as he shed them. She tried to rise. He grabbed her short-cut hair—the badge of a runaway—with one hand. He slapped her face with two quick blows of the other hand.

"No, master," she once more whimpered.

"It's not as if no one has entered here before," he said.

She shook her head wordlessly. She was cornered like some helpless creature. Yes, many had entered before—with pleasure, with joy, with high spirits. But never like this. Never wielding such awful power. Never while she was wife to one man and mother of a tender babe.

What defense had she? She edged toward the corner of the bed, but he flung himself half across her, wheezing. His flesh was soft, but there was muscle beneath it. He grasped her bodice and ripped it off, then he pulled her skirts away. Never had she been so naked. She tried to crawl away. He raised himself on one elbow and struck her jaw with the other. Then he threw his great bulk upon her, pinning her down.

"I don't mind if you fight me," he said gutturally. "Otherwise it is over too soon." Then, heavily, he pierced her while she grieved so that she could not even sob.

The next morning Molly turned from where she sat apathetically by the baby's cradle to see John looking down upon her. Grimly he studied her so that she was sure he could read each of yesterday's events upon her face. The purple stain upon her jaw must blaze out at him. She sprang to her feet with a sob, covering her mouth with a hand, and fled him.

He followed with long strides and pressed her into his arms until she sobbed out her despair.

"I will kill him!" John said between clenched teeth. His face, which for an instant had been deathly pale, blazed red. "I will kill him!" he roared.

Uttering a wail from the depths of her small body, Molly sank into a heap on the bricks and covered her face with her hands. "Ohhh, it be the end of us." She raised a tousled head, crystal tears upon her cheeks, but John was already gone. Quickly she sped after him. A black maid fled screaming out the door. Breathlessly, Molly searched until she found Gower cornered in a parlor. The Virginia sun shone through the red-brocade window curtains, casting

144

a bloody glow upon them. John's whitish hair looked strangely orange.

A pewter candlestick hit the wall with a crash just above Gower's head. Bits of plaster fell. John dashed to the chimney and seized the iron poker.

"You worm! Whoreson! Applesqueak!" John said through clenched teeth. "Bashing your brains out be too good for you."

"No, John!" Molly clutched at his fustian shirt, trying to pull back his hard and sturdy body. "You cannot do this to me! They will punish you! Punish me! Burn us! We never will be free!"

"Never," Gower said coldly, recovering his nerve. "If you strike me."

John's shoulders suddenly sagged. He bowed his head, his muscular neck looking sadly defenseless.

"Oh, God," he said, almost in tears. "Why did we come here?"

Burying her face in her hands, Molly sobbed so that her coarse-linen bodice trembled and her shoulders shook. Her short hair formed a halo of golden curls about her head.

Squire Gower saw that he was for the moment safe and straightened, and his face became purplish with anger. He pushed John's arm aside.

"So, John Martin," Gower wheezed, seating himself in a gilt leather chair. "You have recovered your wits. Now we can begin to deal."

John looked up with surprise. "Deal?" he said. "For what?"

Lettice rode out through the fields on Aurora, her favorite horse from among Charles's limited stable. The chestnut mare pranced daintily, enjoying the beautiful weather as much as did her rider. The fresh air took away the nausea that plagued Lettice. Her green riding dress strained across her swelling breasts.

Her face shaded by a wide-plumed velvet hat, she scanned the forest in the direction of Gower's plantation, awaiting John. She had insisted that Dorothy allow him a conjugal visit, though Wat had muttered and threatened. Dorothy stood in some fear of Wat while Charles was gone, as did everyone else on the place. Lettice knew Wat hated her—and Geoffrey more.

145

She heard the sound of galloping hooves before John's pale hair was visible through the trees. She wondered how he had urged the old nag he rode to such a pace. As he burst into the open, Lettice urged her horse toward him.

He saluted her. "Mistress Lettice," he said. "We must have words."

She wheeled to ride at his side.

He swallowed several times. His face was flaming, and he looked away, embarrassed, but finally he said, "There be bad trouble. Gower has forced Molly to his bed."

"Dear God," Lettice said.

John reined up his horse and looked directly at her as she halted beside him. "I tried to kill him," John said.

"Oh, John, you didn't! What will he do to you?"

"Nothing. We bargained."

"For what?"

"I was to tell you that he would free Molly and buy me free from Squire Charles if you was to marry him. And now I done it, and I tell you that Molly and me'll never let you do it. But I said it like I promised, and so he can't punish me."

"Oh, John." Lettice shook her head. "Oh, John." She found she had never liked him so much. "Were he not such a brute, his offer would tempt me, for I have trouble of my own."

A startled look came into his eyes. "What's that, mistress?"

"I have told no one yet. I am to bear Geoffrey's—you call him Henry's—child. I don't know what I am to do."

"He be a good man, mistress. He will want to know."

Lettice bowed her head. Why was it so much easier to talk to John than to Geoffrey?

John leaned forward, bracing himself on his horse's neck as he thought. "I think we must find Bacon's rebels. Look for them at least. Better to die fighting against the governor than in this slavery."

"Wat will be after you in an instant."

"He must not follow. If we run away, we are already outlaws."

"Yes." Lettice considered for a moment. "Yes, there is a way to do it—if we leave by river."

"On the sloop?"

"Exactly. That is what we must do. I will arrange it with

146

Dorothy somehow. I'll tell her of Squire Gower's bargain. Surely, she'll not want me to wed that man. I'll make an excuse that I go in search of a more suitable husband. We will go to Jamestown. Perhaps Geoffrey can tell us how to find the rebels."

He nodded to her as an equal, which Lettice thought showed more respect than when he had pretended to serve her. They rode off, each occupied with thought. The breezes ruffled the feather on Lettice's hat and spread her long hair out behind.

She knew all their futures were uncertain, but she was drawn to Jamestown the way John was drawn to the rebels. She must see Geoffrey. Her body craved his presence even more since the child was within her. It was as though she were tied to the father in some primitive way, like the cord tied her to the child.

The horses' hooves pounded the rich Virginia soil. But a single thought occupied Lettice—soon she would see Geoffrey.

In the shadow of the rough stable John helped her dismount. He was just turning to lead his horse away when a hand grasped his collar. It was the giant Wat. Lettice gasped.

John became very still. His face was expressionless as he strained to avoid the kind of trouble he had faced with Gower. Wat's bloodshot eyes burned behind narrowed lids. He did not release John. He just turned his square head with its patches of mangy-looking hair slowly as he looked from one to the other of them.

"They all wants her." He laughed with eyes glittering like a lizard's. "The silk-and-satin gentleman was first—the rest follow. Soon it will be my turn, eh!"

Lettice, still holding the reins of her horse, slashed out at him. "You are mad, Wat!"

Wat released John in an instant and lunged at Lettice, seizing her riding dress with both massive hands. For a moment Lettice was raised up off the ground. Then there was the sound of rent cloth. Growling breaths came from Wat's throat. Jerking the cloth again and again, he shredded it until Lettice stood bare-breasted, her petticoats boiling as she lashed out at him with feet and arms.

"Leave off!" John cried, but the giant paid no heed. Lettice could not catch her breath. Her hat sailed to the

147

ground, her head jerked back and forth as though she were a puppet being punished by a child. From the corner of her eye she saw John bend to pick up a horseshoe—aim—and then there was the sickening sound of metal striking bone. Wat sagged. As he fell, he brought Lettice with him to the ground.

Nauseated and jolted, she could not for a moment rise or pull her shreds of clothing about her. Her face was in the dirt of the stable yard, and she gagged, then vomited.

Silently, John stripped off his own fustian shirt that she might cover herself. "This be my day for trouble, mistress," he said ruefully. "Wat will kill me now."

Lettice got up and wiped her mouth on his sleeve. "He will not have the chance," she promised. "Bind his wrist and ankles and drag him to the house that Dorothy may see. My clothes will be undeniable evidence. Even though she fears Charles, she cannot allow Wat to remain here after this."

And she added, "Then we will make our escape."

Robert lay on his great bed, abandoned in the darkness, the curtains drawn about him, stifling. He felt great pain and weakness throughout his body. One day faded into the next so that he was not sure what month it was or how old he had grown.

But he knew that soon it would be time for his wife, the Lady Isobel, to appear. Robert knew that he hated her. Though they had been married some years now, she had never given her body to him. He might have had the marriage annulled were it not for this terrible sickness and weakness.

Sometimes he feared the potions and medicines that Lady Isobel gave him with her own hand. If only Henry, his old tutor, was to be had. He might have helped to discover whether these cures did him good or ill. Robert often suspected that the doctor was in league with his wife.

But Henry had had Isobel though her husband had not. And then he had disappeared, though he had left all his belongings behind. Once Robert thought he had seen Henry riding with Isobel in the park, better dressed than usual. It was all very mysterious. Perhaps it was Henry, after all, who Isobel rode off so often to meet, returning when Robert knew not.

There was a scratching on the door, and the curtains were pulled aside. His old gray-haired nurse appeared with some liquid in a cup in one hand and a candle in the other.

"There, there, now, Master Robert," she soothed. "Be you not better? Drink this now. The Lady Isobel has sent it."

"I do not want it." Robert turned his head away.

But the nurse was used to his moods from childhood. "Come, my dear. The doctor has ordered it. We must have you well. Else I fear you will grow too weak."

Perhaps she was right. The candle shone on her moon of a face, illuminating the suffering concern. Robert had no right to suspect his wife just because she did not love him.

Reaching forth a thin and shaking hand, he grasped the cup and drank. Then he fell back again. "Please leave the candle, Nurse," he said.

His nurse went downstairs to where Lady Isobel sat listless in a chair next to a dying fire in the parlor they called the red parlor because of its furnishings and draperies. The doctor, a silent man who looked himself to be in poor health, sat facing her.

"Has he taken it?" Lady Isobel asked the nurse in a bored tone.

"Yes, my lady," the nurse responded. "And you must care for yourself. You look right pale."

"The doctor advises me to go abroad."

The nurse looked at her mistress with surprise. "And leave Sir Robert alone?"

"Others can continue the medication as well as I. See that you do. The doctor will visit often to make sure all goes well."

"To be sure," the doctor said.

The nurse pursed her round mouth and left the room.

Lady Isobel extended a delicate hand toward the doctor. "Come receive your payment," she said low in her throat.

He came to her side and sank on his knees, covering her hand with kisses, his thin body tense with passion. Then he ran his hand down her silk lavender gown and prepared to reach up underneath.

She brushed his hand aside as she might an insect. "It is too early. You may have the rest when all is over. No one must suspect. You must make sure they continue the potion. I will be far away when it happens and free from blame."

"Oh, yes, my lady," he said in a choked voice. She did not stop him as he lowered himself to the floor and began pressing hot kisses upon her ankles.

X

At sundown Geoffrey slipped through the gates of Jamestown. Lit by an orange evening sky, the wide river shone deep-copper. Water lapped against marsh grass. Dark forest stood beyond.

By the river's edge a cockney servant was studying the ships. He looked around with a start when he heard Geoffrey's step.

"A long way home, ain't it?" He nodded toward the river, his voice floating in the soft air. "That bit of water runs away into the same ocean as does the Thames. It's hard to believe." He sighed. "I'll never see London again."

"Pray God we all will," Geoffrey answered.

"Nay. No one will steal me back the way they stole me here." With a sad gesture, the stocky man saluted and turned back toward the gates to return to his master. The sentry did not question the Londoner. He knew his face well since he often stood there in the evening watching the river.

Gnawing the inside of his cheek, Geoffrey, too, studied the river. Fortunately Charles was spending two days at Green Spring. He had not given Geoffrey leave to quit town. No one would bother him so close to the gates, but should anyone suspect he tried to stow away home again, he would be seized and punished. Geoffrey had seen searchers swarm over departing vessels like ants. He'd seen desperate wretches dragged screaming and kicking back to shore.

Geoffrey was not attempting to escape now. He knew not what might greet him in England. The times were not yet ripe. He studied the slant of the sun, whistling silently.

An unusual amount of masts were silhouetted against the evening sky. Many gentlemen's sloops had borne their masters to the Assembly. But it was one of the English ships anchored out on the waters that interested Geoffrey. He stood with his back against a rough tobacco warehouse, watching. A few wisps of rising mist blew like smoke upon the river. After a time Geoffrey's heart lightened as he saw a boat being lowered. He heard the sound of dipping oars. Then he heard a grating noise as the boat was pulled ashore.

Geoffrey gave a low whistle, and the oarsman looked over to him. A gentle wind ruffled the stranger's hair, which was burnished with the final rays of the setting sun. His shadow long behind him, the gentleman sauntered in Geoffrey's direction. He spoke in a low voice, "Have you got your letter?" The man appeared to be only a year or so older than Geoffrey and he had an air of self-assurance and command.

Geoffrey reached into the bosom of his shirt and drew out several folded sheets of paper, which he had purloined from Master Charles, along with ink and quill. He handed the letter—it was a letter to James, his old friend from Oxford—to the slim figure before him.

"I can think of no way to repay you." He was conscious of his poor appearance compared with the other's elegance. Fine white ruffles showed below the wide cuffs of the gentleman's good claret coat as he brushed aside any consideration of reward.

"It is nothing, my friend. Having heard your story, I am only too anxious to help. I sometimes wonder how many stories like yours one could find in Virginia. But I shall return to the King's court directly upon my arrival, and I shall look for your fellow scholar, James." A genial smile crossed the thin, civilized face.

Geoffrey breathed as though a great load had been lifted from him. He looked with longing at the English ships rising and falling with the gentle ripples of the river. "It would not grieve me to see the last of Virginia, though it has some interest for me. But the treachery I have met gnaws at me constantly."

The gentleman looked up at the palisades of Jamestown and out into the sentinal pines of the forest. He spoke softly, "I do not envy you. It seems to me Virginia is a tinder box at best. I hope the next time I greet you, the country is not all ablaze with war."

Geoffrey thought of much he would say, so many hopes rode on his letter. But he could only manage to add, "I hope your voyage is a safe one."

The gentleman grasped his hand warmly. "Fare you well, Master Finch."

Watching the gentleman's narrow, wine-colored shoulders recede toward the river, the unwitting servant stood in the grip of great emotion. As the Englishman rowed out to his ship, Geoffrey wondered how his ailing mother fared and what had happened to his old home. And Giles. He wondered about Giles. And if he was yet in possession of their father's fortune. Or if his mother had died and Giles was in possession of that which should come to Geoffrey.

The sky was purple now, the James turning black. He was about to go the way he had come when he noticed a number of figures surreptitiously slip ashore from a newly arrived sloop. Indistinct dark shadows—but Geoffrey's curiosity was aroused. Shielded by the warehouse, he saw a man walk casually in through the gates, then pass under the torch. The sentry nodded to him. Smiling broadly, the man slapped the sentry on the back and engaged him in loud talk. Thus two more slipped through. Geoffrey sensed still others concealed near the water. One figure headed toward his own shadowy hiding place. Torchlight touched a bulky shape as it moved in and out of patches of darkness. Geoffrey could see a rag tied over half his face—and an old fur cap.

Geoffrey started from concealment. "It can't be. . . ."

A knife gleamed; the figure half crouched.

"Jud!" Geoffrey hissed. "Is it you?"

There was just enough light to see a smile break out on Jud's face—a smile amazingly pure in the midst of the destruction of his face.

"Henry, is it? How is it with you, lad?" Hurrying forward, he grasped Geoffrey's hand in his hard callused one. Then glancing back, he nodded to Geoffrey to follow him into a place that was sheltered from the sentry's eyes.

"I left you for dead," Geoffrey said softly, full of joy that he was wrong.

"Nay, not me. I'm too tough to kill," Jud laughed.

153

"I never thought to see you live again, Jud, yet you seem much the same."

"Not so," Jud growled, settling himself down upon a beached boat. "My face pains me even in good weather." He reached out to grasp Geoffrey's arm to urge silence while he studied the sentry at the gate. Then he got up and walked to the end of the shed to look out upon the river. Grunting satisfaction he returned.

"Come along inside the gates now, my friend. They are about to close, my old wounds tell me."

Geoffrey trusted to this advice. The pine torch flickered above the sentry's head as he peered into their faces, scratching stiff spikes of black hair about his bald spot and yawning. "Out late, ain't ya?" he said to Geoffrey.

"Just a free bit of air," Geoffrey answered.

Along the dusty streets the two men moved. They tried to avoid the passing gentlemen who were weaving from the too-free imbibing of a town so social that every house served as a tavern. Capped and aproned housewives slammed their doors behind departing friends, work and gossip finished for the day. Sounds of the town slowed.

Geoffrey studied his friend's bulky shadow in the darkness. Jud wore too many clothes for the warm weather. This was his way of carrying all he needed when he traveled. But Jud's pace began to slacken from the effects of his wounds during even so short a walk as this through Jamestown.

"I'm with the rebels now, Henry," Jud said quietly. "Can I trust you?"

Geoffrey's laugh rang out. Then he lowered his voice as he noticed several gentlemen look up. "Why not? His Majesty's government in Virginia has done little for me."

Jud halted in the dusty street and gave him a searching look. He clasped the former gentleman about his shoulders. "Do you still seek to run away? Would you still hide among common men?"

Geoffrey hesitated, his eyes coming to rest on the livid scar showing beneath Jud's makeshift bandage. He had come to value this man's wisdom and his friendship, yet Geoffrey felt he had his own path to follow.

"I have been denied my own fortune, Jud," he said regretfully. "I will lay my hands on it if I can and then leave this place. I am no leveler."

154

Jud grunted. His gaze shifted so that it was impossible to tell if Geoffrey's words had disappointed him. "It is what you are born to," he said gruffly. "But you're a good enough fellow all the same."

As the first stars began to appear, several sudden reports sounded from guns overlooking the river. Jud laughed low in his throat. "The governor's men say no to Bacon's request to come ashore, I think. His sloop'll be skittering along up the river."

"So Bacon lies upon the river in his sloop."

"He's elected to the Assembly with Crews, his henchman. They vow to serve, even if they're outlaws." Jud turned to look at the palisades, chuckling. "But if the governor thinks to drag Bacon off his sloop in chains, he must do it another day. Bacon should be here at Mr. Lawrence's house before us." Jud's footsteps slowed, and he swung his head about so that his single eye peered at a substantial brick house that Geoffrey knew belonged to one Richard Lawrence, a gentleman and keeper of a tavern. Light from many candles shone through the window panes.

"I am sorely tempted to join you all the same, Jud," Geoffrey said. "I long for a life of freedom and action. Had I not just dispatched a message to England, I would become a rebel."

Jud shrugged his shabby shoulders. "Come along, anyway. A man's fortunes can take many strange turnings. Someday you might need a refuge with the outlaws."

Jud lowered his fist upon the panels of the door. Geoffrey found himself too curious to turn away. After a minute or two a pretty black woman in a white cap admitted them. Geoffrey looked at her with interest. It was rumored about the little town that Richard Lawrence was in love with his slave.

"Are they expecting you?" she asked in a low and melodious voice.

Jud nodded.

She seemed not to notice his bizarre appearance. Their footsteps sounded on the tiles of the floor. Her brown homespun skirts swept the floor as she went before them, but she did not speak again. The tavern was empty, but as she opened a second door, her soft eyes sought a man with brown cavalier locks. He sat in shirt sleeves, and his face brightened when he saw her. The gentlemen were gathered in a well-appointed parlor lit from several candles, which were casting weird shadows.

A slender, dark-haired man in his late 20s was just discarding a buff coat in the warm evening. He started when he noticed the newcomers, then he gestured with movements full of restless energy. Since others deferred to him, Geoffrey took him to be Bacon.

"Why do you bring a stranger here, Jud?" Bacon demanded. "Do you want us betrayed."

Jud shrugged. "He saved my life in Maryland. I trust 'im with mine."

Geoffrey saw that he had made a mistake in coming. "I will leave, gentlemen," he said, "if it makes you easier. And do not fear that I shall talk."

Bacon came to stand directly before him, one hand on his hip, looking with his hard black eyes directly into Geoffrey's. "Do not talk," he said. "Else we will hound you for the rest of your life—aye, to your very death." Bacon turned to fix blazing eyes upon each man in turn. His voice rose almost nervously. "Do you hear me, friends? We will have loyalty to the death—from all!" But Geoffrey was his special target. "And sooner or later all will be forced to choose in Virginny between one side and the other. And choose in England too."

Geoffrey nodded, but in his heart he wondered at this man. "The day may come soon when I join your ranks," he said. "I wish you Godspeed."

But Bacon had turned his back on him to continue more important pursuits.

The comely black woman ushered Geoffrey from the white-walled parlor into the dark-paneled dining room. Her candle formed a pool of light in this empty part of the house. One hand toyed with her white apron. Her black, full hair was pulled back from a high, oval brow and tied. Wide-spaced, clear eyes sought his.

"You are a servant?" she asked shyly.

"I am."

Her teeth caught up her full lip, then with a rush of breath, she dared to say, "I beg you. Do not speak of these men here to your fellow servants. They will talk. I do not want my master to suffer."

"I would not betray my friend," Geoffrey said. "And if I should, they will punish me."

Her face softened and relaxed as she nodded.

Geoffrey was deep in thought as he returned through the streets of Jamestown. Few candles still flickered. Householders had closed up for the night. The Assembly was long over. He prayed God that Charles had not returned unexpectedly to find him gone. It galled Geoffrey to serve a man like Charles. To say "yes sir" and "no sir." Still it was better in Jamestown where his tasks were relatively light and he had some freedom of movement and chance to take part in the life of the town. And he was free of Wat.

But the figure that greeted him in the parlor of his inn was not Charles—but Lettice. Her black silk rustled as she rose from a seat near the chimney. Dark smudges under her eyes showed things were not well with her. A single candle shone down, burnishing her hair, but making the shadows on her pale face even deeper. Her creamy-white bosom gleamed, uncovered by any lace ornament about the bodice. Why must she look so lovely? he thought. Even haggard she was a beauty.

"Geoffrey," she said in a low voice. "I have been wondering where you were."

Words leapt from his throat. "My God, woman. What are you doing here?" He saw confusion and disappointment in her violet eyes, and he regretted his hastiness. "I'm sorry, my dear. I did not expect you." He came to kiss her briefly on her forehead. "Forgive me. I have much on my mind."

Then he turned to kick at the dead ashes by the fire. Because of his promise, he could say nothing to her of the rebels whose plans he did not as yet know anyway.

Lettice was hurt by his coldness. How could she, while he was in this mood, tell him he was father to her child? She looked down at her clasped hands, torn. She felt the need of his touch, longed to wrap her arms about him, yet how could she add to his troubles by telling him hers? He was a servant, after all.

"I, too, have much on my mind," she admitted. "I am come here with the excuse to my sister that I hunt for a husband in Jamestown since Gower presses me."

He bit his thumb, thoughtfully, then turned to lean one arm negligently upon the chimney piece. He squinted at her through expressionless, brown eyes.

157

"Yes, my sweet," he said softly. "It were best you found a husband."

She flushed. She had not wanted him to be so agreeable on this point. How dare he be so agreeable? Her hands formed into fists as she choked back angry words. But then she swallowed. Of course he did not know of the child. She saw that he looked down upon her with eyes still cold and masked. Very well. She would not tell him. She would care for the child somehow herself. There were still perhaps gentlemen in Jamestown, after all, who would wed her and be pleased to have a woman of grace and beauty in a land so raw.

"You are pale, Lettice," he said softly. "What is it?"

She wanted to burst into a torrent of words, call him fickle, beat her fists upon his chest. Instead she blurted, "Molly. Gower has raped her."

Geoffrey's face turned white with anger.

Lettice hurried on, somewhat breathlessly. "They are both here—or rather out upon the sloop. John was in a murderous mood. There was no telling what he would do. We must get them away before they are pursued."

Geoffrey stiffened. "They are on the river? My God, those two are star-crossed lovers if ever two were."

"What do you mean?" she said, thinking that she and Geoffrey were equally star-crossed.

"The gates are locked tonight. Ships may be searched. Bacon's sloop lies upstream. They will probably send someone to capture him. But Bacon—" The muscles in Geoffrey's jaw tightened as he cut himself off in mid-sentence. "He is not there," he finished lamely.

"They want to join the rebels. It is the only answer for them."

His moody eyes held a faraway look. With one hand he picked at the wax drips from the candle on the chimney piece, considering something that she did not understand. She felt a wave of sadness. Finally he looked at her directly and said, "Pray God there will be some rebels for them to join. Bacon's fortunes are uncertain."

"So, it seems, are all our fortunes." Lettice settled herself upon a joint stool, her skirts belling about her. She could feel herself droop with fatigue. "I have brought them nothing but trouble," she sighed. "And you too."

Geoffrey's dark eyes blinked with surprise. Then for the

first time his expression softened. "Trouble? To me? No, Lettice. Who was it, after all, who untied me when I despaired? And who found a master for me when Captain Quince threatened to throw me overboard? And besides," he smiled at last, "you have brought me no small measure of joy."

Lettice looked down upon the tiles of the floor. He was grateful to her, it seemed. And that must be all, else why did he stand so far away from her? She would not play upon that gratitude and tell him of the child, she decided. There was nothing he could do. She leaned wearily against the small parlor table.

"But the corners of your mouth draw down, you are tired," Geoffrey said. "Has the landlord given you supper? Charles is not yet returned, I suppose."

She shook her head.

"As your brother-in-law's servant, I must see you are refreshed." Geoffrey strode away into the kitchen to bring her some cold beef and ale. With a flourish, he set them on a little table before her.

"Charles would not like you waiting on me," she said.

"He does not keep me overbusy here." Geoffrey sat opposite her with a tankard of ale for himself. "The landlord is a good fellow who disapproves Charles's miserly ways," he confided. "He has found you a chamber off the kitchen with, fortunately, no other lodger to share it. It is quite close to where I sleep in the kitchen, as a matter of fact."

She flushed and looked down.

Gently he raised her chin with one finger, looking into her eyes. "But I am a surly lover, I fear, Lettice. Would that this was another time and another place and I could woo you myself." Then he withdrew his hand and spoke heartily as though to cover up his softness. "You should see the sights of Jamestown while you are here—and be seen by all these prospective husbands."

"Geoffrey, you anger me." She bit her lip. She would not have him to think her a feckless jade, angling for any attention from a man. But he was lost in thoughts of his own already, his muscles tense, his eyes narrowed. He might almost be prepared for flight. She suspected that behind his almost-forced cheerfulness he was considering some serious matter.

"I'm sorry, my sweet," he said after a time. "I am only pained that I cannot join the ranks of your admirers."

She turned her head so that he could not see her flush and gnaw at her lip in her discomfiture, saying lowly, "So far there are none—except Gower."

"Hmm. An excellent suitor, that!"

She felt her cheeks blaze. "Do you think so? Perhaps I should accept him."

His mouth tightened briefly, then he said, "Do not take my clowning seriously, Lettice. You should know me better. And do not play the lady tease when I cannot respond."

Tears splashed into her eyes. He was telling her she was wrong to follow after him here. It brought back memories of her final scene with Philip. Very well. Though it was impossible for her to marry Gower, she would find someone else. And if she did not, must she bow to Gower's will? She looked at Geoffrey once more, hoping he had not noticed the dampness of her eyes.

"No, Geoffrey, I do not know when you are serious and when you are not, and it grieves me considerably." Feeling sad and weary, she stood. "I would rest, Geoffrey. I can do nothing for John and Molly tonight."

"We will do what we can for them tomorrow," he promised as he led her to the door of her chamber.

She lifted the latch and entered her room. Looking back, she saw him settle on a bench near the fire, moodily studying the flames. Once her door was closed, she took off her clothes and folded them carefully. She stood in her shift, tying her bed gown over it. Then she went to look out the crack about the door. Geoffrey had lain full-length on the bench and spread his cloak over himself. He seemed to be sound asleep. The fact that he could sleep with her close by and yearning pricked her. It was not just a matter of feminine pique—there was the child. But most of all she missed the look of tender and unguarded love upon Geoffrey's face. Her eyes misted over. But she must be practical and plan her moves carefully for the sake of the child.

The sun was just beginning to climb, and the pallisade gates of Jamestown were opening to allow a party of drunken revelers to exit. Though the usual river mists lingered, it would be a fair day. Geoffrey reached to grasp her hand and held her back for a moment.

"What is it?" she whispered.

"There is something familiar about these men," he answered.

One of the besotted group separated himself for a moment. He wore a bandage about his face and a dirty fur cap on his head. Seeing him, Geoffrey nodded. The man gave a very short nod in return, which made Lettice wonder if he were as besotted as he pretended. The men were supporting a cloaked figure who seemed about to fall down with drunkenness. She could not see his face, but wondered that he was so muffled when the morning was already warm.

From out upon the beach other men appeared with horses. Once mounted, the cloaked man seemed to suddenly sober, for he raised his dark head and seized his reins with purpose. They galloped off, raising clouds of dust.

Geoffrey followed them with his eyes. They seemed to be headed up the river. Lettice saw him study the broad James before them. One of the English merchant ships, the *Adam and Eve*, had raised sail and had gone further up the river. Geoffrey frowned at this discovery.

"There seems to be a bit too much drama upon the river today," he said.

Lettice could not understand the meaning of his words, but a chill feeling of danger swept over her.

Urgently he asked, "Where is Charles's sloop?"

She pointed. Ajax and John were standing upon the deck and had already spotted them. Ajax gave them a great wave in salute. Then he got into a smaller boat to row back for them.

Because of the runaways they judged it safest to meet on board, but they must watch the river for signs of conflict. The sloop had a single slanting sail and a cabin jutting back over the rear. There was scarcely room for all of them inside. Ajax's eyes sparkled as he looked at them gathered there. He maintained an indomitable good humor in the face of his troubles. "I would throw in with the rebels with the rest of you," he said.

Lettice was shocked. "But my sister's household must have some workers," she objected.

"I would not be a slave all my life, mistress," he said, his voice soft but steady.

She had no answer for that.

"Do you know where the rebels lie, Henry?" John asked. His face was serious and somewhat drawn as though the consequences of his actions weighed heavily upon him.

Molly sat upon a bunk, suckling her child. She looked rosy and cheerful to be so free and close to her husband and baby.

"I know where the rebels lie," Geoffrey told them, "but it may be difficult to go there."

There was a sudden report over the water from up the river where they could see the sails of the *Adam and Eve*. Puffs of smoke drifted back downstream. Startled faces from all over the river front looked up to discover what was happening.

Geoffrey's face paled. "Let me correct myself. It may be impossible to get to the rebels."

"What is it?" Lettice said.

"Unless I am much mistaken, Bacon is about to be captured by the captain of the *Adam and Eve*."

The five of them looked at each other with dismay.

"Then we be beat afore we begin," John said, placing a heavy red hand on his wife's shoulder.

"Not yet," Geoffrey said. "Even if Bacon is taken, the bulk of the rebels are still up the river. Though how long they will last without a leader I do not know."

Scrambling, they all crowded out onto the deck to see what more could be seen. The *Adam and Eve* was plain enough, as were the figures busy swarming onto the deck of Bacon's sloop, but it was difficult to determine the course of events.

After a time the governor's coach appeared, unsteadily. It had just come the three miles from Green Spring. It halted before the gates of Jamestown. The little party upon the sloop stood boldly watching the scene spread out before them. Other people from outlying farms began to converge upon the gates, dressed mostly in poor homespun clothes or in buckskins. Snowy-aproned women wore kerchiefs upon their heads. There were a few oxcarts ambling toward the gates.

"I think we should return to the town, Lettice," Geoffrey called. "We can discover more there, and Charles may return. If Bacon is truly captured, John must take the rest to the woods to find Bacon's men."

Molly looked up at Lettice with bright blue eyes. "We will be all right, I know it," she said. "It cannot be that we escaped from Gower and then fail."

John squeezed her small hand in his large one. She was wearing a brown petticoat and had Lettice's scarlet ribbons tied upon her sleeves. Lettice could only smile at her and hope that she was right. She handed her a packet of napkin-wrapped bread and cheese and a bottle of ale she had brought from the inn.

Ajax slipped into the boat that was tied alongside and picked up the oars. Geoffrey handed Lettice down into it, though the bobbing upon the water made her queasy. The sun, which had clambered partway up the sky, glinted upon the river, hurting her eyes.

Molly dimpled at them over the sloop rail. "Be careful, Master Geoffrey. What your lady carries be very precious."

Geoffrey's head jerked about, and he looked at Molly with amazement. A deep red flush washed across his face. Lettice gave a little gasp. Molly would never learn to hold her tongue until she was 80 at least. And now she had acknowledged Geoffrey's relationship with her mistress openly—and had used his real name besides.

"Lettice," Geoffrey said. He was all confusion as he settled into the boat beside her. "What is this?"

"Have you not told him, mistress?" Molly's shrill voice sped across the waters. " 'Tis not a secret a woman should keep from her man. Be careful she do not run off to marry that fat pig, my master, out of some strange pride known only to ladies. But if she do not tell you, you will see it soon enough as she swells." Then Molly dimpled once more and waved her hand. Her breasts were falling free of her bodice, and her curls were all falling around her face.

Really, Lettice thought. She would never change. Lettice sat up stiffly in the boat. Wordlessly, Geoffrey took her hand. Ajax looked curiously at both of them as he began to row, the sun glistening on his bare, dark back.

"Lettice." But Geoffrey seemed too stunned by Molly's news to go on. He squeezed her hand.

Lettice felt a kind of sorrow that her secret was revealed and that Geoffrey's response to it was so inadequate. But as he lifted her out of the boat, there was a new tenderness in his touch.

Ajax saluted them and returned to the sloop.

By now an amazing crowd was gathering, streaming from every point of the compass toward the gates of Jamestown. Lettice had not thought there were so many people in the whole colony. All heads turned to look up the river. A party of riders at a gallop led the dark-haired gentleman Lettice had seen feigning drunkenness before. They drew up before the governor's coach. The four coach horses stamped restlessly, tossing their manes and shying away from the snorting saddle horses. The crowd watched silently. Then the coach door opened, and a liveried black helped the somewhat stiff governor to the ground. Sir William wore a plum-colored velvet coat and his full, long periwig. He stood much upon his dignity.

"Bring the gentleman here," he ordered coldly.

Bacon dismounted, and two men seized his arms to lead him to Sir William. Before his cousin he fell upon his knees, an attitude that seemed unnatural to him. The stiff breeze off the river disordered his dark cavalier locks. His face was the color of old paper.

The governor lifted up his hands and eyes to heaven.

"Now I behold the greatest rebel that ever was in Virginia!" he said. He stood there for a time while his cousin looked down upon the ground, trying to control his emotions. After a time, with no word from Bacon, the governor spoke again. "Sir, do you continue to be a gentleman, and may I take your word? If so, you will be at liberty upon your own parole."

Bacon drew in a deep breath, his eyes masked and without expression as he looked fully upon his cousin for the first time. "I will submit to you, Sir William," he said, "and give you written proof of my disobedience. Thereby I will ask your pardon and your favor."

The governor nodded, a look of approval upon his face. "Now you shall see a penitent sinner," he announced with fervent voice to those standing about. "You may present your confession to me formally." He was helped back into his coach as Bacon was led away under the guard of pikemen. But the crowd kept coming, murmuring its discontent.

"That is not the last of it," a voice said behind them.

Geoffrey and Lettice turned to behold the scar-faced man with the fur cap.

"Jud!" Geoffrey said. "You are not captured with the rest."

"Not I," Jud said. "There is much to do yet in Jamestown."

Geoffrey nodded at him, a pleased expression on his browned face. "But you have not yet met Mistress Clifford." He turned to Lettice. "This is my old comrade in arms."

"My lady." Jud swept his fur cap off his bald head, revealing still more of his mutilation. But Lettice could see enough of his remaining good face to judge that he was a sound and reliable man, though none too pretty nor too washed.

"Now I see why you hang back, eh Henry?" Jud said.

Lettice flushed. Whatever did he mean, hang back?

But Geoffrey ignored her discomfiture and seized Jud's shabby arm, speaking rapidly, "We have need of your help, Jud. Two escaped servants and their child seek a hiding place."

Jud looked behind himself, narrowing his single eye. Then he spoke in a loud whisper. "I will go to the troops in the forest soon and will guide your friends—if the man be willing to fight."

"He is."

Jud nodded. Then he studied Lettice carefully before speaking more. He dug into Geoffrey's ribs with a sharp elbow. "A good woman, this. She will never betray us, I think. But before I can help your friends, I must hang about Jamestown to see how our commander fares. He does not submit as meekly as he pretends, I think."

"That suits our purpose well," Geoffrey said. "Should the rebellion end, we would have no refuge."

Nodding, Jud raised a finger to his lips, then melted into the crowd. Geoffrey glanced briefly at Lettice, then led the way, walking silently through the gates. Now and again he studied her, then looked away, deep in thought. Apprehensively she thought that soon they must discuss the matter of the child. If only he would share his thoughts with her. But what, after all, could he do? She could not blame him for disinterest while he was a powerless servant.

But before they could say a word to one another, a man

with brown cavalier locks blocked their path. He threw Geoffrey a bitter look, and his voice was equally bitter. "A servant who speaks as a gentleman," he said. "And now our leader is captured." He made a gesture as though he would strike Geoffrey, but he restrained himself.

Lettice looked at Geoffrey with amazement. His body was rigid, his face flushed. "It was not I, I swear, Lawrence!" he said.

"Was it not?" Lawrence said, rage gurgling in his throat. "What brought you, then, to my house last night—and to the river's edge so early this morning?"

Before Geoffrey could answer, Lawrence had turned on his heel. As they watched his retreat, Geoffrey's hand upon Lettice's elbow was cold. What new trouble was this? she wondered.

They had passed the few frame houses of Jamestown and had come to the newer brick ones. They found Charles inside the inn where they were staying before they spoke more to each other. Charles was in a foul temper.

"Charles," Lettice said, dissembling prettily. Normally she would not deign to try to influence him in this way. "Your good wife has sent me here upon some errands."

"Why does she not wait for some trade ship to come up the river? There is precious little to be bought in Jamestown." Charles's sour expression made Lettice suspect he suffered from a bad stomach.

"The poor woman is quite distracted. Young William is . . . not well . . . though it is not serious," Lettice added hastily.

"Then best you return soon to aid her," Charles said. He did not offer any brotherly welcome. "And what have you been doing with my servant?"

Lettice prayed she was not blushing. What had they been doing, indeed! In a few months it would be plain.

"We did see the taking of the rebel Bacon upon the beach," Geoffrey said, offering his master the very slightest of bows.

Charles clutched his head as though a headache threatened. "Indeed? Oh, if a man only knew which side to back! Nay, Gower is right. I must walk a middle course. But come along upstairs, Henry. I will send letters. You can help me and then deliver them."

Geoffrey looked at Lettice with the same serious, abstracted expression he had worn since they left the sloop. "I will return later, Mistress Clifford, to help you with your errands," he said.

"If I give you leave," Charles whined, wiping his nose on a limp handkerchief.

Lettice woke late at night to find Geoffrey's lips upon hers. He had set his candlestick nearby on the floor, and it threw his shadow large and black upon the wall behind him.

"Geoffrey," she said sleepily, automatically reaching her arms about his neck. It seemed perfectly natural that they were together again.

"Little fool." He kissed her forehead. "Why did you not tell me about the child?"

"It will only make trouble for you, Geoffrey," she sighed. "I have thought so much about Molly's troubles that I have had no time to think of our own. And then I did not know what you would think."

"There are some troubles worth dying for, my pet. But enough of this. I must leave soon on a matter of life or death—my own, perhaps. I have time to ask you one question only. Will you marry me?"

"Marry you?" she asked, so surprised that she forgot his other words. She tried to clear her head of sleep. Then after a moment she said, "No, I will not."

"You will not?" His voice rose in exasperation. He lowered it again. "How not?"

"You are a servant, Geoffrey, and it will only add to your time."

"Well, it is plain that you do not love me. It is not surprising that you cannot love a servant." The anger in his voice surprised her. He gestured so impatiently that the candle flickered wildly, sending his shadow dancing upon the wall.

"Oh, I do love you." She sat up in her bed and smoothed back her long, silken hair so that she might look at him more directly. "And I do not care that you are a servant."

He smiled then, his teeth gleaming as he reached to grasp her hand. "And I dare to love you, mistress, though I am but a servant, and our love has brought difficulties to us both. But if I can give argument why we should marry, will you?"

She looked upon his candle-lit, sun-darkened face and saw that his brown eyes were warm once again and half-laughing with tenderness.

"Oh yes, Geoffrey," she said. "With joy."

He bent to kiss her lips, then sprang to his feet. "Swear that you will marry me if I can give you reason."

She raised one hand, then saw that he was laughing. "I will not if you laugh," she said.

"Very well. I will not laugh. Now swear." He tightened his lips to remain serious.

"I swear!" she said, watching to make sure he was not merely teasing.

"Good! Then I shall come for you tomorrow."

Her mouth dropped open with surprise. "Geoffrey?"

He stopped at the door to look back at her. "My dear?"

"You have given me no argument."

"I am afraid that will have to wait until after the fact. My errand is, at this moment, even more urgent than love."

"Geoffrey!" she insisted, pounding her fists upon her knees. But he was gone out the door and had closed it behind him.

She lay back on her pillow with her hands clasped behind her head. Was he teasing once again? No, she thought not. The corners of her lips turned up. It was a mad plan all the same. She prayed his arguments were good ones, and then she spent some time thinking what they might be. But soon the child within her dragged her down into sleep.

Geoffrey hastened through the streets, checking now and again to make sure he was not followed.

"You!" the black woman hissed as she opened the door to Lawrence's house. "How dare you?"

He reached out to take her hand, looking truthfully into her eyes. "It was not I who informed, though I know Lawrence thinks so. Is Lawrence taken, or may I yet speak to him?"

"Face him if you have the courage." She flung open the door to the parlor. Then she slammed it shut behind him.

Several of the gentlemen from the night before were clus-

168

tered about a single candle. Curls of smoke rose toward the ceiling as they indulged in the native plant, giving them the look of plotters in hell. Lawrence rose to his feet. His lean, muscular body was shaking with rage. Two others sprang upon Geoffrey and threw him into a Russian leather chair. One twisted his arms behind his back and held them. Geoffrey felt his palms grow clammy, though he had expected just such a reception.

"Why did you do it?" Lawrence asked through clenched teeth, glaring down upon Geoffrey.

"I have told you it was not I," Geoffrey said patiently. "That is why I have come—to prove myself."

"A spy," another sneered.

"Not so," Geoffrey said.

Lawrence began to pace about the room. Then he seemed to make up his mind about something and came to stand before Geoffrey again. "This makes our work easier," he said. "Now we do not have to seek you out as Bacon promised."

Geoffrey watched him closely, as though they were about to begin some game—or were circling about each other as fencers.

"I said I would prove myself to you." He felt himself grow calm.

"We will ask you some questions," Lawrence began, pacing again. "What do you do in Jamestown?"

"I am an indentured servant. I have come here with my master."

"And he is—?"

"Squire Charles Albright, of Albright's Point."

"Squire Albright. Yes, we know him well. A close man with a coin. Close, too, with his words when we ask him to support us. And whose side is Squire Albright on in this dispute, my man?" Turning on his heel, Lawrence pierced Geoffrey with his eyes.

"I am not sure." Geoffrey's face whitened as the man behind him jerked his arms up and back. It took Geoffrey a moment to catch his breath.

"We will want to know for sure," Lawrence said grimly.

"I am not sure that Squire Charles has made up his mind." Geoffrey hesitated. He did not want to bring trouble down on the house of his prospective brother-in-law. For Charles himself he cared nothing.

"He lies," the man beside him said, twisting his arm again. Geoffrey could not suppress a grunt of pain.

Lawrence resumed his questioning. "Did Squire Albright send you out near the river this morning?"

"No, I was out on other business, business which in part brings me here."

A heavyset man burning papers by the fire looked up abruptly, revealing a pock-marked face. "Liar!" he called.

"It is not a lie. I was. . . ," Geoffrey began, but halted as his arm was twisted again. "How can I explain if you will not let me speak?"

In answer one of his captors struck him alongside his head.

His arms clasped behind his back, Lawrence paced. "Let us begin the questions again," he said evenly. "What do you do in Jamestown?"

"I have told you already!" Geoffrey cried impatiently. "And I have come here to plead that you help friends of mine, and. . . ,"

Lawrence stepped toward him. Lightning-fast his hand lashed out and slapped Geoffrey across the mouth. Geoffrey could feel his teeth bit into his lip. His courage left him. He had been so confident that they would listen to his story.

"Let us begin the questions again," Lawrence said. "Whose side is Squire Albright on?"

Geoffrey tried to marshal his thoughts. It was well past midnight now. Whose side was Charles on? For that matter, what was Bacon's dispute with the governor to him?

"What do you do in Jamestown? Who is your master? How, if you are a servant, do you speak in the accents of a gentleman?" On and on the questions came, repeating, going round in circles. Geoffrey fought to keep a clear head.

"Why were you by the river so very early this morning?"

"It was another matter," Geoffrey said doggedly.

Lawrence nodded to the man who was burning papers. It seemed strange to see a fire on such a warm night. The man placed the tip of the iron poker among the coals. Geoffrey began to sweat. The men formed a ring about him and watched silently. Lawrence took the poker from the fire and placed its glowing tip to Geoffrey's arm just

170

below his shoulder. There was the smell of scorching cloth, of skin. Geoffrey drew in his breath sharply, stifling a groan.

The door was flung open suddenly! Jud stood there.

XI

Marry her? And tonight? How would he dare? Lettice sat bolt upright in her bed. Sunlight streamed through the many panes of her casement. She buried her face in her hands and tried to think clearly.

A knock interrupted her thoughts, and she realized that an earlier knock had awakened her. She opened the door a crack to find the landlord. Beyond, she saw that the bench before the fire in the already-stifling kitchen was empty. Geoffrey was gone. If he really intended to marry her, how dare he go off and leave her like this with so many unanswered questions?

The landlord flushed a brilliant red. "Henry sent a message, mistress. He will meet you at the Statehouse. You are to go to the Assembly to learn Bacon's fate."

Lettice nodded. Perhaps Geoffrey would answer some of her questions at the Assembly. And they must plan for the fugitives as soon as possible. They had planned to sail up the river overnight to hide in an inlet lest Charles discover them, but they could not hide on the sloop forever.

Since the day promised great heat, she donned a striped blue-and-white dimity skirt, a jacket of the same material and a blue-silk waistcoat. These were more suited to the Virginia climate than most of her English clothes. She combed her long silken hair and picked up a blue-velvet pocket to carry.

The landlord gave her a strange look as she came into the kitchen. What on earth had Geoffrey told him? After she had eaten a hasty breakfast, she slipped forth into the oppressive heat.

The town buzzed. A crowd was already gathered before

the Statehouse, which was several brick buildings joined with common walls under a tile roof. The center of much of the government and commerce of the colony, it served as a residence for the governor, as well, whenever he stayed in town.

She forced her way through the people who had flocked by the hundreds to offer Bacon support. Many faces burned as colonists made inflamed gestures and shouted defiance. A red-faced man wearing a smock seized a fellow by the elbow, crying, "All's over; Bacon's taken!"

Indeed, she hoped that all was not over, for John and Molly's sake. But a familiar face caught her eye. It was Daniel! She had not seen him since they had landed in Virginia. Hastening to catch up with him, she waved and called. A peculiar expression crossed his face. Then he melted away and was lost from sight among the throng.

Most of the crowd seemed content to stand outside in the street, but Lettice was determined to go inside. Following the flow, she was pushed along until she entered a chamber over the general court. Lettice struggled past several idlers standing against the wall. She prayed her condition would not overcome her since there was no air in the place. Lettice searched the faces about her. There was no sign of Geoffrey. Her heart sank with disappointment.

These gentlemen were better-dressed than most of those outside. Some wore broadcloth coats, too heavy for the Virginia warmth; others wore bright silks and lace; still others had on the common leather hunting clothes and light shirts. They took their seats amid the scuffling of boots, little coughs and throat-clearings.

The governor sat at the head of the room. He was wearing the same plum coat as the day before. His huge periwig seemed to burden him in the heat. A look of irritation marked his pouchy eyes. Sir William's demeanor was old and sorrowful as he waited for silence. When the rustling had finally died in the hall, the governor's dry and aristocratic voice penetrated the room. "Bring on the rebel Bacon."

There was a deep hush. The assembled Virginians waited, turned expectantly toward the back of the room. Lettice had a glimpse of Charles among the burgesses.

Bacon entered to considerable stir. His dark head was bowed and humble. In his hand he held a rolled-up paper.

174

He sank to one knee before the bar. Silently he handed his paper to his cousin.

A dangerous man, Lettice thought. His back was straight and tense even as he bent in pretended humility. Plainly many busy thoughts buzzed in his brain.

But the governor seemed to see no threat now in him. Genially, he smiled down at the kinsman. "If there be joy in the presence of the angels over one sinner that repents, there is joy now, for we have a penitent sinner before us."

Bacon then spoke in a voice so low it was difficult to hear, though the room was hushed. He seemed to have trouble parting his clenched teeth.

"Before God and bowing to the King's Majesty, I do beg your pardon, your honor."

The governor's wig slipped as he nodded. "God forgive you, I forgive you," he said, and repeated it twice more, obviously much relieved that his young relation had returned to the fold and would listen to wiser and older men.

At this, a newly elected burgess, one of those representing the more popular element, called out, "And all that were with him!"

The governor nodded. After a minute of silence he drawled, "Mr. Bacon, if you will behave civilly but till next quarter court, I will promise to restore you again to your place there." He leaned to point to Bacon's empty council seat.

"And now, gentlemen." Sir William looked from one to the other of the burgesses. "I would have you, as the first order of the day, consider means of security from the Indians and a method of defraying the cost of defense that may be more to your liking. Meddle with nothing else until the Indian affair is settled."

With these words the governor prepared to depart, and the burgesses rose to their feet until he was out of the room. Walking with hard-muscled elasticity, Bacon followed his cousin. Sir William's walk was stiff and old.

Once they were gone, a hum of conversation filled the room. And Lettice turned to leave, praying she would find Geoffrey somewhere outside. She jolted up against someone, and with a shock she recognized Charles's brittle form. He wore an old moth-eaten coat with a new waistcoat to impress the Virginia gentlemen. His face was somewhat pale, but his long bulbous nose was red as usual.

"Sister, I would have you finish your errands soon and return to Albright's Point," he said in his unpleasant voice. "The town is full of rabble."

"Oh, I shall, Charles," she lied. Fortunately he sighted a fellow burgess whom he particularly wanted to see, and he pushed away through the crowd. Lettice blushed as she thought of all the startling secrets she kept from her brother-in-law.

"Mistress Clifford," a voice beside her said.

She turned to look directly into a mutilated face. She steadied herself, for though she had seen this face before, it was still a shock.

"Jud," she said with a strained smile. "And so it seems the rebellion is over. Where can my servants hide?"

"We'll find a place for them." Jud did not look at her as he spoke, but studied the burgesses one by one as though to take their measure. "But I ain't sure that the rebellion is over. A flame burns in Bacon that ain't so easy to quench. The governor has humbled Bacon before his supporters, but Bacon's clever." Jud shook his head. "No, I think we will have more of this."

He stood back to let her pass before him out of the stuffy chamber. But as she was leaving, she halted as a curious figure met her eye—the first Indian Lettice had yet met in the colony. She could only stare. Like a crown, the dark-skinned woman, who seemed to be some 40 years of age, wore a band of black and white shell beads three inches wide fastened about her glossy, black hair. A mantle of dressed deerskins cloaked her from her shoulders to her feet. The hair on these skins were turned outward, and the ends were slashed into a six-inch twisted fringe. She passed close by Lettice and Jud.

"She looks like a queen," Lettice said.

"Aye," Jud said with a certain awe. "The Queen of Pamunkey. They say an English colonel fathered her son."

"That man beside her?"

"Nay. He looks to be an interpreter."

"Then the other is her son. What does she do here? I thought the Indians were our enemies."

Jud's scarred face twisted into a smile. "Nay. More likely we are theirs."

His words made Lettice draw back in surprise, but Jud went to look about the door frame into the chamber the queen had just entered. Lettice stood by his side, as fascinated as he. A group of burgesses were meeting there. At the head of the table sat the chairman in a yellow coat and blue embroidered waistcoat. His eyes were fixed upon the queen, who walked regally to the far end of the table. She sat down in an empty chair. The interpreter and the queen's son took up their posts on either side of her.

"Your Highness," the chairman said, breaking the silence. "We have called you here to ask what men you will lend us for guides in the wilderness and to assist us against our enemy Indians."

The queen turned to her interpreter with a questioning look. He wore slashed sleeves that showed his muslin shirt sleeves. His wide-topped boots were English, but his breeches were made of Indian buckskin. The queen's dark-haired son, too, was dressed in a mixture of modes.

The interpreter bent toward the queen and talked rapidly. Then he addressed the chairman. "She would have you speak through her son," he said.

The chairman drew an impatient breath and mopped his brow with his handkerchief. He jerked about to face the son. "What men will you lend us?"

The son looked toward his mother and said a few words. There was silence lasting several minutes.

"Please, madame," the chairman said after a while.

At this the queen began to breathe heavily, and her face took on a look of anguish. It seemed as though she were about to burst into tears. Instead she burst into a torrent of words, words none of the assemblymen could understand.

Lettice looked with amazement at Jud, who seemed to be nodding as he listened to the queen.

"Can you understand her?" she asked with surprise.

"Only a little," he said. "There's many Indian tongues. But she chastises the English for the way they behave. I think she says, 'Tatapatamoi is dead.' He was her husband, as I recall, who led a hundred of his braves to help the English against hostile Indians some years ago. He was slain with most of his men. The queen would have compensation for his loss."

The chairman idly tapped his forefinger upon the table. He had fixed a cold look upon the queen. His long periwig and his brow were dripping moisture.

"Well, madame," he said at last. "What Indians will you

now contribute to our new war against the Indians? You have sworn to be an ally."

The queen turned her head half away with disdain. Finally she answered a single Indian word in a slighting voice. The chairman looked toward the interpreter.

"Six," he answered.

"Madame!" the chairman exploded. "It were just as well you sent none."

The queen sat sullen for a while longer. Then she answered again with a single word.

"Twelve," the interpreter said.

"Madame!" the chairman uttered while his fellow assemblymen muttered in the background. Some were scratching under their wigs. "Either you stand with us or against us. You have sworn by treaty to aid us. There are a hundred and fifty men in your village."

But the queen did not answer him. She rose to her feet and gravely walked away, obviously not pleased with her treatment. The two men followed her.

Lettice stood back to let the Indians pass through the door. She and Jud followed them into the hall.

"It is the first queen that I have ever seen, and the first Indian," Lettice said.

"Aye," Jud said. "She is a real queen. But she will have to hold fast to her crown in these storms."

Lettice turned to look at this strange friend of Geoffrey's, a man whose face was half-gone, his cap moth-eaten, his clothes ragged.

"You sound as though you believe the Indians are right in this war," she said.

"In some measure they are," he answered gravely. "It is the same in every war." But then his expression changed, and he smiled at her. Several people looked at them; they made such an odd pair.

"Come along outside, mistress. Henry—or Geoffrey—has sent me to tell you he cannot come, though we were up together most the night."

"Up all night?" Lettice asked indignantly. "Were you carousing, then?"

"No, lady," Jud laughed. "But it took much persuasion from me to convince Lawrence that Geoffrey was never a spy. Now, it seems, they are the best of friends—for however long it may last."

"But he promised me he would come. . . ." Lettice bit her lip with vexation, blushing furiously. Did a proposal of marriage mean so little to him? But she would not mention this supposed marriage to Jud.

"He will come," Jud said. "But you would have but half a man had I not persuaded him to rest. And it did take hard persuasion."

Lettice supped alone. The black maid lay a trencher of meat before her. The landlord stood by the chimney, smiling nervously. Charles came in the middle of the meal with his face pinched in from one of his headaches. The heat and the crowds had been too much for him. He went upstairs complaining that Henry was always gone and demanding that Lettice bring him a cup of hot metheglin, a drink made from honey.

Lettice sighed. Geoffrey might at least have the courtesy to tell her how John and Molly fared. But the midnight proposal must have been one of his warped jokes.

Charles was lying in a great curtained bed, deathly pale. Lettice set the hot drink on the wash table beside him. Then she pulled the bed curtains well open so he might have more air. She looked out upon the Jamestown houses pensively. No sign of Geoffrey.

Charles looked at her. There was a frown between his slightly crossed blue eyes. "And why is Dorothy not here?" he grumbled.

"Because she is at Albright's Point, brother-in-law," Lettice said sweetly, turning to lean on the wash table and regard him with deceptively bland eyes. Now was not the time to tell him that they had turned Wat off.

"And Henry. His errands take him twice as long as they should."

"The town is very crowded." In truth, her irritation at the absence of Charles's servant was greater than the master's. It was hard to maintain her soft expression at the thought. "Everyone is waiting to see which way Bacon will fall."

The recollection seemed to give Charles pain, for he clutched the wispy hair of his head. "Oh, Gower was right, I think. The governor will win out in the end, and we must stand with him—if only we do not offend the others at the same time." He turned over, doubling up under the coarse

179

bed sheets. Lettice smiled at him. This was not an easy time for a man of Charles's temper to be involved in politics.

"If you will excuse me, brother," she said. "I will withdraw now and let you rest."

She descended the stout oak stairs again with listless tread. She desired nothing further to eat; so she lifted the latch and entered her room.

Molly, her maid, stood inside, looking wild and disheveled as usual. She carried a basket on her arm, and she had a most ridiculous expression on her face, as though she plotted some prank.

"Molly!" Lettice said in surprise.

"Mistress!" Molly set the basket upon the floor and came to kiss her mistress's cheek, an unusual familiarity. "Why be you idle here on this night of all?"

Lettice flushed.

"Has not Master Geoffrey warned you to be ready? Oh, I praise God I was able to be with you on this day." Molly chattered on without noticing Lettice's confusion and uncertainty.

"But does he really mean to marry me?" Lettice said finally.

Molly blinked her bright eyes with surprise. "Of course. He has the minister standing ready."

Lettice bit her lip. It sounded much more perilous now than it had last midnight. She sat down upon her bed. "Oh, Molly," she sighed. "Do you think we can?"

"You must, mistress," her maid said steadily. "Love rules us this way."

Lettice hesitated, then a mood of recklessness swept over her. After all, had she not gambled in coming to Virginia? And now she would gamble on love. She had vowed to marry here, and her wish was coming true, though in a form not anticipated. She prayed God she would not live to regret it.

"Quickly, mistress, else we will not be ready. Is Master Charles about?"

"He lies in bed with one of his headaches."

"We be blessed." The maid then stepped into the kitchen to see how much warm water was left in the kettle. Lettice gave herself up to Molly's hands. Her maid washed her hair with water to which she added lavender. Then Molly combed the long, silken tresses until they were smooth and beautiful. Next she went to Lettice's leather-bound box and laid out fresh underpetticoats.

"Oh, mistress, have you brought the plum gown and the blue-silk petticoat?" she asked.

"I have," Lettice said. "I have never yet worn it, Albright's Point being as dull as it is."

Molly carefully drew these garments out, chuckling to herself all the time. "Oh, Master Geoffrey be a hard man in bed if I'm not mistaken."

"Molly!" Lettice said.

"Better hard than soft," her maid answered.

This set her mistress to giggling so that she had to halt in her preparations for a moment. Molly burst into laughter.

"Shhh," Lettice warned. "Charles may hear your voice."

When Lettice's hair was dry, Molly judged her ready. Then she ran her mistress's comb through her own wild hair. Lettice slipped a pair of pattens over her thin-soled shoes. Molly picked up her basket.

"Oh, Molly," Lettice said. "Find my mask and my silk cloak. That way no one will know who goes through the streets." Molly nodded and opened the box again to find it.

They stepped into the kitchen where the long, lean landlord gave Lettice another strange look as she stood there, the leather mask dangling from one hand. Lettice wondered at his strange, almost secretive, behavior. But she knew Geoffrey liked him well enough. Silently, the landlord lit a lantern for the two women, who let themselves out through the back garden. The night was warm.

Molly helped Lettice fasten on her mask. Then she led the way to the church, which dominated the 30 or so buildings inside the palisades. They passed through silent streets since the events of the day had exhausted the colonists. Only one man upon horseback and another on foot passed them, stirring up the dust. Lettice wondered where the crowds that flocked there earlier slept that night.

She swallowed nervously before the red-and-black buttressed walls of the church with its single square tower. The slate roof sloped up from each of the four walls to a peak in the center surmounted by a cross. As they stood before the arched doorway, Lettice looked up to see six

181

ominous loopholes. Even the church was fortified in Jamestown.

Molly opened the door a crack, then nodded to her mistress. Lettice took off her mask. She gasped with surprise when she stepped inside and Geoffrey gripped her firmly to pull her to his side. She stole a closer look at him and saw that he wore a good claret-colored coat with wide cuffs ending well above the wrist as was the fashion. But it seemed a bit tight in the shoulders.

He smiled when he saw her surprise. "Master Lawrence lent it to me," he whispered.

It suited his dark hair and warm brown eyes. Ah, her husband would be a handsome man, Lettice thought, even if he had no money.

"Why is it everyone knows more of this wedding than I?" she asked.

"So that you will not think so much upon it that you lose your nerve," her intended responded.

Lettice tilted up her chin. It seemed she was all but abducted into this wedding.

John was carrying the baby, and Jud, too, was there, smiling so widely that his bandage threatened to slip. He swept off his fur cap and bowed. Ajax nodded and smiled to her. But the minister was coming between the pews down the tile-paved aisle.

"Mistress Clifford?" he asked gravely when he came to her side. "You are a free woman, unbound?" He looked to be a fairly vigorous man with austere features accented by his black clothes.

"Of course," she answered a bit shortly, wondering how Geoffrey would answer this question. "I am sister-in-law to Squire Albright of Albright's Point. He lies ill this evening."

The minister then turned to Geoffrey. "Master Geoffrey Finch," he said. "Are you also free and unbound?"

"Geoffrey Finch is a free man," Geoffrey answered. "I have met my bride in England, and we would return there as soon as possible, hence our haste. Mr. Lawrence will vouch for me."

The minister nodded. Lettice reflected that Geoffrey had actually told no lies to mar their marriage before God. But then God would surely understand their plight. The minister smiled at them. It was as though the sun appeared in a watery sky.

"Upon this spot many years ago, before this church was built, the Princess Pocahantas was married to an English gentleman, John Rolfe."

"Think of that, mistress!" Molly exclaimed, her eyes wide and bright. But when the minister had retreated up the aisle, she whispered, "Who be the Princess Pocahantas?"

"A daughter of the Indian Emperor Powatan," Lettice answered. "She died in England and was very famous."

At this point the minister nodded to indicate that he was ready, and Geoffrey and Jud went down to stand in the front of the church. Molly tore the napkin off her basket and lifted out something inside. It was a wreath of honeysuckle and wild roses.

"Molly," Lettice said. "How lovely."

"It took me a good part of the day to find a place where I could pick them," Molly said, placing the wreath upon her mistress's silky hair. Then she reached into her basket for a handful of rose petals and herbs, which she strew before Lettice. Walking slowly up the aisle, Lettice smiled to see Molly so happily employed when she had, before, been so defeated and exhausted at Gower's. At the end of the aisle Geoffrey reached to take his bride's hand. She noticed he moved a little stiffly, as though he were protecting his left arm.

But when the time came, they realized they had no ring. Jud cleared his throat while he reached into a pouch that was belted at his waist. He drew out a little packet, which he unwrapped. Inside nestled a common circlet of gold, which he handed to Geoffrey. Geoffrey tenderly slipped it onto Lettice's finger. It was too large.

"I took it off a dead man at the Indian battle," Jud whispered.

Lettice's eyes widened. But she could hardly give it back to him. Geoffrey's fingers tightened on hers, and she thought he stifled a chuckle. It was all very well for him to laugh. He didn't have to wear a dead man's ring.

But another sound, a stranger sound, came from Molly. Lettice turned to look back. The little maid was sobbing. Tears ran down her dainty cheeks. Lettice felt a catch in her own throat, and she reached to nudge her maid's ankle with her slippered foot.

As the ceremony concluded, Geoffrey bent to kiss his wife. At this point the babe in John's arms gurgled pleasantly as though wishing to join in the ceremony. The sound seemed to sober Molly. "Oh, sir," she said to the minister, though she still sniffled loudly. "Could you christen the babe? Though we be but poor folk with naught to pay for it," she added.

Lettice said that she would pay, and she and Geoffrey stood godparents to the child. It was named Henry as its parents had decided before Geoffrey started using his own name again. These happy events were duly noted in the church records.

Lettice slipped on her pattens again, but she did not don her mask now the deed was done. The whole party left the minister and exited the church in smiling accord.

"Wait, now, mistress," Molly said, handing baby Henry to John and seizing her basket again. Then laughing uproariously she began to strew her petals and herbs once more in the bride's path along the dry Jamestown street. Ajax, who was holding the lantern high, guffawed loudly.

"Molly," Lettice whispered, stifling a giggle. "All of you! The whole town will know. This is a secret event, and you are fugitives."

These words sobered her maid somewhat, for she threw no more petals until they stood on the back doorstep of their inn. Then she emptied the contents of her basket upon her mistress's head.

They all entered the kitchen in gales of laughter. Lettice shook her head to free it of the pleasant debris. Then she drew in a deep breath of surprise. Garlands of flowers had been hung from the beams overhead and about the pots and frying pans upon the walls. There were bottles aplenty of drink upon the table. A pile of unshelled oysters was heaped upon a trencher. The maidservant had set two mince pies nearby. There were venison pastries too. The landlord's face was beaming; it was no longer mysterious or strange.

"Our landlord has been keeping secrets from me!" Lettice exclaimed.

"He has given us this feast as a wedding gift," Geoffrey

said. "He says that if this event drives away the patronage of Squire Charles, all will be worth it."

The landlord bent his bony head on his stringy neck in embarrassment.

"Besides," Geoffrey went on, "he will put much of it upon our master's bill, since you are his sister-in-law."

Even Lettice could not but laugh at that.

"No, no," the good landlord said, turning redder. "It is my gift to the bride and groom." At this he began to pour the drink, handing Lettice a glass of claret.

"A toast to the landlord." Geoffrey placed one booted foot upon a joint stool, raised his glass and smiled madly at them all.

"No, no," the landlord objected. "We must drink to the bride and groom first."

"To the bride and groom *and* the landlord!" John said, handing the baby to his wife while he drank.

Geoffrey placed an arm about Lettice, and she felt as though she were an ordinary, happy bride in ordinary, happy times. If only all their days would prove as good as this.

They were interrupted by a pounding on the ceiling from the floor above. They all looked up at once. "I will see what Master Charles wants," the landlord said. The party became quiet during the time that he was gone, but the servants dug into the food, which was finer than their usual fare.

"Well, dear wife," John said to Molly, "I think that we should soon leave and let this marriage begin. Master Lawrence promises us a bed by his kitchen fire."

"And the landlord will guard us from Charles tonight," Geoffrey said.

At that moment the landlord himself entered. "He asks for you, Mistress Lettice," he said.

Geoffrey frowned at his wife. "You shall not go."

"Oh, Geoffrey, I think I should. I shall return shortly." Lettice turned to the black maid. "Lend me your apron, please." The girl shyly untied it. Lettice took it and tied it on over her finery. Then she took the wreath from off her head and set it on the table.

Her head was spinning somewhat with wine, and her candle wavered as she climbed the stairs. She opened

185

Charles's door softly. He was in an angular heap under the sheets.

"Oh, sister Lettice," he groaned, clutching his nightcap. "There is such a noise below I cannot sleep."

"It is a wedding party," Lettice said.

"Really? The landlord did not tell me of it."

"It was quite unexpected, I believe."

"Has my servant Henry returned at last?"

"Yes, I think he readies himself for bed." Lettice could hardly keep from giggling at the double meaning of her words.

"Indeed." Charles's eyes grew heavy. "Indeed. Well, I will rest now so that the pain will leave me."

"Please do, brother." Lettice withdrew with her candle. She bit her lip to keep from laughing as she made her way down the stairs.

When she entered the kitchen, the guests were standing in the open door. Molly came rushing into the room again to embrace her. "Oh, mistress," she said. "God bless you for all you have done for us. And for your own happiness. I know we will all be happy together some day."

Lettice's eyes grew moist. In many ways Molly had always been her closest friend.

"Do look after her, Master Geoffrey," the maid said, then she followed her own husband into the night.

A chill breeze seemed to come in through the door, perhaps from off the river, for it was very late. The landlord nodded to them, red-faced, and then departed.

"Oh, Geoffrey," Lettice said. "I am suddenly afraid."

He put one strong arm about her and seized the remaining candle with the other. Then he led her into her room. His face was serious, but his brown eyes were alight with love.

"We have been very bold, my love. But I do not intend that our lives shall continue as they have these last months. I told you that I would give argument for our marriage after the fact." He set the candle down upon the table and looked into her eyes. The corners of his mouth quirked up. He could never remain serious for long. "But which would you have first—the loving or the arguments?"

She clasped her arms about his neck, laughing, still reeling a little with wine. "Oh, I would have the loving first. There is, I hope, the rest of our lives for argument."

She touched his arm and he started as though in pain, "What is it?" she said.

"Believe me, it is nothing, and I thank God it is not worse."

He pulled her to him and pressed his mouth upon hers, savoring her lips in a more unhurried manner than he had ever been able to before.

"Oh, Geoffrey," she said after a time. "If only you could hold me always."

"That is my aim," he answered. These few words settled many of the doubts she had felt throughout the day.

Geoffrey tilted his head sideways to look at her. "Well, then, wife, would you go to bed with a wreath upon your head and wearing an apron and silken gown?"

"No, husband. I will lay aside all those."

When she stood before him, naked, he ran his fingers over her bare back, following the line of her spine. "Would you wear what I would desire, you would be a thrifty wife, for I prefer your own fine skin to any gown."

"It might be chilly on a winter's night."

He sat upon the bed, staring at her. "Not with a good fire and a warm man between the sheets."

She knelt then beside him so that her breasts were at the level with his face. "And are you so warm, then, husband?"

"No, I am hot for a fact." She cupped her hands about his head and drew him closer. Sighing, he lay down, and she lay beside him.

"Tonight, at least, I do not have to worry about making a child." He placed his hand upon her belly. "Where does it lie?"

She shook her head. "I do not know. It has yet to move, but it does terrible things to my stomach each morning."

"Poor sweet." Then he moved his hand down to feel her femininity, and he bent his head to kiss her breasts.

"Ah," she groaned. "I would have the father enter to be closer to the child." And she raised her hips hungrily to meet him.

They had no more words after that, since their bodies spoke for them. In time they fell into deep sleep. She awoke to hear the birds begin their noise in a gray-pink light that marked the beginning of dawn. Geoffrey's bare muscular back was presented to her, and she bent to kiss it and thought how luxurious it was for them to idle together like this.

He awoke with a start and turned to face her. "Lettice. I was dreaming of your face, and now I see that unbelievably it is really here." He half sat up and peered through the window curtains. Then he leaned back to kiss her. His eyes met hers. There was some strange expression on his face. He seemed almost apprehensive.

"It is almost light, my sweet, and I must leave you."

"Leave me? Where are you going?" Lettice's drowsy calm was shaken.

"Oh, my pet, it seems the time for argument has come. I am leaving with Jud and John and Molly to join Bacon's men."

"Today?"

"Yes, today."

"And I?" Lettice asked with a sinking feeling.

"Return to your sister to care for yourself and our child until things are more settled."

"I would rather go with you."

He slipped his arm about her naked shoulders and kissed her cheek. "To bear our child on a riverbank? I think not, my dear. I regret I cannot provide a better place for you at the moment."

"But what am I to tell my sister?"

"Nothing until it is necessary. Then confess that you are secretly married."

Lettice shook herself free and turned her back upon him. "It seems there is no point in my having married at all," she said. At least that would have left her the option of marrying Gower, though it was an option neither she, nor Geoffrey nor her sister wanted.

Geoffrey reached to turn her back again so that she must meet his eyes. "I will argue that you are wrong," he said. "I told you that I had thought much of the matter. I would not have married you if it was all risk for you and no benefit. Though there are risks. It is a risk for me to join the rebels. If I survive the fighting, I may be hung."

Lettice's eyes widened with shock. "I did not think of that! And does John, too, run this risk?"

"Somewhat less, since he will be of lower rank. Some of Bacon's men trust my abilities since they are Oxford or Cambridge men like me. I spoke with them yesterday, which was one of the things that kept me away from you. But at any rate I will give you the name of a highly placed friend of mine in England. He knows the law and will make sure that my brother Giles will not cheat me of my just inheritance from my mother. If my friend James can relieve me of my bondage in some way, I feel sure he will, though I don't know how he can do it unless I can buy myself free. But beware of Giles should you ever go to England without me, for I do fear him, though he is my brother. James will look after my interests in secret."

Lettice was about to speak, but he placed a warning finger across her lips. "There is not much time. I must give you all the arguments. So if I die, there should be some inheritance for you and the child, and you can still seek out your rich planter to marry."

"I would have you live, Geoffrey. Surely you do not intend to die."

"In the event that I live, there should be enough to set us up on a piece of land here, though the life would not be easy. Yet I admit much could still go awry with all these plans. My letter to James may go astray. Or Giles may be more cunning than I guess. Though I cannot guess why he must take what little is mine. Or the law may be more unjust than even I believe.

"But still there is some hope, else I would not have married you, much as I love you. I cannot, though, continue to serve Charles while you are near and chance his taking legal action against me. There may be some expectation for advancement if Bacon's men win out. Many slaves and servants have joined him because of this."

His flow of words ceased for a moment, and he caught up her chin and kissed her, parting reluctantly. "I was known as a wild youth, Lettice, yet I tell you this is the biggest gamble I have ever made. The stakes are high—you, our child and my freedom. I pray that you will not be sorry you have married me."

She shook her head. "Never. For me, too, it is a gamble. And for me, too, the stakes are high."

Geoffrey got up and began to dress. She drew in her breath sharply. "Geoffrey, there is a burn upon your arm." It was the size of a small coin, but it looked drawn and ugly.

"It was the price of my life," he said.

"How so?" she demanded.

He would not answer. He only smiled.

"How so, Geoffrey?"

"The story is too long," he said. She was filled with misgivings for him.

He reached into a leather pouch he wore at his belt and pulled out a folded paper. "James's name and probable location are written here," he said. "I have also written a will."

"This is so solemn," she said, "for the day after our wedding."

"Aye, sweet," he agreed. "I hope your sister will protect you well. I know she is fond of you. Otherwise send word to me, or to Jud's woman, Sal. Molly will go to her if things grow too hot with the rebels."

"Geoffrey." She watched as he finished dressing. "I know you must leave, though I wish you would not. But . . . ," She bit her lip. "I do not trust Bacon. I would fear to rest my fortunes upon him."

"Oh?" Geoffrey spoke somewhat absently. "I do not know him well. Yet at the moment he is all I have."

She nodded. Her head ached slightly from the wine she had drunk, and her stomach was queasy as it usually was in the morning.

There was a low whistle. Then from the back garden she caught a glimpse of Jud's fur cap. She shook her head to clear her thoughts. Her life was moving entirely too fast at the moment. She could not digest it all. She barely had time to realize that she was married—and now Geoffrey was leaving.

Geoffrey unfastened the casement and leaned to wave to Jud. Then he lay down upon the bed to hold her tight against him. "Sweet," he said. "Try to remember that we will have a life together."

"I pray so, Geoffrey," she said. "And I pray God will protect you. Do not be gone too long or I swear I will seek you out even if my belly is as big as the governor's house."

"You shall not," he said. "Even though I die of loneliness for you." Then he went into the kitchen to gather up his few belongings, and he left her.

She was so stunned by this rush of events that she did not cry or feel anything at all for a while. She put on her shift and her bed gown and found a dry piece of bread in the kitchen to chew to keep her stomach settled. Then she looked up above, as she heard Charles thumping upon his floor.

She sighed deeply. Soon she must explain to him that he had lost his slave and his servants and his overseer and that there was no one to sail his sloop back up the river.

But she would not tell him until the fugitives were well away and hid.

Two days later the news swept the town that Bacon had fled from submission to his cousin. On June 23 he returned to Jamestown at the head of some troops. Swearing "Damn my blood, I'll kill governor, Council, Assembly and all," he seized the commission against the Indians he had coveted for so long. The Assemblymen trembled until he left.

XII

Both horses and men found the Great Dragon Swamp hard going. Geoffrey and Jud were on horseback, John afoot. Heat bore down heavily; mosquitoes devoured them. They were aware that the day before one man had been bitten by a poisonous snake. They had left him lying on the ground with a comrade to watch while his leg swelled and his breathing grew short.

Gone now was the hard-baked bread, and scarcely any game had been sighted. Some days before, John had stumbled upon a she bear standing erect and menacing in his path. A lucky shot had brought her down. They had searched for her cub, but they'd never found it. But now the meat was long gone.

Bacon gave a rousing speech, pacing, gesturing nervously. He warned that this would be a difficult expedition and that those who were of a mind to should leave. Few had.

Molly and the other camp followers had been sent away. Molly went to stay with Sal, who could shoot a musket as well as a man to protect the two of them and little Henry. The men were forced to cook and mend and clean their clothes themselves on the march. They ate poorly and slept dirty in their clothes.

Geoffrey noticed Jud's silence as they rode. There was little to be heard but the soft pounding of hooves and the creaking of saddles. Since the patch of ground they were crossing was solid, Geoffrey rode up next to him.

"How is it with you, Jud?"

Jud shook his head thoughtfully, pursing his lips so that his ugly scar was drawn down. "I don't like this. The only

Indians Bacon chases are Pamunkeys, and they're our closest allies."

Geoffrey heard these words with reluctance. Once again there seemed to be no logic to these Indian skirmishes. "Perhaps he has some reasons," he said after a time. He wanted to believe in Bacon.

Jud shook his head, moisture oozing down his face from under his fur cap. He smelled even worse than usual. "His only reason is that he hates Indians and loves himself."

"Perhaps I should talk to him." After all, they had much in common, Geoffrey thought. Both were university men, not too far apart in age. Bacon seemed to have taken a liking to him.

Jud turned to look into his face. "Has he ever listened to you?"

Geoffrey did not answer.

Jud fixed his single eye on his horse's ears. "Nay. He listens to no one, only some buzzing in his brain. Our general is a bit mad. And it's his madness that leads us."

Geoffrey studied his friend carefully. Jud was seldom wrong, he had discovered. But if Bacon was a madman, it would go hard with all of them. Their fortunes were tied to his. Geoffrey felt a great desire to believe that Bacon was what he would have him to be.

Suddenly a musket shot rang out. The three men stopped in their tracks. Then cautiously they proceeded around a clump of reeds and bushes.

An Indian woman lay bleeding to death on the ground. One of her hands was carelessly flung into a swampy pool. Beside her cowered a small girl. One of Bacon's men was reloading a wheel lock musket, watching the girl as she raised a plump brown hand to cover her dark eyes. Her elbow was rounded with baby fat.

Lightning-fast John sprang forward to seize the child. "Stop!" His deep, rough voice tore through the silent swamp.

About to take aim, the musket man hesitated. Geoffrey guided his horse between the man and his target, then he reached both arms down. John handed the child to him. Geoffrey placed the plump, shivering figure on the saddle in front of him. "What kind of war is this?" he demanded.

The musket man shrugged, tossing back his long, greasy locks. "Ye got t'get them all," he said. "Else they'll just come back. There's too many Indians in Virginny." Then he climbed back into his saddle and rode on. They could see his back disappearing through the pines.

"Was it to kill women and children that I left my master?" John exploded. Blood rushed into his face, which was still peeling and sunburned in patches, but had at last begun to tan.

The child jerked with convulsive tremors. Geoffrey raised one hand to gently smooth her hair.

"This war is going wrong," Jud muttered. "We must end it soon, one way or another."

The party continued slowly on into the deep ooze of the swamp. The horses tossed their reins and rolled back their eyes to see if their riders would truly urge them on to such treacherous footing. Bacon had employed about ten Indian scouts to seek out the Pamunkey in their cabins. Their shots were heard in the distance as they caught glimpses of other Indians sent out by the queen. Bacon's English troops clustered together to avoid being picked off as stragglers.

The commander himself rode up to where Jud and Geoffrey had halted. A rare smile flashed. "I think we have them now. I think we've found their village." He rode forward eagerly, gaining the solid ground. A little clearing opened in the midst of the swamp. The open area was rimmed by a thicket of small oak, saplings, chinquapin bushes and grape vines. This growth masked the settlement from prying eyes.

More horsemen followed close behind Bacon. One by one those on foot filed into the clearing and looked about with bemused smiles as they discovered the cabins of the Pamunkey. They looked empty. Full baskets of corn stood in the doorways, hatchets cleaved into chopping blocks, earthen vessels still contained water. But no one seemed to be there.

Nor was there sound or movement. The men grew uneasy, expecting a trap. Then, bit by bit, they began to relax. One of the men started up an off-key whistle. Flint and steel came together with a scratching sound, and a fire was lit. Soon kettles boiled, and the delicious smell of cornmeal mush wafted through the clearing. Men burst into the cabins, dragging out furs and bits of jewelry, wampumpeag— the Indian money—baskets and mats. Some men were lucky enough to find broadcloth and other English goods of which the Indian queen was very fond. A few hiding prisoners were dragged forth.

Jud smiled as he dished some mush into a wooden bowl for Geoffrey. "A full belly is victory enough," he said. He set the child prisoner on his knee, feeding her from his own wooden bowl as the tears dried on her cheeks.

A long wail cut through the quiet domestic noises. It came from a clump of bushes. The man who had earlier shot the Indian woman stood with this musket pointed down toward the ground.

Geoffrey dropped his basin and raced over to follow the musket man's narrow-eyed glance to his target. A gray-haired woman with a wrinkled and prominent chin and no teeth in her gums lay on the ground. Geoffrey placed a hand on the man's rigid shoulder. "Easy now," he said softly.

The woman began to whimper with terror, then seemed to gain control of herself and fell silent. By this time Jud had set down the child and was now squatting on his heels at the woman's side. He began to speak hesitantly. He did not really know the language of the Pamunkey. But the woman knew some English.

Bacon seeing the commotion, strode over to study the woman. "Who is she?" he demanded.

"She says she is the queen's old nurse."

A gleam shone from deep within Bacon's dark eyes. "Is she?" he breathed. "Tell her we will let her live if she leads us to her mistress."

Jud's eyes met his commander's. He hesitated. Then he directed some words toward the old woman.

But she had understood Bacon well enough. The look of animal fear left her black eyes, and she stood unsteadily. Gathering a deerskin cloak about her shoulders, she nodded, happy enough, it seemed, to know that she would live.

Bacon ran back to the fire and stood with his habitual cavalier attitude, one hand on his hip while the other gestured with fierce energy. The men hastily finished their mush and packed up once more. Some of them, however, remained to thoroughly loot the Pamunkey camp.

A small party of horsemen followed the old woman into the swamp. They sank deeper and deeper into the mire as they progressed. A day and a half later they shot her when they discovered that she had lead them astray. But her toothless mouth was fixed into a smile when she died.

Lettice had thought to do some riding early that morning before the unbearable August heat settled down. She had sewn a new loosly-laced bodice for her green riding costume to allow for her expanding figure. She did not intend to ride away from Albright's Point, for it was rumored that there had been some fighting and that some Indians had been captured not too many miles away.

The whole place seemed sad; her friends, Geoffrey, John, Molly and Ajax were gone. Visitors were rare, and she had no notion of how the rebellion progressed. Charles doled out news whenever he was home as though it were part of his precious hoard of silver. Thank God the business of the Assembly kept the master of Albright's Point away.

Neither the unrest in the colony nor that summer's drought had added to his prosperity or sweetness of temper. The loss of so many of his servants had hit him hard, though he had some 15 left. The last week he had spent at home, he had been plagued by constant headaches, and he suffered, too, from much uncertainty about where his political sympathies should lie. Charles had let himself be persuaded to be a loyalist, yet he worried. But Gower counseled Charles to be cautious. His Majesty's weight would be behind Berkeley in the end. The Stuarts had no love for rebels. It would only be a matter of time.

Just as Lettice arrived at the rough-hewn stables, she heard the clopping of hooves. Gower, who had risen early, had reined up at the house. His fat body was heaving and panting. She had no desire to see him of all people. He had stormed over upon her return from Jamestown and had accused her of conniving with her maid to escape. Lettice had denied everything, though Dorothy had looked at her strangely.

The slave who looked after the horses saddled up Lettice's favorite mare, Aurora. As he helped Lettice into the saddle, she wondered how much longer she would be able to crawl up onto a horse.

She vowed she would rather be captured and tortured by Indians than encounter Gower that day. With that in mind she flicked the little whip she carried, and the horse stretched out at a gallop toward the uncleared forest. Lettice reined up, glancing about uneasily into the green, shadowy depths of the trees. Insects hummed ominously. In the heat the mosquitoes and flies swarmed in a way that made riding in Virginia not the pleasure it was in England. Aurora began to trot into the welcome shade. Lettice felt herself grow short of breath as she often did lately. As the infant within her grew, it seemed to be pressing upward as though seeking the mother's heart. She had felt its first movement with a great joy that, distressfully, she could not confide to Dorothy. Yet the knowledge that here lay Geoffrey's child, that she had captured him into her very body, thrilled her. She sighed. She had had no word of her husband since he had left Jamestown.

Drawing up Aurora, she looked about cautiously as she thought she heard the bushes rustling. And for an instant, she thought she had a glimpse of straight, black hair. Her throat closed over in fear. She pulled Aurora's head about sharply and headed for home, cantering toward a break in the trees. As she burst into the cleared space before the tobacco fields, her way was blocked by the bulk of Gower upon his horse. This real obstacle seemed anticlimatic after her terror of the phantom Indians. He reached a bloated hand to grab her reins. "So, mistress," he hissed. "I thought it was you I saw ride out."

Wild-eyed, Aurora tried to pull free, dancing nervously. But Gower pulled the reins until his fat knee rested upon Lettice's thigh. She looked up into his purple-red perspiring face. He dropped his own reins and reached obscenely with stiff fingers to feel her breasts. Then he slid his repellent hands on down her body. Panting, Lettice struggled to free the reins, but his plump, moist fingers would not loosen. He narrowed his bloodshot eyes.

"It seems my lady swells. Where have you done it, my lady? Have you lain with the missing servants? Perhaps you and your little maid did lie with them together."

Lettice raised her whip and slashed him across the face. His hand fell away, and his horse started back. "That for the rape of my maid, Squire Gower!" she cried. "And much more if I have my way."

Gower's face turned an unbelievable shade of purple. "I'll have you before the magistrate for aiding her escape.

And we'll see who has given you an illegal brat. We do not sanction looseness in the colony."

"Looseness?" Lettice could not restrain herself, but burst into peals of laughter, throwing back her head. She could not have injured Gower more had she plunged a knife between his ribs. An interesting thought, that, the fat old slug, she mused. She gathered her reins and straightened her hat. But as she rode off, gales of laughter once more overwhelmed her. She felt Gower's mean pig's eyes pierce the back of her green riding dress until she was out of sight. And she heard his voice. "I thought to marry you, mistress. But not swelled. Not swelled. I will go to the magistrate instead and have you dragged into court. We do not want Virginia filled with bastards. We have laws to maintain decency."

Whatever else he said, Lettice could not hear it as Aurora pounded toward the stables. When she dismounted, she felt the child within her lurch. Poor mite. She must be careful not to risk him. Gower was a disgusting fool, yet he was cruel enough to wage war on her, even if it meant using the hypocritical laws. She was not ready to tell him yet that the child was no bastard, and she did not know if judgment would go against her for marrying a bond servant.

Parched with thirst, she thought to go to the kitchen to drink and get water to carry to her room to wash away the dust from her blazing face. She sighed. She must confront Dorothy squarely one of these days and warn her of possible trouble.

On the kitchen doorstep she halted. She could hear scurrying sounds from within. The hair on the back of her neck raised in fear. The sounds were not like those of an animal, and she knew of no one else who could be in the house. Chloe, she knew, was weeding the kitchen garden. She would recognize Gower's heavy movements immediately.

She tried to reassure herself, yet the sounds were furtive, frightened. Cautiously she leaned to look through the door. Seeing nothing, she stepped inside. Then she saw an Indian boy of about ten years of age, who was crouched down behind the table. He clutched a piece of corn bread.

Lifting up a fry pan from off the table, she ordered,

"Come out of there!" He must understand her meaning if not her words.

Slowly he backed out and raised himself to his feet. He fixed frightened black eyes upon her, which glazed over as he fell in a heap onto the floor. She banged the iron pan down on the table and went to kneel by him, studying him closely. He wore an English linsey-woolsey shirt and breeches. His glossy dark hair was rough cut. About his neck he wore a string of shell beads. He had obviously once been well cared for by a people who had had much contact with the English. But now he looked thin and dehydrated—on the verge of starvation. He was also excessively dirty.

She filled a noggin with water from the bucket, then propped his head upon her lap, forcing liquid between his lips. He might have been a pretty child in other circumstances. He stirred, his eyes opened, then he smiled when he saw that he was not killed. Gently, Lettice let his head down and went to fetch some turkey broth. Propping him up again, she began to spoon it between his lips. He sucked eagerly on the spoon, gaining strength with each mouthful. Then he got up and reached for the bread that had fallen on the floor. He pressed it into his mouth.

"Poor child, you're starving," she said. "Where have you come from?"

If he understood he did not answer. She saw that his dirty feet were cracked and bleeding, and she thought to get some water to wash them. But as soon as she bent over the bucket, he made a pouch of his shirt, stuffed it with bread and ran out.

Lettice stood in the doorway, her hand shading her eyes. Now the sun shone so bright and hot that even her plumed hat failed to protect her from the glare. She saw the boy make for the trees across the fields. Biting her lip, she told herself she should have made him stay to rest. But perhaps he had someone hid out there. She wondered if she should tell Dorothy and the men. Still, the child by himself was harmless. She could not make herself betray his presence to the others. She only prayed no one else would follow him back. She peered again toward the forest, then shrugged and stepped forth to go to change her clothes into something better for work. Dorothy was cleaning the parlor that day and had no one to help her.

When Lettice stepped back into the kitchen later to fetch some water, she saw the boy standing just inside. Earlier, she had stuck a heavy pistol under her apron band in case anyone came back. The boy's face was very worried.

He reached out to pluck her sleeve. "Come. Come, missus. Take bread. Take water." He reached to pick up more bread. "Take. . . ," he gestured toward the stew kettle.

Lettice stared for a moment, then decided to trust him. She dipped some broth into the bowl as he snatched a noggin. He was evidently planning to fill it at the stream along the way. They must have made a strange sight as they walked through the fields. A black field worker straightened to stare, bare feet planted solidly in the moist, rich earth.

As she walked boldly into the dark shade of the trees, Lettice felt a quiver of fear. She fingered her pistol. They had not gone far around the huge roots and dead limbs, stepping upon a rich fall of decayed leaves, when Lettice saw a figure lying unconscious on the ground. Lettice stared with surprise. It was the Queen of Pamunkey! Gone was her elegant, savage cloak. She wore a much-soiled scarlet petticoat and Indian buckskin bodice with many beads and pearls about her neck.

The boy ran to the stream to fetch water while Lettice chafed the queen's cold hands. Finally her lifeless eyes fluttered open. Gesturing to the child to lift the Indian woman's head, Lettice raised the cup of broth to the queen's lips. She drank gratefully, slowly at first, then gaining strength. Then she looked into Lettice's eyes to judge her character.

Lettice grasped her hand and felt a firm palm, neither over-soft like many ladies', nor rough and hard like those of work-worn poor women.

"Come, Your Highness," Lettice said. "We will find you a soft bed. You must rest and regain your strength."

The queen parted her stubborn lips. "Nowhere safe," she whispered. "All against me."

"No!" Lettice protested. "I'm sure the governor would be appalled at your condition. But we will talk of that when you are rested. Are you and the boy alone?"

"All alone," the queen said sadly.

Lettice ran to beckon to the slave working in the field. He flung aside his hoe and came running down the long rows. He looked down with some relief and surprise when he saw the middle-aged woman and young boy resting upon the ground. Lettice asked him to help carry the queen to the house. The royal lady was not an easy burden, yet they managed without encountering Dorothy. Lettice thought briefly of secreting her in the hidey hole, but decided she would boldly give her up her own bed. She herself would sleep on the trundle bed. She settled the queen and helped her wash while the boy curled up beside her in the great curtained bed. He was soon asleep, his dark lashes resting against his brown cheeks.

"How have you come to this state?" Lettice asked the queen. "I know the governor values you as an ally."

"The governor matters no more," the queen began weakly. Then she became roused with the kind of irritated anger she had shown the Assembly, and she began to spill out her story. She knew much English, though she had not admitted it to the Assembly.

When Bacon's volunteers had come to harry the Pamunkey, the queen was very frightened, but she was determined to offer her allies no resistance. She gave orders that no shots be fired upon her old ally, the English. Instead the Pamunkey fled into the woods. "I find myself alone—all alone—only with small boy," she said. "Very quiet. Many trees. We not know who will kill us."

But she had decided to return to throw herself on the mercy of her English attackers, who, after all, had no reason to harm their allies. But before she had gone any great distance, she came upon a dead woman. The flies were thick about the congealing blood from her head wound. This sight struck terror into the queen's heart, and she fled back into the swamps and wild woods, the child at her side. Soon they found themselves lost and without food. Finally the boy pounced upon a terrapin when, after several days, they were both so desperately weak with hunger that they gnawed upon this creature's leg to keep themselves alive. They thought they had been wandering and lost for about two weeks, but they could not approach any settlers for they no longer knew who to trust. They had seen no Indians since the dead woman.

Lettice was deeply disturbed as she left the queen sleeping. From what she had seen of Bacon and his war against Indians, Lettice had lost sympathy for this cause. Yet all those she loved most were deeply committed to him. With hesitant step, she went back down to the separate kitchen to find Dorothy and Chloe busy with preparations. They had noticed none of the commotion in the main house.

"Dorothy," Lettice said. "I must talk with you."

Dorothy studied her sister's face, then came without hesitation. The two women sat themselves down in the great hall.

"I have brought an Indian queen and a boy into the house," Lettice announced.

Dorothy's eyebrows rose. Her sallow face took on a tinge of pink. "Sister. You do the strangest things."

Lettice related the story to her. "I do not think this brings us any danger," she added. "The main body of the Indians seems some distance away. Even if Bacon does not kill them, they will probably not attack. I ask you to give the queen your hospitality."

"Well." Dorothy's faded eyes probed into Lettice's, unwaveringly. She drew up her lips, showing the wrinkles that would form there one day. "I thought you were about to tell me of your pregnancy."

Lettice swallowed. "So you know."

Dorothy's fine forehead creased as she plucked and played with her apron. "I wondered how long it would take you to tell me. I suppose Master Finch did the fathering." She looked down nervously at her lap.

Lettice felt freed of a great weight. "But it is all right, Dorothy, because we are married."

Dorothy met her eyes once more. "It is illegal."

"I'm sure the marriage is good," Lettice said with alarm.

"Probably." Dorothy's dull complexion blazed, as did her eyes. "But Master Finch has committed a crime. A bound servant may neither marry nor flee."

Lettice leaned to place a hand upon her sister's forearm. She spoke with soft persuasion. "Sister, Geoffrey was kidnapped from England. He had no desire to become a servant."

"But he became one." Dorothy rose to pace the room. She idly fingered her spinning wheel, some weapons on the wall, a pewter platter upon the table. "We were so close once. Now we seem quite different, Lettice. You have become quite lawless. But you and Philip were always a little that way."

203

"Philip is a world away," Lettice said. "Geoffrey and I plan to make a life together, in time."

Dorothy came to take her hand. Her eyes were moist. "Oh, my dear, I hope that you may. I have become hard, I suppose, with the realities of my life here. It is not easy to be a planter's wife in so new and raw a land."

Lettice kissed her cheek. Her arm embraced the thin shoulder that already hunched, though Dorothy was still in her 20s. Then Dorothy pulled away.

"Oh, I do fear what Charles will say. He has . . . oh, I must confess, my dear." Dorothy turned to look at her through watery, blue eyes. "He has told me that you must leave Albright's Point. The business with the servants put him beside himself with rage. But I implored him, said that soon enough a woman as lovely as you would marry—not Gower!" Dorothy raised one hand in horror at the very thought. "But of course it is too late for that. I do not know how I can defend you from Charles now."

Lettice stiffened. She felt her cheeks grow hot. "I am sorry to make your life more difficult. As soon as the queen is strong enough, I intend to take her to the governor."

"Lettice, how can you?" Dorothy made a veritable knot of her apron with her twisting. "Charles has the sloop. Besides, there's no telling where to find the governor the way the war goes. It is mad. You cannot travel without protection."

"I must go. I will take a pistol. And I may gain word of Geoffrey."

Lettice noted a look of relief in Dorothy's eyes. As usual, when feeling pressed, her sister changed the subject. "Well, I pray you do not strip me of any more servants."

"I do not intend to. But Molly had to leave. Gower was forcing her to his bed."

Dorothy's forehead wrinkled in pain. "I do not like to hear these things."

"If you live among them, you must know," Lettice insisted, trying to contain her anger and disappointment. She would wind up with nowhere to lay her head when her child was born. She would not think of it now. She would take one step at a time. But Albright's Point was no longer a shelter, and there were Gower's threats to be considered too.

Since Dorothy had developed the gift of not knowing what distressed her, she pushed the hazards of the trip from her mind. Once, she stopped Lettice on the narrow stairs to protest the effect of the journey upon the unborn child.

"The child sits well," Lettice replied.

Surprisingly, Dorothy grew fond of the queen while she stayed with her. Dorothy found her quite entertaining. The queen had an amusing and blunt way of telling stories in her broken English. But then she had had at least one English lover and had been a clever diplomat until this latest disaster.

When it was time for them to go, Dorothy stood twisting her hands in her apron, a look of guilt upon her face. Charles would be angry about the horses they were borrowing. But he'd be glad Lettice was gone. Characteristically, she said nothing aloud, but merely cautioned them about the night air. When she saw they were determined to go, she wished them Godspeed.

Lettice took Aurora, and the queen was on another horse. The boy rode behind each of them in turn. They had their baggage tied onto a packhorse. As much as possible they stayed beside the river, though the many low-lying marshy areas made this difficult. The women were hooded and masked as ladies often were when riding. But their real purpose was to disguise the queen. The boy they would pass off as an Indian slave. They made slow progress, perched as they were upon ladies' saddles, their skirts draped over the sides of the horses.

The first night, when the stars were out, they stopped with squatters, since they were afraid to approach a large plantation. If the squatters recognized the queen as an Indian under her mask in the misty night, they said nothing, but shared their rations in a friendly manner. The next nights the three travelers slept upon the damp ground, hid only by ferns and the protecting white clouds that were spreading peacefully from the river. Fortunately the nights were still warm as late summer turned to fall. The queen still tired easily from her recent ordeal, but her basic fiber was tough. Watching her with admiration, Lettice forgot her own discomfort. She was determined not to be stopped.

But in time they ran out of food. Lettice grew faint. And

the queen seemed even weaker. Lettice decided they must seek shelter and ask for food no matter how dangerous it might prove. She turned off the path that followed the water's edge and headed toward a large stone house. She paused for a moment, wondering at the loud voices drifting out the open door and past a neglected garden. An unusual amount of horses grazed on the lawn.

Lettice glanced at the queen who was swaying slightly in her saddle. A close inspection might reveal the color of her skin, but the mask and hood covered much. Some men at the door had already spotted them. Lettice's hands turned clammy as she tightened her grip upon the reins.

A short, mean, green-complected man stepped forward, tensing his compact muscles, narrowing his brown eyes. "Don't bring that Indian in here," he ordered.

Lettice stiffened, then saw that the speaker was watching the boy. "He is my servant," she said. "He can watch our horses if you will but spare my aunt and myself a bite to eat. We are headed for Jamestown and have run out of provisions."

The man shrugged, but he did not relax his wiry tension. "Go to the kitchen," he said.

Lettice dismounted with what grace she could. She was conscious of his eyes. She raised her mask as she neared him, praying that he would find her so interesting he would ignore the queen. The queen walked silently at her side, a brave and clever woman. But the mean-faced man was intrigued enough to follow them into the kitchen. It was attached to the house so that they had to walk through the great hall where many men and some women were lounging. Pikes and muskets were stacked on the floor. Chests that obviously belonged to the owner gaped open. Their contents hung out.

It appeared as if the house had been seized by one side or another of the rebellion, but which side? Lettice worried that first she must get the queen settled. Then she would try to find out what had happened here.

"Is there a place my aunt and I can rest?" she asked.

The man shrugged and threw open the door of a small bed chamber just off the kitchen. Once, before it had been walled off, it must have been part of the kitchen itself. "Some other women stay here," he said, "When they're now warming the beds of the men upstairs."

Lettice prayed that these camp followers warmed them well and that the men would not return for a while.

"Oh, do lie down, Auntie," she urged. Fully clothed, the queen lay herself down on one of the two small, curtainless beds. Quickly Lettice shut the door.

The wiry man stood just behind her. Lettice bit her lip and walked past him, hoping he would not touch her. She searched for something to eat, though she almost gagged as she looked about the room. Everything told of great disorder. Corn was spilled upon the floor; bloody spots were swarming with flies where game had been hacked apart to fry or place upon the spit. Heat from the fire, hunger and nausea almost overcame her. But she did find some discarded pieces of Indian bread and some dried meat, which she gathered together on a trencher.

The man watched her every move through beady eyes. She must discover whose camp this was. But first she must get some food to the queen. Smiling nervously, Lettice ducked into the chamber. Whispering into the queen's ear, she urged food upon her, swallowing some herself at the same time. She must get something to the boy too. With relief she saw the queen slide into sleep.

But when Lettice stepped into the kitchen again, the man was still there. He was sipping from a noggin of small beer. Eying her, he belched. She put on a nervous smile as she edged toward the door. He seemed to be an overseer or landowner. Dirty locks of black hair hung about his sallow face. He scuttled over near the wall and blocked her exit.

"Come upstairs, mistress." He smiled without warmth, revealing brownish stained teeth, half-rotted. "There's nobody in the chamber where I sleep. We needn't bother your auntie, eh?"

"I must look to my horses." Lettice spoke as steadily as she could.

"Look to them after. Here, now!" He pressed narrow beer-smelling lips upon hers.

"Let me go!" Lettice tried to shove him aside to make her way out of the kitchen.

He grabbed her arm, wrenching it back behind her. She kicked out at him with her riding boot. His face contorted, and he tangled his fingers in her long hair. Though barely taller than she and with a look of sour meanness, his muscles were of iron.

"If you aren't friendly, we'll do it fast, in here." He gestured with his sharp chin toward the room where the queen slept.

Lettice fought not to faint. She must keep her wits about her. She suspected that these were Bacon's men and more lawless and uncontrolled than if they had been Loyalists.

"No," she said. "Leave her alone."

"Then come willingly, or I will have you on the same bed as your auntie. Perhaps she may join, eh?"

Lettice blanched. If she went with him into the great hall, would someone aid her there? She nodded to him quickly, not trusting herself to utter a word.

The great hall bustled with noise. Yellow afternoon sun slanted into evening, casting wild and menacing purple shadows. The room seemed full of writhing forms. Lettice stepped over sprawled bodies until she reached the center. Then she looked about wildly for someone to aid her. It seemed as though she looked into the jaws of hell, a place where all the deadly sins were being demonstrated. A drunken woman clung to a leather-clad volunteer. Her sandy hair hung in greasy corkscrew locks. One breast fell out of her bodice while the man pumped and squeezed the other. Lettice halted in dismay.

"Come along, now," Lettice's companion ordered.

"No! I'll not!" Lettice cried loudly. "I will not go."

Raucous laughter filled the room. "Let him pet your cony, mistress," the blowzy woman urged. " 'Twill make it quiet as a little rabbit." Then she broke into ghastly laughter that revealed half-rotted teeth. Lettice's skin crawled.

"Leave her alone," a woman's voice cried from the corner. "Brutes, rogues, thieves!"

Wild laughter greeted her protest. She was a dark-haired woman who wore a housewife's white cap and apron. A soldier reached to pinch her thin buttocks.

"Take her upstairs instead," said the man who was kneading the blowzy woman's breast again. He raised his other hand in an obscene gesture toward the housewife.

The woman shrank, then straightened with a surge of anger. "Whores, trulls, cowards, braggarts! Were my husband here, he would take a pistol to you!"

A thin, drunken officer with a steel gorget about his throat staggered to the woman's side. "He lies with the

208

Loyalists, Mistress Ursula. I believe they will do you much good, being famed for their bravery."

"They're less cowardly than you!" the woman screamed. "They do not war on women."

"Enough of that scolding tongue. Push her over. Let's have a look at a Loyalist bum!" someone called. Mistress Ursula's hands came up jerkily with fear. In an instant two men had seized her and bent her over a chest. Whipping up her skirts, her thin shanks and defenseless private parts were displayed.

"I say take her here and now!" snorted a drunken wretch.

"No! Enough!" the officer said. "Chase her outside to cool her heels."

Sobbing in great gasps, Mistress Ursula fled out onto the lawn among the many grazing horses.

Lettice's wiry companion tightened his grasp. She was dizzy with fear of the besotted crew among whom she had fallen. How would the queen and she escape? She was being pulled toward the stairs again. They would only laugh at her protest. The hall, filled as it was with tobacco smoke and with the low angle of light, looked even more like an engraving of hell. But she could not willingly sink to their level.

"Please," she cried. "My husband is one of you. He is Bacon's man." The black-haired man regarded her with doubt.

"Hold!" a harsh voice said.

Lettice looked up. The shadowy figure of Wat, the giant overseer, loomed above her. She swayed, almost lost consciousness. She clung to the panels of the wall, breathing heavily, filled with dread. Nothing more was heard but drunken laughter as the sousing and tousing continued.

Silently, Wat twined his fingers into her hair and brought his florid face closer. He smiled, resting his narrowed eyes on her breast and hips. "What, mistress, have you not been used enough, you struggle so? Has your husband not taught you? You say the silk-and-satin man has married you?" His great hand shot out to grab her wrist.

"No, Wat!" she begged desperately. "I am with child."

"Then the way is well worn by the silk-and-satin man, and you cannot be got once more. Now is Wat's turn."

"Eh?" Her first assailant spoke with indignation, but Wat had only to look down at him from his great height. The man remained helplessly where he stood.

Wat pulled Lettice's hair sharply so that she cried out. He pushed her down onto the first of the stairs, then reached up under her skirts to feel the place he sought. "I will have it. You owe me much."

She lashed out with her feet, but he only jerked her head back harder until her eyes streamed with tears.

"Lie still!" he ordered, but she struggled even more. He freed his hand from the tangle of her skirts to strike her twice, brutally, in the face. Would he beat her until she lost the child? He twisted her arms behind her back and heaved her up so that he could carry her. To the vast man she was an easy burden. There were a few low laughs from those close by, but most were too drugged by their own pursuits to notice. Lettice dug her fist into Wat's hair and flailed about so that he was forced to set her down on the top step. Then he struck her so hard she fell headlong onto the floor, half sobbing for herself and her baby.

"Come, dearie, I would have you show me what you showed the silk-and-satin man," he whispered passionately, jerking one of her arms to draw her to her feet again. He kicked open a door and shoved her so that she fell onto the floor.

The room held only a chair, a chest with an ax-shattered lid, and a red-curtained bed. He yanked her off the floorboards and half threw her through the curtains onto the bed.

But it was occupied. A naked woman lay there. Her knees were drawn up as a thin and wiry man plunged between them. Lettice screamed, but the couple payed no heed.

Wat dragged her back onto the floor. "It must be here, after all." He forced her knees apart, whipping back her petticoats, then pressed rum-smelling lips upon her mouth. She struggled to turn her head aside.

"Please! Take me to Bacon! Surely he will not allow this!"

"He's miles away," Wat said, lazily unfastening his breeches. "With the silk-and-satin man. But you are a Loyalist like Mistress Dorothy. You both owe me much." His right arm covered her shoulders like an iron bar. One knee held her legs apart. He breathed heavily. His face blazed with ugly triumph. No willing love could stir passion such as this in him. She shrank away, but there was no escaping him. He found his way in, and it was immediately over as he exploded. Then surprisingly he jerked and sagged with his full and loathsome weight upon her. Her mind whirled, half mad. Had his rum-soaked exertions stopped his heart? She felt as though she had fallen into a stifling pit, and she desperately struggled to free herself. Someone was aiding her. Was it not over yet? She strained back to look, a sob in her throat. A ghastly scarred face met her eyes.

"Jud!" she breathed with relief as Wat's stocky body slid in a heap at her side. Quickly she smoothed her skirts and turned so that her face was hidden. She could not look into Jud's face. She could not even bear the feel of her own body.

"Nay, lady," Jud said, reaching with a soiled and shaking hand to smooth her tangled hair. "There is no time for tears. This place is like hell itself. We must be gone before this pig comes to, though I should have killed him for a fact like a poisonous snake."

Lettice dried her tears on her sleeve. She must pull herself together. Warily, she glanced toward the bed. The curtains still shook as the couple within exerted themselves.

"The queen," she whispered, rising shakily. "We must get the queen."

Jud's grotesque face took on a strange look. "Have you lost your wits, mistress?"

Lettice leaned closer to the scarred face, a face that looked strangely pure and wholesome compared to the giant Wat. "It's the Queen of Pamunkey in disguise. She lies below near the kitchen. I cannot leave without her."

Jud chewed the inside of his lip. His one eye shifted about the room. "How did you come here?"

"By horse. With an Indian boy and the queen."

"Without a man or a weapon, girl?"

"My pistol is still tied to my saddle, I pray."

Jud tore aside the bed curtains and reached in to yank a blanket off the bed. A hand reached from inside to angrily pull shut the curtains, but otherwise the pair seemed undisturbed.

"Trust me, mistress," Jud said in his low, gruff voice. Then he prepared to wrap the blanket completely about her and to lift her to his shoulder. "You are with child," he said even more gruffly.

"Some six months or more," she said.

" 'Twill make it all the harder."

She tried to hang as limp as she could over his shoulder, bending half sideways. She felt him grope his way carefully downstairs. He had not the strength of the huge figure of Wat, yet he had a backwoodsman's wiry endurance. Once again she heard the noise of the great hall. She could feel Jud brace his free shoulder against the wall for a moment. She trembled with fear. Would they discover her? Would it happen all over again?

"What have you there, fellow?" someone called.

"Booty for General Bacon," Jud growled, lurching forward.

"Let's have a look," a slurred voice demanded.

"Not unless the general says." She felt Jud's steps falter as he reached the door, but he stepped over the threshold and out onto the lawn, breathing with deep, rasping breaths. Finally he set her down. He had surpassed himself.

"Pray God they are too besotted to follow," he said. "I am too old for this work."

When he had freed her from the stifling blanket, she discovered that they were concealed by some shrubbery. But his voice was urgent and unrelaxed. She shrank from his touch, yet she felt almost like clinging to this friend as she fought for self-possession. She could still feel Wat's body upon her and prayed she would not vomit up what little she had eaten.

"Be calm if you can, mistress," Jud said, and she knew she must for his sake as well as the queen's.

He looked about cautiously, judging the danger. "Where do your horses lie?"

She pointed them out and was relieved to see the Indian boy standing nearby, unharmed. Jud pointed to a clump of trees near the river. "Meet me there. I will bring them."

But as she crept away, she looked back and saw the boy stubbornly refuse to give up the horses. A good boy, though overloyal this time. Jud bent to whisper into his ear, but the boy shrank from his ugliness. Finally Jud pointed to her direction, and Lettice showed herself for an instant. This seemed to work, and the man and dark-haired

212

boy ambled across the open space, leading the horses. They aroused no more than casual interest from those watching the house.

"The queen," the boy said as soon as they were close enough. His eyes shone intense with worry.

"I will bring her around the back," Jud said.

"But she does not know you," the boy said. But he did some fast thinking and quickly tore the string of beads from about his neck. He handed it to Jud. "Tell her Mistress Lettice and I say come."

Jud placed a hand upon the boy's straight blue-black hair and nodded. Then Jud sped off on foot. It seemed an age before he returned with the queen riding sturdily behind him on Jud's horse. She showed no sign of fear.

"Quickly," Jud called as the queen dismounted and climbed into her own saddle. "Let's be gone before they come after us."

Some of the tipsy, pipe-smoking loungers about the door looked up lazily as the little party rode into the open for a moment on their way down to the river. As soon as they were sheltered once more by the heavy foliage, Jud spurred his horse, and they sped away through the forest. Jud halted suddenly, bidding them pull aside from the trail to hide. A solitary rider pounded away toward Jamestown. Once he was well gone, Jud urged the women on again. It was far into the night when, satisfied, he allowed them to stop.

"I am very hungry," the boy said as his feet touched the ground.

"Oh, the poor child," Lettice cried.

But Jud soon remedied this with some pieces of hard bread from his saddlebags. The queen was in excellent spirits, and she soon settled herself to sleep, rolled in a blanket.

"Jud," Lettice said softly, coming to his side. "I must go down to the river to bathe. I must wash that man away, nay, scour."

Jud scratched his head. "I'm not much for washing myself, but he were an ugly scum. I'll watch the bank. Seems a dangerous thing to do, especially with a moon this bright. But if you need to do it, girl, go. I should have killed him for a fact, as Geoffrey's friend."

"What will Geoffrey say?" Lettice said lowly, looking across the moon-silvered river.

"He will kill him if he knows."

Then Lettice walked away, sheltered by the rising mists, and shed her clothes at the river bank. She waded out until her hair floated on the water. Then she scoured her skin with ferns and reeds from the bank until she burned and pained. But she thought it would be some time before she felt clean again.

"Can I trust you, Jud?" she asked when she returned to where the shabby figure stood with his back honestly turned from the river. "I must get the queen to the governor's protection."

"That's not so easy, mistress."

"But surely if we go to Jamestown. . . ."

"The governor is not in Jamestown. And Green Spring is in the hands of the rebels."

Lettice was shocked and disheartened. "Then how will we find him?"

"We will go to Jamestown and wait. He will be there soon."

"But how do you know that?"

"Because now I am a spy for both sides," Jud said.

XIII

By the time they arrived at Jamestown, the governor had retaken it from the rebel garrison, and the town was bursting with troops. By some miracle Lettice's old benefactor, the landlord, found room for her. She, the queen and the boy cooled their heels at the inn for several days. Finally Jud came to tell her the governor had said she might meet with him.

"You've seen him, Jud?" she asked with curiosity.

He shook his head sadly. "I would be on the side of the poorer men who follow Bacon were he not butchering Indians, raping women and killing children. Most like myself are good enough fellows, but those few madmen force their way to the center until the fight becomes theirs. And all they want is to loot and the blood of Indians. Nay, there's nothing for it but that I must support the governor, at least for a time."

"Then what will happen to my husband?"

Jud shook his rag-wrapped head again. "Honest, mistress, I dunno. But the governor trusts me; so I may be able to speak for Geoffrey—and John and Ajax too. But Bacon cannot hold out forever since troops will arrive soon from England."

A short time later, clad in a light muslin gown, Lettice followed the hot, dusty street toward the Statehouse. Jamestown was crowded with newcomers. Sun glinted off pikes and helmets, musket men crisscrossed their chests with bandoleers. One leather-clad soldier sat cross-legged on the ground. He was tootling a flute while a crowd stood about, laughing at his sour notes, cheering when his melody took off and flew. The crowd parted as a man drawing a cart laden with household goods made for the gates.

White-aproned goodwives bustled about airing and washing and snapping at their children. They were all preparing to flee if necessary. They knew that if Bacon should come down upon them, there would be a battle. Most townspeople had supported both sides at one time or another. Lettice must arrange quickly for the queen's care and then return to Albright's Point. In some few weeks she would bear the child.

She had just arrived before the Statehouse when a freckle-faced boy ran up to tug at her beribboned sleeve. "Please, mistress!" he cried. "A man told me to ask you to meet him outside the town gates, over by the water's edge by the big pine." He tossed a penny into the air, his reward for carrying the message. His fine, sandy hair blew half over his eyes.

"A gentleman?" Lettice questioned in surprise.

"Please, mistress. He said he was your husband, though in truth he is not as finely dressed as you."

Geoffrey? Lettice's heart lifted. It was foolhardy of him to enter the town. Yet she was touched that he took this risk to see her.

"But how did he know I was here?" she asked, more to herself than to the boy.

The boy shuffled his feet and wiped his nose nervously with the back of a hand, snuffling loudly. "He saw you, mistress," he said finally. "But he is gone now."

"Was he truly my husband? What did he look like?"

The boy was at a loss.

"Like most men. Tall. Wearing hunting clothes."

"You are a good boy." Lettice reached into the blue-velvet pocket she carried to toss him another coin. She looked up at the Statehouse with regret, knowing she must abandon that errand until this one was completed. She could not endanger Geoffrey by her delay.

"Be careful, mistress," the sentry warned as she slipped through the gates. "Bacon's troops wander about."

She nodded, not trusting herself to speak, afraid she would cry aloud that her husband was near. As she walked, she heard the sound of axes. The Jamestown defenders were extending a palisade from the James to the back river. She had not expected to walk so far. Her slippers were soon coated with dust, and she felt every pebble through her thin soles. Heavy and ungainly with the child, she hurried toward the sentinel pine. She stopped uncertainly, biting her lip. Low brush surrounded the tree, and all seemed dark and strangely menacing in the deep shadows of the foliage. Then she thought she saw a blur of brown and white. Awkwardly she began to run, bursting into the thicket.

A heavy hand closed over her mouth as another grasped her about her neck. Wildly she struggled to see who had captured her, biting the thick palm. Her eyes turned upward, her body froze. She knew those florid features well. She knew the perpetually narrowed eyes that at this moment were but slits. Oh, God, had she not escaped him after all?

"There's no way out this time, mistress," Wat said.

She tried to scream, but she could scarce breathe with his immense hands covering her face. A second man brought a rope. Once her hands and ankles were fast, a cloth was stuffed into her mouth, and another tied over it. Wat's muscles bulged as he lifted her to carry her through the brush. She could still hear the governor's men behind her, hacking and clearing in preparation for war.

She shrank from his touch as Wat raised her to the front of his saddle, then sprang up behind. Waves of revulsion swept over her. Her stomach churned so wildly she feared she would gag and suffocate. Tears filled her eyes as she thought of the child. It could not take much more abuse. Perhaps she should give in to Wat—promise him anything—so that she might protect herself while she carried this child.

She was close to fainting. Wat's elbow was crooked about her throat. But she heard two men speaking. Bacon was expected at a rendezvous. She began to hope. She prayed. If Wat did not rape her, if she did not lose the child, Geoffrey might yet free her. Then she remembered Wat's madness and hatred, and she feared for Geoffrey too.

The horse picked up speed as it crossed a large, cleared field, carrying her farther and farther from Jamestown. They passed a tall brick chimney of a building long ruined. As they burst into the trees at the other side, a voice called out, ordering them to halt. She could feel Wat tense.

217

"Is this lady an enemy?" someone demanded waspishly. "Or do you divert yourselves before the battle?"

"She is of Squire Albright's family," Wat answered.

Lettice's disordered hair covered her face so that all she could see of the gentleman whom Wat addressed were black boots and the sides of a dark horse. But she recognized the nervous, forceful voice as Bacon's.

"Squire Albright," the voice came, thoughtfully. "He has gone over to the governor, we have heard. The lady may prove useful in that case. Set her safely beneath yonder tree. She is my prisoner now. And if you would serve under me, you will take axes immediately and begin to build a palisade before we hear more from the governor. And hurry. If we fail here, the game is over." Then Lettice heard his horse's hooves pound away toward Jamestown.

Cursing under his breath, Wat slid from his saddle and placed Lettice beneath a half-grown pine, binding her fast, though he allowed her to sit upon the ground. Then he and his companion slipped off their shirts, drew hatchets from their saddles and set to work. Wat returned for a moment to tower over her, squinting down, his impassive face stiff with suppressed emotion.

"Do not mistake, mistress," Wat said. "I will return. You owe me, I think." Then he was gone. Dogwood, ferns and cedar grew lush about her, yet she was left with a clear view across the field to the town. Other figures thrashed through the brush. Behind her a few tents were thrown up as camp was prepared. A new party rode up hailing the general, as Bacon was now called. Lettice searched futilely among the men for a glimpse of Geoffrey or John. A few cast curious glances in her direction, but for the most part they seemed unmoved by her plight. Their interest was in their leader.

"What news?" Bacon demanded. He was standing at the doorway of his tent, arms akimbo.

"The governor sent out a party to scout our movements."

"Hmm. Does he now." Even from where she sat, Lettice could see a light of excitement fill Bacon's eyes. He sprang into the saddle of his black horse, which was grazing nearby. Then he raised one arm over his head. "Come on, my hearts of gold. He that dies in the field lies in the bed of honor. Let us greet the governor."

218

The men laughed and cheered as Bacon galloped off over Paspahegh Old Fields with a handful of others toward the governor's palisades. Dimly, Lettice could hear a trumpet sound, then shots as one of the men fired a carbine. There seemed to be no answering fire from the governor's forces. After a time, horses' hooves pounded back. The men were as excited as schoolboys set to a prank by their leader. Bacon dismounted, paced about and gestured wildly, planning his defenses.

By this time more and more riders had ridden to rendezvous under a grove of cypress, not far from a sandy crescent of beach. Some had already dismounted and were making camp. Women camp followers gathered fagots, piling them together to make fires. Soon blazes sent trails of smoke into the clear sky. Iron fry pans were produced, and stewpots boiled. These women paid no attention at all to Lettice. If only she could speak to them, she thought. Her mouth was so dry her lips began to crack.

As the sun rose higher, the shade shifted. Lettice found herself in full sun and growing faint, stifled by the gag. Her head sagged forward until her long tresses trailed upon the ground. She thought she saw her husband's face. He was smiling, well dressed. He raised a goblet of wine to his lips and whispered her name. The women's voices became suddenly loud, then dimmer as she lost consciousness.

The world whirled and blurred with the light-green foliage of Virginia as she came to again. She found herself looking into the concerned eyes of a leather-skinned, hard-eyed woman with a dirty kerchief tied over her hair. A clay pipe of tobacco hung from one corner of her mouth. With callused fingers she removed Lettice's gag.

"Don't these men know how to treat a woman carrying young?" The pipe moved only slightly as she spoke through tight lips. "Prisoner or no, it ain't right."

A wooden water bucket hit the dirt with a thud, overturning and spilling. A thin, bedraggled figure stood, wide eyes upon Lettice.

"Mistress!"

"Molly! Oh, Molly." Tears of relief filled Lettice's eyes. She would have reached out to her had not the bonds cut into her flesh.

Molly rushed to her aid, and in no time Lettice was free. Molly's blue eyes seemed even brighter with worry. Her lovely skin was coated with a thin film of dirt. For a moment there was silence between them as though there was too much to tell.

"Oh, mistress, how came you here?" Molly asked finally.

"Wat," Lettice whispered, looking over her shoulder.

Molly straightened and stared about, shielding her brow with her hand. Then she turned back with a gesture of a chin grown sharp with deprivation. "He's here? We must warn the men."

"Geoffrey?" Lettice whispered.

"Back behind, foraging for food and supplies. John and Ajax too. We have only just arrived. Cursed be that Wat should be here too."

Lettice leaned against Molly's shoulder. "Wat is mad, Molly. We must be very careful."

"Do you stay with us, then, mistress?"

The woman with the pipe lay a restraining hand upon Molly's arm. "She'll stay, yes, indeed. Unless the general says she can go."

"If you say so, Susanna."

Molly's worried eyes met Lettice's. The woman, kind as she was, was loyal to Bacon. They said nothing as Susanna returned to her chores. Then Molly brought Lettice a bit of dry bread and a cup of water. She lay a hand on Lettice's belly. "You are growing big now, mistress. The babe should be here in a month or two."

Lettice nodded, studying her former maid. Molly's golden hair was all snarled from traveling with the troops. Her dainty wrists looked fragile, even brittle. There were deep hollows about her eyes, and her skin had lost its sheen.

"How is it with you, Molly?" Lettice whispered. "Where is the babe?"

A stricken look crossed Molly's face, and she lowered her eyes without answering. Lettice reached out to grasp her arm.

"Molly . . . what is it?"

"Little Henry be gone, mistress."

"Gone?"

"It were a flux, all green and awful. Sal and I done our best, but he wasted and died."

"Oh, Molly." Lettice stared at the turbulent curls of the bowed head. "You will have other children."

"P'raps," Molly said, her face all woebegone. "If we ever find a corner of the world to call home. But enough." She sprang to her feet. "Now it be your child we must think on. We women will keep Wat from you."

Molly brought her a blanket, and Lettice lay down to rest as she was bid. She watched the women at work under the trees as they cooked and began to scrub clothes for the men and for themselves. Soon clean linen covered the branches of trees and bushes. The men were busily at work cutting trees and hauling them to build a shelter above the ditch of Bacon's French works. Now and again a man would return to pinch the thigh of a shrill woman or silence a nagging complaint with a kiss. Like most armies, Bacon's could not function well without its women.

A party of dark-skinned, dejected men and women were being led, roped together, past the campfires. Dressed in a mixture of native and European clothes like the queen, they made Lettice wonder if they were captured Pamunkey.

Shortly afterward Bacon rode into the camp, shouting more orders and directions for the building of the French works across Paspahegh Old Fields. "We will work through the night," he said. As he dismounted, his eye fell upon Lettice.

"Why is this prisoner unbound?" he demanded.

Molly came running, her apron fluttering. "I did it, General, sir," she said. "She be pregnant, you see."

"Make sure she is not lost," Bacon called over his shoulder as he headed toward his tent.

"Oh, I will, sir." Molly curtsyed. "I will watch her well." She sank down beside Lettice, covering her mouth to stifle her giggles.

"You may be able to protect me against Bacon," Lettice said, sitting up, "but Wat is another matter."

"Have no fear, mistress," Molly said. "You can sleep with the women. Even Wat be too much of a coward to brave the wrath of all of the women together, and the men will work all night."

The moon rose full, and Lettice lay down among the eight or ten camp followers, her fatigue deep and her heart heavy. How did the queen manage in Jamestown? Geoffrey—where was he? In the distance she could hear the sounds of spades and axes and men's voices calling to one another as Bacon prepared his defensive positions.

She awoke with a scream in her throat! In the eerie light Wat's face appeared above her. His foul and heavy breath was on her cheek. There were groans and rustles as the other women awoke. Lettice screamed again. Wat's hands were upon her breasts. Lettice saw Susanna stretch her long, gaunt body and stand. Molly sat up from her snarl of blankets.

"Wat!" Molly cried as she scrambled over on hands and knees to pummel him upon his enormous back. Wat turned and struck her a blow that sent her sprawling upon the other women, who were all wide-awake now.

Lettice lashed out with her feet, crying, "You'll not rape me again! I'll kill you first! You'll not touch me! I'll kill you!"

But Wat's huge hand seized a flailing leg, and he dragged her along the ground toward the brush. She could feel the fine cloth of her bodice tear. She screamed.

At this all the women screamed together. "Is that a way to treat a woman?" one yelled.

"Ugly brute!" another called.

"She's with child, you pig!"

One of the women lashed out with her fingernails and raked them across Wat's face. Susanna ran to the ashes and picked up an enormous fry pan. Lettice's petticoats boiled as she kicked and struck out, slowing Wat's massive bulk only a little. Wat fell to his knees. He struggled with her. His enormous hands darted among her clothing, seeking a handhold.

Then the ringing of the iron pan as it struck Wat's skull echoed across the fields. The women burst into cheers. Lettice lay still for a moment, then scrambled free. A couple of men ran up to see if Berkeley's forces had attacked in the night, but they only shrugged when they saw it was a fight with the women. They laughed and pointed as they recognized Wat. Slowly he sat, shaking his head dazedly. Then he began to creep toward the shadows to safety.

Cursing like a band of witches, the women charged Wat in a body. They seized stones from off the ground to hurl at him. Shaking his head again, he struck out, wildly, once, twice. Then he ducked and ran for cover.

"Sot! Whoremonger!" Susanna cried, throwing the fry pan after him. It landed with a thud on the ground.

"These men won't let a body rest. They're after nothing but lust!" cried another. But her man came to her side. He pinched a cheek, stroked a thigh, gentling her like a horse as he led her away behind the bushes.

"Oh, mistress," Molly sobbed. "Be you all right?" She helped Lettice to her feet and dusted off her muslin petticoat.

"I only wish it was my hand that had cracked his skull with a fry pan," Lettice said angrily.

Susanna patted her awkwardly upon her back. "Stay close to us, lady," she said. "We'll keep that great lout off you."

"Be the babe all right?" another woman called as she finished kissing a lean and smiling man.

"I pray so. And I pray that his life in the world is more peaceful than his beginnings," Lettice answered.

"I'll make you a cup of blackberry-leaf tea," Susanna said, poking up the fire.

Bacon stayed awake during the whole night. The men worked with good spirits, flagging toward dawn though their general had no desire to rest. At last he would face his cousin; face one of the many old men who had plagued him and stood between him and his desires throughout his life. This old man would know his mettle.

With dawn, Bacon saw that a goodly number of ships had sailed up before the entrance to the town. Their guns were trained on his fortifications. But the men were undaunted. Truly they were, as he called them, "hearts of gold."

"Let's let the governor know we're here," one cried, seizing a loaded wheel lock. Five others, who had been resting after the night's labors, leaped to their feet. They sped off across the fields toward Sir William's palisades. Bacon smiled to see them go. He heard shot as they fired upon the guard. There was no returning fire. Bacon frowned. Sir William must have ordered his men to refrain from shooting. Would his cousin ignore him? He could not, must not, this time.

Bacon thoughtfully studied his newly built fortifications. He would display his captives—Pamunkeys—there. Then the governor's supporters would see that he could war against Indians while they shivered behind their palisades. And he, Bacon, would decree that all captured vermin would be slaves for life. If the governor would have done the same years ago, the savages would be subdued by now, and the colony much advanced.

The six men returned, panting and laughing at their own daring. "The governor will beg us to let him surrender. See if he don't!"

"If they offer a treaty, we will throw it back in their teeth," Bacon said coldly. "We will not bargain, but prevail."

The men staggered toward the camp to lay down. Looking after them, Bacon thoughtfully felt his chin with a thumb and forefinger. Then he spurred his horse toward his own fortifications. He must have time to build them higher before the attack. The governor had much force at his command. Bacon narrowed his eyes. When the lion's strength was not sufficient, he must augment it with the fox's brains.

A face flashed before Bacon. It was Squire Albright's pretty girl relation, heavy with child. Then the commander straightened in his saddle as a brilliant thought came to him. Where were the wives of the other Loyalists? The wife of the elder Nathaniel Bacon, another cousin of his, for instance?

Turning his horse, he rode back to camp. There he sought out the most aggressive, most brutal of his men— Wat among them. Drawing them aside, he lowered his voice. Pleased with his instructions, the men nodded agreement. Then they chose mounts from the horses grazing near by and rode off toward the Loyalist plantations.

Throughout the long day the camp followers bickered among themselves. One would look up now and again to hurl an insult toward the men. But the men only laughed. They loved the women well enough, but it would not do to take them seriously. At the sound of returning horses, the women fell silent. They began moving closer together. Molly came to stand beside Lettice.

None of the grim riders deigned to glance toward the camp followers, but rode instead toward Bacon's tent. Seated on their horses, before each of the eight riders, were ladies of various ages. Their wrists were bound, eyes wide with terror, clad in light gowns and petticoats for the warmth of the fall weather. And each still wore her snowy-white apron.

Susanna's brown eyes showed surprise, almost fear. "What, do we war on women?" she called out. "I thought 'twas Indians we fought."

"That's Mrs. Nathaniel Bacon, the elder," one woman whispered.

"That's Mrs. Thomas Ballard," said another.

Hearing the hoofbeats, Bacon emerged from his tent. One of the older ladies on horseback cried out, shaking herself free of the restraining grasp of her captor. "Is that you, Nathaniel? Do you dare to hold *me* prisoner?" She dug an elbow into the man seated behind her as he tried to subdue her.

Bacon came to stand before her horse, his arms on his hips, his dark cavalier locks lifted by the breeze, his eyes fanatic and black. "Yes, Cousin."

"Let me assure you," the lady cried with rage, her broad face reddening, "you will never receive a penny of my husband's estate after this! He was good enough to make you heir. But now I would rather he had left it to the poorest beggar on the streets of London!"

Bacon flushed. "We shall see, Cousin. I gamble for high stakes."

"I have told your mother you would end up on the gallows. . ."

"Please, Mistress Bacon," another lady called fearfully. "We are in his power. You will only drive him mad." The voice came from a young woman who shivered, seated astride in fear before Wat. Wat's meaty hand lay clenched high on her thigh. Her dark-blue skirts were raised halfway up her legs.

Bacon turned blazing black eyes upon the lady. "I am glad you understand your peril better than my cousin. Since you understand so well, I will have you released." He nodded toward Wat, who impassively dismounted and set the lady upon the ground.

"Free her hands," Bacon ordered.

Wat took a long knife from his belt and slashed the leather bindings.

"Now, good lady," Bacon instructed while the woman cowered. "If you wish to see these other ladies again, listen

225

carefully. I will send you to the governor and to your husbands, who support him. Tell them that General Bacon would improve his position here without interference from the old men of Jamestown or the governor's tame sea captains out upon the James. Therefore I need a shield between myself and my cousin the governor. These ladies here," he nodded toward the rest of the party, "will serve well. I will bind them upon my ramparts. If he wishes not to soil their pretty white aprons, he will order his men to hold their fire."

"You are mad, Nathaniel," Mistress Bacon whispered, turning white as her apron. "I pray they pay no heed to us and shoot every one of you. I would rather die than be your pawn."

"Silence, Cousin," Bacon ordered. Turning to the other woman, he said, "Now be off. Tell the governor that the white flags he sees upon my ramparts do not signal surrender and that these ladies' aprons make good targets. Meanwhile we will build our fortifications deeper. Now take these ladies away."

The horsemen spurred forward across the fields with the ladies helpless before them. Bacon's messenger stared at the ground, her hands trembling.

"Well, mistress," Bacon demanded as a flush swept over her throat and bosom. "Do you understand your errand?"

She raised brown eyes, which were blind and soft with fear. "The ladies. You will use them as a shield."

"You are a most excellent student. Show us how well you can march to the gates of Jamestown!" Bacon ordered

Unsteadily, the lady turned, wiping her palms upon her skirts. Those watching saw her figure grow small as she picked her way on foot toward Jamestown. Bacon's eyes never left her until, seeming satisfied, he turned to go back to his tent. Then his gaze fell upon the silent, huddled camp followers.

"Where is the other prisoner—Squire Albright's kinswoman?"

The women moved aside, leaving Molly and Lettice standing alone.

"Let her join the other ladies," Bacon ordered.

Molly let go of Lettice's hand, crying out involuntarily, "No!"

"Silence!" Bacon said. "I will have obedience."

226

Molly opened her mouth to say more, but something in the burning eyes of the commander silenced her. A sob escaped her as she turned away. But she did no more work that day, for her eyes kept returning to her former mistress.

Geoffrey rode into the encampment. John and Ajax were behind him with a squealing ox-drawn cart of supplies, much of which had been plundered from Green Spring. As the party broke clear of the forest, they saw the smoking campfires and the women about the fire. Molly straightened, shaded her eyes, then came running. John stepped forward to embrace her, but her eyes were on Geoffrey.

"Geoffrey . . . you must . . . oh, it be awful!"

"What?" he called, reigning up.

"Mistress Lettice. And the other ladies." She pointed toward the ramparts in the distance.

"What the devil!" Geoffrey peered in the direction she indicated, but the women were shielded from view by Bacon's rough palisade.

Molly came to grasp his reins, looking up in entreaty. "He's bound them there, all the ladies. Mistress Lettice too!"

She stood back as Geoffrey spurred his horse and galloped across the fields. He swung wide so that he rode directly under the line of fire from Sir William's guns. The ladies' fluttering aprons and flying hair met his eyes. Lettice was at the very end, sagged down against her ropes, swelled with pregnancy, half fainting. Geoffrey sprang from his saddle to support her.

"Sweetheart!" he cried. In an instant he whipped his knife from his belt and slashed her bonds.

"Geoffrey," she whispered. Her hands clutched at his shirt. And then she lost consciousness. Her husband tenderly lowered her to the ground.

"Please, young man," Mrs. Nathaniel Bacon, the elder, called. "Please cut us free."

"Please," a stocky woman with a hint of mustache on her upper lip added. "I'm so full of piss I think I will burst."

Geoffrey quickly cut them free and bade them aid their sisters. Then he lifted Lettice into the saddle before him

227

and returned to camp. He had only gone a few steps when Bacon, Wat and some others mounted and thundered down upon him. Bacon raised one arm, and the others halted.

"How dare you go against my orders!" Bacon cried. "I ordered that lady bound."

"And I disobey you. This lady is my wife. The child she carries is mine." Though Geoffrey's voice was cool, his face was drained of blood as he barely controlled his rage.

Bacon looked truly startled. "She is Squire Albright's kinswoman."

"I believe mine is the closer tie," Geoffrey said grimly.

Bacon sat silent, obviously discomfited. Out of the corner of his eye, Geoffrey saw a figure run across the fields, a figure with hair and rumpled apron. Molly reached up to grasp Lettice's cold hand.

"Would you stand here talking?" she cried. "I pray God she does not lose the child. And you," she turned to screech at Bacon, "can you do nothing but war on women? What kind of a man be you? Or be you one at all?"

A slow blaze engulfed Bacon's face. Molly hesitated. His eyes glowed as he turned to the men behind him. "Let the women go," he ordered.

Lettice, who had been drooping as limply as a puppet, stirred and sighed and opened her eyes. She looked from Bacon back up at the man whose arms held her so tightly.

"Perhaps you are a Loyalist like your wife," Bacon sneered.

"Not yet," Geoffrey answered coldly. "Nor do I think my wife has any politics at all."

"Then I offer you this choice: Return with your wife to Jamestown, or send her alone and remain to serve me. I would have you prove your loyalty."

The muscles of Geoffrey's jaw tightened. "I will remain," he said at last. "But as you see, my wife is not well."

"Well, I'll not remain," Molly's shrill voice cut into their talk. "It be beyond me how you men do go on. But I'll not stay with brutes who hide behind women's petticoats. I'll go along to take care of my mistress."

Geoffrey could not help but smile at her. "Molly. You will land back into Gower's tender care."

"Oh, Molly," Lettice sighed, shaking her heavy head to clear it.

"My mistress needs me. And I'll not stay among men who treat women so!"

Geoffrey looked down at her. There was a look of tender respect in his eyes. "What can I say to these arguments? Except that they make me seem a coward to myself. And that John will miss you."

"And I him," Molly said shortly.

"I would have the wench gone," Bacon said. "I do not like women who argue."

Geoffrey gave him a sharp look. "I hope my commitment to your cause will bear a closer look," he said. "As for now, I would like to take these women to the gates."

"No," Bacon said. "I do not trust you."

Geoffrey drew in a great breath as though he would object. Then he looked off toward the ships upon the James, his brow troubled.

"Tell John . . . ," Molly began, but she did not complete her sentence. She turned instead toward Jamestown, biting her lip.

Geoffrey bent his head so that he spoke into Lettice's ear. "Sweetheart. Things are all awry, it seems. You must leave Jamestown for some safe place. Do not think of me or of this foolish war until the child is born. Do you promise me?"

Lettice raised her eyes and saw that Bacon watched them closely. She tightened her grasp upon Geoffrey's arm, nodding.

"Enough of these secrets," Bacon cut in. "I want these women gone so that I may prepare for war."

Geoffrey helped Lettice dismount. His hands were gentle under her elbow. He kissed her hair just above her ear, defying Bacon's cold gaze.

"Can you walk, Lettice?"

She nodded again, though in fact the fields wavered before her eyes. Molly came to her side, and the two women walked hand in hand over the uneven ground. Geoffrey's eyes never left them until he saw them reach the gates of Jamestown.

Lettice awoke once more in the bed she had occupied before as a guest of the landlord. It was dark, and her eyes fixed upon an approaching candle. Images swept through her brain while she fought to remember how she had left Jamestown only to return to her bed.

Molly's face, her curls touched by candlelight, hovered over her. "How be you, mistress?"

"My head is splitting. I can barely remember all that happened—Geoffrey—the other women. If only I would wake to find Geoffrey's arms about me. But I know he is loyal to Bacon, and so is John."

"I have found it a poor choice between Gower and Bacon, mistress. But John and me will be together some day. I know it. And you and Geoffrey too. But we must hurry, mistress. The fighting be almost upon us. The landlord has already packed up all his valuables and run off."

The two women looked up as a step was heard in the kitchen. Jud stood there. He had respectfully removed his fur cap so that his ugly scar was fully revealed. "How is she, then?" he called softly.

"Oh, I shall live, and the babe too. 'Twas only too much time without water or food in the sun. I can feel the babe's restlessness; so he is well. It is only that my head pains so."

He came forward shyly to pat her hand while Molly fluttered about, straightening her pillow. Then Molly hastily began to pack up their belongings.

"You have had much to bear of late, mistress," Jud said. "I hope you will bear the child as well."

"The queen, Jud. What has become of her?"

"She is well. Sir William arranged an escort for her back to her own lands. The treaty with the Pamunkey will be repaired, I think, and we have much to thank you for."

"I hope I shall see the queen again, for I count her as a friend."

"She sends you this." Jud reached into his worn leather pouch, then opened a callused palm to reveal a string of glowing pearls of particular regularity and beauty. The Indians were fond of them, and they searched among the oyster beds to find them. "She says she knows English ladies value pearls."

"How lovely!" Lettice said.

"Oh!" Molly cried, taking them from Jud's hand to display them by candlelight.

"There are few valuables left in my family," Lettice explained. "And never such an extraordinary string of pearls as these."

230

Jud looked up, for the sound of guns were heard. A second later the two women jumped as a loud splintering noise announced that Bacon's cannon had made a breach in the palisade.

"Bacon grows impatient," Jud said. "Ah, the governor could hold here forever were not his men faint-hearted and on the verge of mutiny. Well, nothing is simple, and it's plain I must be off, my dears. Where I go, I won't say, and I beg you to say naught of me and my sympathies to anyone."

Lettice nodded, though her heart feared for Geoffrey.

Jud nodded approval at Molly's hasty preparations. "The governor prepares to abandon the town. You're safest with him at Accomack upon Virginia's eastern shore. But leave with haste, my dears."

Bacon planned to enter the town after dark. He was beside himself with excitement when at last his troops poured through the gates. But the town was all but deserted. As many goods as the burdened ships out upon the James could hold had been evacuated. A thousand of the governor's troops had deserted to the rebels, swelling the ranks that now surged through the short, narrow streets.

Fingering his chin and preceded by a lacky bearing a lantern, Bacon surveyed his conquest. Behind the palisade were some 12 new brick houses and a considerable amount of the older frame ones with brick chimneys. A few horses had been turned loose in the streets, and two or three sellers of wine still hopefully awaited business.

"We will burn the town," the general decided. "I do not want to provide a place of refuge for my cousin's forces another time."

A burly soldier looked up, astonished. "Burn it?" he cried. " 'Twould be a shame, General."

Lawrence and Drummond, two of Bacon's most ardent supporters in Jamestown, strode up to their commander's horse.

"What say you, my friends?" Bacon asked. "Will you stand with me and burn the town, taking your losses, or will you prove as soft as the governor's men?"

"We will stand," they both answered. Neither bent nor wavered.

"Nay, Mr. Lawrence," cried a rebel who stood holding a

231

torch high to illuminate the empty houses. "Burn you own?"

In answer, Lawrence climbed rigidly into his saddle and spurred his horse, pausing only to seize the torch from the man's hand. His dark mount shied and screamed with fear of the flames. Lawrence galloped a short distance. The crowd followed on foot. He flung himself from the saddle and leaped to his own doorstep. The door burst open. His black maidservant stood there. Her eyes were wide with fear.

"Master Lawrence!" she cried.

"Stand aside!" he ordered, then stepped within to touch his torch to the heavy brocade curtains at the windows. Those outside could see the casements flare with the orange-colored light of flames, and beyond, the onlookers could see one or two good pieces of furniture ignite.

"Master!" the woman screamed, bursting into terrified sobs.

Lawrence exploded out the door. There were sparks upon his sleeve, which he shook away. Glancing at his dark love briefly, he said, "Hasten down to the river with the other women."

"But all my clothing . . . all . . . everything is inside!" she cried, wringing her hands.

"The women will care for you. Go!" he ordered.

She fled into the night, apron strings flaring out behind her.

The sight of the flames seemed to intoxicate the men, for they seized up whatever came to hand and lighted new torches from the old. Running between the houses, they touched piles of straw with their lights and broke through windows to set curtains ablaze.

"The Statehouse!" someone screamed just as Drummond cantered up. Lawrence looked up the street with concern.

"Don't worry," Drummond chuckled, his face aglow in the firelight. "I had the records and documents secretly removed several days ago."

There was a sudden burst of light as a new building flamed.

"The church!" Drummond cried.

"No matter." Lawrence turned his horse's head in the direction of the river's bank. "We will all find new fortune following our most excellent rebel leader. One cannot always take the safe way."

In the morning, two days after Bacon's men had attacked, Jamestown lay a pile of smouldering ashes—as destroyed as it had been from an Indian attack many years ago. Bacon and his men withdrew to Green Spring to plunder and to wait.

Lettice was given a room along with some other refugee ladies and her maid Molly by the owner of a prosperous plantation in Accomack County. Sir William's troops were quartered in tents nearby. Lettice opened her box to change into fresh clothing, for since the flight from Jamestown she had not had a moment to herself. Sadly, she reviewed the events of the past several days. She and Geoffrey seemed further apart than ever. And now John and Molly were separated as well. Her only consolation was that the queen had been returned to her own people.

Through the open window Lettice heard voices, both men's and women's. A fiddle tuned; a flute joined in. There was a clapping of hands and a country dance was struck up.

What on earth! Thrusting her head out the window, Lettice saw ladies and gentlemen filled with a holiday air as they enjoyed themselves so far from Bacon's forces. A new party seemed to have arrived from the English ships that were anchored out upon the river. Several couples pranced joyously to the music out upon the lawn.

Then the music changed to the more stately sounds of a courante. Lettice's eyes roamed over the pleasant sight and came to rest on a dark-haired figure in a wine-velvet coat. She gasped with shock and started forward to call down. Then she checked herself. There was no doubt that it was Geoffrey, yet if he were dressed so formally, it must mean that he was here secretly to gather information. She must proceed with the utmost care, yet she did not mean to let the opportunity of speaking to him pass. And she would dance with him, since she never had—unless one considered their pairings in bed.

She drew back into the room as a fine ruse occurred to her. She selected her plum gown and blue-silk petticoat. She sighed. There was no disguising the fact that she was

233

pregnant. She laced everything loosely so that it fit. Lastly she slipped on the Queen of Pamunkey's string of pearls. Though barbaric in origin, they enhanced the creaminess of her skin, and she noticed they made her eyes softer and larger. Hastily she chose a star-shaped silken patch and placed it upon her chin.

She next dug into her box and brought out her mask. It was not very beautiful, being made of leather, like a comedian's mask. But she slipped it on and walked down and through the crowd to watch Geoffrey more closely. He danced with obvious pleasure. She would wish, in fact, that he showed less, since he must certainly be longing for her, his wife. Then the dance ended, and he turned toward the crowd, and his eyes lightened on her. He did not recognize her, even with her pregnancy showing so obviously. But the mask intrigued him. She smiled at him slyly, piquing his interest. He turned briefly to excuse himself from his partner, then walked over to Lettice. He bowed before her.

"Your mask does make me wonder what beauty lies beneath, mistress," he said. She pursed her lips and flashed her eyes at him.

"The face beneath must be most appealing. And the lady, for all her disguise, must have some vanity, for there is a patch upon her chin." His fascination was so obvious that she began to resent it, since it was equally plain that he did not yet recognize her. She licked her lips flirtatiously. He smiled.

"The mystery of your beauty overwhelms me. You must promise me this dance."

She smiled. Perhaps he had been joking all along. Geoffrey was such a tease. Out upon the lawn they faced each other for the figure of the dance. He bowed. His hair was arranged with a care that was unusual for him.

"Though so far from their native shores, the ladies of Virginia are great beauties, I believe."

"Really, Husband, you overdo," Lettice burst out with pique.

"Husband?" her partner said. "But mistress, I am not your husband."

She looked cautiously about to see if anyone had heard, but by now she was thoroughly nettled. How could his dark eyes appear so cold? "Well, I am not your wife, then, if you say so."

"My lady," he said. "You thoroughly confuse me. But not so much that I cannot tell that you are surely not my wife."

She stopped dead in the midst of a figure and glared at him from behind her mask. Really, when he teased so unmercifully, she wondered why she had married him.

He smiled a strange smile, then looked about to see who was observing them. "I see that we shall have to discuss this at a more quiet place."

At last he seemed to understand. No doubt it had been a bad joke on his part. She had begun it by slipping on the mask, but she had not expected him to go to such lengths. But it were better they sought privacy, for of course it was dangerous for him to be here. She felt contrite for her carelessness in possibly exposing him.

He took her hand in his and led her through the crowd. Turning back, he nodded to the lady who had been his partner. She followed them. The three walked without speaking into the house.

"These people have been kind enough to offer shelter since Jamestown is no more," Lettice said, trying to break the silence.

Lettice looked at her husband carefully, beginning to feel very strange. What on earth was Geoffrey up to, and who was this woman? But he ushered her into the great hall. Then he leaned back upon the chimney piece to regard her before he spoke again.

"Take off your mask, my dear." He gestured toward her with a tense, almost aggressive, movement that was unlike him.

She did as he bid, then stared at him. Fear and unease began to crawl about her spine. With a sinking feeling she finally understood.

"Giles," she whispered.

XIV

Giles nodded. His eyes—the dark eyes she so loved in Geoffrey—glittered.

Well waxed and polished, the paneled room seemed serene compared with the emotions stirring there. The herringbone patterns of the floor tiles were well scrubbed. Dark portraits of men and women of earlier days, orange-colored faces framed by white ruffs or lace collars, hung upon the walls. A sewing box sat open upon the carpet-covered table.

Giles and Lettice regarded each other silently, taking measure in this comfortable room.

"You are—were—Mistress Clifford?" Giles said.

"I was."

"She is pregnant, Giles," the lady drawled. She had just arrived in the doorway. She appeared flushed, and there was a wicked glint in her beautiful eyes. When she smiled, she revealed spaces between her teeth that gave her a wolfish look.

"So she is." Giles lowered himself into a turkey-work chair. His hands clutched the arms. He stretched one booted foot out before him, bending the other, lounging negligently. For a moment he leaned his dark head back and closed his eyes.

The lady laughed a brittle laugh as she swished into the room with a great rustle of petticoats. "What a shame your lady wife does not share her condition," the woman said.

"Yes. It is a shame," Giles replied.

Swinging her hips, the lady walked closer to inspect Lettice. She bent to finger the pearls, then the silver lace on her petticoat. Lettice started in surprise. Where had she seen that tall figure, that yellow hair, before? The lady was clad in a yellow-silk gown trimmed with blue ribbon. Her elegant, puffed undersleeves were of the finest quality. She straightened to look down into Lettice's eyes. "So you did buy it, after all. I scarce thought you could afford it."

"Of course! You are the lady in the London shop!" And she had thought to see the last of her, to put an ocean between them. She remembered she was called Lady Isobel. But Lady Isobel was right. The lace had been too expensive.

The lady smiled, changing her perfect beauty into the look of a hunting animal. "Think of it, Giles. I have already met your sister-in-law in London."

Giles said nothing. He looked from one to the other of them before finally breaking the silence. His dark eyes were curiously dead and sullen. "I might know Geoffrey would get some wench with child as soon as he set foot in Virginia."

"But Giles," Lady Isobel reminded. "You do not ask the most important question. Where is your brother?"

Giles's eyes swung back to Lettice. He did not repeat the question.

"I do not know," Lettice said.

"What, has he left you already?" Lady Isobel drawled, dimpling and nibbling at the end of her forefinger.

"Be silent, Isobel," Giles commanded. "He is doubtless among the rebels. That is why the lady was surprised to see me here."

Lady Isobel sauntered about the room, fingering the pewter and the candlesticks. There was a restless tenseness about her that made her walk catlike. "Well, then," she said. "This lady will be a widow soon, for he will be hanged if he should live that long."

Lettice gritted her teeth. "That will please you mightily, no doubt."

Lady Isobel paused. She raised one graceful arm. "Please me? And have Giles lose his double?" She sighed a deep and exaggerated sigh. "I only wish I could keep them both. Their thighs are so strong, and their thrusts so deep."

Lettice's cheeks blazed. She straightened and looked back over her bare shoulder at the odious woman. "What do you mean?" Lettice demanded.

238

Giles turned a steely eye upon his companion. "Enough," he said.

Lady Isobel grinned, revealing her wolf's teeth again. She lounged back against a heavy oak table so that her smooth, round breasts were raised, framed to advantage by the low-cut bodice. Lettice had the impression that she displayed herself as much for her benefit as for Giles's. Lettice could not look away from a pulse that was beating in Lady Isobel's long, stretched neck. It was fortunate she carried no sharp weapon. Lady Isobel moved her shoulders sensuously so that her breasts rippled. "If it upsets you, Giles. But I beg you both to remember that if he dies, this lady can treasure his memory with the child."

Lettice sank into a leather-upholstered chair, conscious that her figure had lost much grace with her condition. And that Lady Isobel had had many new gowns since they had fought over the silver lace. As for this lady's insistence that Geoffrey would hang, why, she would not believe it. Geoffrey was well able to take care of himself.

But had Geoffrey really carnally known this lady? Lettice had a vision of his tanned hand parting her long and elegant thighs. Her face flushed. It was no good telling herself that he had known Isobel long before falling in love with his wife.

"We seem to be offering poor company, lady, for you look so grim. But what is your name? Giles will want to address his sister-in-law in a warmer manner."

"Her name is Lettice Clifford." Giles spoke almost absently. His mind was occupied with private thoughts.

"Finch, Finch, my sweet. Now she is a Finch."

Giles raised a threatening brow. "Leave off, Isobel."

"Yes, my dear." She began to walk again. "I see that you are disturbed. The discovery of your brother's peril and the finding of an unexpected kin 'twould try any man's nerves."

"Isobel!"

"Yes, my dear. I am overfond of talk." Then surprisingly she fell silent and ceased her pacing. Standing at rest, her lovely coloring and graceful form were breathtaking. Lettice would have willingly strangled her.

But it was Giles and his silence that frightened her most. Giles, the probable betrayer of his brother. Giles, whose

239

form was so like that she loved, but whose spirit distorted every glance, every gesture.

"Why have you come here?" she asked.

Giles started as though awakened from slumber. "I don't know," he said.

This answer frightened her more. Giles was not the man to leave his estates for a whim. For the Lady Isobel it was something else. The yellow-haired witch went to embrace his muscular shoulders. She smiled into his face. Her artfully arranged curls swept his cheek. "Adventure, my dear. It is a great adventure," she reminded him.

"Speak for yourself, Isobel. I have not your strange tastes."

"Not all." She laughed throatily, throwing her head back so that her long neck was vulnerable. "Some of your tastes are strange indeed, my love. But I do wonder if it was, after all, the Lettice Clifford about whom I have heard so much who has become dear Giles's kin."

Lettice looked up, frowning. She felt herself become a plaything of this perverse lady. But her duty was to seize the chance to see if and why Giles had had his brother abducted. She owed it to Geoffrey.

"Why, whatever have you heard of me?" she asked, fighting to keep her face composed and bland.

"Ah, that is another story." Lady Isobel crossed the room to grasp Lettice's hand and raise her from her chair. Gracefully, she half turned to consult Giles. "May I?" she asked.

He looked at her coldly. "Whatever you wish, Isobel."

"Then we ladies will seek sanctuary above."

Lettice had half a mind to say she would go nowhere with Lady Isobel, but curiosity got the better of her. They were no sooner on the stairs than Isobel halted and placed one slender hand upon Lettice's shoulder.

"Such lovely breasts," she sighed, looking down into Lettice's cleavage. "Of course they are swollen because of the child. You must be careful they are not ruined if you nurse your babe."

Lettice shook the lady's hand free, making no bones about her dislike. "I hardly think it's any concern of yours."

"Ah, but you fascinate me, my dear. You are so pretty. You must tell me how it was that you and Geoffrey be-

240

came lovers. I was astounded to discover Geoffrey had a double in Giles. Though Giles was my lover first, I admit. I could not wait to compare them when Geoffrey returned from France and Venice. Of course there was not time for a real test, for Geoffrey unfortunately came to Virginia."

"You mean he was abducted." Lettice's face flamed.

"Hmm." The Lady Isobel turned and proceeded up the stairs. Lettice could have bitten her tongue. She should not have let Lady Isobel sting her into admitting she knew of the abduction. She would have to watch her step. But she sighed, reflecting that there was much she did not know of Geoffrey, that he had been to the Continent, for instance. Certainly that he had made love to Lady Isobel. Since he was a servant, they had very little chance to talk, and lovemaking had been more compelling.

Lady Isobel led her down a hall and through an empty chamber. Then she knocked at a door.

"Come in," a voice said.

Lettice turned pale. The Lady Isobel opened the door. Inside the chamber Lettice saw the expected light hair and haughty expression as she came face to face from the first time in many months with Philip.

Lettice swayed as though she would faint. She sat down on the great bed, clinging to the bedpost.

"Oh, my dears," Lady Isobel crowed. "How you pale and then burn! You must love each other very much indeed."

Lettice looked at her with shock. Could Lady Isobel be right? Was she still in love with Philip? She had thought that Geoffrey had driven all concern of Philip from her mind. He came across the room to take both her hands in his. "You are even more beautiful," he said. "Your face is softened." Then he looked down upon the bulge of her pregnancy. "Someone has got you with child," he said with horror.

"Indeed," Lady Isobel said. "The lady says that she is married."

"Married?" Philip uttered as though he could not believe the word.

"Don't worry," Lady Isobel said. "In all likelihood she will be a widow soon enough—when Geoffrey is hanged as a rebel."

Lettice's gaze shifted to her. Lady Isobel fingered the

241

brocade of the bed curtains, then went to the window to look down upon the dancers. She returned to touch the lace of Lettice's bodice. Then she felt the velvet of Philip's jerkin. A most restless lady. More and more catlike.

"You do run on, Lady Isobel," Philip said.

"So I have been told," the lady sighed.

Philip frowned. "Perhaps we should walk outside. The house is crowded with refugees."

Lettice stood without speaking.

"What, would you spoil my pleasure?" Lady Isobel said, an exaggerated look of pique upon her face. "Oh, well, there is nothing for it but that I must return to entertain Giles. He sulks below, but I believe I know what will cheer him." Her face took on an absent look as she followed them downstairs. Giles had left the great hall, and she went in search of him.

Philip led Lettice by the hand past the gracefully bowing couples and the laughing spectators outside into a young orchard where a few withering apples and pears still clung to the branches. Philip seated her upon a wooden bench, then stood with one booted foot against the edge to regard her in the autumn sunlight.

"It grieves me that someone has had you before me, Lettice," he said huskily.

Lettice frowned. He was his usual tactless, arrogant self. "After all, Philip, you did have your chance," she said. "And you have no right to address me in this way. We are both married."

"No, you are wrong," he answered. "Mary has died, leaving me with an heir. My father is dead too."

"So now you control both fortunes, yours and hers."

Philip nodded. His features were as fine and handsome as ever, though he seemed to have thickened somewhat about the neck and jaw. "I have everything I want now in life, except you."

Lettice felt a pang. If she had but waited in England, she could have had all that Philip offered. She could have been mistress of a large house, never been raped nor mistreated, nor seen her husband separated from her by war and servitude. She sighed. Had she stayed in England, she would never have known Geoffrey's laughing brown eyes, nor his teasing wit, nor the tenderness of his touch. Nor would she have carried his child.

"But you see, Philip, you cannot have me, for as I warned, I have married someone else."

"Geoffrey Finch, I have no doubt. It was insane of you, Lettice. He has only a small fortune from his mother. And I have heard that he is a servant here to your brother-in-law."

"It seems you receive very good information in England." Lettice flushed. "Geoffrey did not ask to become a servant. He was abducted. And Philip, I must confide to you that I believe Giles has done it. If you do still hold any affection for me, I wish you would help me find out if he has."

An odd expression crossed Philip's fair-skinned face. He seized both her hands and looked directly into her eyes with his light-gray ones. His expression changed to a bland and sincere one.

"Lettice. I don't know how to tell you this. How well do you know your husband?"

"What do you mean, Philip? As you see, I bear his child. And I have known Geoffrey, at least by sight, all my life."

"But how well do you really know him?"

Lettice felt her face blaze. She was aware that Philip had noted her discomfiture. Alas, there was much she did not know of Geoffrey.

"I thought as much, my poor innocent. You see, Giles has confided to me very unhappily the truth of his brother." He hesitated.

"Go on," Lettice said with a sinking feeling.

"Have you not wondered why Geoffrey came here with a false name, or did you not know that he was called Henry Cooper?"

"I did," she said.

"And you know he has spent some time in France and Venice."

"I did not," she said.

"And you never wondered, my poor sweet." He freed one hand to stroke her long, silken hair. He seemed to consider his words carefully. She did not like it that there almost seemed to be a twinkle in his eye. "You see, when Geoffrey returned from his flight to Europe, Giles heard that his brother had been discovered."

"Discovered? What on earth are you talking about?"

"You remember, I am sure, that the Finch brothers were always fond of pranks. Giles sobered somewhat, but Oxford did Geoffrey no good at all. With some of his drunken friends Geoffrey took to the road one night. They all had cloths tied over their faces. They stopped a heavily laden coach that night but soon discovered that it was defended. Geoffrey's two companions perished. Geoffrey himself took two men's lives. You see, my dear Lettice, Giles had his brother abducted to save him from the hangman."

"A very pretty story," a melodic voice cut in. The two of them looked up to see Lady Isobel standing there. "And I am afraid that if Geoffrey escapes the hangman in England, he will only meet him here in Virginia—as a rebel."

Bacon sulked in Gloucester County, one of his strongholds. He had billeted his men inside a large Loyalist house. Some, though, shivered in tents outside. Winter was almost upon them, and little had changed in the colony. Bacon had vowed to be victor and sole possessor of Virginia, but it was clear that so far he had failed. Sir William was still a force to be reckoned with.

Of course it would be necessary to assure the king of Bacon's loyalty and fitness to govern if he were to come into his full powers. But at this great distance from the throne it would be hard for the king to interfere. And Bacon and his men and influential friends at home would present their case in the right light.

Bacon frowned. He watched two drunken wretches outside his window fight over the caresses of one of the women. He must somehow control his men. The looting and drinking and wenching were turning the countryside against them. Only yesterday a man had sought out the general to complain that not only were his house plundered and his sheep destroyed, but that Bacon's troops had barbarously taken prisoner his wife, who was big with child, and beaten her with a cane. They snatched the childbed linen from her hands and forced her and her children out of doors. They had since been made to live on corn and water and lie upon the ground.

Yes, he must enforce discipline, Bacon told himself, before all was lost. He rose from his solitary seat near the fire and opened the small parlor door. Before the huge chimney of the great hall stood a cluster of tattered, serious-faced men. Bacon gestured to the dark-haired Geoffrey Finch, noting that he wore new buckskin breeches and a buff coat, which, till recently, had been the property of a Loyalist.

Geoffrey approached his commander with a questioning look. Bacon closed the door behind him. He gestured toward a table set so that the gray autumn light through the window fell upon it. "I would have you act as the clerk," Bacon said.

Geoffrey sat and picked up a quill. He dipped it into the inkwell. Bacon stood for a moment in thought, fingering his chin.

"Sometimes events race so that I feel I am losing control." He turned to point a finger toward Geoffrey's paper. "Write," he said and began to talk and pace again. "Whereas Sir William Berkeley, Knight, late Governor—make sure it says late Governor—hath in a most barbarous and abominable manner exposed and betrayed our lives, and for greediness or sordid gain did he defer our just defense. . . ," Bacon paused, then the phrases flew from his lips as his face darkened and his gestures grew more excited, "he left the country in a small vessel, it being unknown to all the people to what parts of the world he did repair . . . our army, upon his departure, betaking themselves to the care of the frontiers, did march out against the Indians and obtain a victory. And—ah—as yet not withstanding, Sir William with forces raised in Accomack did invade the country. We protest against him unanimously as a traitor and a most pernicious enemy to the public. . . ."

"And I want you to write this next most plainly: We swear that in all places of His Majesty's Colony of Virginia we will oppose and prosecute him. He hath endeavored to set the heart of our sovereign against us by false information and lies. . . ."

Geoffrey did as he was told, though wondering mightily at the strange turns of his commander's mind. This man of the blazing dark eyes, who was a few years older than himself, seemed to take the least doubt as to him or his cause as a grievous personal attack. Geoffrey kept his face blank and expressionless as he pushed back his chair and stood awaiting further orders.

Bacon read it over, made a few changes, then nodded to himself as though agreeing with an inner voice. "Instruct the men outside to come in to take this oath," he ordered. "Then take a party into the countryside to bring in all the men still here to swear loyalty. I will not be surrounded by men loyal to my cousin, and this oath will be a test."

Geoffrey looked at him for a moment, trying to form a sentence to discourage the commander from this project. If only swearing allegiance to a rather outrageous statement would keep the men loyal, then the fight was indeed lost. But he could do nothing but nod and go out the door. He tightened his buff coat about him, for there was a chill in the air.

The great hall was jammed with humanity. Men stood shoulder to shoulder. The few women remaining were subdued. Guards prevented anyone from leaving. Despite the cold weather it was stifling hot.

Bacon stood upon a stout oak table. There was a feverish look in his dark eyes. Characteristically, one hand rested upon his hip as the other gestured wildly. The men looked up at him, faces frozen in lines of surprise. A few muted whisperings were silenced under Bacon's stare. In his hand he held his proclamation and oath of loyalty. None would be able to leave, he swore, until they had signed.

The paper was then set upon a table near the door, and one by one the men dazedly signed and were released under the watchful eye of the general.

Suddenly all looked up, their tension making them react as one, as the door was opened and a bound figure thrust within. The man struck the floor. A moth-eaten fur cap flew down among the men's booted feet. A dirty cloth that was tied about the man's face slipped away, revealing a livid, puckered scar and eyeless socket. The battered man, no longer young, lay dazed.

A florid giant with wisps of unhealthy-looking hair that seemed to stand up with excitement stepped over the prone form, crying, "We've got 'em, General. He's been spying for both sides."

Bacon still stood upon the table looking down. His eyes darkened, his gestures grew more abrupt and nervous. "A one-eyed spy, eh? I have never trusted him wholly. He looks too sharp with that eye."

246

Jud attempted to rise and to speak, but Wat placed a foot upon his neck.

"Well, my hearts of gold," Bacon cried. "What shall we do with this flea-bitten fellow?"

"Kill 'im," called one drunken old man. He lifted a ceramic bottle of ale to his lips, and the liquid ran down his unshaven chin.

The rest of the room fell silent. Reluctant to play Judas, the men looked away from one another and stared down upon the floor. It was not an occasion that made them proud in their manhood.

"One says we should kill the spy," Bacon said. "And I am of that mind. But I am a fair man. Will any here speak for him?"

Still the men's heads bowed, and they shuffled their feet uncomfortably.

Bacon fixed a look of contempt upon them. "Very well," he said. "I wash my hands of it. Take him out and hang him. Let him be a lesson to all that we will allow no turncoats to live." He gave one of his nervous gestures toward the door, then sprang from off the table and pushed aside the men in his path to return to his private parlor.

"I'll enjoy hanging him," Wat said. "And I'll not forget the one who protects him—his friend, the silk-and-satin man."

But Bacon did not hear him.

It was twilight when Geoffrey and his party returned, turning away from the river and riding through the trees. They brought with them two old men and a boy to take Bacon's oath. None spoke. There was only the sound of saddles creaking, horses snorting and hooves upon fallen leaves.

It seemed a senseless kind of war to Geoffrey, but then much of his life since leaving England had been senseless. The only thing with any meaning was the woman he had taken to wife. Soon she would have his child. He tried to imagine it and prayed she was safe at Albright's Point.

He wondered if, as he had many times in the past, if James had received his message. He had told him to answer care of the landlord in Jamestown. God alone knew where the landlord had fled after the burning.

Geoffrey raised one arm, and the party halted. Through

the twilight he noted a curious shape among the trees. A feeling of dread swept over him. It appeared to be a hanged man.

A wave of weariness engulfed Geoffrey. He ordered the rest of the party forward, but he himself sat at rest in his saddle, rubbing his brow with a tired hand. Then he rode to discover, almost against his will, upon whom Bacon had taken his vengeance.

Unmanly tears filled his eyes as he looked upon the ruined face, which was distorted even more by the hangman's noose. The fading light softened the rumpled old clothes and the horror of the single darting eye. Thus was the end of a man once supremely civilized, if unwashed.

Geoffrey heard a twig snap behind him, and a voice, almost soft in the quiet air, spoke out, "He was your friend, wan't he, silk-and-satin man?"

Geoffrey pulled his mount about and searched the shadows until he made out the huge, misshapen figure of Wat. An old cloak was wrapped about him so that in the dusk he looked like a giant bat.

"No one defies me," the sullen voice came. "And your lady lost me my place. Not that I don't like soldiering as well. But no one goes against me if I says so. I told myself you owed me—as did your lady until I made her pay."

Geoffrey stiffened. He checked his saddle holster and felt his pistol.

"She did not tell you I made her pay with a thrust between the legs, eh?" And Wat, who never smiled, laughed hollowly. "I dragged her in the mud. 'Twas only this dead dog here who stopped me from taking more. Did she not tell you, silk-and-satin man? I thought of you much at the time."

Geoffrey had a quick impression of Lettice, all smooth and graceful, full of silken curves and large violet eyes with endless depths. He swallowed as rage rose within his throat to choke him. He forced words from between clenched teeth. "I have beat you once, Wat. I will do it again."

Wat's hollow laugh sounded once more through the dusky shadows. "I'll meet you over there under the oak tree. I would not want the general to hear our fight and interrupt us." Then he lapsed into his usual, sullen silence. His eyes were upon Geoffrey.

As he gathered up his reins, Geoffrey's hands trembled

with a desire to choke the life out of Wat. Grimly, Geoffrey rode into a clump of saplings and young pine, a blaze of red rage half blinding him. His emotions made him careless, almost so careless that he failed to hear a click behind him. Quickly he reined his horse and moved aside. A pistol ball sped through the semi-darkness, grazing his shoulder.

Geoffrey turned in his saddle, cocked his pistol, took aim and shot. Wat made a large target. He crashed to the earth like a fallen buck. Geoffrey rode over to look down on him. It was still light enough to see the pool of blood pouring from his heart.

"A very interesting drama," a drawling voice said.

Geoffrey recognized Lawrence. The gentleman stepped through the gloom to stand before Geoffrey's horse. "Wat is better dead, I think," he said. "He would have all of us killing each other did he live. But come, my friend, I will help you cut down your friend to bury him."

Geoffrey nodded, and the two of them busied themselves about this unpleasant work until it was done. It was pitch-black with a few stars overhead by the time they had finished. Geoffrey muttered a silent prayer. He was filled with a bleak despair.

"I must mark the spot well," Geoffrey murmured, "so that Sal, his wife, may find it."

"Do that, my friend," Lawrence said, clapping a hand upon his shoulder and leading him back into the hall. "But he was the governor's spy, you know. I hope you are more loyal than your companion."

"I don't know what I am," Geoffrey said.

"An honest man, at least," Lawrence replied.

It was unseasonably cold, and though the year had been one of drought, rain had plagued Bacon and his forces of late. Some blamed Indian sorcery.

And Bacon lay dying. The men not out on patrol were clustered in whispering knots; the women were all gone. It would be an ignoble death. A bloody flux wasted the general, and his body bred such swarms of vermin they could only be destroyed by throwing his shirts into the fire as often as he shifted himself.

"I see God's hand," said one grizzled man in a low monotone. He looked fearfully back over his shoulder as though he thought if God did not strike him, Lawrence or another of Bacon's most loyal men might. "At least a thousand times a day the general swore 'God damn my blood.' Now God has so infected his blood that it breeds lice in such number that for 20 days he never washed his shirts, but burned them."

A clergyman prisoner huddled against the scarred panels of the wall. He had barely escaped Bacon's hangman, and now he muttered with a half-smile, "Bacon is dead. I am sorry at my heart that lice and flux should take the hangman's part."

"Shh," the grizzled man said. "He's not dead yet."

A door banged. Heavy footsteps pounded down the stairs as a swarthy, squat messenger came from out of the sickroom to the corner some distance from the fire where Lawrence and Geoffrey stood. He pumped his short, muscular arms self-importantly as he walked.

"He wishes to know if frigates and forces have arrived from England," the messanger said. "He is much unquiet in his mind."

Lawrence sighed, dipping a pinch of snuff and sneezing violently before speaking in his bored and drawling way. "Tell him no. Though if more ships have arrived in Chesapeake Bay, we would have no way of knowing. And," Lawrence leaned closer to the messenger, "let the men plainly know that the general is still lucid and not breathing his last. We shall have trouble enough holding this rabble together until the commander dies."

The squat man nodded, then returned whence he had come.

"How long will it be?" Geoffrey breathed through lips that barely moved.

"Not long at all," Lawrence answered in the same manner. "And soon after, all will be lost for us."

"We have gambled and lost."

"But we must wait till the body is cold before we can conclude all this. Bacon intended to resist the king's forces if they arrived."

"Surely not!" Geoffrey said, startled.

They heard the messenger's determined footsteps running toward them again. Was this it?

"The general would have you make sure the guards are well posted about the house," he said.

* * *

When the death came, the inner circle of Bacon's men kept it secret. Instead, they left the crowded great hall one by one to allay suspicion. Grim-faced, dry-eyed, they spirited their leader's body to a secret hiding place near a grove of cedar. There they gathered, draped in dark cloaks, voices hushed in the dead of night. Geoffrey was among them.

" 'Twill not be well enough hid," Lawrence judged. "If Sir William's men find the body, they will hang it as long as there is enough to suspend from a rope."

Without complaint the men picked up the shrouded body and walked farther for some half-hour through uncultivated land. Finally, discovering a clear space beneath a large cypress, Lawrence was satisfied. Geoffrey carried a spade and was designated gravedigger. It was the second grave he had dug in a short space of time. The first he had made with grief and respect. He was unsure what he felt about Bacon's finish, and too weary to care. A chill light drizzle had fallen for most of the day so that the ground was softened. Geoffrey could hear others hacking about in the brush as they prepared for the funeral. A silent fellow relieved Geoffrey at his digging.

The men scratched together flint and steel to light torches of pitch-pine branches, which blazed up brilliantly until the setting was bathed in a warm and glowing light, though the shadows lay deep. The body was lowered into the grave without a coffin.

Then each man, acting as a family member, seized a freshly cut bough. One by one they slowly walked to the edge of the pit to drop their boughs upon the body. They stood about the grave, staring down at what could be seen of the white gleam of the shroud. Then they looked at one another, uncertain who would deliver the oration. Lawrence stepped forward to the head of the grave.

"Let us say simply, 'May he rest in peace,' " he said.

"Amen," the men responded together. Each in turn extinguished his torch in the earth.

Blinded by the sudden loss of light, Geoffrey was too dazed for a moment to begin the work of recovering the grave. He heard men moving about him as they left to walk back to their quarters, but he knew that someone remained beside him. When his eyes adjusted to the darkness, he saw that it was Lawrence.

"This is the end of all for me," Lawrence said. Yet though his brown cavalier locks were disordered and his well-cut clothes shabby, his face still wore its arrogant look. He would carry it to the grave.

Geoffrey answered him with silence. He, too, felt this to be the low point of his life. When Captain Quince had threatened to kill him, there had only been himself to consider. But now there was Lettice—and very soon the babe. He sighed. A pretty husband he had proved.

The walk back through the penetrating chill of the night seemed endless, but though their bodies were stiff with cold, neither was anxious to enter the great hall again. The drizzle had grown lighter, icy. Here and there a few snow-flakes fell. When they burst into the warm and lighted room, they found a faction of the men clustered excitedly about one Joseph Ingram, who was Bacon's lieutenant general, not long in Virginia.

"Is the general buried, then?" Ingram called.

"Buried?" Lawrence asked. "I don't know what you mean. He must be dead before we can bury him."

But the men about Ingram, a particularly loutish lot, continued to watch him with unblinking stares. Obviously Ingram planned to take command. Others were coming down the stairs and from outside to stand in the circle about him.

"The lion has no sooner made his exit, but the ape steps upon the stage," Lawrence whispered.

And Geoffrey thought with honesty that the country, which had for some time been guided by a company of knaves, now was to be governed by fools.

A youth of some 14 or 15 years, his face gray with fatigue, approached them. "Mr. Lawrence, the general is not dead like they say, is he? I do not believe God would let him die."

Lawrence hesitated. "Nay," he said finally. "He is not dead."

The boy smiled, then he went to lie down by the fire.

"He will not serve Ingram, it seems," Lawrence said. "But we are divided into further factions every day. God knows what the troops in the other counties are doing. And the king's forces will arrive soon."

"I must confess to you that I would leave this faltering war had I anywhere to go," Geoffrey admitted.

Lawrence's eyes sharpened. "What? Turn traitor?" Then he laughed. "Traitor to what? I am become traitor to my own dream of becoming a great lord here in this new land. I, too, would leave had I anywhere to go."

"I would find my wife," Geoffrey said.

Lawrence paused midway in the act of dipping snuff, bemused. "Yes. The women make it hard." Then he completed his act and sneezed again.

They jerked about as a hiss was heard. Some of Ingram's men were moulding bullets and had just emptied the hot lead pellets into a bucket of cold water. Ingram looked across the room at Lawrence. His face had a look that strove for dominance.

"Ah," Lawrence said quietly to Geoffrey. "I think that this is the final act for me. It is time for me to bow out."

"Where will you go?"

"I will disappear." Lawrence picked up the edge of his cloak to mask himself like a stage villain. "It may be that I shall disappear in the direction of Carolina where I have cousins. Then the name of Richard Lawrence will be heard no more in Virginia—nor in Carolina, either, for I will disguise myself."

"It is a difficult journey. And it is snowing," Geoffrey said.

"I shall take a few stout companions. Will you join me?"

Geoffrey shook his head regretfully. "My wife will be brought to childbed soon."

"That way ends the plans of many a man," Lawrence said.

Word reached the men in Gloucester County of Drummond's death upon the gallows. He'd been executed by Sir William within two hours of his capture. Rumor had it that the Duke of York had sworn to hang Bacon and his men. But Bacon's flux had saved him from the noose. Some days later Geoffrey and Lawrence, with four other desperate men, set out from Ingram's rebels. The small group traveled together a day before Geoffrey parted from them. Wearily hunched in his saddle, Geoffrey watched as all who were left of Bacon's most loyal followers marched away ankle-deep in snow. They were headed toward an uppermost plantation. Heavily armed, they led their laden horses. Geoffrey watched until the large, damp flakes blotted them from view. Then he turned his mount toward Albright's Point.

Lettice sat sewing close by the fire in the house at Accomack. She glanced up now and then at the wintry sky through the casement. Molly stood before her, glaring in a way that ill suited a maidservant.

"You be drifting into trouble, mistress. You'll rue the day you trust one sweet word from Sir Philip. And Lady Isobel be a snake. And Giles such a villain that I wonder how he was born by the same woman as Geoffrey."

"Hush, Molly." Lettice moistened a silk to rethread her needle. She was making over a deep-green gown that Lady Isobel had given her to cut down. The silk was so lustrous that the highlights were bluish, while the shadows black. Lettice's prettiest things had become tight in the bodice, though she loosened the lacings.

"I'll not hush," Molly insisted, stamping a diminutive foot. "Not while you head into danger. Do not let the babe lull you to sleep. Think of what Geoffrey would say."

Lettice sighed, her face grave. "Philip says that we were right about Geoffrey when we first saw him bound in a coach. He is a murderer and will be hanged if he goes to England."

"Mistress!" Molly placed her hands on her hips. "What Sir Philip says be of no account. What does your heart tell you?"

Lettice was about to silence her maid, but instead she sighed again. What, indeed, did her heart tell her? She was afraid to face it squarely, yet when she listened to its dictates, she was moved to tell Philip and the world that Geoffrey was her husband and she loved him no matter what crime he may have committed.

"I say again, mistress, you will rue the day you trust one sweet word from Sir Philip."

"Sir Philip has been my friend all my life, Molly," Lettice said, biting off a thread.

"Will he love you, mistress, once he has had the use of you? Nay, it be your denial that keeps him hot."

Lettice flushed hotly. "Enough!"

"But, mistress, the time be growing short. Soon you will be too far gone to travel."

Lettice looked down at her hands. "You are right,

Molly. But I keep thinking that if I stay here, I will hear something of Geoffrey. And besides, I do not want you to place yourself back into Gower's hands."

Molly bowed her curly head for a moment. "There be no other way, mistress," she said finally. "Staying here won't help your husband. And John will never find me in Accomack."

Lettice mused, still lethargic. "I wonder if I can persuade Gower to let me buy you back. Though he will ask a great price." She brightened. "Perhaps I can sell the queen's pearls."

"I will not ask it, mistress," Molly said, her eyes beginning to hope.

"We shall see," her mistress said. She fastened down a last bit of fragile white lace at the neckline of the dress. Then she looked up at Molly and smiled. "The babe tries to persuade me that all is well and I can rest here. I have been sunk into lethargy too long. We shall go."

Molly dipped a curtsy. Her blue eyes shone bright. "Thank you, mistress. But swear to me first you'll never say a word of this to Sir Philip, nor anyone else."

"It is well not to tell Giles, I think. Geoffrey never trusted him. But perhaps Philip could help find us a sloop. Otherwise I confess I can see no way of traveling."

"We don't need Sir Philip," Molly said triumphantly. "I have already found a sloop on its way up the river. And men to steal your baggage from the house. If you sit quietly through the day, mistress, you can meet me at midnight at the river's edge."

"You take much upon yourself, Molly," Lettice said. But she smiled again. It was well to have the way smoothed, for the child within her told her constantly to rest.

Nevertheless, as the door closed behind her maid, Lettice thought it would be well to speak to Philip at once. She might hear more of the abduction. She was not satisfied with what he had told her. And she did not have long to wait, for Philip came knocking at her door.

"Ah, Philip," she said. "I would ask you some things before—"

"Before what, my dear?" He fixed a piercing gray eye upon her.

But Lettice decided that she did not want to speak to him after all.

It was difficult for Lettice to judge when midnight had arrived, for there were no church bells to sound here. She had laid out a heavy wool cloak, and she took it up now to wrap about herself, moving quickly and quietly, for there were other women asleep in the room. Regretfully, Lettice must leave without thanking her host, who had rescued them. But in fact he must be pleased whenever any of the refugees left, since it drained his resources severely to feed them.

Downstairs the heavy bolt was stiff, and it squealed in the darkness as she drew it out. Did a shadow move out in the garden? She stood listening. Were those footsteps? She hoped the men had hidden her baggage well by now.

But there was no crime in leaving the house. She was not a thief. She flung the door open. The grass was cold and wet, and a thick fog arose from the frosty ground. It was thicker still over the river. She could barely see the sloop near the shore. She saw nothing moving. Biting her lip, she was tempted to snuggle back into the warmth of her chamber.

But Molly, her faithful servant, was right. She could not tarry here. Molly had promised to wait on the bank, but there was no sign of her. Yet she might already be on board with Lettice's box.

With a sigh, Lettice drew her cloak close and set forth, thankful that she had worn her stoutest shoes in the cold damp. The fog seemed to close in, enhancing her sense of unease. Wherever had the silly wench got to? The sloop bobbed at its moorings like some ghost ship. Lettice's throat felt dry. She feared to call out.

Staring about, she at last dimly saw a dark, cloaked shape heading toward her. She stepped toward it, anxious to be under way. But no, the figure was too tall. And then she saw the light shoulder-length hair, which was dripping with moisture, and the damp aquiline features. A flash of alarm swept through her.

"Philip," she said. "You surprise me."

He reached for her hand with a cold, damp one. "The boatmen have happily changed their plans—upon receiving the proper amount of coin. Did you think to meet your maid, my dear? She waits upon the *Anne and Mary* with the rest of us."

256

Lettice felt herself go white with shock. "The *Anne and Mary*? Why, that is Captain Quince's ship."

"Why, so it is," Philip said, leading her away.

XV

Charles sat close to the great-hall fire, feeling dyspeptic and ill at ease. Almost without ceasing, he dabbed at his long, red nose with his handkerchief. Finally he blew into the linen cloth with an irritated blast. Physical ills were bad enough, but he had other worries too. Confound it, the governor must conclude this mess in the colony before they were all ruined. The tobacco market was all but destroyed now. There seemed no doubt that Ingram and his rebels were finished, still. . . .

Outside a wind howled. A deluge—half rain and half snow—assaulted his casement. For this reason it took him some time to hear the pounding upon the door. Dorothy was asleep, Chloe had gone to her cabin, and he did not keep a manservant in the house overnight. With a sigh that was half a groan he rose stiffly and shuffled past the stairs, past the parlor door to open the heavy door to the outside.

For a moment he did not recognize Captain Quince. Slushy snow clung to the broad shoulders and half-grown beard. The captain entered, laughing heartily. He doffed his black hat, unconcernedly shedding mud and water upon the floor that Dorothy prided herself in having kept spotless.

"This is a surprise." Charles truly relished company from the outside world. "I had no idea you were in these parts. Come sit by my fire." Walking unsteadily, Charles led the way to the cheerful corner where the fire sparkled. He blew a final blast into his handkerchief, then tucked it inside his ruffled sleeve.

Quince sat with a grunt.

"How did you come here?" Charles asked. "We do not

often see visitors, especially in the midst of bad weather and with the rebels below."

"I've three men upon a sloop. 'Twas as perilous a passage as any I've sailed." The captain showed his strong teeth. But it was not precisely a smile.

Charles chuckled. "Then you'll want some warmed ale, or a bit of rum."

"Rum, d'you say?" Quince's eyes glistened.

Charles poured him a tumbler, and though his own stomach was queasy, he poured a drink for himself. Once seated, Charles regarded his guest with expectation through watery blue eyes. His left eye turned in more than usual as it did in moments of excitement.

"Well, sir," Charles said. "What have you to sell me tonight? It must be something special to bring you through the storm?"

"Sell?" Quince laughed a low, gurgling sound deep in his throat. Drops of melted snow fell from the ends of his beard. "Why, nothing to sell, Squire Albright. I've come here to . . . buy." He dragged out the last word so seductively that it grated in his throat.

"Buy?" The word made Charles uneasy. "What would you buy, my dear Captain?"

Quince sucked at his glass with a gross and vulgar sound, then exhaled with pleasure. "What I have already sold. One Henry Cooper, known in England as Geoffrey Finch."

Charles began to tremble with distress, for he would not offend so good a man of business as Captain Quince. But he knew not what the offer signified, and he preferred things to be predictable and controlled.

"My dear Captain," he began timidly. "It seems you will be disappointed. The man you seek has fled to the rebels."

Quince nodded his shaggy, dark head as though he had half expected this. "I have heard it rumored so. But the war ends, and sooner or later he is bound to return."

"That may be, but . . . I am very short of servants with all the trouble. . . ." Charles looked acutely uncomfortable. "Well, I may as well admit it to you, Quince. My wife tells me the man has become a family connection. It is most embarrassing. I have no love for the man, nor for my pesky sister-in-law. They've caused me to lose both servants and horses. Much more and I shall be ruined."

"To be sure." Quince laughed, though his bloodshot eyes

narrowed. "He is a most insinuating fellow. I should have watched him more closely on my ship." Quince's hairy hand reached to his belt where a moneybag was tied. Smiling, he poured a pile of silver and gold coins near his by-now empty tumbler onto the table. He drew back his hand, which cast the shadow of a huge spider upon the wall.

"It is a great deal of money, you see, Squire. Much more than you gave me."

Squire Albright did indeed see. His eyes widened at the sight of that much coin, and he wondered at his former servant's sudden value. Silently he peered at the captain, who looked quite blurry by now, as Charles's eyes crossed more and more with stress and drink.

Quince pushed the pile of money toward him, whispering, " 'Tis for the delivery of the man called Henry Cooper, live, or if misfortune strikes, dead."

Squire Albright had been about to reach out to test the coin, but Quince's last words gave him pause. "Dead?" he blurted. "What means this, sir, 'dead?' "

Quince made no answer; he merely jingled two coins together in his fist and closed one reddened eye in an elaborate wink.

Charles swayed to his feet. "Dead, say you? What do you think I am, a Judas? I am fond enough of coin, sir, but this smacks of something much against the law. The magistrate shall want to know of this."

Quince's face turned purple. He had misjudged the man. "Do you threaten, Sir Charles?"

Charles's bony forehead wrinkled. "If you offer me what no magistrate would swallow, and speak of delivery to you of a dead man for coin."

"You will not take care of your new family connection?"

Charles paused for a moment. He was for a fact angered at his former servant. And he was in need of coin to help overcome his recent reverses. Yet someone wanted Lettice's husband removed very badly. Charles smelled money here. No, he would not be a fool and involve himself in this unsavory matter. And his sister-in-law, wherever the silly girl may have got herself to, might in fact be carrying the heir to something of value should the father not survive the rebellion. Yes, it were better to go with caution.

Charles shook his head.

Without ceremony, Quince grabbed the bottle of rum from the table and raised it to his lips, drinking so rapidly a trickle ran down his chin. Charles was startled to see the paleness beneath the captain's weather-beaten skin. Could so strong and brutal a man know fear?

Quince set the bottle down and steadied himself. "No, Squire Charles," he said, rising to his feet. "I won't let you cry off. They are very hard people, you see. Harder than any seaman I ever knew. . . ."

"What's this?" Puzzled, Charles was beginning to grow frightened of his guest.

"They are mad folk. 'Tis not the love of coin alone that drives them. But something else."

These words made Charles more convinced. "It sounds very perilous, Captain. I will have nothing to do with it."

"What must I do, then?" The captain's face showed true distress.

"Report the offer to a magistrate," Charles said coldly.

"Report. . . ." The captain's bloodshot eyes flamed. "Report! Are you mad, Albright? Think you I could explain my plight to a magistrate so tidily? Explain to him where I have got all these servants that you and the other planters so delight to buy?"

Charles swayed once more, his head pounding. There were only a few inches between the two men. "I think, Captain, I must ask you to return to your sloop. I know of no illegalities in your trade. If they exist, they are your own affair."

The captain swelled. He reached two meaty hands to grab Charles by the arms, and he began to shake him. "You know of no . . . why, you idiot. . . . You are as mad as any Tom O'Bedlam. 'Tis a convenient ignorance, isn't it! Isn't it!" He shook Charles especially hard. " 'Tis nice the way you planters close your eyes in a way we seamen cannot."

"Please, Captain," Charles whispered. His head pounded, his stomach lurched, he felt himself growing faint. "Please."

"And now you beg!" The captain released Charles suddenly and shoved him away with the heel of his hand.

Charles's bony legs buckled, he sagged and fell back. He struck his head upon the andiron and lay still in a heap on the floor.

262

Quince straightened in surprise. Some of the crimson faded from his face. "That's done it, Quince," he told himself. "Best hurry away." He shot out an arm to scrape up the coins, spilling some on the floor. Then he burst through the door, not even stopping to close it from the howling wind and rain.

"Well, lads," he told his sailors upon the dark and rain-swept deck of the sloop. "We sail in storm tonight. We must be far from here by morning."

The door was still open when Geoffrey arrived. He had told himself he was a fool to travel on so stormy a night, but he was drawn by Lettice. The open door disturbed him, for Squire Albright and his wife were very careful people. Geoffrey shut it softly, and the candles in the hall ceased their wild dancing. He had only taken two steps into the room when he saw Charles sprawled on the floor. Quickly Geoffrey came to kneel at his side, feeling for his pulse. Charles was not dead, but deeply unconscious. There were a few coins scattered about on the floor near him. Geoffrey picked up one of them, deep in thought.

It was at this moment that Dorothy let herself down the stairs. Her thin hand was clutching at her thin chest, her nightgown trailing. Her expression was flushed and dazed as though she were not fully awake. Her eyes widened slightly as she saw Charles full-length on the floor and Geoffrey fingering the coins. The bridge of her nose whitened with fear, and her pale eyes seemed to start from her head.

"What have you done to him?" she cried out hollowly.

"Done to him?" Geoffrey dropped the coins with surprise.

"Did you think to rob him?" she half sobbed. "And after you have seduced my sister?"

"Where is Lettice?" Geoffrey rose, one hand extended to reassure her.

Dorothy shrank. "Do not think you can molest me because I am all alone. I have all my life feared something like this, especially when father. . . . He would return drunk from some tavern wench . . . Lettice was never afraid . . . she took after the Cliffords. But I was. I thought to be safe with a sober man like Charles. But Lettice has destroyed it all . . . and you. . . ."

"Where is Lettice?" Geoffrey asked, thinking his wife might be able to calm her sister's growing hysteria.

"Gone! Like all our servants. We haven't even a decent overseer! And now Charles. . . ."

Geoffrey reddened. He had never been over fond of Dorothy, yet he had never meant to injure her. Clutching her nightgown more closely about her, she was sliding down the stairs, her back against the paneled wall. When she drew opposite Geoffrey, she stared at him. Once more Geoffrey reached out to reassure her.

Dorothy shrank away, then ran screaming down the hall to the door. "Help! Oh, help! Your master is killed!" she cried into the stormy night as she disappeared in the direction of the servants' quarters.

Geoffrey cursed. Foolish woman. How would he explain this nonsense to Lettice? Squire Charles could well die for all the attention his wife gave him. Yet Charles was not dead, it seemed. Since Geoffrey had no desire to encounter the servants, it was best to depart. Running to his horse, he vaulted into the saddle and headed into the forest. He knew an old cabin deep in the woods where he could rest for a day with any luck. Then he must set out in search of his wife. He hoped the governor's hangman did not catch him first.

Meanwhile, he prayed Charles would recover his wits soon and explain to Dorothy that her new brother-in-law was innocent of any attack.

Dorothy returned, followed by three stout men. She had them wrap Charles in a blanket and carry him upstairs. There she sat chaffing his wrists and massaging his forehead until at last he opened one eye slightly. But he seemed to scarce recognize her. And he seemed unable to move his limbs or talk.

Tomorrow she must send someone for a doctor—and a magistrate.

Four hundred English and Negroes were garrisoned at Colonel John West's brick house. Word had been received that West's Point, on the other side of the York, had already surrendered under Ingram's orders. Captain Thomas Grantham, master of the ship *Concord,* was serving as go-between for Sir William and the rebels. He sought a ceasefire until such time as troops and officials of His Majesty arrived on Virginia soil.

John and Ajax crept out of their icy tent to thaw their chilled fingers near the fire. They were a study in contrasts. John's fair skin had lost much of its summer color, but his hair was still sun bleached on top. Ajax's ebony skin no longer gleamed with health, and his black hair grew wild and unruly, offending his naturally neat and precise soul. He was forever seeking someone with shears to cut it for him, but it had become a secondary matter in the war.

"Since the rebels are promising freedom to slaves and servants, you'd think they would find a place by the fire inside for us," he complained.

John looked up at the house that the men jokingly called Bacon's Castle. The ornamental brickwork proclaimed it to be solid and comfortable. Smoke rose from the many chimney pots. It would be warm. "Nay, we be gulled, I think," he said. " 'Tis the richer men bask inside. We poorer folk remain on the bottom."

When Grantham came clattering up on his horse, the door of Bacon's Castle burst open, and some of the officers stood tensely on the porch with drawn pistols. Grantham smiled and diplomatically held up his hands to prove he was defenseless.

"Stay where you are, Grantham," an officer called. "We know you've betrayed us."

"No, gentlemen," he answered. "I think you will discover that I have saved your lives."

"Saved our lives?"

"He's a spy for Sir William, 'tis plain." The gentlemen were growing desperate and disheartened.

"Don't listen to 'em, sirs," one old servant called from the tents, wiping his frostbitten nose on a ragged sleeve. " 'Tis well enough for you, but we'll be back with our masters with even more years."

Discomfited, the gentlemen looked from one to another of their fellows, knowing not what to say, and each afraid to speak first.

"Never fear," Grantham called. "I am authorized to offer pardon to the freemen, and freedom to the Negroes and servants."

Shamefaced, the gentlemen, each of whom in years to come would never admit to being the first to surrender, lowered their pistols. They beckoned to Grantham to dismount and come in.

As the door shut behind him, John and Ajax met each other's eyes, not daring to hope that Grantham's words were true.

"Freedom for slaves and servants?" Ajax asked.

"If only Molly could be free," John said. "She marched alongside us, after all."

"You can't believe what them gentlemen says," the old servant said, approaching the fire. "Grantham's face be too smooth, I'm thinking."

John's eyes met Ajax's. The two men nodded agreement. They could not really believe this luck. Warily they watched Grantham reappear into the cold, wintry afternoon. He began to direct the removal of the weapons. Some of his own sailors were marching up to aid him. Grantham produced a barrel of brandy for the men in the tents. Warmed by drink, they hastened to dismantle the arsenal until a great heap of hundreds of muskets and fowling pieces lay on the riverbank. Then the men began loading a chest of powder, a thousand weight of bullets and shot and three great guns onto the ship. It had taken the rebels months to assemble all this. But Grantham, alone with no weapon but his tongue, had seized it all.

Some of the servants and Negroes who still had desperate memories of their pasts refused to surrender their arms, even as they saw their comrades head toward home.

"What? Will you not?" Grantham asked John, who would not give up his weapon. "Then how will you live? You are only a few blacks and 20 English servants. You cannot take on the whole of the colony and His Majesty's forces alone."

" 'Tis true, but I still will not surrender," John said.

"There's nothing worse than slavery," Ajax added, "since there's no end to it."

Grantham stood with his legs apart in a seaman's stride. He sighed with irritation. "I really must ask you to leave this place," he said. The Negroes and servants stood mulishly silent, only moving closer and closer together until they presented a solid wall of obstinacy. They stared at Grantham, and he at them. Then a grizzled black with three front teeth missing smiled and pointed to a large sloop nearby.

"We can leave by river, Cap'n. We take sloop'n go on up river. There be some of Bacon's men there."

Grantham looked thoughtful, then nodded. "If you insist on going down river, I will tow you."

The men conferred for a moment, however the thought of a free ride appealed to them. But when John and Ajax climbed aboard the sloop, they found themselves staring into the mouths of some of Grantham's 30 great guns and the triumphant smiles of his sailors.

"He's foxed us," Ajax said.

A day later, unarmed and footsore, slave and servant began the wintry walk back to Albright's Point. They met many others walking and riding home, some still armed and hoping their absence among the rebels would not be noticed.

"Now I be neither free nor have a wife," John said. "Nor do I know when I'll ever see Molly again."

Governor Berkeley sat studying papers and reports on board Captain John Martin's ship at Tindall's Point. He nodded coldly when the rebel Ingram was ushered into his cabin. Bacon's successor sank down on one knee before His Majesty's representative in Virginia.

"I'm here to receive your pardon, Sir William," Ingram said.

"I do not intend to give it," Sir William responded. "I shall hang you instead."

All that could be seen of Molly were her tumbled curls and the dull-brown cloak that was wrapped about her. For a moment Lettice's heart stopped within her. Then she saw that the little maid who was lying so still upon the bed did in truth yet breathe. Molly slept soundly—curiously in the same cabin on the *Anne and Mary* they had occupied before. It was as though the events of these many months past had never occurred. Only Philip stood with a lantern at Lettice's elbow in the doorway.

Lettice crossed the short space of floor to shake Molly's shoulders. There was no response. Lettice turned, accusing, "I will never forgive you for this, Philip. She is drugged."

"She was very restless, sweeting," he said with a cold smile. He seized his old love's hand to press to his lips.

Lettice pulled her hand free, chilled. Looking about, she

did not even bother to answer him. All her belongings, including the gowns she had made with Lady Isobel's aid, lay about the cabin. Once more she tried to arouse Molly, who still lay limp as a sack of flour.

Lettice fixed angry eyes upon her abductor, wondering how Molly and she would get out of this new trouble. It was hard to be frightened of Philip, since they had toddled as babes in leading strings together. No, it was more wrath she felt than fear. Were she a man, she would have challenged him to fight.

"My dear, I think you should rest. Your, ah, condition." Philip avoided looking at her belly. Her pregnancy obviously distressed him and cooled his ardor.

Lettice sat upon a joint stool, pushing back her hood so that it fell about her shoulders. She was tired—it was well past midnight—but she would not submit meekly.

"Explain yourself, Philip. I have not been overfond of some things you have done in your life, but never have I seen you stoop to anything as bad as this."

He raised his hand with its narrow wrist to his head as though her words might pierce his temple and give him a headache. "Please, sweeting. We can talk in the morning." He pulled a splinter from the doorframe and lit her candle from his lantern.

"Philip, by tomorrow I expect to be on my way to my sister's house with my maid at my side. I will leave as soon as Molly is revived."

"Do not excite yourself, Lettice. All will be well. You will see." He bent to plant a soft kiss upon her hairline.

Lettice found herself gasping with anger. "Philip, would you kidnap me and my maid only to tell me that we will talk in the morning!"

"Sweeting!" He raised her hand passionately to his lips.

"Oh, stop, Philip." Snatching her hand away, she stood and whirled about, her mantle whipping around her. "Abduction, it seems, has become a habit among your circle of friends."

His face grew grave. "I could not have you steal away, Lettice. I have thought of you long and traveled far to see you." He slid his hands down her body, wincing as he encountered the by now enormous swelling of her pregnancy.

"I can see I attract you less while I carry the child," she said. "But pray you understand that the child is a part of me, a very important part, the more so since the father may be imperiled."

Philip's eyes narrowed, and his fine-boned face turned white. "Do not speak of that rogue."

In her heart she felt a kind of pain that Geoffrey was not there to defend her. She sighed, daring not to admit that they should never have married—nor bedded. It had been mad, every bit of it. Yet the strength and sweetness of his body returned to her even now.

Philip sensed her thoughts and gripped her shoulders. "Stop thinking of him!" he hissed. "Or if you must, picture him with his face all purple and his tongue lolling out, for he will be hanged."

"I cannot believe that he will be hanged, Philip. But if it should happen, then I must be by his side. He must not die alone. Let me return to find him. Please."

His fingers bruised her wristbone. "Giles has remained on shore. He will see to his brother's consolation."

Impatiently, she pulled herself free. There was no consolation in Philip's touch. "How very good of him, seeing how thick he is with the captain who carried Geoffrey off."

Philip fought to control his tone. "I have explained that to you, sweeting. Besides, Giles must stay behind, because he has invested part of the family fortune in trade to Virginia. This trade will bring him more wealth than land would."

"A pretty trade—that involves human flesh," Lettice spat. "Pray find someone to help carry Molly ashore. I will not wait until she awakes."

The lines about Philip's mouth tightened, and when he spoke, it was with a sob of rage. "I lose all patience with you. Tomorrow we will speak of it, but no sooner. And let me warn you, my dear, that a very large man is guarding the shore side. I hardly think the man you call your husband will try to rescue you here."

"Then tell your good friend Giles to beware. Geoffrey will not be easy to hang."

Philip came to her once again. He gripped her arm painfully. "Do not speak of him. I will never forgive him for having you first." Philip's eyes glittered with an emotion that actually made her gasp and shrink from him. Then he fought to draw a more civilized mask over his finely sculpted features. "In time I will teach you to respect what

I tell you about him," he said. "Obviously you are still too angry at me for marrying Mary Wells to listen. In time you will see."

How typically self-centered of Philip to ascribe her feelings of love and concern toward Geoffrey to jealousy about himself and Mary. "Philip, you are impossible. . . ," Lettice began, but he raised a hand to cut her off.

"No. Rest tonight. We will speak tomorrow." He kissed her briefly and then departed.

Lettice sat hugging the bulk of her pregnancy. There was no way she could see to escape with Molly unconscious. Then she started up as a great commotion arose upon the deck. She opened her door to peer out past the wide shoulders of her guard. In the black night Captain Quince and three ruffians appeared through the mist on the shore. One held a lantern high. She heard splashing sounds as a boat set out for them. With a sigh she closed the door. She had no desire to see the odious captain again. Surely she must make Philip see reason tomorrow.

There was a bottle of wine and a cup on her table. She would have a sip. But she set it down again. It could be drugged. She bent to take a taste of water from the bucket instead. Then, fully dressed, she lay down beside Molly, hoping the maid would wake soon.

In the night Lettice rose sleepily and absently reached for the bottle of wine. Then she slept, half waking now and again with strange visions parading before her. After awhile she thought her door opened. Philip appeared. His face was lit strangely from below by his light.

"Lettice," he whispered slowly. "I will have you long . . . and hard . . . in pay for not waiting for me. I will teach you all that I taught Mary, to fear me. In time you will open yourself to me. First I will try persuasion. But only for a while. I have suffered long. I will wait only a little longer . . . only a little while."

The light in his hand seemed to swell, to burst. Her head began to ache, and then another image took his place, a toothy monster! And she thought the Lady Isobel rose up like a sinuous sea serpent wedded to a mermaid. Then lights burst within Lettice's head, and strange flowers bloomed.

Far into the afternoon of the next day she awoke. She felt her belly to see if the child still moved. She was reassured, though the babe seemed more sluggish than usual. She must let no other unknown substance pass her lips. Looking about the now deserted cabin, she felt the motion of the ship. They must be out upon Chesapeake Bay, or even at sea. She ran as well as she was able to the window.

A noise from the door spun her about. She breathed a sigh of relief to see Molly. Had the maid not been carrying a napkin-covered basin, her mistress would have embraced her.

"I thought perhaps they had thrown you back on shore," Lettice said. "How on earth did you get here?"

The maid brushed a curl out of her eye and shrugged as though nothing surprised her. "Those low men from the sloop turned on me—paid off by Sir Philip I have no doubt. Though I kicked and screamed, they carried me on board. Then Lady Isobel said I must drink a cup of wine. And I woke up here with you beside me. I never should have drunk it."

Lettice picked up the bottle and held it to the light. "It is certain we must be careful. I, too, sampled the wine, and now it seems we are on our way to England."

"I won't eat anything from that witch's hand," Molly said. "She be here, you know. That be why I went below to flirt with the cook. He do remember me well from the voyage out." She stripped the napkin from the bowl, revealing some mutton stewed with mustard. "He made it for the captain and Sir Philip."

" 'Tis far better fare than on our last voyage," Lettice said thankfully. The two women shared the feast without speaking, slicing the mutton and eating with their fingers.

"But, Molly," Lettice said at last, "I fear I have involved you in trouble once again."

"I can't have much more trouble than I had," the little maid said gravely. "And Lord knows where John be. But I know John and me will cling together as man and wife again soon. It be a feeling I have."

Lettice put an arm about the maid's delicate shoulders. "They are telling me Geoffrey will be hanged."

Molly reached back to pat her mistress's back. "Don't believe them, missus. Geoffrey be too clever."

Lettice gave her a faint smile. Then her face fell into a pattern of worry. "If only I could send Geoffrey a message. Yet perhaps I am fated to return to England. His friend

271

James is close to the king and will surely intercede on Geoffrey's behalf." Lettice raised her head defiantly. "If necessary I will go to the king himself. My husband has been treated basely, and that is why he turned rebel."

Lettice bit off her words suddenly as the door burst open. Lady Isobel stood upon the threshold along with her child servant, a small black boy she had somehow acquired in Virginia. She had dressed him in an exotic turban. She was training him to dog her footsteps. Lettice felt sympathy for any child left in Lady Isobel's tender care. He bore a tray of food.

Quickly Lettice made a pretense of straightening her skirts as she sat upon the bed, but instead she covered over the basin. She hoped they did not reek of mutton.

"You must be ravenous by now," Lady Isobel said, laughing gaily. "I have brought food." The boy set the tray on the table. There was no expression in his eyes. Lettice thought it too bad for a child of seven or eight to show no expression.

Then Lady Isobel came to sit next to Lettice, taking her hand. Lettice prayed she would not dislodge the empty basin. Lady Isobel's fingers were fine and clammy-cold. "I do so want to know everything about you, my dear," she said. "You have not yet told me how it was that you came to marry Geoffrey."

"Do you want to add spice to the fact that—so you tell me—my husband will be hanged?" Lettice asked tartly. She took this moment to withdraw her hand.

"My dear," Lady Isobel showed her wolf's teeth in one of her endless smiles. "You must have some special charm to attract two such interesting men as Philip and Geoffrey." Her long fingers played with the satin ribbons on her puffed sleeve.

"I'm afraid two are rather too many for me," Lettice responded.

Lady Isobel threw her white hands into the air in a gesture of mock despair. "A pity that Giles takes all my interest of late. Geoffrey, of course, I have already had, and he makes Giles all the more interesting. Knowing what I know, it is a pity that I cannot witness the hanging."

Lettice's throat constricted. "That is a perverse wish."

Lady Isobel smoothed her long yellow hair back from her shoulders so that her gleaming bosom was exposed.

Her tender lips curled. "I have never claimed to be other than perverse. But Philip does not suit me. There is much understanding between us, but we are too much alike, even to our fair coloring."

"Philip does not show his fangs so readily."

Lady Isobel colored as she rose. "He is not so open in his strangeness as I." The little servant followed the swish of her petticoats as she left.

"Oh, but she be a witch for sure!" Molly exploded as soon as the door had closed.

"How could Geoffrey ever have had anything to do with her?" Lettice said.

Molly brushed the thought aside. "Oh, she be lyin'. Or if not, it be no great matter after all, mistress, if he loves you."

"Or if he is hanged." Lettice bit her lip to keep back tears.

As Molly was removing the napkin from the tray of food, Lettice placed a warning hand on her arm. "Don't eat anything! And surely do not drink anything."

"Here be an apple." Molly held it up for inspection. "That be hard to poison, I think."

"Except in fairy tales." Lettice watched as Molly took a large bite. "How is it?" she asked. "Let me try it."

Molly tossed her another. "Here be some mutton stew," she said, sniffing. "It be made of the same mutton we had, and may well have a potion added."

"I shall not touch it," Lettice declared. "My head still feels strange and dull, and it may damage the child."

"She can't put potions in everything. But still, I always knew her for a witch." Molly went to unfasten the window, then stuck her head out to see if anyone was visible upon the deck. She seized the dish of stew and heaved it toward the gray sea.

Despite herself, Lettice began to laugh. She in turn seized a bottle of wine and tossed it over the deck. But it had no sooner left her hand than she doubled over in pain.

"Mistress!" Molly said. "Do be careful!"

Lettice found she could not straighten as a cramp engulfed her body. "It was careless of me," she whispered. Then her face contorted as a pain shot through her back. She groaned.

Molly took her by the shoulders. "We'll not escape the ship this day, it seems. The babe has come at last."

"It is almost time," Lettice said uncertainly as she reached for Molly's hand. "Oh, Molly, do not leave me. And do not let the Lady Isobel near me."

"I'll kill her if she tries, mistress."

Molly did not have to try, for Lady Isobel did not seek to interfere with the process of birth. It was a long labor, unsurprising in light of the mother's recent adventures. But the dark-haired child emerged at last—a dark-haired boy, whom Lettice named Geoffrey immediately. Molly began ripping petticoats apart to make clothes for him.

Lady Isobel came at last to ask about the child, sticking her elegant blond head about the door so her fashionably dressed curls swept the doorframe.

"It be a boy," Molly said.

Lady Isobel smiled a strange smile. "A boy. Most interesting. Giles will be so charmed."

Lettice and Molly looked at each other with dismay.

XVI

The coach jolted around a corner and down a treelined drive that led to the wide arched entrance of a substantial stone house. It was a beautiful house, Lettice admitted to herself, even with gray and lowering clouds weighing down upon it. Two graceful, symmetrical wings extended in classic simplicity from what must have been the original Tudor house. Ballustrades and classic statues stood upon the square roofs. All the opulent newer parts must have been added at about the time King Charles regained his throne.

Lettice shifted the baby, who was clinging to her breast. She could only see the edge of Lady Isobel's curls and the back of her red hood. The lady had one tense hand on the studded-leather lining of the coach. The other was clutching the window curtain. This must be the place that Lady Isobel Ashley called home—a larger by far and more finely constructed house than Brookside. Even Philip's house or Finch's Fortune was less grand, though she had only entered Geoffrey's family home once as a small child.

But she suspected that in fact they were not far from the scenes of her childhood, a day's ride perhaps. With a sigh, Lettice let the leather window curtain drop.

If only she might find refuge in her old home with her cousin, but he was a cold and parsimonious man. Still, there might be some way to appeal to him. Philip had sought to have her live with him, but she had pleaded possible scandal and taken her chances with the offer of Lady Isobel's hospitality. At this he had turned quite sulky, as he had as a boy, and said he would give her until the baby was weaned. But she did not want to think of Philip. Her mind was constantly occupied with thoughts and fears about Geoffrey. Though penniless at the moment, her goal was to take Molly and the babe to London to seek out James. Philip, she knew, would never let her go again once she placed herself in his hands. If James could not help her, the only chance would be to throw herself upon her cousin's cold mercy.

She glanced down at the sleeping abigail all flushed and disheveled. She envied her. Molly could sleep through a battle.

Lady Isobel turned from the window to flash her wolfish smile. Then she pulled her scarlet hood farther forward over her yellow hair as the coach came to a jolting halt. "Well, my dear, you have arrived at your haven."

"I hope it will prove so," Lettice said, looking directly into the hood-shaded eyes. "You seem not to have tampered with our food or drink once we were well out to sea."

Lady Isobel tossed her head and did not answer.

Molly awoke and was the first helped down by the coachman. Lettice handed the babe to her, not trusting Lady Isobel's touch upon the child. Lady Isobel descended last. As her feet touched the ground, she straightened her tall figure to peer toward the imposing doorway of her house. Her eyes widened; her glowing complexion turned ghastly white.

"My dear!" she gasped.

A slender, sallow young man dressed in riding clothes walked toward her, a frown upon his face.

"Why, Robert! I am astounded to see you looking so well," she cried hoarsely.

"No doubt," he said drily.

Lady Isobel's hands fluttered nervously. "And where is Doctor Herbert?"

"Dismissed." The short answer lay like a dagger between them.

Lettice had never before seen Lady Isobel discomfited. Indeed, the lady seemed unable to speak or move for several moments. Then she came to place a chaste kiss upon the young man's cheek, bending slightly to do so. She turned to extend a slender gloved hand to Lettice, turning from one to the other of them so that her skirts swept some damp leaves that had blown across the walkway. She began to rattle off words as though she dared not think too deeply.

"Mistress Lettice, you must meet my dear husband, Robert, who has surprised us by making what appears to be a marvelous recovery from a very serious illness. Robert, how may I best explain? This is Lettice Finch, wife— or widow—of your tutor, Master Cooper, or as appears he was really named, Geoffrey Finch."

Robert stared at Lettice for a moment, digesting all this. Then a smile crossed his sallow boyish face. He bowed. "Henry's wife? You are very welcome, mistress. Henry and I were . . . very close at one time."

Lettice decided that she liked this young man who must be only a year or two younger than herself. He would prove a friend in this strange household.

"But why does she say 'widow?' " Robert frankly met Lettice's eyes.

"I hope it is some of Lady Isobel's nonsense," Lettice said with what lightness she could muster. "Though with the rebellion over, it could prove real enough. They will hang some of the rebels."

Robert nodded thoughtfully.

"Well." Lady Isobel was still too unsteady to challenge them or prod with the barbs of her words. "I do think we must go inside rather than stand in the chill."

Leaving her husband behind, she proceeded into the house where a number of servants gathered to greet her in the entrance gallery. They bowed as she passed, but she took no notice. It seemed to Lettice that the many portrait's of Robert's ancestors must look down at her reproachfully.

Robert drew Lettice aside into a small parlor. "Henry will be all right," he said softly. "He is more clever than my wife thinks. Though we had a falling out, I still have a good deal of respect for him. The more so for marrying a woman graver than has been his usual taste."

His words vexed Lettice somewhat. What had been Geoffrey's taste? And gravity, after all, was something she had learned after Philip had cast her aside.

Supper was to be sent up to Lettice's room so that she and the baby might rest from the journey. Lettice insisted

277

Molly share her bed. She did not feel safe alone. Lettice lounged behind the great curtains, the babe at her breast. Molly sat upon a stool, looking about at the furniture, which was carved so intricately with flowing vines, beasts and flowers and inlaid with glowing patterns in wood. It was far finer than the stout old turned furniture of Brookside.

Lettice raised her eyes from the baby's downy head. "We could have gone with Philip," she said.

Molly shook her head. "No. He would never let you go again, but lock you up."

Lettice sighed. "There seems nowhere safe in the world for us. Nor for our men."

Molly's bright eyes turned speculative. "If Geoffrey really be hung, you could marry Philip in the end, mistress."

Lettice said nothing.

"Though I hope you will not," the abigail muttered under her breath.

There was a knock upon the door, and Molly opened it to reveal Lady Isobel bearing a candle. Beside her stood a wrinkled old woman with a tray of food. "Nurse Smith and I thought you would want to rest without coming down," Lady Isobel said.

The nurse set the tray upon a table and came with her rustling apron and petticoats, like a great ship, to beam down upon little Geoffrey. "What a lovely babe!" she gurgled. Her brows rose with delight, which cast many parallel furrows across her brow as she waggled a finger at the little one. And then the nurse bent closer. "But such a poor gown and bonnet."

"His birth caught us far from home," Lettice explained.

"The poor dear," the nurse said. "But I still have some of Master Robert's old things laid away. And I will set the maids to work." She bent to chuck the baby under his chin. They cooed and smiled at each other, though little Geoffrey was just learning how.

"You are very kind." Lettice couldn't help smiling. Nurse Smith obviously yearned for a babe to care for, and Lady Isobel had none. Nor did she seem interested in infants. The mistress of the house parted her glistening teeth briefly, then nodded to them before turning to close the door behind her.

Once she was gone, Nurse Smith seemed to relax. "Be you really Master Henry's wife?" The nurse clasped her plump hands together, fixing large, vague, near-sighted eyes upon them. "He was a good man and a real friend to Master Robert."

Lettice smiled. She had heard no good words of Geoffrey except from Robert and the nurse. Then she frowned, recalling that Geoffrey had made love to his charge's wife. Robert was indeed generous.

The nurse lifted the covers from the food, and Molly and Lettice sniffed the delicious odors of a dish of chickens with puff paste, a custard and a pear pie. Molly's bright-blue eyes met Lettice's violet ones. The two women were afraid to eat. The nurse gave them a look of understanding.

"Don't be afraid, mistress," she said. "I watched over the cooking very carefully myself. It is safe."

Lettice felt her extremities grow cold. If there was peril here, she should have chanced it with Philip. "Then you are saying all is not safe here," she said through stiff lips.

The candle upon the table revealed the nurse's flush as her apple cheeks turned brighter still. Her wide brown eyes showed honest distress beneath the rim of her white cap. "I couldn't say, mistress," she said modestly.

"But I must know if it is safe for me and the babe."

Nurse Smith peered cautiously into the dark shadows of the room, then leaned closer to whisper, " 'Twas not for Master Robert. 'Twas a potion of that black-haired foolish doctor, who is besotted with love for Lady Isobel. My poor babe weakened daily until he was close to death. Then I decided the cure itself might well be killing him. So each night I poured it into the slop pot. After then, Master Robert grew stronger. The first day he was able to rise from his bed, he sent the doctor packing."

"A good thing too!" Molly exclaimed. "But, mistress, what if the same happens to us?"

Lettice narrowed her eyes while she removed her nipple from the babe's tiny lips. "I think we are safe for now." She pulled her silk nightgown over her bosom and set the babe down to rest.

The nurse looked puzzled. "Why would Lady Isobel harm you, mistress?"

"I think she would not for the moment," Lettice judged. "My presence somehow bedevils Giles—mine and the babe's. After all, should Giles die, Geoffrey or his son would be the heir to Finch's Fortune."

"I don't understand, mistress," Nurse Smith said.

"Nor do I," Lettice assured her. "Only that Lady Isobel delights to bedevil Giles.

In the flickering light from the comforting fire the three women stared at each other.

Bare black branches swayed in the bitter wind. Dried grasses and bits of skeletal leaves scattered about. There was no snow upon the cold ground.

Geoffrey stood beneath the gallows not far from the governor's house at Green Spring, which was now the seat of government. Which of the rebels hung there, he could not be sure, since the body was badly decomposed. A crowd of crows had risen and were flapping and cawing at his approach.

A poster upon an oak at Middle Plantation had sent Geoffrey hurrying away—a poster announcing that one Henry Cooper, alias Geoffrey Finch, a runaway servant, was wanted for an attack on Squire Charles Albright. He cursed Dorothy and her foolishness and hoped he would not be spotted here. Now Virginia had become as dangerous for him as England, more so, perhaps. Three lone coins nestled together in his leather pouch. There was little to buy in the raw colony at the best of times, and almost nothing in a land half ruined from rebellion. The night before, he had shot a rabbit and roasted it over a campfire. A few other servants who had delayed in returning to their masters drifted from the forest like ghosts to join in his feast. Then they faded away into the night again.

If he could but find Lettice, Geoffrey thought, she could perhaps deal with her sister until the time came when he was able to reach James. Otherwise he must head south toward Carolina, hoping to catch up with Lawrence. He had a sense that his life was rushing by with speed and little accomplishment.

And then there was the child. He frowned. He had been thinking only of the mother, but winter was well upon the colony. Lettice had never told him plainly when the child was expected, but surely it must be born by now. Where on this earth was she? He felt a great longing for the fresh beauty of this woman he had taken to wife in such an unplanned way. Had she found shelter somewhere? Perhaps she was too weak to travel sensibly back to Dorothy's care. At least Wat would trouble her no more. And he knew that Molly would guard her mistress to her death.

About to mount his horse, he froze, his hand upon the saddle. He had had a fleeting vision of Lettice, silken hair spread out about her, lying in a pool of blood. What if the birth had not gone well? Oh, God, he never should have entered her if it were only to prove her destruction. But if Lettice was dead, where then was Molly? This thought calmed him somewhat. No, the two of them must be resting some place, along with the babe. He prayed that it was so. But he could not relieve himself of his anxiety.

He sprang into the saddle and rode, gnawing his cheek all the way, toward Green Spring. There he came upon what appeared to be a village of tents clustered about the governor's enormous bulk of a house squatting under the heavy gray sky. Finally he spied a familiar figure walking upon the grounds. It was the boy who had asked Lawrence and himself about Bacon's death.

Geoffrey gave a low whistle. Startled, the boy looked over toward the trees. Geoffrey whistled again, and the boy came hesitantly toward him. When he spied Geoffrey, he halted, scratching his head with its disordered brown curls. He did in fact appear quite astonished.

"What's the matter, boy?" Geoffrey said. "Seen a ghost?"

"No-no, sir," the boy stuttered. "It's just that I'm surprised to see you here." He drew his old cloth coat more closely about his scrawny chest. His bewildered eyes never left Geoffrey's face.

Geoffrey smiled, then leaned to pat his horse's neck as he spoke further to the boy. "I've never been known as a governor's man, it's true. But at this point I am quite beyond politics and faction."

"Oh, it's not that, sir." The boy halted in confusion, scratching his head once again and snuffling loudly as his nose ran in the cold. "Still, if you're beyond politics, sir, why did I see you just now talking to the governor inside?"

"You are mistaken," Geoffrey began with a laugh. Then he halted. His brown eyes narrowed.

The boy went on, his adolescent voice seemed confused.

281

" 'Tis beyond me, sir, how you changed clothes so fast and came out here. A man cannot be two places at once."

"No, he cannot. You are very observant." Geoffrey spoke slowly, taken aback momentarily. Then his heart began to rise. "Though years ago my brother and I gulled one or another ignorant farm girl to think so." Geoffrey rubbed his chilled, sun-browned hands together, blowing on them. Then he reached into his pouch for one of his remaining coins. Holding it pinched between thumb and forefinger, he extended it toward the boy.

"This is yours, my boy, if you listen to me carefully and do as I say." The boy nodded eagerly, and Geoffrey tossed the coin to him.

"I think," Geoffrey said, "that if you go inside the governor's house, you will find, amazingly, that I am also there—not so browned by the wind and sun, perhaps, nor so lean and starved, certainly better dressed."

The boy gawked at him in amazement.

"No, 'tis not witchcraft, but something more natural. We are twins, or were as infants. Our minds and our spirits have grown apart."

"Why, yes," the boy exclaimed with relief. " 'Tis a miraculous likeness, sir."

"But you must swear to keep this fact a secret," Geoffrey warned.

The boy's face clouded over. "I will," he promised.

"I want you to go to find this man you took for me, but speak to him only if he is alone."

The boy nodded his understanding.

"Tell him his old playmate waits him anxiously here. But he must come without friend or servant."

"Yes, sir," the boy said as he strode off.

"Wait!"

Pulled up as though at the end of a tether, the boy returned obediently, clutching the coin.

"Does the gentleman stay at the governor's house?"

The boy nodded respectfully. "Yes, sir."

"Tell me which room he occupies."

"The third one to the left at the top of the stairs."

"Can you see the window from here?"

"Yes, sir." The boy raised a grubby finger to point. "You see, the panes are cracked in several places, because the rebels half destroyed the house. The governor himself

282

had to borrow a bed to sleep in when he came home. And Lady Berkeley will be angry."

Geoffrey nodded his understanding. "Now do as I have bid you," he told the boy, who raced away across the frost-silvered lawn that was grown ragged.

When he was alone, Geoffrey rubbed his hands until they glowed red. He slapped his shoulders and generally tensed and relaxed his muscles. Then he led his horse far back into the brush where he tied it. He crept closer again. He must not let Giles surprise him.

How lucky it was that he had discovered his wily brother before Giles had discovered him. Their pranks as children had been competitive and heedless, yet often filled with a reckless humor. Giles of late no longer amused his brother. His games had become grim indeed. Giles had commanded the situation too long. Today would be Geoffrey's play.

Geoffrey saw the heavy door to the governor's house open and a figure the very shadow of himself emerge. Only the body looked softer and more carefully cared for. Upon the gentleman's heels trod the oafish figure of Daniel, Philip's servant. So Giles did not have the courage to face him alone! There was little cover at this time of year; so Geoffrey huddled near the ground, watching. He did not intend to give Giles the upper hand.

Giles looked about, his body tense. Then he said something in a low voice to Daniel, who returned to the house. He looked back only once from the door before he obediently entered. Giles strode purposefully across the lawn, leaving dark footprints in the frost. He seemed filled with a kind of excitement so that his step sprang from a source of tension. Geoffrey did not stir while his brother walked some ways into the undergrowth. Giles halted, looking about, then called out slyly, "Have no fear. I have brought no one with me."

Geoffrey moved not a muscle, the smell of the cold, damp earth was strong in his nostrils. He could see Giles's tension grow.

"Come now, Geoffrey," Giles called suavely after the silence had grown unbearable. He wore a dark hat, its feather bowing to the wind. His long, curled, dark hair swept across his square cheekbones, almost obscuring his brown eyes, which under a threatening sky looked black.

"I know it is you, Brother, and I know your tricks. We have played these games since we were children, after all. We may eliminate the opening moves and go to the heart of the game."

"So we may," Geoffrey said as he rose and stepped into a clearing to face Giles at last. He prayed his body was not so stiffened from his chill wait that it would let him down.

"Why, Brother." Giles smiled. "You have grown thin and shabby."

"At least I am not dead," Geoffrey said grimly.

"No," Giles was thoughtful.

"And you have received poor value for your silver."

"I, Brother?" Giles laughed mirthlessly, coming toward him. His blunt-fingered strong hand was outstretched.

Geoffrey unsheathed his sword.

"What?" Giles's eyes glittered with malice. "Would you attack an unarmed man?"

"I was weaponless when your ruffians seized me, Brother."

"My ruffians?" Giles laughed again.

Geoffrey lunged so that the tip of his sword touched the elegant white ruffles at Giles's throat. Giles glanced down at the blade then back into his brother's eyes so that each mirrored the other in shadowed umber depths.

"If you must challenge me, Geoffrey, do so more fairly. I have left my sword inside, because you were ever the fair and honest one—too proud to take advantage."

"You may have misjudged." Geoffrey's face felt stiff as he struggled to keep expressionless. "Much has happened since we last met."

Giles tilted his head to one side and regarded him mockingly. "No, I have not misjudged you, Brother. You cannot kill in cold blood."

Once more their eyes met. Geoffrey's muscles tensed. He willed himself to complete the thrust so that Giles's white neckcloth would be spotted with scarlet. Geoffrey clenched his teeth, his muscles strained, his hands shook. He must prove Giles wrong.

He lowered his blade. He could not do it.

Giles laughed. "I thought not. You are a coward when it comes to villainy," he said and arrogantly turned his back upon his brother.

Geoffrey lunged forward to grasp him by a handful of

his claret-colored velvet coat. "Hold on," he said. "We are not done yet."

Giles turned once more, seeming faintly amused. "What? You seek to challenge a man such as I who has many valuable friends inside the governor's house? Will you be hung as an outlaw in Virginia?"

"Perhaps," Geoffrey said between his teeth.

Giles gave him the special smile with raised brows that had always goaded Geoffrey to madness. "You would challenge a man better fed than yourself?" Giles questioned.

"And softer," Geoffrey said shortly.

"I have beat you before."

"And I you. Who else could prove such an even match?" Geoffrey thought of his fight against the giant Wat those many months back. He had won because of his agility and endurance. But Giles was equally agile and, as he had pointed out, better fed. Geoffrey had eaten nothing but bits and pieces of rabbit for the past several days. He saw Giles glance toward the house, and he judged that Daniel was posted there in case of trouble.

"We'll move farther from the house," Geoffrey said, "lest your friends make the fight less equal."

Giles's lips tightened. "If you wish," he said. His eyes narrowed, and Geoffrey knew that by now his brother was truly angry. Seeing this, a kind of weariness swept over Geoffrey. Giles, after all, was only an obstacle in his path to freedom and his search for his wife. Yet Giles did indeed deserve some kind of justice.

They walked in silence, neither feeling the cold nor hearing the crackle of leaves and twigs underfoot. When at last they turned to face each other, Geoffrey reflected that he had at least learned a few tricks from the sailors on the *Anne and Mary* and from Bacon's ragtag army.

They fought on a bare patch of black, damp earth. There was no sound in the forest, save for their gasping breaths. Giles's temper flared, dulling his caution, as they rolled on the ground, now one dark head on top, now another. Giles's cavalier locks were ground into the dirt; Geoffrey's hair was wild and matted. The winter sun slanted low.

A ragged figure crept out of the forest and witnessed one man rise from the combat. He had delivered a blow to his brother's head, rendering him unconscious.

"You beat 'um," the ragged figure uttered, his eyes glinting with pleasure at Geoffrey's triumph. He was one of Bacon's servant soldiers who'd been reluctant to go home. He had joined Geoffrey last night.

Geoffrey nodded, breathing deeply, jaggedly. He swayed, for the lack of food had indeed weakened him sorely.

"My brother has grown soft," he said when he was able.

"Have you any food, friend?" the ragged man whined.

Geoffrey shook his head. "None," he said.

The man rubbed his hands across his sunken belly. "That rabbit you roasted last night whetted my appetite for more."

"And mine," Geoffrey said. "But we can, I think, help each other."

The servant came forward eagerly. He took off his cloth cap and crushed it in his hands. Geoffrey rolled Giles onto his back and began stripping his fine clothes from him. He then dressed Giles carefully in his own worn buff coat and hunting clothes. When the switch was made, he attached Giles's money pouch to the belt he wore. Then he sawed away at Giles's cavalier locks with his own old hunting knife. Brushing aside some dead leaves, he buried his brother's hair between the roots of a tree. That was easy enough. His own hair would prove more of a problem.

"Give me a hand," he called to the soldier. Each grabbed one of Giles's shoulders, and they dragged him to where his horse was tethered. Heaving him over the saddle, they tied his hands over the withers and his feet under the belly so that he rode with his face over the beast's tail.

"Take him into the forest and lose him," Geoffrey said. "Here are two gold coins, and the horse is yours."

"You want me to kill him, friend?"

Geoffrey sighed. "No. But do not let him escape easily. I must be a week gone from here by the time he arrives back upon this spot."

"I pray I can find someone to sell me bread. If not, I shall eat the horse."

"You'd do better to use it to ride to Carolina," Geoffrey said.

"Then, could I have the use of your pistol, sir?" the servant asked humbly.

"I am in need of it myself," Geoffrey answered. "See you do as I ask."

The man nodded and seized the reins. At this Giles awoke and called out. Geoffrey snatched his sword from the ground and touched it to Giles's now-naked throat, which was helplessly exposed against the horse's flank.

"Do not trust your luck too far," Geoffrey hissed.

"Nor you yours," Giles whispered. "I am the only one who knows where your wife can be found."

Geoffrey halted in his tracks and saw an expression of cunning cross Giles's reddened face.

"Untie me, and I will lead you to her," Giles gasped.

Geoffrey dropped his sword and closed his hands about Giles's throat. "Damn you! Where is Lettice?"

Giles strained to look up into his brother's eyes. For a moment fear showed upon his face, then he assumed his usual look of sulky pride. "So I was right. He who owns her owns you. She is quite safe. Untie me, and I'll tell you more."

Geoffrey hesitated, studying his brother. "No, Giles," he said finally, his heart sinking. "If you will not tell me where she is, I will find her without you. I know how you tease. But now is your chance to taste bondage." With that he tore a strip from the ragged shirt Giles wore and forced a gag into his mouth. Too late, if Giles would really tell him about his wife. But Geoffrey knew his brother well. He would torment him to death with the secret and never say more.

Geoffrey turned to the ragged and shivering servant. "Now go," he said.

"Yes, sir." The servant touched his cap. "I will do what you have said, sir. You can rely on me."

As he watched the two of them disappear, Geoffrey reflected that the servant had been the first in several years to call him "sir." What a difference a velvet coat and white neckcloth made. But those inside might not be so easily fooled. The first hurdle would be Daniel.

The cold was beginning to bite deep now as the sun dimmed behind the increasingly heavy gray layer of clouds. Geoffrey sauntered toward the house, pulling the hat as far down as he was able to cover his hair. The fine velvet of his clothes was besmirched with mud, but that was easily explained by some tale or other.

287

Did the door to the governor's house open a crack? Geoffrey had a vision of the gap-toothed servant standing just inside. But first there was the intervening open space of lawn to be crossed. Geoffrey rubbed his cold, stiff hands and blew on them. He didn't take his eyes off the door. He would wait, he decided. His patience was rewarded when, after awhile, the door opened again, and Daniel tentatively crossed to stand in the middle of the lawn, looking about. The house rose behind, square, ungraceful, but large enough to accommodate a hundred or so men behind those many windows, which were now staring blankly in the light of a cloud-laden sunset.

He could not wait forever. His stomach caved in with hunger, and the cold was unusual for Virginia. Now was the time to cast his dice.

He gave a low whistle. Daniel looked up. His swarthy face broke into a wide smile. Walking fast, he headed into the brush. He did not see Geoffrey poised with his pistol upraised. In an instant the butt cracked him across the skull. Daniel immediately fell unconscious.

"Sorry," Geoffrey murmured. Daniel, it seemed, had a knack for being about the wrong errand at the wrong time. Geoffrey hoped he would not rouse too soon and that his head would not ache too badly.

Geoffrey had seen several gentlemen enter and leave the governor's house, since it was a center of activity in a colony that was all but ruined by the rebellion. He would be but one more gentleman visitor. Yet he hesitated a moment, his regained gentleman's identity sitting uncertainly upon him. Then he took a deep breath and sauntered toward the house. He could not suppress a chill of danger as he set his hand upon the heavy iron latch and pushed in the door.

"I was wonderin' if you was comin'," a low voice said.

Geoffrey's head jerked up. He relaxed. It was the boy. Geoffrey reached two fingers into the pouch at his belt and fished out one of Giles's coins. It was only fair to steal back some of the inheritance Giles had stolen from him.

"Some supper in my room, boy," he commanded.

"Did you leave the other gentleman outside, sir?" the boy wondered. "And change clothes?"

Geoffrey leaned toward him. "Is the difference so obvious, then?" he whispered.

"The hair, sir," the boy said. "And you are so brown. But, mind you, I know now you are twins."

Geoffrey sighed. "Bring me a basin of hot water to my room, and we will see what we can do."

He did not look back as the boy sped away toward the kitchen, but instead climbed the solidly paneled stairs to the room the boy had indicated. Geoffrey did not hesitate. He threw open the door as though he had just left it.

It was unoccupied, though the bed curtains hung in shreds, victim to Bacon's men. When he, fully clothed, lay back upon it, he felt strange lumps. Pulling the bedclothes aside, many mended slashes were evident even in the cold evening light. Truly Bacon's troops must have had an orgy of destruction here.

Still, the bed was softer than any upon which Geoffrey had lain in months. He lay back again with a contented sigh.

There was a knock upon the door, and the boy entered with warm water and food. As Geoffrey gnawed hungrily upon a roasted beef bone, the boy described the activity of the house. His eyes were sparkling with the excitement of this game they played. It seemed the gentlemen and a few ladies were gathered down below, discussing the hangings and generally celebrating the return of order to the colony. The mistress of the house was still in England, though the governor was in residence.

Geoffrey picked up a piece of wheat bread as he listened—the first such he had tasted since the rebellion. His stomach was so shrunk that he was soon full and drowsy. But he went to wash his hair and remove the worst of the dirt from the rest of him. Then he attempted to form cavalier locks with little success. Though not as shorn as a Roundhead, his hair hung only to a little below his ears.

The boy gossiped on about the way one Drummond had been sent aboard a ship in irons, and then taken off again to be hanged. He'd complained all the way of the cold, since the hangman had taken his fur coat to wear himself.

Geoffrey turned to look at the boy as he sat at the end of the bed, swinging his legs as he listened to the boy's story. "Has the governor hanged so many, then?"

"No," the boy replied. "He has pardoned most. There was a court-martial upon Captain John Martin's ship, and three or four were sent to be hanged. Drummond was taken later in New Kent County."

Geoffrey reflected that it might have been this same Drummond he had seen swinging upon the gallows.

"I wonder how many more will be condemned," he said slowly. All the more reason to hasten. Geoffrey frowned. Here he was taking his ease without knowing what fate had befallen his wife.

"Tell me," he asked the boy, "did you see my brother here with any ladies?"

"Ladies?" Shaking his head, the boy looked puzzled. "He has only been here some two or three days though."

"Be a good fellow and ask—carefully, mind you—where he has recently been and if there has been a lady and her maid in his company. But mind you, let no one know what you know about me. If you serve me well, there will be more in it for you."

"Yes, sir." The boy rose with sparkling eyes. " 'Twill be almost as good as serving General Bacon."

"And do not mention that name," Geoffrey cautioned.

Geoffrey lit a candle from coals lying in the chimney. Then he built up the fire, enjoying the warmth. Spring came early to Virginia, but for Geoffrey it could not come soon enough. He carried his candle over to a looking glass upon the wall and stared at his face. Giles's velvet coat suited him, hollow-eyed and hollow-cheeked as he was. The dark-brown eyes that stared back at him were his brother's, or did they show the beginnings of a few light lines about them that denoted a warmth and humor foreign to Giles?

There was nothing he could do to fatten himself in the brief time he had to escape, even were he to steadily feed from the governor's well-stocked kitchen. But the hair and the nut-brown color of his skin must be disguised somehow. Carefully, he opened his window and glanced out. Below was the light from many blazing candles, but the windows immediately next to his were dark. Once more he would play the thief—this time with no Captain Quince to catch him.

Geoffrey peered past his door before opening it wide. Several candles burned in sconces upon the paneled walls, casting wild and ominous shadows. He was halfway down the hall when he heard faltering footsteps behind him.

290

Starting, he half turned, shielding his face. The gentleman was staggering badly, his periwig askew. Geoffrey smiled to himself, all but rubbing his hands with anticipation. It was a most excellent periwig, all dark-brown curls long and flowing. Geoffrey bowed to the gentleman, then lay an arm across his shoulders.

"My dear sir, you do appear to be in need of help. May I conduct you to your room?"

"If you please," the man whined. "The walls do swim."

"Let us hope they stand straight in the morning," Geoffrey soothed. "Which is your door?"

"That one." The man pointed, his eyes crossing with the effort. He pointed again. "No, that one."

"I pray you are right." Geoffrey guided him toward what he hoped was the proper and unoccupied room. He kicked open the door. This bed, too, had its curtains slashed. Bacon's men were very thorough.

When Geoffrey closed the door, they were in pitch blackness. Geoffrey led the man slowly to the bedside where the man slid from his grasp and collapsed. Fortunately he fell across the bed. Geoffrey raised his feet, praying the whole body would not slide back onto the floor. Then he pulled off the shoes and removed the periwig. It was a masterpiece of the wigmaker's art. Geoffrey prayed the man did not have nits. He was almost safely to the door when it opened, and a middle-aged woman appeared. She was equally drunk and carrying a wavering candle.

Geoffrey did not falter. "I have put him to bed, madam." He bowed obsequiously, holding the wig behind his back.

"How kind!" the lady said, her words slurred. Then she set her candle and herself before her pier glass and removed her wig, which she set upon a stand. The stand next to it was naked, awaiting the gentleman's wig. The lady's own hair was sparse and graying.

She was also, Geoffrey noticed as she sat in her little circle of light, exceedingly pale. Too pale for the hand of nature. She turned back to regard him. "You needn't stand there gawking, sir. I am about to retire."

Wig-laden hands behind his back, Geoffrey bowed and retreated. Once in the hall he sped to his room and buried the wig in Giles's box. Then for a time he paced before the fire, bone-weary, but too keyed up to rest. When he adjudged the house slept, he crept again into the by-now black hall. No light shone from beneath the gentleman's door. Carefully Geoffrey lifted the latch and entered. The smallest glow from the overcast moon entered the window. Geoffrey made his way to the lady's looking glass, feeling about until his hands encountered powder and paint. He lifted them to smell to make sure. Then he sped to the door. But not fast enough. He heard sounds from the bed.

"What?" the lady murmured sleepily. Then, "What? Who's there? Thief! 'Tis a thief. Stop! Oh, my diamonds! Stop!"

Geoffrey raced, half stumbling, to his room, while startled rustlings seemed to thunder through the silenced and darkened house. He slammed his door behind him with his heart beating wildly. He dove for his bed, covering himself and slipping the boxes beneath his pillow. He lay there for some minutes, the thumping beneath his ribs as loud to his ears as the sounds of the search in the hall.

His door was flung open by a figure carrying a candle. Geoffrey opened one eye and let out a bellow, "What is this disturbance? Can you not see I'm trying to sleep?"

"Oh, yes, sir. Sorry, sir." The figure backed again.

As he lay his head down upon the soft pillow, Geoffrey smiled. Then he fell into a sleep deeper than any he had enjoyed in many a month.

He awoke in the morning to the sounds of the boy building up the fire. Geoffrey sprang from his bed and dug the boxes of powder and paint from beneath the pillow.

The boy had also brought food—Indian corn bread and some warmed ale. Geoffrey downed these hurriedly. He was still famished from his long fast. Then he set himself before his glass, which bore a crack across one corner, no doubt courtesy of one of Bacon's men. Carefully, Geoffrey began to apply the white paint and powder, not so much that its use would be obvious.

Watching, the boy stared at him, open-mouthed.

"Well, my boy," Geoffrey said. "What have you discovered?"

"Your brother, they told me, landed on the eastern shore, sir. He had a yellow-haired lady with him, and a light-haired gentleman, too, from England."

"That's not my lady," Geoffrey said with disappointment. "My wife's hair is ash brown, and she is . . . was . . . expecting a child."

"Oh, that one!" the boy cried. "She was there too."

Geoffrey turned to look at him. "Are you sure?"

"Yes. And she had a maid with her. Everyone said the lady's time was near."

Geoffrey frowned. "She must have gone somewhere to have the child."

"Yes, sir," the boy said cheerfully. "On board ship with the other lady and her maid and the gentleman from England. Then they sailed back home."

"To England?" Geoffrey's heart dropped to his boots. Would Lettice leave without a word or a message? Urgently, he grasped the boy's arm. "Do you know the other lady's name? Or the gentleman's?"

The boy shook his head. "Not the lady's. But the gentleman was called Sir Philip."

Of course. Philip's father must have died. Geoffrey sat back motionless in his chair. He was well aware that Philip had long coveted Lettice, for he had spoken rather grossly of his passion for her since they had all been half grown. But once Geoffrey had gone away to Oxford, he had seen little of Philip. Dimly he remembered the elegant fair-haired cavalier one Christmas telling how he had stolen with Lettice into her mother's closet and then slipped his hand into her bosom to feel her smooth, young breasts.

Geoffrey burned with anger. He had not remembered this story till now. Would Lettice really have left him for a man so vain and callow? He closed the paint and powder and threw them into Giles's box. Placing the wig upon his head, he turned to face the boy.

"It's very good, sir," the boy judged. "No one will know the difference, especially if you wear a cloak."

Both started at a knock on the door.

"Who is it?" Geoffrey asked boldly.

"I have a message, sir."

"Yes?"

"Captain says thank you for agreeing to his terms for the return voyage, sir. We will be ready to sail in three days."

"Three days?" A sly smile tugged at the corner of Geoffrey's lips. "Well, well. Tell the captain my servant and I will see him on the morrow." He paused to wink at the boy. "To set sail for England."

A servant from the house carried his box as the boy led the way down to the wharf at the river's edge where the English ship was tied up. Mist from the river was so heavy it took them some time to discover the two figures who were looking down upon them from the deck. One of them was Daniel. Geoffrey swallowed. This would be more difficult than he had imagined. Still, the mist might aid him.

Geoffrey raised a hand to his mouth to shout to be taken aboard. How well did Giles know the captain? No matter. He would treat him as a servant. That's what Giles would do.

"Hurry with that box," he ordered the man whose back was bent carrying Giles's belongings. "Get along, now, don't tarry," he called to the boy, whom he had promised to take with him. The boy flashed a quick grin but suppressed it quickly.

"Where are you putting me?" Geoffrey snapped at the captain.

"The same place, sir. Up there." The captain pointed. "But we won't sail for another two days."

"Very good. In the meantime I don't want to be disturbed." Geoffrey did not look in Daniel's direction, but strode off purposely to the cabin, hoping it was the one the captain had meant. He trusted that Giles had already paid for his passage and would not reemerge from the forest too soon. If not, he would pay with Giles's money. And even if Giles did show up, they would take the word of a dandy like himself over a person who looked as disreputable as Giles must by now. At the door he turned to call back, "Hurry, boy!"

Through narrowed eyes he saw Daniel hesitate as the boy ran across the white-curtained deck. Daniel opened his mouth to speak. Then after an endless moment he closed it again. With fast-beating heart, Geoffrey shut the stout door. Now he must wait and pray until his feet touched English soil again. But the idleness would not be good for him. He was already tortured by phantoms of Lettice's body with Philip's long, fair hands upon it.

XVII

Molly dawdled downstairs one morning, fingering and admiring the carved stair rails with their twined leaves and flowers. She stopped to touch the urn of blossoms upon the stair post, wondering how the clever wood craftsman had made them so like the best from a real garden. Only a real garden would not make you as conscious of wealth and power as this did. Then she saw Nurse Smith hurrying along the gallery, a look of anxiety upon her plump, pleasantly wrinkled face.

"Master Robert be low again," she whispered.

"That witch, the Lady Isobel!" Molly hissed.

"Do you think so?" The nurse's round eyes were troubled. She grasped Molly's arm and drew her back and about to the kitchen. "I dared not think it, yet it seems to me it must be so. He refused his tray when Lady Isobel and I went up last night. He must eat something. The poor lad will starve."

"Take him something you know is safe," Molly urged in her shrill voice.

Nurse Smith placed a warning, gnarled finger over her lips. "I dare not. I must go to Lady Isobel to help her sew. She has forbidden me to go near Master Robert."

Molly looked about the large room with its black iron pots hanging from huge beams and its scrubbed wood table. "I'll do it," she whispered.

At that moment Lady Isobel entered the steaming kitchen and eyed the two of them suspiciously. "Nurse," she said, "I have told you I must have your help. My new gown is all wrong and must be done over."

"Yes, mistress." The nurse dipped a knee, then followed

after her mistress, her plump body bent in submission. Once, she turned back to look at Molly with an agonized expression of worry.

Molly looked hastily about. A large caldron of pease porridge bubbled over the fire. Surely such a large amount could not all be poisoned, or the entire household would fall ill! A fish pie cooled on the big oak dresser—an uncut pie. She decided to chance it, though the cook would kill her if she discovered the theft.

Quickly Molly sank a knife into the pie, which smelled of carp and eel and nutmeg and other savory good things. She loaded all the food onto a tray, placing a spoon alongside. Then she stuck her white-capped head through the doorway to make sure no one was coming. She did not walk, but raced up the flowery carved stairs again, halting at the top while the dishes trembled dangerously.

Which was Master Robert's room? She knew Lady Isobel was downstairs in the parlor, but she had only a vague suspicion of the direction where Sir Robert might lie. For a moment she stared at the closed, many-paneled oak doors about her. Finally, drawing a deep breath, she turned the handle of one of them. There was a startled gasp. A young maid of about 15 turned hastily to face her, waving a dustcloth over her head. She was almost buried in an enormous apron.

Molly gasped also, for about the throat of this mere chit hung an enormous diamond necklace. Obviously she had been admiring herself in the glass. Blushing wildly, the girl clumsily unfastened the diamonds and lay them in a small casket. Molly backed out again. She barely noticed out of the corner of her eye the glowing petit-point flowers of Lady Isobel's bed curtains. But one thing was certain. The maid would not dare betray her.

If that was Lady Isobel's room, the next should be Sir Robert's—unless they were even stranger than most married folk, which could well be true of course.

But luck was with her. As she entered the room with its damask-covered walls, Robert sat up weakly. His eyes seemed huge in his thin face. He was almost lost in his great-curtained bed way off in the corner of the enormous room. And the elaborate white-carved plaster ceiling seemed to threaten to crush him.

Molly closed the door hastily and came to his side.

"Nurse Smith sent me, Master Robert," she said. "I chose the food myself."

Robert's face brightened as he reached for the spoon with a yellowish and transparent hand. He stammered, "Oh, thank you." Then he spoke no more until he finally set his spoon aside, his fish pie and pea porridge gone.

"I hope I have not made trouble for you, but I was prodigiously hungry."

Molly nodded, wondering if she should gather up the things. But curiosity got the better of her, and she sat on the edge of the bed, tucking one foot up under her skirts. "Why be the Lady Isobel trying to poison you?" she asked conversationally.

Robert frowned. "Do you think she is? It does seem the only explanation, though she will have nothing to gain from my death. A small bit of my fortune will go to her, true enough, but she has a large one of her own. Of course I am sure she has a lover."

"Oh, yes," Molly blurted. "Giles Finch, Geoffrey's twin. You knew Geoffrey as your tutor."

"So that's it." Robert straightened in his bed and smoothed his nightgown over his thin knees. "But she has loved my tutor too." Robert darted a glance at her and flushed. "Though I dare say it was her idea rather than his. Still, I was humiliated because . . . because. . . ."

Molly leaned forward so that her rosy bosom swayed toward him, threatening to burst free of the shift she wore next to her skin. "Go on. You can tell me."

"Well, you see. . .," Robert hesitated. His deeply shadowed eyes looked pained. "Though she is my wife, she has never bedded me. Or I her, I should say."

"Never!" Molly drew back in surprise. "Well, I never. I always knew Lady Isobel be a witch!"

Robert went on seriously, deepening the frown line that had prematurely formed upon his young face. "And if she is trying to poison me, it is because she does not love me."

"Hmm," Molly said. "I think it be more than that. It be that someday she would have Master Giles as her husband."

"Perhaps. Be that as it may, I have never had her—or anyone warmly and softly—and I burn and yearn so from this lack that it scarce matters I am poisoned by potions as well."

297

"What?" Molly's shrill voice rose with surprise. "No one ever, then?"

He shook his head and looked down upon his silk coverlet.

"But you look to be the same age as me, and I've had a husband and babe and many other men in my bed besides," Molly confessed.

"My tutor did say my education was neglected," Robert admitted.

"And so it be." Molly sat regarding him with a rush of sympathy. "No wonder you sicken, Sir Robert."

Robert made no answer. He only flushed again.

Molly had a momentary vision of John. He would not mind, she told herself. But to make sure, she would not tell him. Her face blazed. "Sir Robert," she whispered, her eyes all glistening, "I, too, am suffering for lack these many months."

He raised his moist eyes to hers, but he could not speak.

"Mayhap I can cure your trouble," she breathed, crawling on her hands and knees over the vast bed until she leaned over him. She seized one of his cold, limp hands and placed it into her bosom. Then she lowered her mouth upon his. His body stirred; he sighed. She reached down to where he stirred, and he stiffened beneath her fingers.

" 'Tis as good a size as any I've seen, Sir Robert," she assured him. "You need not be ashamed."

He sighed again as she tucked up her petticoats and sat astride him so that his hopeless longings found a home. But he had barely entered when he was spent with a great convulsion. His sallow face grew beet red.

"Oh," he groaned. "I did not think it would be so fine."

Molly lay back at his side. " 'Twas only a tease for me. Now that the first bloom is gone, we must do it again, more slowly, so that my wings may beat against yours."

He sighed luxuriously. "I am ready," he said.

Reaching a hand out to him, she found that indeed he was. "Young men be always ready," she laughed.

They spent a good hour at this play. Finally they lay back rumpled and warm with sweat in the cool room.

"Well, it seems you be well again, Master Robert."

"I have never been better," he answered seriously. "And I owe you everything. But I must escape this room and become a man upon my own estate. My wife has taken charge of all."

"You must truly become a man," Molly said severely. "And we must somehow take care of Lady Isobel." As Molly gathered the dishes together, she saw Robert's face cloud over. "Do not fear, Sir Robert," she said. "My mistress and I will help you."

But as soon as she shut Robert's door behind her, she glanced toward Lady Isobel's and found it half open. Lady Isobel was seated before her mirror. Great tapers on tapersticks shone down upon her. Her eyes met Molly's in the glass. Molly felt a chill of fear. She recollected what she had told Robert. If Lady Isobel wanted Robert out of the way to marry Giles, she might want Mistress Lettice and the babe gone too, so that Geoffrey's portion would go to Giles. Molly stopped in her tracks. Giles was still married. She frowned. It was something else Lady Isobel wanted, some sick excitement. And she, Molly, was but an unimportant obstacle in the face of all the Lady Isobel's schemes.

Lettice, too, descended the flowery stairs, for Philip had come calling. She frowned and bit her lip. Philip was becoming a nuisance. Yet there might be some way she could use him. She had already entrusted a servant with a letter for Virginia, explaining things as best she might to Dorothy. But her sister was often worse than useless.

Lettice threw open the door to the small red parlor, and Philip sprang to his feet. He crossed the room rapidly to seize and fondle her hand.

"Don't, Philip!" she cried. "The baby has been fretful all morning, and I am in no light mood."

At the mention of his rival's infant, Philip let her hand drop. Lettice sat herself in a high-backed chair, regarding him. She gave an exasperated little sigh. The red parlor was the most comfortable room in all the great, vast house. The effect of the warm wood paneling and the cheerful red draperies were hard for even Lady Isobel to chill, and indeed it was her favorite room. She had sat here earlier in the day, sewing with her maids. Later she would come down again, for she was having another portrait painted, this one with the small black page she had brought from the colonies.

Standing at the fire, Philip had his back to Lettice. He ran his slim hand over the white alabaster chimney piece, then turned to face her. "I cannot offer you a house as fine as this," he said abruptly, "though I may yet make a fortune in trade."

"You cannot offer me anything," she objected. "I am married to someone else."

"If he still lives."

"Yes," she said lowly.

"But I would like you to come to me whether he lives or not, Lettice. You are not safe with Isobel."

"You told me in the colonies that they were charming and reliable friends and that my husband was the villain." Why did he always manage to antagonize her? How could she have ever considered loving him?

He gazed at her moodily before speaking in a voice so low she could barely hear. "I do not trust Isobel."

"Surely she has nothing to gain by harming me."

"Her mind takes strange paths."

"She says that you and she think alike," Lettice accused.

"Perhaps that is why I do not trust her."

Lettice rose to her feet and began to pace. Finally she turned and stretched her hands toward him. "Philip, you must help me. I must somehow discover how Geoffrey fares. I think perhaps I should go to the king's court in London to—"

Philip uttered a short, cold laugh that was almost a bark, and he loosened her hands. "I help you? I owe him no favors for having you first. I shall rejoice if they hang him."

"Philip!" she cried. "How can you speak so? Why, you are my oldest friend!"

Philip's laugh died in his throat. He lunged to grasp her wrist, jerking her toward him until her face was but a few inches away. "I did not manage to discover all I would of you all those years when we played," he said between clenched teeth. "I play more seriously now."

"Oh, leave off, Philip," she said wearily. "You were ever the child, and these poor theatrics do not dignify you."

Glaring, he released her, his narrow, fine-boned face a surly red. "Mind what you say, Lettice, else I make you pay for it one day."

"If you will not help me, Philip, please go. Now that I am a mother, your childishness does not amuse me."

The ugly flush of his face blanched away. "Very well." He snatched up his hat from a walnut-topped table with legs supported by gilt caryatids. Lettice thought these fanciful golden creatures looked as foolish as her erstwhile lover. Philip pulled his cloak about his shoulders and sped to the door where he paused to look back.

"As I said before, I will give you until the child is weaned," he said. "But do not think to put me off again." Then he slammed the double doors together.

When he had ridden away, Lettice climbed the stairs to her chamber with relief. Philip did indeed distress her. She must make haste to search for James. Yet the babe was tender still for a journey so far, especially when his mother had no resources.

Young Geoffrey slept soundly in the cradle that had once held Robert, or so Nurse Smith had told her. Lettice thought the softly wrapped child grew more like Geoffrey every day, though his eyes when open were her own dark-lashed violet ones.

Lettice looked about the too-quiet room. Strange Molly had not returned. There was little about a house so filled with servants that could keep her away from her mistress. Fighting the fears that seemed to creep forth from the shadows, she settled into a padded chair near the fire and soon drowsed. When she awoke, the fire was out. Molly still had not returned. Lettice rubbed her hands together, but neither her hands nor her heart could warm. Each day she spent in the proximity of Lady Isobel filled her with greater unease. What lay behind the lady's hospitality and open-handed generosity? These softer virtues were unnatural to her.

Lettice stood and smoothed her skirts, trying to order her thoughts as well. Robert. Perhaps Robert would know where Molly was. They were friends, she knew. Cautiously, Lettice crept out into the passage toward the young man's room. Softly she knocked. No answer. She lifted the latch.

Robert lay sodden with sleep upon his great bed, his face a pale blur in the shadow of the bed curtains. She walked across the room to grasp his hand. He was drugged.

Lettice felt her own hand grow icy. Could Lady Isobel poison so freely?

But where was Molly?

Her next thought was Nurse Smith. She must find her. Entering the passage again, she began to run, speeding through all the great and narrow hallways of the house. Into the kitchen, the great saloon with its enormous pictures of Roman gods and goddesses, into the red parlor where the painter was setting up. But the servants merely rolled their eyes and shook their heads when she asked about the two women.

Lettice raised shaking hands to her mouth. Something dreadful must have happened to Molly, and to Nurse Smith too. Then another thought struck her. The babe! Oh, why had she deluded herself that all of them were safe in this great house? She raced up the stairs, threw open the door.

Lady Isobel stood in the center of the room. Her yellow hair hung down her silken back, her pearly complexion glowed, her eyes glinted. She parted her lips to reveal animal teeth. In her arms little Goeffrey nestled uneasily.

Lettice stretched out her arms as though Lady Isobel's touch would do him harm.

"You may have him, my dear." Lady Isobel relinquished him. "He is wet."

Lettice took a deep breath, looking down into the child's eyes to see that he was safe and well. Then she looked up. The expression on Lady Isobel's face was ironic.

"Where is my maid?" Lettice asked.

"She was not well," Lady Isobel said smoothly. "We are caring for her."

"Not well? Then you have arranged it! Robert is drugged!"

Lady Isobel's eyebrows arched. "Is he? Then think how fortunate you and your child are to enjoy such excellent health."

Waves of faintness swept over Lettice. She put out a hand to touch the paneling to steady herself. Then, hearing a sound, she looked toward the door. It opened slowly. A servant appeared supporting Molly's dainty feet, while another bore her head and shoulders. They lay the unconscious abigail upon the bed. There Molly, rested, blond curls all tousled.

"How soundly she sleeps," Lady Isobel sighed. Then she nodded curtly to the servants, who departed. When Lady Isobel turned to smile upon her, Lettice wondered how she could ever have envied her beauty. The corruption of her soul seemed to hang like a haze about her.

"My dear," Lady Isobel said. "Do not betray my hospitality by allowing your servant to pry into what does not concern her. So far you and your child are safe and well. It amuses me to care so for Giles's family. But do not try me." She stood silent for a moment, watching Lettice's face.

"I see you understand me," she said finally. She then crossed the room with sinuous movements and silently opened the door and shut it behind her.

Lettice closed her eyes with pain as she felt the whole vast bulk of the house press in upon her. She lay the babe in his cradle, then she breathlessly came to Molly's side to chafe her wrists. The maid did not stir. The babe cooed softly and kicked his tiny feet. Lettice saw that his fine, delicate eyelids were heavy. Soon he would be unconscious with healthy sleep rather than drugged stupor. But how long would he remain healthy?

They must leave this place, soon, this very day. But who would help her? With a pang, Lettice left Molly and the babe in search of Nurse Smith. Lady Isobel must be below, posing before the painter. Her self-love should keep her occupied for a while. The young artist, too, had fallen victim to her charm. It would please and entertain his yellow-haired patron to toy with him an hour or so, especially with Giles still so far away.

The house was a labyrinth of halls and rooms. However would she find the nurse? Gray shadows shifted about the high-ceilinged rooms as the windows reflected the heavy clouds that were blowing across the sky. Lettice longed to be free of this pile of stone and marble. She longed for the open air, longed for the bustle and life of London. For there she must find James.

As she passed by the great saloon, she heard a noise through the open door. A young housemaid was scrubbing the marble floors. She started when Lettice came up behind her. Lettice had never seen the girl before, and she thought this all very well. In her innocence or ignorance the girl might tell her the truth. But the girl seemed almost dim-witted, the result of Lady Isobel's discipline rather than an inborn slowness of the brain, Lettice judged. Their words were scarce intelligible to each other. The girl began to gesture with rough and uncouth movements until Lettice understood how it was that she could find Nurse Smith.

Lettice stole past the red parlor. The door was ajar. Lady Isobel's back was to her. Her long, yellow curls were swept back over her bare shoulders. The young painter was intent upon his work, tracing the large and sparkling diamonds that were about Lady Isobel's fragile throat.

Hurry! while they were engrossed. Lettice hastened up the stairs, then up another flight to the smaller rooms on the third flooor. Some of the maids and servants had cubbyholes up where the wings were joined to the main house. Lettice threw open a door. A cry of fear greeted her! Nurse Smith's plump, wrinkled face with its apple cheeks was so drawn in fear that it actually looked gaunt.

"Mistress Lettice," she whispered, sinking to her knees in agony. "Please, please let me alone, or she will make me pay!"

"No, Nurse, I will not," Lettice answered. "For your sake, for Robert's and for the babe's. Molly is drugged just like Robert, and we must all escape from her while we can."

"No, no," the nurse moaned. "I never believed she was so hard. She will kill me—or worse."

"We must find where she hides her potions," Lettice insisted, "so that Robert and Molly can escape with us."

"Escape," the nurse whispered. "Yes." Dazed, she stared at Lettice until her old eyes grew clearer and she seemed to gather courage. Shakily, she rose.

Lettice began to pace the tiny room, which was furnished with only a poor hard bed, a chest and washstand. In her anxiety she bit her lip until it was raw.

"Oh, Molly or Robert must not prove too weak to travel. We must rouse them somehow. Lady Isobel understands me well, I think. She knows I will not desert my maid after all we have been through. And the babe, too, is tiny for journeying. We must find a shelter somewhere."

"Nurse Brown," Nurse Smith muttered.

Lettice stared at her, wondering if the old woman had lost her senses.

"Nurse Brown, my dear old friend, nurse for many years

to a good family some miles away. We were friends as girls, and then we lost each other as we grew up. Now she is set up in a cottage of her own so that she may live peacefully in her last years. She visited me while Lady Isobel was gone. Surely she will take my poor Robert in, and the babe, and I can hide there safe from Lady Isobel."

Lettice came to grasp her hands. "Oh, Nurse Smith, if only we may! That way I could go to London to plead my husband's case at Court. Oh, is it far?"

"But two days' journey."

Lettice exhaled with relief. "Then we shall do it, somehow! Tonight!"

"Tonight?" The nurse seemed ready to sink to her knees again. "But how can we move Master Robert? And Lady Isobel will not let me near him."

"If we stay longer, she will have us totally in her power. First, if we can, we must discover her poisons. But we may not be able to speak again. Plan to meet us at the garden house tonight—say midnight. There is plenty of shrubbery there where we may hide."

"But how will you manage, my dear?"

"I don't know," Lettice said. "But I must."

"Then I shall be there at midnight," the old woman said, summoning up all her courage. "But pray you, mistress, do not abandon Master Robert. I could not love him more were he my own son."

"I understand," Lettice agreed. "And I know your good heart. I will place my child in your hands while I go on to London."

Lettice left the old servant's room, wondering how she would carry out the awesome tasks before her. There would be no problem if Robert and Molly were themselves. She must see if there was any chance of rousing Robert. Surely he must wake to be fed. Or would Lady Isobel allow him to starve to death while unconscious? The halls were growing darker as the gloomy day drew to a close. But thankfully she saw no other soul. She held her breath as she passed Lady Isobel's room, but though she could see yellow candlelight seeping under the door, there was no sign of the witch lady herself.

Cautiously she opened the double white paneled doors that led to Robert's room and his prison. Poor young man, she thought. There was a single candle burning atop a cabinet, which reflected in the highly polished wood. The thin, sallow form was lost in his great bed in this sumptuous and over-large room. What good was his wealth to him? She went to his side to feel his wrist and discover his condition. His pulse beat . . . was it slow? His body seemed cold and clammy.

She smoothed his sheets, then stiffened as her hand came in contact with a strange object. Stifling a scream, she drew it forth to examine it by candlelight. It was a strange and twisted root with the tiny clothes of a man upon it and hair fixed to the top. She dropped the object to the floor. How loathsome it was! Its touch would haunt her always. But she knew from stories well enough what it was. It was a mandrake root. The root could work for good or evil. It could cause a man who could not perform to become erect. But surely that was not Lady Isobel's motive, though who else would have placed it there like some obscene joke upon the husband she spurned? Were it the old days, Lady Isobel would be burned as a witch.

But what drug did Lady Isobel use? Lettice looked about. If only she could find the source, she might stop these poisonings. She must find a way to set Robert free.

Cautiously she peered through the great double doors of Robert's chamber. She heard footsteps in the passage. Lady Isobel moved languidly toward her room, bearing a candle. Her lips were moist and parted, her hair all disheveled. Her left hand trailed behind her, and a fan was dangling from her wrist. Behind her panted the lank-haired painter. He reached to play with the fan as courting gentlemen were known to do. With his free hand he tugged at his waistcoat, leaving it in a heap upon the floor. Then he grasped the fastenings of his breeches. His mouth, too, was open, and he panted audibly. Lady Isobel let out a throaty laugh. She freed her closed fan, and opened it to wave at the young man's burning face. As she disappeared between the doors of her chamber, he moaned loudly and fled after her as fast as his faltering legs would carry him. He only took time to bang the doors shut behind him.

Lettice smiled. Lady Isobel would obviously not be free for some time. But on the other hand it would be impossible to search her room. Yet the rest of the house would be open.

Lettice stopped in her chamber just long enough to find

Molly regaining consciousness. "Hurry," she warned the sluggish maid. "Gather up the babe and whatever we can carry with us. We will leave at midnight, come what may. Can you travel?"

"What?" Molly shook her heavy head. "I'm not sure, mistress. But I will try to place one foot before the other to walk. As long as that witch woman be far from me." The thought seemed to waken Molly's memory. Her eyes sharpened with fear. "Oh, she does turn my heart cold. She wants no one to spoil her game with Master Robert. Oh, I'm lucky to be lyin' here talkin' to you. And I do fear for him." She shook her head.

"You must be ready," Lettice said urgently. "We shall have trouble enough with Robert, and we do not want to abandon him."

Molly rose up off the bed at this and set her feet upon the floor. But at her second step she sank to her knees.

"Oh, Molly!" Lettice cried. "Whatever shall we do?"

"I be all right, mistress," Molly whispered weakly. "I swear. I must get away from her."

Lettice watched as Molly raised herself and went to the water pitcher. Reluctantly the mistress left her maid, hoping Molly's dogged determination and unquenchable love of life would restore her in time.

But there was other business at hand. How she would love to search her hostess's room for evidence of poison to take to a magistrate. She hurried down the broad stairs and looked into the red parlor. She had not really expected the lady to have left anything there. Two objects met her eyes: There was the diamond necklace, carelessly discarded when passion had overcome the artist and his model; and Lady Isobel's velvet pocket. The lady carried it with her at all times about the house. Lettice snatched it up. Sure enough, there was some sinister-appearing vials inside. The lady had gotten careless indeed. There was also a packet of folded papers, which appeared like the household recipes Lettice's mother had written in her spidery handwriting and bequeathed her daughter on her death.

But these recipes were of another sort. One struck Lettice with a particular chill. "To make a sleeping apple," it began, "take opium, mandrake, juice of hemlock and the seeds of henbane."

But which of all these potions the lady used was impossible to know. They could not wait to revive Robert and bring Molly to greater wakefulness. They must flee that night. If only one of the menservants might aid them and carry Robert from his bed. But the Lady Isobel had thoroughly frightened them. Lettice was about to go up to drag Robert from his bed herself when a strange sight met her eyes: Lady Isobel's diamonds had risen off the tabletop and were suspended in midair! With a sudden swish they began making toward the window. Lettice, who had been standing near the wall, lunged to close her hand about them, feeling eerily as though she were wrestling with the spirits of the dead.

But as she neared the window, her eyes met the startled ones of a lean man looking in. The light from the tapers on their stands and from the fireplace made it plain that he was not a ghost, and that the chill she felt was not from a spirit. The window stood open a crack, and sweet night air wafted in.

Their eyes locked together. Each tugged. Lettice pulled upon the diamonds, and the thin man was pulling upon a fishline and pole he held. Lettice now saw the fishhook caught among the gems. The man gazed at her steadily. She found that she was quite unafraid of him—less than of the Lady Isobel.

Lettice moistened her lips to speak. "I am afraid I cannot let you have the diamonds. But if you will step inside, I will speak with you."

The young man tested her once more with his warm eyes, then nodded, opened the window wider and stepped in.

"Please sit down," Lettice said, coolly gesturing toward an elegant chair. "I have never spoken with a thief before, and I am uncertain how to begin."

The young man, who was halfway to the chair, straightened and flushed. "I ben't no thief, mistress. I be Alf the angler. 'Tis a much more skilled trade, after all."

Lettice felt the corners of her mouth twitch as she controlled herself to keep from laughing. Alf was a very serious person, and she found she quite liked him. But she must not let herself be fooled, for whatever he said, he was a thief after all.

"I'm sorry," she said. "Please sit."

Alf did so, his over-large hands clasped between his thin

308

knees. He had left his fishing pole outside. She noticed that though his clothing was road soiled, his waistcoat was of good-quality silk and richly embroidered. No doubt he had angled it out of some gentleman's window.

"I've taken a great risk to come inside like this," Alf said ruefully.

"I have taken a great chance inviting you in," Lettice reminded him. She, too, sat and began conversation with some urgency. "I am almost a prisoner here, you see, and must escape. But I need the help of someone who can go upstairs to carry away a man who lies unconscious."

Alf sat back. His lean face twisted up. He exhaled a low whistle. "Sounds very dangerous to me, mistress. I be afeared I cannot do any such darin' thing unless the price be very good." His hand stole toward the diamonds lying on the caryatid-supported table.

"Please!" Lettice said. "Not the diamonds. We might be traced through them, and I refuse to steal from Lady Isobel."

"What then?" Alf lowered his hand to trace along the gilt breast of a caryatid.

Lettice bit her lip, then brightened. "Pearls. A string of pearls."

Alf nodded. "Pearls be good and hard to trace without a setting."

"These are lovely pearls," Lettice said. "They were given to me by a queen."

"Think of that." Alf's eyes grew dreamy at the thought. He seemed less the thief and more the tender poet.

Lettice leaned toward him to lay a hand on his arm. "I hope that I may trust you, Alf, whether you are a thief or not."

Alf sprang to his feet and tugged at his forelock. "Of course you can trust me, mistress. Angling be my livelihood, but I always stay loyal to my friends. And I think you will be my friend."

"Good," Lettice said with a smile. Then she rapidly gave him instructions. Once he understood them, he nodded, then exited the way he had come in. Lettice shut the window, carefully leaving it unlatched. For a moment she stared moodily into the blackness of the night. She had no way of knowing how this day's work would end, but merely moved step by step, praying they would all be

309

saved. Alf she took to be a gift from God. He had softened some of her worst fears. Quietly she moved back to the table where Lady Isobel's pocket lay. Reaching inside, Lettice removed one of the vials. She prayed it was not deadly poison, for she would not be a murderess. Then she opened the double doors to go out. In the dim light she did not notice a small turbaned figure rise from its resting place behind a heavy cabinet in the corner.

Lettice stood before Lady Isobel's door. Her heart was racing and the candle in her hand was trembling. This was the most dangerous task of all. The vial was safe within a pocket fastened to her girdle. Lettice knocked loudly. There was a moment of silence, then the painter wrenched open the door and fled down the hall. Lettice entered to find Lady Isobel bare-breasted behind the gold-satin lining of her petit-point bed curtains. Smiling sardonically through the glowing flowerets that were surrounding her, she seemed like the serpent in the Garden of Eden. She seemed not to care who knew how many occupied her bed. Nevertheless, she looked as beautiful as ever.

"It is time I talked with you," Lettice said as she walked toward her hostess. "I must know whether you have heard anything from Giles or Geoffrey."

Lady Isobel stretched languidly. "Nothing, the poor dear. I quite pine for Giles. That is why I must console myself."

"Indeed," Lettice said. She moved to the bedside quietly enough, but her mind was busily planning. There was a Chinese lacquer table before Lady Isobel's mirror. Upon it sat a half-full glass of wine. Dare she chance it, or would the poisoner herself be suspicious of others? She must be sure Lady Isobel did not discover Alf when he came to take Robert away.

"Geoffrey must be well, else we would have heard something," Lettice said.

Lady Isobel pursed her lips and looked out of the corner of her eyes. "A pity to miss the hanging if there is one. They say a virile man's organ becomes enlarged."

"Beast!" Lettice hissed, springing toward the side of the bed with her hand upraised to slap the leering beauty's face.

Lady Isobel laughed deep in her throat and leaped up,

anxious, it seemed, to display the rounded curves that had so recently been caressed. Lettice bit her lip. She must not let herself become Lady Isobel's toy. Cautiously she felt inside her pocket for the little vial.

Lady Isobel went to the wardrobe to draw out a shift and a pink-silk bed gown. While she was pulling the shift over head, Lettice pulled the cork, and her hand darted out over the goblet of wine. Before Lady Isobel could free her mocking eyes, Lettice had dropped the vial upon the floor. With her toe she nudged it gently toward the bed curtains until it was well hid.

Lady Isobel turned once again to smile her wolfish smile. "My dear, you must learn to adventure a bit with love. Philip sits morosely in his hall, panting for you, and you do nothing but throw Geoffrey into his face. Though Geoffrey is indeed a worthy lover, Philip is not to be scorned. He has a fascinating imagination, I am sure."

"I do not care for the kinds of imaginings you seem to relish," Lettice said. Do not let her provoke you, she reminded herself. Her own game was far more important.

Lady Isobel glided to her mirror. The tapers from their stands on either side shone down, bathing her peachy beauty in golden light. She removed a patch from off her cheek and began to comb her long, yellow curls. She settled lightly on a little chair.

Lettice held her breath as Lady Isobel's elegant fingers with their sharp nails reached for the goblet and drew in a long drink. She set it down and opened her mouth to utter one more barbed remark. Then her eyes widened, and she struggled to her feet. As she turned to fix accusing eyes upon Lettice, her knees buckled, and she fell headlong in a flurry of silk.

Lettice drew in a deep breath. She knelt by the lady's side. Lady Isobel did not appear to be dying, but there was no way to be sure.

Lettice grasped her under her arms and pulled her onto her bed. Then she opened a drawer in the inlaid chest and searched through the contents until she found some yards of ribbons. As she bound the lady's hands and feet, she reflected that binding her was even a greater pleasure than freeing Geoffrey had been. Lastly she seized one of the lady's stockings and tied it about her mouth as a gag. Then she arranged the witch woman so that she faced away toward the back curtains of the bed, her hair covering her face and the gag.

Lettice stepped back, dusting her hands together with satisfaction as she admired her work. When she stepped out into the passage, her heart rose with a feeling of freedom and joy she had not felt since the night she had married Geoffrey.

All was dark as a tomb as Lettice, holding the babe in one arm and supporting Molly with the other, approached the garden house. Would Alf carry out his task as promised? The fact that Molly moved yet so sluggishly made Lettice suspect that Lady Isobel would not rouse for some time. Yet she could not be sure. A low whistle came from the bushes. She could barely make out Alf as he stepped forth. Another figure emerged supporting Robert, and yet another bulkier figure that was obviously wearing women's dress.

"Who's there?" Lettice whispered in surprise.

" 'Tis my good friend Jack and his mort."

"His mort?"

"Lady friend, you would say, mistress."

"Well, the more the merrier," Lettice said hesitantly. "But where is Nurse Smith?"

"Here, mistress," the good woman said, coming about the side of the garden house. "But I must say we've fallen among strange folk."

"We are lucky to have them." Lettice drew forth the Queen of Pamunkey's pearls. "Here, Alf, these are for you."

But he brushed her hand aside. "Nay, mistress," he said. "Keep them till the journey's end. You will trust me more then."

"I am beginning to trust you very much indeed," Lettice said. But he tightened his grip upon her hand, hissing for silence. Approaching light footsteps were plainly heard. After some moments they could barely make out a small turbaned figure—Lady Isobel's page.

"Please, mistress," a light voice cried out with a half sob. "Do not leave me with *her*."

"But however will we hide you?" Lettice objected.

"No mind," Alf said. "We'll take him away to hide

among the actors. No doubt they'll pay some for the favor."

With a sigh Lettice agreed. "Then let us put as many miles as possible between ourselves and the Lady Isobel," she said.

XVIII

It was Giles who untied Lady Isobel. Her servants had carefully crept around her as she slept through the day. But Giles hesitated before removing the gag. "I think I like you better silenced, sweet Isobel. Your tongue has a most cruel edge. But where is my brother's wife?"

Lady Isobel moaned behind her gag and writhed in an agony of frustration. Her numb hands struggled with the stocking. Giles reached to grasp the slender wrists while her eyes showed that she would willingly kill him.

"I take it it was she who bound you, then escaped." Giles gave a short laugh. "Ah, my dear, you have never been lovelier than with your tongue gentled. God did indeed err when he allowed women to speak."

Isobel lashed out at him until he relented and uncovered her provocative lips. She seemed about to break into an angry torrent of words, but instead her tones softened, and her eyes as well. "Giles, my love, you have been away a most incredibly long time."

"I had a devil of a time convincing the authorities in Virginia that I was myself. I had to borrow money for my passage home. But even so, Geoffrey is ahead of me by a week or more, and must be stopped. He may even come here; so it is well his wife is gone."

"You have suffered, my poor dear," Lady Isobel said softly as she leaned to press her mouth upon his.

Giles breathed deeply and clutched her to him. He ran his hands down her straight, silk-covered back, whispering huskily, "The thought of you has tormented me these many weeks. No matter how perverse you are, my love for

315

you is like a fever." His arm curved about her as though she were of incomparable value.

"You love me because I torment you." Half laughing, she showed her rapacious teeth, though he could not see them.

"Then why do you love me?" he asked as his mouth sought the throbbing pulse in her throat. As though they had a life of their own, her long, narrow hands stole along the muscles of his back.

"Because you know me so well, and yet cannot stop loving me. And yet," she added, "there is much you fail to understand." But if she subtly warned him, he did not hear her, for he was blinded by his love for her and his passion.

When they rested spent and quiet upon the rumpled sheets behind the gold lining of the petit-point curtains, he gazed about the shadowed room, then hoarsely said, "Tell me truly, Isobel, that it was not Geoffrey who emerged first from our mother's womb. I know now that it is but one of your tricks."

"Why, Giles," she murmured with a wolfish little smile. "How can I tell you that? I would not reveal my tricks."

"You will drive me mad one day," he said seriously, bending his dark head to kiss her again as though he were a man in the desert sucking water from a spring.

Lettice came to value Alf's company, for he opened a whole new world to her. Traveling awkwardly with children—the babe and the small African page—and the victims of Lady Isobel's potions, it had taken almost three days to reach Nurse Brown's cottage. She was a very thin, frail, old woman whose mind wandered now and then. But Lettice was overjoyed to discover that the family Nurse Brown had served for so long was the Finch family, Geoffrey's own.

"Think of that," Nurse Smith said, raising her plump hands in wonder. "I never realized the babe Nurse Brown loved so well was Master Henry."

Nurse Brown told Lettice many tales of Geoffrey's baby and boyhood ways, though at times she confused him with Giles. "Oh, such a sweet mite! So like Master Geoffrey," she cooed over baby Geoffrey.

Lettice was able to leave her child with light heart, satisfied that the only danger from the two old women was that

316

they might smother him with too much love. Robert revived and strengthened daily in this simple though happy setting, and Molly, too, grew stronger. But Lettice was determined to make the journey without her. Molly and Robert could get along well together and aid the old women. And Molly was a country girl at heart and happy to be free of Robert's overwhelmingly large house to walk in the meadows and breathe the spring air.

For the journey, Lettice borrowed some shapeless old clothes from Nurse Brown, though the hems and seams had to be let out. Alf smiled to see her, but declared her as beautiful as ever. Looking into the glass, Lettice doubted him.

Finally, as Lettice and her little band of friends were ready to leave for London, Nance, who was Jack's lady friend and who had come along with Alf the night they'd escaped, threw an arm protectively about Lettice's shoulder and confided to her that they had all just elected Alf as "upright man," or leader of their little pack of rogues. Further along the road they were joined by Rolf, another of Alf's friends, who appeared to be an old maimed soldier. He survived by seeking out former Royalist commanders whom he would pretend to have served under, until, with misty eyes, the military men pressed alms into his eagerly outstretched, shaking hands. But inside a rowdy tavern Rolf would shed his bandages and run his fingers through his hair, loosening the graying powder. Then he would smudge away the painted wrinkles and stand tall to reveal a youthful body. Delighted, the barmaids flocked to surround him. They'd sit upon his knees while he pinched their luscious curves with hands now firm and strong.

Along dusty roads under the fresh green leaves of May, Tom O'Bedlam, another of Lettice's little vagabond band, staggered ahead of the troop. He had foxes' tails sewn to his clothes to feign madness. But he never forgot to keep his hand outstretched for whatever was offered, and his eye slyly was alert for an unguarded pocket to pick. He once winked at Lettice, then stumbled into a ploughed field, frightening a skylark from its nest in a cup of grass.

But Nance and her lover, Jack, had the most interesting scheme of all. Whatever was Jack's real name had now been long forgotten, for he was indeed a "Whip Jack," or counterfeit mariner who presented his mort as a poor creature he'd saved from shipwreck through his heroism. Jack told this tale with such art and embellishment that the countryfolk and prosperous merchants of the towns and villages listened with open mouths. Then they would ungrudgingly give up coin. He had curly, dark-brown hair, ruddy cheeks and a flashing smile. Jack should have been a man of the theater; he had in fact many friends among England's strolling players and puppeteers. One band of puppeteers, footsore along the country roads, happily took charge of the slave boy, thinking he would attract trade at the next village fair. And the boy went happily, fascinated by the little wooden-faced figures that could be made to move and dance like men.

Lettice laughed at her new friends' antics, yet she admitted that she had never felt so safe when traveling as with these folk. Though they had their tricks and their vanities, they were kindlier than most gentlefolk she had met. But Alf warned her that all rogues and vagabonds were not as good hearted as these who were his special friends. Often as they walked the dusty roads, she would have misgivings as she found Alf's adoring eyes upon her. He revered her and never lay a hand upon her, but most times whistled cheerfully as he trudged along beside her, carrying her bundle of belongings as well as his own.

One morning as they neared the outskirts of London on the Southwark side of the bridge, he confided, "I must admit to you, Mistress Lettice, that I've given many a lass a green gown—and not all light skirts at that—yet my heart never has gone out as it does to you, nor has any maid seemed so fair—"

"I am not a maid, but a wife . . . ," Lettice began, raising her hands toward his lips as though to shut off the flow of words. His hand met hers, his thin brown face was screwed up with the effort of explaining his emotions.

"Oh, well I know, Mistress Lettice, that you are wife, not maid, and I would do anything to help you find your man again." He released her hand and walked with his eyes upon the ground for a moment.

"No," he continued, "you are like the sun and the moon to me, high and above me, and not fit to be wed by jumping over a dead horse hand in hand the way we of the road are promised to one another. No, alas, I shall probably never wed."

318

"Oh, don't say that, Alf!" Lettice cried, looking upon the rough, short-cut locks of his bent head. He was barely as tall as she, having lived upon scraps for most of his life.

"But I do have my wedding clothes put away," he confided. "And I want you to know of it."

Lettice was taken aback and could not understand his meaning. His blue eyes met hers, and all the cunning of the road dropped away.

"Then you will marry?" she said hesitantly.

He shook his head and reached up behind his decorated waistcoat to scratch his back. "No, mistress. In all likelihood hangin' be my fate."

"Oh, I pray not." Lettice bit her lip. What had been Geoffrey's fate these many months? Oh, if only James could help discover what had happened and clear Geoffrey's name and set him free. With these thoughts the look she cast upon Alf was doubly sad.

" 'Tis nothin' to grieve over," he said. "We must expect it. It be a good end for many a rogue with his friends gathered 'round to watch. That be why I have white wedding clothes, all clean and pure, laid by in a tavern not far from Tyburn. If ever I be hung, mistress, since I love you so awfully, I would ask you to bring my wedding clothes to me that I might die in style."

"Oh, Alf!" Lettice cried. "Who knows how far apart our paths will carry us? And I would not want you to resign yourself to hanging. Surely there is a maid as sweet as yourself who would walk the roads by your side and bear your children to look after you in your old age."

"Bear them in a ditch, mistress?" Alf shook his head. His eyes had a kind of innocence that belied his trade. "No, never. But if I thought your hands might bring my wedding clothes to me in the jail, 'twould lighten my heart."

"I will if I can, Alf," Lettice promised. "Though it grieves me to think of it."

"Your answer be good enough, mistress." Alf closed his eyes for a moment as though seeing a vision of his future. " 'Twill comfort me."

Lettice glanced once more at her wiry, sunny-natured companion of the road with his fishing rod slung over one shoulder. He began to whistle, at first slowly and mournfully, but soon happily again. He broke off to grin at her.

Lettice smiled back. She would miss this man once she got to London and to James.

Nurse Brown tottered to the door, thinking to look out over the fields for Molly. But before she could open it, the stout oak panel was pushed in, and Giles, her old nursling, stood there, panting. His dark hair hung in disordered locks, his face was suffused with blood and rage, his gait unsteady. There were wine stains upon his rumpled shirt.

Nurse Brown shook her head and pursed her thin lips with disapproval. The knot of gray hair at the back of her skull slipped loose. She did not do things well anymore. But Giles refused to be chastened, and he seized her thin, brittle arm.

"Nurse!" he cried. "I have ridden this long way seeking you. I cannot stand it anymore. You must tell me the truth of the matter."

"Do sit down and rest yourself," Nurse Brown half soothed, half scolded as though he had never left the nursery. "You seem all but demented. You know I have always warned you not to grow too excited." The nurse settled herself into a chair. She was excessively tired that day, unused to having extra people and a babe once more about the place. Waves of gray fog seemed to infect her brain so that it was hard at times to see or hear or think clearly. Then the fog would lift again, and she would be her old self.

Now what could be agitating Giles so? She found that her gnarled old hands were shaking. She could no longer cope with the strong emotions of younger folk. If only she could leave all that caring and worrying behind, but it seemed never to be. There was always someone in need. And she dearly loved Geoffrey's little babe. Yes, Geoffrey had always had a sweeter temper than Giles. But Giles was looking at her with burning eyes. With a trembling hand, she rubbed her wrinkled forehead and looked about at the simple, substantial walls of her cottage.

"What was it ye want, Master Giles?"

"Nurse," he demanded, bending until his wine breath washed over her frail face, "you must tell me. Was it not I who came first from our mother's body?"

"Why, yes, Giles. Certainly. It was your way to be ever first if you could."

Giles straightened to look down upon her. "Are you sure

320

Nurse? *She* has told me otherwise. But did my mother tell you?"

"Not your mother, Giles. The mistress was very ill. She remembered nothing of the birth."

"But you're sure it was I who emerged first?"

"Why, of course, Master Giles. I was in the chamber where your mother had her lying-in. A lovely lady, the mistress. I hope she is well. Yes, I'm sure it was you." Nurse Brown paused for a moment. "Or was it Geoffrey? He was a happier babe than you, Master Giles. Very much like the babe upstairs." Nurse Brown glanced up toward the stairway, then trembled even more. Giles, too, looked up with a serious expression upon his flushed face. They had told her not to tell anyone the babe was there. That was the trouble with age. It was very hard to get anything straight in your head. Now look at the strange way Giles looked at her! As though ever so many thoughts raced through his handsome head.

"The babe . . . here . . . ," he said. Ah, he could see right through her.

There was a step on the threshold, and a lady appeared, all silken and yellow-haired. In one hand she carried a half-drained goblet of red wine. Through the door Nurse Brown could see a coach drawn up outside in the bright spring sunshine.

The nurse could see that it was not Giles's wife, despite the gray mists that threatened to close over her. Ah, but the ways of the gentry were beyond her. But Nurse Brown did not like the look of this lady's eyes, which were cold enough to make you shiver. Yes, they glinted with an awful kind of mischief. The nurse had seen that look on a woman's face once before, years ago, when as but a bit of a girl, she had stumbled into a moonlit glade to find a circle of silent witches there. Fascinated, she had hidden to see one strip her body bare before a flame and reveal her most private parts to the moon. The memory had given the nurse nightmares for the rest of her life.

"Nurse," Giles said. "Before this lady you must tell me which of us was first."

There was a buzzing in the nurse's ears, which rose to a pounding. "You, Giles," she said weakly.

"You see, Isobel," Giles said triumphantly, turning to the lady.

"But, Giles." The lady dimpled as though all were a huge joke. "She is nothing but an old fool. Can you not see that she is very old and that her memory is gone? There were others at the birth. They may have other stories to tell. I may keep what I have discovered a secret, or I may not." Isobel took a sip of wine, her eyes provoking him over the rim of the crystal.

The edge of the mist turned to flame as Nurse Brown's pulse quickened. She saw clearly what it was between the two of them. "Nay, Giles. You are a fool. Can you not see that she tries to bedevil you with the story?" The nurse gave a cackling laugh. "She would keep you under her thumb that way. Of course you were first." There seemed to be a buzzing about the room—flies, or evil spirits? Sometimes her old ears did ring these days. But the two of them were speaking. It tired the nurse to listen to them. She must close her eyes before the fog engulfed her. Yes, life had become too much, and soon, dear Lord, she would be lost forever in the fog.

Giles's mouth tightened, his reddened eyes hardened. Slowly he turned toward Isobel. "Would you bedevil me, Isobel?" he asked gruffly.

She laughed, stretching her long neck. Her limp fingers loosened about the stem of her goblet, and it fell to the flagstone floor, smashing and crimsoning the shards of glass.

"You could have had me with your body alone," he said.

"But, Giles." The lady parted knifelike teeth. A bead of saliva glistened on her lip as she laughed. "You know how I like excitement."

"Excitement," he whispered. "Did it excite you that I feared to lose everything that matters to me? Did it excite you that I had my own brother abducted and would have killed him?"

"Yes, Giles," the lady whispered. "It did excite me. I would be the puppet master. The grander the passions, the more I am thrilled." She whirled away from him with a little pirouette. Her scarlet dress was cut incredibly low, and the tucked-up skirts revealed a petticoat striped round with red and blue. The high heel of her slipper ground into some of the broken glass.

"Oh, but it has been such fun," she chortled, eyes dancing with glee. "Geoffrey bound and sold, the two of you seething with hatred. Such excitement! If only I could have had both of you in the same bed."

He rushed toward her, drunkenly, but she easily avoided him. He leaned on the heavy plank table, head bowed. "I will kill you, Isobel," he said thickly.

"No, my darling," she said. "You are too besotted, and besides, I fear that you are too weak to play a master villain. And it begins to bore me. Philip would be stronger, but alas there are no surprises between us. If only I could loosen Geoffrey from his lady wife. To make a man love me against his will is delicious indeed."

"You will not lie with him again," Giles snarled.

"Perhaps." She turned about, thoughtful, to look out the window. "But there is something about him. Something . . . although you are cut to the same pattern. Yes," she sighed deeply, "something you do not have." Dimpling, she turned to regard him again. She tossed her long, yellow curls flirtatiously over her shoulder.

"Of course you will have the most of the estate . . . unless . . . unless. . . ." She burst into gales of laughter.

"You will not make trouble for me, Isobel," he said with a warning in his tone.

"I adore trouble!" she cried, stretching her graceful, long arms toward the ceiling. "Trouble is my aphrodisiac. It excites me so that if I loved all day, I would not be satisfied."

He held one strong hand toward her, a bitter smile upon his face. "Come here, and I will show you true satisfaction," he challenged.

"What can you show me new?" she said, half intrigued.

"Come kiss me and see."

"Should I?" She cocked her head to one side. "Perhaps. I will try you once again—though you are growing well worn." She stretched her long, elegant arms to him.

He drew her close. Their lips joined as though the blood of one would flow into the body of another, as though a single heart beat for both of them. Her hands fluttered, then flattened against his back as passion gentled her. He clutched her narrow shoulders. Then slowly his hands rose until they were closed about her throat. Her eyes widened, her face changed color.

"Giles, I beg of you!" she choked as she recognized the

323

drunken rage he had disguised seductively. He gave a little laugh, and his fingers tightened. She tried to scream, but could not. Her fists beat upon his back. She jabbed at him with the heel of her red slippers, biting into his shins. Pained, he flung her from him until she landed in a heap upon the floor. A shard of glass gashed her wrist. With a shock, she looked upon the blood gushing forth.

"Giles!" she cried, raising the dripping hand beseechingly toward him. "Stop the flow, or I will die!"

"Do you not enjoy the sensation?" he said, his voice all ice. "After all, death will be new to you."

"Giles!" she begged, beginning to sob. "Please, Giles! I did not mean those words I said."

"Not while you fear for your life."

"No, Giles!" she cried, hugging her wrist to her petticoat pressing with her free hand. "Get me a bandage. The cut is deep."

Roughly, he grabbed her wrist free and watched as her blood dropped upon the floor. She looked at him with horror, then screamed and kicked out at him. He made a bar of his forearm to force her back upon the floor. "Struggling only makes you bleed faster, my sweet," he said between set teeth. "Now tell me—who was first, Geoffrey or I?"

At this, peals of laughter swept over her, and all her lovely body shook with hysteria. "Oh, but you show me something new, Giles," she gasped. "No one has ever made me fear so far my life." She drew a deep breath. "And I thought you weak, my darling. But this move is yours, and you have humbled me. I know you will dare anything. I love a man who is strong."

Giles's grim expression did not change.

"Giles!" she pleaded when she saw he did not relent. "Giles, I grow faint." And then with all her might, she tried to free herself from his weight. Her jaw tightened, she clenched her vicious teeth, then opened them to scream with rage, "You fool! You worm! You are not half the man your brother is! I would he had killed you while he had the chance!"

Still the expression of his face did not change, but he reached down beside himself to grasp something from off the floor. Wide-eyed, she stretched her head back to see what he was doing so that she bared her long, white neck.

It was very easy for him to plunge the knifelike shard of glass into her throat. She uttered one gurgling groan.

Unsteadily, he arose and looked at his hands almost in surprise. He shook his head as though dazed. Isobel's eyes were already glazing over. Nurse Brown seemed sound asleep, but her thin lips began to move. She spoke as though from another world.

"So the witch is dead. So much blood. You were always one for rage and jealousy, my boy."

He looked at her blankly, as though not knowing quite where he was. Then he came to kneel by her side as he had so often as a boy. "Nurse." His voice was hoarse with urgency. "You must remember. Which of us was first—myself or Geoffrey."

"You, Giles," she said reassuringly, patting the hand that rested upon her knee. Then, after a pause, she added, "Or was it Geoffrey?"

Giles picked up her hand and found it chilly. She spoke no more. Her old eyes closed. Her breathing became that of a sleeper. The whole scene had upset her aging wits. Giles swallowed. He loved the nurse as he did few other beings.

He returned to Isobel. The nurse had seen through her, and now his love was already growing cold. She had provoked him to many crimes. Her own death was merely the latest. What must he do next? There was the matter of Geoffrey's child. If Lady Isobel had not lied, the child would be heir after Geoffrey. God knew where Geoffrey was by now. Giles, stood, staggered, then turned toward the stairway that went up along the rough stone wall.

He started with shock as he looked directly into the muzzle of a cocked and loaded pistol. "You have killed my wife," a young voice said. "I take it you are Giles Finch and not my former tutor."

Giles saw that his mistress's husband was very young and very frail and that his character was still half formed. His hand shook as though he had been ill. "Why, no, master," Giles, said engagingly. "No, Sir Robert, I am indeed your tutor."

"You lie," Robert insisted, his thin jaw firming. "Henry would never have killed Isobel, no matter how angry she made him."

Giles came to the bottom of the stairs and placed one

foot upon the step. He held up one hand, offering it palm up, as though Robert were a horse or a dog he was trying to tame. "My dear boy, it is obvious that you do not understand."

"I am no longer a boy," Robert said. "And now it seems I am a widower. But you cannot come up here. They warned me to keep you away from the child."

Giles chuckled. He began to relax and took another step upward. "Have you primed your pistol properly? It may misfire, you know."

Robert's narrow shoulders tensed and hunched. His rich clothing seemed too big on him. "I think that it will not misfire," he said. Giles's eyes narrowed. The effects of the drink were gone. "The child is kin to me. And if you shoot me, you will be in great trouble."

"I think not," Robert said evenly. "After all, you have murdered my wife."

The word "murder" surprised Giles. It had all happened so fast. He turned to look back to where the Lady Isobel lay all sprawled, yet still beautiful. Then he turned again to face Robert's pistol. "I will have to take my chance."

"Very well," Robert answered without hesitation as he pulled the trigger.

Nothing happened. The click of the poorly primed pistol was barely heard in the still cottage. Robert looked down at it with dismay. Bursting into laughter, Giles wrenched it from his grasp and struck him alongside the head. Robert's slim body fell with a crash.

The sound roused Nurse Brown. She looked about dazedly until her eyes found her nursling once more. "Ah," she said, shaking her head. "You always did want to be first, Giles. But now that I think on it, I am not sure which of you came first from your mother's womb—you or Geoffrey. It was too long ago."

"What on earth is happening? The babe and I could not even sleep!" a thin voice cried.

Giles smiled grimly as Nurse Smith came to the top of the stairs with the babe in her arms. Her eyes went wide with shock as she saw the fallen Robert and the blood-soaked Lady Isobel. Giles pointed the pistol at her. The innocent woman did not realize that it could not be fired until it was reloaded. Trembling, she let him take the child, then sank to her knees, sobbing.

But she raised her head to stare at the open door as hoofbeats were heard approaching. The fair-haired Philip paused on the threshold to discover Giles and the infant. Philip's eyes darted about the cottage, probing into every corner of the rustic room. His expression was calm as he discovered Lady Isobel. He barely moved as Giles brushed past him and made for his coach.

"It seems I have followed them too late," Philip said aloud. "The fools. One should not play these games of passion and power unless one intends to win." He studied the room once more, then with a swift gesture he snatched a little shirt of the babe's from off a table and stepped over Lady Isobel's body. He bent down and dipped the shirt in the blood.

Then he turned on his heel and fled as though the devil himself were after him. "Giles!" he called toward the coach, which had just lurched into motion. "Hold! All is not lost yet! I have a plan!"

Molly, who had been walking out in the fields, did not happen upon the scene at the cottage until some time later. As soon as she was able to make out what had happened, she burst into sobs, wringing her hands and displaying emotions that had been locked frozen within her when her own babe had died. Then she bathed Robert's head. In time, Lady Isobel's servants came to take the body away. And a magistrate questioned all in the little dwelling. But no one knew where Giles had taken the child.

"Why did I pick that hour of this day to walk about the countryside?" Molly mourned.

Robert, white-faced and guilty, comforted Molly as best as he could. "It's my fault. I could not defend you all against my wife's lover. I don't know how anyone can tolerate me."

Then Molly, in her turn, comforted him, and they found some consolation and pleasure in the task.

They lay spent and drowsy, and he reflected upon how often he had laid alone in the great bed. He drew her to him and kissed her tousled curls. "My dear Molly," he said. "I do love you so dearly that I have a mind to make you my wife."

"Your wife!" Molly sat up with dismay. "Master Robert, what can you be thinking of? I be married already."

A crease appeared between Robert's tender eyes. "But he is in Virginia, and whoever would know?"

"Why . . . ," Molly cried, sitting up in agitation so that her naked breasts were revealed. "Why, I would. I be married in my heart to John. And Mistress Lettice has written her sister and told her much. We hope John is back at Albright's Point by now. Good men like John be rare in Virginny; and so they will need him there. All I need now be passage to Virginny and a way to keep free of old Gower, my cruel master."

"I would send you to your husband, if that is truly what you want," he said. "I love you too much to keep you against your will."

"Robert!" she said with swelling heart. "Truly you be the bravest and kindest man in all the world." She leaned against his thin, bare chest in gratitude, then sat up again to cry, "But I cannot leave Mistress Lettice here alone until the babe be found. Oh, why do we idle here? We must search for the babe. Look into every cottage in all the land if need be. Pray that wicked Giles does not harm the sweet mite. But it is his own flesh and blood, after all." And then she added, "At least Lady Isobel will never threaten us again."

Lettice stood in the garden at Whitehall. James was at her side. James was close to the king's circles and thought that Geoffrey's problems would be solved finally and without question if His Majesty intervened on his behalf. The king had the power to pardon all, regardless of crime.

When he had told her this, Lettice had dredged up all the doubts Philip's story of Geoffrey as a highwayman had raised in her. James merely laughed. "I can assure you, my dear, that Geoffrey is innocent of that charge. He changed his name for other reasons. The only crime he committed at Oxford—aside from a little dalliance and drunkenness— was the crime of being poor."

Lettice felt some relief, and she chided herself for her doubts. She studied the small crowd of ladies and gentlemen waiting in the garden for the king's arrival. His Majesty was rowing upon the river, a sport he enjoyed, much to the scandal of the more sedate of his courtiers.

Whitehall seemed not so much a palace as a disorganized cluster of buildings with Inigo Jones's classic white

328

banqueting hall, the only building of great distinction. But upon the walk-crossed green grazed many animals: deer, cattle, goats and gazelles. The menagerie gave all a country atmosphere, which Lettice would have enjoyed had not so much been on her mind.

The ladies and gentlemen gathered seemed in a holiday mood. Many were hoping for a word with the king. James had spent some time arranging this meeting for Lettice. His Majesty's bedchamber was guarded by the page Will Chiffinch, whom rumor had he acted as confidant, spy, procurer and pawnbroker for his master. Chiffinch was an ardent drunk, and he let no man change his habits. But he was never too drunk to pass on information to His Majesty.

It was Chiffinch who had suggested that Lettice speak to His Majesty here in the garden. Lettice wore the deep-green silk with the blue peacock-feather highlights that Alf had carried so carefully in her bundle all along the road. It made her smile to think of him now walking paths so different from the one she now tread.

"Ah, hah!" There was a little smile upon James's lips. He nodded toward a fashionable group of gentlemen approaching, some leaning in bored and elegant manner upon walking sticks. Five or six dogs raced in circles about them as they sauntered toward Whitehall. Lettice could easily pick out the king, who was taller than the average and had a head of gloriously healthy black curls, all his own. She also thought she recognized the Duke of York, the king's brother. She did not know which of the three women trailing behind the group might be mistress or mistresses to the king.

James had tutored her on King Charles's tastes and habits; so she was not surprised when Geoffrey's friend drew her over to be acknowledged and introduced. Lettice curtsied as her king took her hand and studied every feature upon her blushing face. He was expert in reading character, she sensed. She found his dark eyes shrewd, the expression of the mouth cynical, but she quite liked him.

"Sire, I hope my poor features pass inspection," she said at last.

The monarch smiled. The lines about his mouth deepened. She was conscious that though his lean face was too deeply chiseled in bitter and dark lines to be called handsome, his body was excellently made. She felt the attraction he had for unusual women.

"I see a loyal nature and a passionate heart all hid behind a face like a pale English rose," the king replied. "You are a lady who dares much, and I would want you on my side."

"Oh, Your Majesty, I would plead for my husband," she said.

"Indeed," the king said cooly.

In a rush of words Lettice described how Geoffrey had been deprived of his liberty and his inheritance and spirited away to a strange land. Finally she confessed that her husband had been forced to join the rebels—without any particular politics, she hastened to add—merely to escape his servile condition.

"My family are not fond of rebels. We have suffered much at their hands," the king said after a silence.

"Yes, Sire," Lettice whispered. "Both my husband's and my father's family were ever loyal to the Stuarts."

"Yet I understand young Finch's plight, and that old fool Berkeley has hanged enough of my subjects."

Lettice nodded, wondering at her sovereign's harsh words concerning the governor who had served him so loyally. But James had told her that the king was dead set against Berkeley; so she dared not speak for Sir William.

"I will give instructions that your husband, Geoffrey Finch, be given amnesty and relieved of his bondage, that is, as long as he commits no further crimes. And please inform him that he has a most appealing and well-disposed wife."

"Thank you, Your Majesty." Lettice curtsied once again. She should have been elated, but her spirits sank. She had no idea where on earth her husband rested. When she found him again, she would tell him much—and love him long. As soon as the king's documents were drafted, she would dispatch them to the new governor in Virginia, then return to her babe to wait for the father.

As the king departed, James gave her his civilized smile. "It has gone very well, I think. Your husband will, in time, come into his own. With the king's favor upon Geoffrey, I would, were I you, go to his parents to see if they will once again grant him his allowance. His mother is very fond of him, I know, and has grieved over his disappearance. Now if you will wait for me in the little room where you waited before, I have one more errand."

Lettice nodded. "You are very good to us, James," she said. But as she moved toward the cluster of government offices that formed a part of Whitehall, she gave a little gasp. She had no particular desire to see Philip, yet strangely here he was in London. He looked much the same with his gay, almost dandified, clothing, his many scarlet ribbons and fine, fair face. But his gray eyes were cold. She looked about for some way to avoid him, but he had obviously seen her and was headed her way. Ardently he took her hand.

"Lettice, my dear." He raised her fingers to his lips.

"I am not pleased that you have followed me," she said coldly. He dropped her hand with an abruptness that Lettice would have found amusing had not his next words caused her such unease.

"I wanted no one else to bring you the dreadful news," he said.

Lettice's heart turned to ice. "What news?"

His face reddened. He blurted, "Your husband is hanged!"

His words seemed to echo among all the brick and stone of Whitehall. Lettice reached for his arm to steady herself. "No!" she cried. "It cannot be true. Oh, can I have been too long and they declared him a rebel after all?"

"It was not that," he said.

"What, then?" she asked with stiff lips. The placid animals and strolling gentlefolk still circled languidly about the garden. His words were too sudden. They could not be real.

"No, my dear," Philip said smoothly. Was there too much satisfaction in his tone? He did not look at her. Instead she stared at his elegant, thin profile. "It was not as a rebel he was hanged. He had returned to England. Once here, he returned to an old mistress and killed her. A mistress you well knew—the Lady Isobel."

Lettice paled. "Lady Isobel? Oh, Philip, how can I believe you?"

"It seems that they were lovers long ago. I always warned you he was a rogue."

"Of course there is much of Geoffrey's life I do not know, yet I cannot believe this of him," she said slowly.

331

"It seems there was some lovers' quarrel between them that concerned his brother, no doubt." Philip faced her at last, a slight flush upon his cheeks. She stared into the eyes of her old playmate.

"What other explanation is there?" he asked with raised eyebrows.

"Then he must have sought me at Robert's house. If only we had known and stayed. Oh, Philip, you must tell me the truth. I know you have lied to me before."

Philip placed an arm about her shoulders, an arm that felt somewhat stiff and tense. "I would not lie about anything so serious, my dear. It did not happen at the Ashley house, but at the cottage of the Finch's old nurse."

"The cottage?" She grew dizzy with apprehension.

"And Giles was there too," he added silkily. "I arrived too late to set things right."

She pulled away from him and looked with fear into his face. "But my child—"

". . . was in the way of the struggle between the two brothers. They fought with swords." At this, Philip reached into the bosom of his shirt and pulled out the bloodstained little garment. "I have placed it next to my heart," he said.

Something in these words rang false to her, for whenever had he loved the child? Yet all logic was swept away as she took the little shirt into her hands. She had sewn it herself; so there could be no mistake.

"So much blood for such a little body," she whispered, then buried her face in the hands that still held the stained relic. Dry-eyed, she raised her head. All feeling was gone as though she were dead. "Philip," she barely uttered. "Take me away from here."

He smiled. "That was exactly what I had in mind, my dear. My coach waits near the banqueting hall." His arm steadied her, for her knees threatened to give way. As they walked about the cluster of outlying buildings, she lay her head upon his satin shoulder. It seemed she walked an endless distance until the coachman slipped down to help her inside, opening the black leather-lined door. She felt as though she was entering her coffin.

"My dear, they will drive you to my house where you can rest," he said. "I will catch up with you as soon as possible, but first I have an urgent matter to attend to."

She scarce heard his words.

* * *

Geoffrey stood impatiently in an anteroom at Whitehall. Although it felt good to stand a free—or almost free—man in London with good clothes upon his back, he fretted with impatience. All the fine furnishings and glowing mirrors and rich carpets did little to soften his mood.

Their ship had blown off course in the spring storms. No sooner had he set foot on shore than the boy who had escaped with him from Virginia had been seized at the docks. Geoffrey had not known whether his captors had been man spirits or authorities who would have returned him to his master. Fuming, he had searched for several weeks. He'd questioned old crones, light skirts and sailors until he had discovered the boy trussed up at the back of a particularly filthy and squalid tavern. And so he had freed the good lad who had helped him to escape.

He next thought to locate James and perhaps seek the king's pardon, but soon after arriving in London, Geoffrey had stumbled upon the governor. Sir William's appearance shocked Geoffrey, and so he explained his situation to this brother of a lord.

Sir William's pouchy eyes betokened gloom as he shook his periwigged head. "I have lost my king's confidence," he said. "He will not speak with me. All my long years of service count for nothing."

Though he had served with the forces of the other side, Geoffrey could see the justice of the governor's complaint. He himself had grown disillusioned with Bacon and had sensed that Jud had come to feel that the governor had the greater right.

Yet what were all these affairs of state to him? Geoffrey thought with impatience, gnawing upon a thumbnail. He had an inheritance to regain and a wife and babe to locate. Yet he could not resist the governor's plea to put in a word with James, or with the king himself if he saw him. But it had been difficult enough to find James. A servant had just informed him that his old friend was awaiting the king in the garden, but would arrive shortly.

Geoffrey walked to a narrow window to brush aside the curtain with irritation and look below. He inhaled with surprise. It was she—there was no mistaking her—Lettice, his wife, in a peacock gown and gold petticoat. She did not look well, and a gentleman supported her. It took him a moment to recognize Philip, whom he had not seen for several years.

So there had been no mistake! Damn the wench. She had left with Philip, happy enough no doubt to shake off the dust of Virginia, though she had carried his child with her. No, she was a scheming vixen after all, and she had fooled him badly. She would probably deny their marriage, carried out as it was in semi-secrecy so many miles away. But there was the child, his child, somewhere. Or had the poor babe not survived?

Look there below how she—his wife—leaned her head upon Philip's shoulder. But then Geoffrey had discovered long ago that that demure rose-petal look of hers was deceptive. Now Philip was handing her into a coach, a far more luxurious vehicle than any owned by the Finch family!

Well, it mattered little, Geoffrey thought, bitterly turning away. The world was full of women after all, and he had tasted the charms of only a few of them. He had half a mind to celebrate the shattering of his illusions in some riotous tavern. But, no, he would see James first. His pile of coins was growing low, and he must settle matters with his family. Giles might even have landed in England before him.

He had just arrived at this decision when the door burst open and two guards entered. Philip was upon their heels. He was all velvet and satin and ribbons and feathers. A feverish look of triumph filled his eyes.

"Seize that man for the murder of Lady Isobel!" he cried.

"Lady Isobel?" The words stunned Geoffrey so that he made no attempt to escape. "Why, I have not seen her for years."

"You were seen entering and leaving the cottage where she died," Philip said. "What luck that I spotted you here!"

"I?" Geoffrey looked about wildly, realizing the trap. "You are mistaken. It must have been my brother once again."

"No, my friend," Philip said grimly. "Giles himself will testify against you. He will say how jealousy caused the two of you to duel, how the lady tried to intervene, how in a rage you cut her throat with a piece of broken wine-glass." Philip smiled an icy smile. "Of course the two of you look so much alike it is hard to tell one from the other. Your old nurse has become so senile she is not sure. But Giles knows. Giles knows."

It was some time later when James entered the room, eagerly searching for his old friend, Geoffrey. He had just heard of his arrival. Once there, James stared about in surprise, for the room was quite empty, and there was no explanation for Geoffrey's absence.

XIX

Philip's family had built a new house some 20 years before after the old Tudor manor had been partially destroyed by fire. The new brick house stood classic and graceful with its hipped roof centered by a white cupola. Two modest wings balanced either side. Yet it was a far smaller and less overpowering family seat than the Ashley house she had escaped from those few weeks ago.

Servants, some whom she had known since childhood, welcomed her and showed her to a room upstairs. Philip, it seemed, had been very sure she would come. The bedchamber allotted her was not as awesomely large as those in Robert's house, and the bed curtains showed signs of wear. Not surprising in a house without a mistress. The dark, satiny paneling glowed with the light of a cheerful fire almost too warm in the beautiful midsummer weather.

But nothing could warm Lettice's heart. In travel-stained clothes she lay upon the embroidered coverlet of the bed as though dead. Her thoughts were frozen. If she allowed her mind to wander, her husband's or her babe's face would appear before her, and that was too painful to bear.

Quiet footsteps announced an elderly maidservant who urged her to slip out of her clothes. The old woman's gnarled hands seized the fine covers and drew them over Lettice's aching body.

But this luxurious comfort failed to soothe her. Lettice's eyes burned, but she could not cry. In time the servant reappeared through the dark room with a sleeping potion. Finally Lettice slept.

The following morning a message was brought to the effect that Philip had now arrived and awaited her in the parlor. Lettice shook her head, then turned to the wall. The distressed servant wrung her hands for a moment, then disappeared.

That evening Philip sent a message saying she must come down to a light supper. With a deep sigh, she arose. She must eat some food, she supposed. And sooner or later she would have to face Philip.

When she walked into the dining room with its carved panels, she was just in time to see a nurse present Philip's child to him before bedtime. Lettice was startled. She had forgotten that Philip had a child, and this little one, who was showing promise of inheriting his father's fine bones, must already be walking. He seemed healthy enough despite his mother's sallow coloring. Lettice closed her eyes for a moment in misery, steadying herself with her fingertips placed upon the polished table.

"I hope you will become fond of my son," Philip said without warmth as she sat in a high-backed chair on his right. The candles glistened upon the tabletop and upon the tears in her eyes.

"Emotions are difficult for me now," Lettice answered, folding her icy hands in her lap as she sat and stared down at her plate.

The child uttered a few soft words before disappearing behind the paneled doors in the arms of his doting nurse.

"We all have our losses," Philip said as he poured himself some ale. She noticed that dry, little lines were forming at the corners of his well-shaped, sensuous mouth. They were unpleasant lines that would draw his lips down sourly with age.

"It does not strike me that you mourned poor Mary to any great degree," she observed.

"So it is 'poor Mary' now. I know. I would suggest that we both forget what is past and go on."

"I cannot," she told him seriously. "It is too soon."

Philip's fine-skinned face turned red. "And am I nothing to you?"

She sighed. "You are a very old friend," she began, "and have given me a haven . . . ,"

Philip flung down his two-pronged fork and his knife and sprang to his feet. "Please understand, Lettice. I have given you a haven for one reason only, that you might

338

become my mistress, and perhaps if things work well and you subdue some of the tendencies you have shown of late—my wife."

Lettice rose with a rustle of her skirts and regarded him steadily, though she was faint with exhaustion. Staring at the handsome face, she wondered how she had ever thought she loved him. "It seems you and I had this very discussion years ago," she murmured. "If indeed I could find a haven here and you offered me friendship through this trying time, I might feel again for you. But since you're as you are, I will go to Robert, who has proved more loyal than my old friend. And Molly will be wondering about me."

With the side of his hand, Philip swept aside his tumbler of ale so that its contents washed across the glistening surface of the table. His narrow hand shook.

"I have been patient with you," he hissed. "But no longer. I followed you, my precious sweet, all the way to Virginia, something I would do for few women. I myself paid your passage home. . . ." His eyes actually misted over, which she thought strange since in her grief she could not cry at all.

"All against my will," Lettice replied. "And had I stayed, I might have prevented Geoffrey's trouble and his death. But I have lost my appetite. I will return to my room, if you don't mind."

The fine lines of his face distorted into ugly rage as he lunged to seize her wrist. She had seen such tantrums when they were children.

"Let me tell you, Lettice, that every time I took Mary's body, I saw your face. Later, lying alone, phantoms of your form appeared to me as though sent by the devil himself. In my mind I did perform such acts on you that made poor Mary shudder when I tried them upon her insufficient, yellow form. But Mary was weak and died, freeing me, but making my imaginings worse. I swore to myself over and over that I would have you . . . in time."

She bowed her weary head. "Philip, your antics would amuse me were I not heartsick and exhausted. Please inform your coachman I shall leave tomorrow."

"Tomorrow?" Philip gave a short laugh and tightened his grasp upon her wrist. "You seem not to understand

what I would do with you. Well, Mary learned in time."
After she did not respond, he added, "Give me a kiss, my
dear. You owe me at least that."

His soft words and his mood began to frighten her, as he
meant it to. A mere kiss would hardly satisfy him.

"Please, Philip. I could not bring myself to kiss anyone
under these circumstances."

He raised his fine eyebrows, but his expression was neither amused nor gentle. "I'll not let you go unless you do."

She gave an exasperated sigh. "You really mean it, don't
you? Lady Isobel did say your mind was as strange as
hers."

"My purpose is steadier. Lady Isobel was like a butterfly
or moth. I never let go of an idea once I have it. And I
have had ideas of you since I first knew what it was that
men did to women. I will have my kiss, sweeting, if I must
wrap you about with rope until you cannot move."

"A kiss is hardly worth that labor," Lettice said wryly.
"Have it if you must, but a kiss won by threat has little
meaning."

"It means I have forced you to submit." His eyes stared
into hers to judge any weakening as he drew her closer.
Then he pressed seeking lips upon hers.

But it truly means nothing to me, she thought. I am as
though dead. It is a petty price to be free of him.

He slid his hand into her bosom, but it only reminded
her of other, dearer caresses. She began to weep great,
rending sobs.

He pushed her away so that she staggered. "Cold bitch!"
he cried. "I will leave you alone for a day or two to see if
you heat up a little. If not, I will teach you in my own way
to respond. In time even Mary learned."

"You promised to let me go!" Lettice cried angrily.

"Ah, I see a spark in you, after all. That shows some
hope." At this, Philip threw open the door to reveal a
thickset, burly man just outside. Philip picked up a candlestick with one hand and grasped Lettice's elbow with
the other. "Come, Will. Show Mistress Lettice to her
room."

Light flickered upon the man's lowering face. His dark
hair grew low upon his forehead, a forehead misshapen
and full of strange lumps and bumps, bulging and swelling.
His eyes shone black with an almost subhuman light. She

340

turned her head suddenly as she thought she saw another shadowy form move at the end of the passageway. How many men would he set upon her?

"I have asked Will to sleep outside your door, my sweet, lest you take to walking in your sleep. Much would have been prevented had Lady Isobel taken like precautions."

Lettice said nothing. She was done with arguing. But she would not lose her head. Meekly she trailed through the corridors, which were filled with the glowing light of evening. Only in the deepest shadows did they need the candle on this midsummer night.

But once she had closed her chamber door, waves of rage swept over her. Philip had brought her feelings to life in a way he had not planned. Oh, but she would use this anger to give her life new purpose! And if, as she suspected, Philip had lied to her about Geoffrey's relationship to Lady Isobel, might he not be lying about other things as well, about the whole story?

But there she stopped. The little shirt had borne its own testimony. Blinking back tears, she swallowed, then stilled herself. There was no way to bring the child back. She would not think of her grief, but let her burning rage guide her to free herself from Philip.

Suddenly she found that she was hungry, after all. She would need strength, she knew. Opening her door a crack, she saw the hulking figure blocking her way. She would find out how malleable he was. "I should like something to eat, Will," she said meekly.

"The master said you was to have nothing," he answered tonelessly. Then he shifted his feet and stared down upon the floor.

Well, she thought, shutting the door. He would be of very little help, though his slow wits might be an advantage. But she was surprised that even Philip sought to starve her into submission. By now her stomach gnawed and ached with hunger, and she thought of the roast shin of beef upon Philip's table, and the dish of peas in oil with herbs. Philip had always drunk ale of a particularly good brew. A drink of it now might steady her. But there was not even water in the room. They had taken everything away.

After the sun set, a grayish-blue light came through the window, for it was not long after midsummer eve, and the evenings were long. She blew out the candle that stood on a washstand near her bed. Stripping herself of the only gown she owned at the moment, she slipped under a beautiful spread, which was worked intricately with strange birds and flowers. Had poor Mary made these many tiny stitches, sitting here all unloved by the fire, dreading Philip's call?

After a time Lettice rose again, clad only in her shift. Hunger gnawed and agitation made it impossible to sleep. If only she could think of a plan. She began to pace about the room, wrapped in the embroidered coverlet. It trailed behind her upon the floor.

Through the casement she saw the moon now full upon the summery countryside. Lettice started as a shadow crossed her window. It paused and then completely blocked the light from her room. It disappeared, then swung back again. Fearful and mystified Lettice walked closer, then gave a gasp of shock. A face looked back at her. There was a tapping upon her casement.

"Mistress Lettice!" a low voice called urgently.

"Why, who on earth?" Lettice began, then broke into nervous and relieved laughter, which she hastened to stifle. She recognized the dark, curly hair of Jack, who amazingly was here. Lettice didn't see his mort, Nance.

Quickly Lettice unlatched and opened the window, and Jack swung inside, boots first. He had suspended himself on a rope fastened in some unseen way under the eaves. She pressed her finger to her lips, nodding toward the thick door.

"Whew," Jack whispered, drawing shut the brocade curtains. "No one saw me, I think." Then taking a tinderbox from his pocket, he worked away with flint and steel until he struck a spark and lit the candle. "It's good to see your face, mistress," he said, though without his usual flashing smile.

"And yours, Jack," she answered quickly, though in a whisper. "I am in the most awful mess here."

"So I found out. When I crept about the house to find you, I saw that the gentleman had set a guard on you."

"So you were the mysterious shadow I saw."

He nodded his rogue's head, his smile subdued. "I'm glad to arrive to help, though my errand be a sad one."

Lettice's brow clouded. She reached to take his hand.

342

Jack's forehead creased. " 'Tis Alf, mistress. He wants ye t'bring his hanging clothes."

"Oh, no, Jack. They could not hang him! Not Alf too."

Even in the midst of tragedy Jack could not tell a story simply, though he did it with fewer embellishments than usual. He struck an attitude as he usually did whenever he was before a crowd, then glanced toward the paneled door. He ducked his head and began to whisper.

"Thieving be a hanging matter. I only pray we be not too late," Jack said. "It were hard to find you, though I searched from your friend Master James's house clear to Whitehall. God himself must have forgiven me all my crimes, for I was guided to speak with a footman who remembered you and could tell whose coach had swallowed you up like the whale that swallowed Jonah. With great good luck I stumbled over Sir Philip, and with craft I struck up a conversation upon a false concern. He come out of Whitehall just behind two guards who were dragging a dark-haired man away for some crime against the king, no doubt. Those nasty fellows looked at me with such ugly suspicion on their faces that I drifted away, but kept an eye on Sir Philip all the same. Then later I saw him talking to the same dark-haired man as the guards held him, though he struggled like a true rogue."

Why did her heart leap so? The world was full of dark-haired man. Jack himself had a full head of dark curls.

"But a groom told me where Sir Philip lived. Once I knew, I leaped upon the back of a horse and galloped all the way here, close on the heels of Sir Philip himself. I stopped only to change horses now and then. My last mount gave out under me, too winded and weak to stand the strain. It lies a few miles back, quite dead. It was such a poor nag that its owner lost very little.

"Then I looked the house over carefully and saw Sir Philip set that ugly fellow to guard you. I must say, mistress, I never liked the look of Sir Philip. We rogues of the road get a sense for the heart of a man."

"But can we not save Alf? Is there nothing we can do?"

"He's set for hanging, mistress. But he would have you bring his hanging clothes and stand by him. A man likes to see his friends about him when he meets the executioner, and perhaps God will be impressed if he sees that Alf has loyal friends, though he be a thief."

Lettice closed her eyes to banish her thoughts of Geoffrey swinging from the gallows. But though he had died alone, Alf must not.

"Of course we must go at once," she said. "But there is a great brute guarding my door, and I am, I confess, weak, since I have not eaten in some days."

"We must do something about that, missus," Jack said, frowning. "I'm well used to days without a morsel to pass between my teeth. And so is Nance, my mort. But you, mistress, a lady like you must eat." He flashed her his grin. "For that matter, I could do with a bit myself. But we must not idle. Can you sit astride a horse?"

"Astride?" Hastily she glanced at the door, realizing her voice had risen. "I can ride well enough," she whispered into Jack's curl-covered ear. "But astride?"

"If you can handle a horse ridin' like a lady, it's sure you can ride like my younger brother, who you'll be. Now bundle up all you have but your shift in a bed sheet, mistress." He grinned again to acknowledge the humor of their strange intimacy. "Forgive me my crude, low ways. Yet 'tis just as well I never was an honest man, for I have need of all my skills of thievery tonight." So saying, he sprang to the door and silently opened it a crack, then pulled it wider with a sudden movement. With a sturdy fist he encountered Will's large, misshapen jaw. Will went down with a grunt.

Jack turned to flash his disarming grin. Then he stepped over the unconscious servant and silently sped down the hall.

She had her bundle all assembled when the door opened silently again. The welcoming smile on her face froze as she saw that it was Philip. His fine eyes narrowed and glowed with a light she had never before seen in them.

"My man seems to have suffered some accident," he said. "A difficult feat for a woman no stronger than you."

"How very strange," she said stiffly.

He walked slowly into the room. His body was tense as he stared into every corner. She would not have been surprised to have seen him raise the bedclothes to look underneath.

"I find it equally strange to find you tying your clothes

344

into a bundle," he said. "Perhaps the two things are related."

Unlike Jack, who smiled in the unlikliest circumstances, Philip almost never smiled. It was hard to believe he could be a threat to her, since she remembered their childhood play. She merely shrugged. "Perhaps there are some things of Mary's I might borrow. I have come off with only the clothes upon my back."

He whirled about, the lines about his mouth drawn down and ugly. "That does not explain my manservant's accident."

"Nor can I explain it. I heard nothing. Perhaps. . . ." She was about to urge him to look to his valuables, but thought better of it. Jack would still be about somewhere.

"Then explain to me why you greeted me so warmly, more warmly, I believe, than any time since I parted from you at Brookside—was it truly three years ago?"

"I thought you would be happy to see me feeling better," she lied.

The muscles about his eyes tightened. She still stood with the embroidered cover about her, and he seized her and threw her with such force upon the bed that the bed curtains whipped about. Her head snapped back suddenly. She was dazed.

"Treacherous bitch! I will not have you be all ice to me, only to melt when the first man comes along. Who is your accomplice? Who?" With each word he slapped her face until her eyes stung with tears and the bones of her face ached. She tried to draw breath to scream her rage, tried to strike out, but his blows kept her breathless, and the coverlet bound her close about.

"Who is it?" he demanded once more.

"Why, it's me," a masculine voice said softly. Philip jerked about to see Jack standing in the doorway, a stout piece of firewood in his hand. Philip sprang toward the door. But not fast enough. The stout piece of oak in Jack's hand cracked against the gentleman's skull and brought him down at the feet of the rogue.

"Oh, Jack, you are a friend!" Lettice cried. Springing to her feet and clutching the cover about her, she did not even look closely enough at Philip to see if he were alive or dead.

"Well, if I be a friend to Alf, I must be off upon the

road. And you too, mistress," Jack said. He stepped over the two unconscious men to pick up what was left of the shin of beef and some fresh bread that he had dropped. He tore a strip from the beef, then handed her the rest. Scooping up some clothes that were lying there, he beckoned toward the shadowy stairway.

"Lift your bundle, mistress, and let's be off. It will be safer if you dress down by the stables in the dark. These fallen birds may soon begin to chirp."

"I am ready," she said, dragging along in her coverlet. "Though it does bother me to steal Philip's horses."

"He was willing enough to steal you, it seems, mistress," Jack pointed out.

In the silent darkness they sped along the road with a feeling of urgency. Jack sported a blue broadcloth coat with many buttons, which had recently belonged to Philip. He also wore a new pair of boots, which, despite their softness, pinched his toes.

Lettice wore a long cloak over a man's shirt and a pair of breeches that bagged ungracefully over her slender thighs. But she had never ridden with such freedom. If only they might not arrive too late! Or if there were some way to save Alf. All fatigue left her as she thought that for this space of time, at least, her life had purpose again.

The summer breezes refreshed her, the horses' hooves pounded. The midsummer night seemed to lack the blackness of a winter midnight or of the velvety Virginia nights. Despite their determination as dawn broke, the two riders swayed with weariness until they halted to hide their mounts. Like brother and sister they curled together in a farmer's haystack. It was the only rest they took until they reached Southwark at the next dawn. The city glowed pink. The Thames, still as a mirror, reflected the many arches of London Bridge.

Once across, they rode to a tavern where they abandoned their horses to proceed on foot. It would not do to be arrested as horse thieves on their way to Newgate.

"We best gather up Alf's hangin' clothes, mistress," Jack said.

"But if we hurry to Newgate, we may yet find a way to save him," Lettice objected.

Jack was fatalistic like many another rogue. " 'Tis later

today he's due to be hanged; so we are in time after all. But not by much. He will be terribly disappointed if he be hanged without his white clothes or the faces of his friends about him."

A coach dashed by, and they shrank against the wall of a house to avoid being splashed by mud. The industry of the city began: shops opened, rumbling carts shook the ground. Sedan chairs were carried past with languid ladies and gentlemen surveying the scenes about them.

"Rally up, ladies! Rally up! Buy! Buy! Buy!" the street vendors began to call, breaking the early-morning stillness. "I ha' white radish, white hard lettuce, white young onions"

Lettice and Jack dodged about some barrels that the brewers were lowering into open cellars. A dirty little chimney sweep reached with a black hand to press upon the back of Jack's new coat, then ran laughing away with delight in this trick. Jack shrugged. "He must know the coat be too good for me."

He left Lettice standing outside the tavern while he dashed inside to retrieve the hanging clothes from the landlady. That good woman, with a round, claret-colored face, followed him outside, weeping at the thought of Alf's fate and declaring that she would go to Tyburn shortly for the hanging.

Ceremoniously, Jack placed the clothes, all white and folded, carefully into Lettice's hands. Someone had lovingly embroidered them with silver thread.

"It's you Alf wants to carry them to him," Jack said. " 'Tis his dream." Then he threw a penny to a flower seller and took a nosegay that Alf might have something sweet to smell as he went to his death.

As they neared the Newgate prison, the crowds grew thick, for two hangings were expected that afternoon. Vendors hawked ballads of famous criminals' last, dying speeches. Jack spent another penny thinking to ask Lettice to read to him later a bulletin about the murderer who would end his life today alongside Alf.

Newgate Prison was built centuries ago as the fortification about one of the medieval gates of London. Every child knew these gates of old and could recite them in a singsong—Newgate, Ludgate, Aldersgate, Cripplegate, Moorgate, Bishopsgate and Aldgate. But a large fire had

347

destroyed much of the area. The prison itself had been first patched and then rebuilt. Yet all dreaded to come within its doleful confines. A stay there was expensive for whomever could afford it; a misery for whomever could not.

The keeper of Newgate allowed them in for a small fee to visit the condemned man. Inside, a mass of caged bodies writhed. Women tried to wash in dirty buckets while their children screamed and crawled about the filthy stones of the floor. Tasty victuals were carried in to well-dressed gentlemen rich enough to afford good food, while the grizzled and leprous poor folk starved in the same cell.

Alf's large-knuckled but handsome hands clung to the grill so that Lettice saw them before she saw his face.

"Mistress Lettice," he said joyously. "I had no doubt you would come. Now I can meet my end as a man should."

"Oh, Alf." Lettice grasped his warm, hard hand. "How did you come to be in this place?"

"It were the pearls, mistress."

"The pearls!" Lettice gasped.

"Yes, mistress. When I took them to a fencing cully to turn them into coin, he whispered aside to the magistrate. So he made a double profit."

"But I gave them to you, Alf! You should not hang for that!"

As usual, Alf's face looked as innocent and cheerful as a masculine child's. "I always expected to hang, mistress. And who would believe such an unlikely story?"

"Someone must!" Lettice insisted as Alf lowered his manacled hands from hers.

"And how did you come by the pearls, mistress?" a sardonic voice asked from the shadowy depths of the cage. "If I may call someone a mistress who is so strangely dressed. But perhaps pearls mean nothing to you. Some lover has draped you with other jewels."

Thoughts were whirling in Lettice's head, and she turned pale. She clutched the grill, doubting her own senses. The phantom voice seemed part of her despairing dreams of the last few days. Slowly she raised her head. Her lips moved, forming words she could not utter. Her startled eyes strained to see past the others crowded into the cell. At the very back wall a dim figure was chained. Her lips parted.

"Geoffrey," she sighed, half fainting.

A bitter laugh answered her. "So Philip was not my only rival!"

His words shocked her like a bucket of cold water. She choked back passionate words, then stood straighter, eyes wide with surprise.

"Your rival? Why, Geoffrey, you fool. Philip was never your rival. Never."

"Nor I." Alf cocked his head to regard his cell mate and softly said, "And it seems you be the lady's husband."

"And the pearls were given to me by the Queen of Pamunkey!" Lettice cried. "And Philip tricked me from Virginia, and told me you were dead. . . ." A sudden thought stopped her. She stretched her fingers through the bars, but she could not touch him. "Oh, Geoffrey. Oh, darling. He told me our babe was killed. Can that be false too? He said you and Giles fought after you killed Lady Isobel, and the child accidently fell before your weapon."

"I never saw the child," Geoffrey answered softly. "I never saw the Lady Isobel, except for years ago when I was very young and foolish. But I have wronged you, sweet. I should have trusted my heart."

"Gentlefolk be worse rogues than us," Alf said. "With us it's just a little thievery to live."

Standing under the glowing torch, Jack scratched his curly head and raised the bulletin he'd purchased to stare at the crude wood-block picture. "So 'tis *your* husband who's to hang with Alf!"

"Hang!" Lettice paled again. "Oh, Geoffrey!" Her eyes searched the darkness for his face. Torchlight glinted dully on his chains, but she could not make out his features. "There has to be a way to save you."

"And it seems your friend here does not deserve a hanging—at least for this crime," Geoffrey said. "Let me see the paper."

Jack rolled it up and handed it through the grill while the rest of them stood, tensely watching. Alf walked over to hold it near Geoffrey's face, since the shackles prevented him from holding it himself. Others in the crowded cage looked on with interest.

"Faugh," Geoffrey said. "It is too dark."

Lettice blinked back tears. "Let me have it. Oh, if only I had read it sooner." She held it under the torch.

The story printed there with much gusto was of two gentlemen—twin brothers—who had sought the charms of the same married lady. The younger, though barely younger, had driven a piece of glass into his paramour's throat so that she died in a pool of blood. The elder had arrived just in time to see his brother leave.

"That is the story my brother told in court," Geoffrey said.

"But, Geoffrey," Lettice said. "There is nothing of the babe."

"The babe was stole away," a breathless female voice cut in. Lettice and Jack jumped in surprise.

"Nance!" Jack exclaimed, pulling her to him and giving her a smack on the mouth. His mort was as buxom and lively as ever, though her dark eyebrows framed a frown of tremendous worry.

"Mistress Lettice." Nance reached for her hand. "It is not so bad as you might think. I set out for Nurse Brown's cottage to see if I could find you there while Jack sought in another direction. And Sir Robert and Molly told me the awful story. But the babe was well, at least then, but stolen away by some gentleman—Giles, they called him."

"Giles, once more," Geoffrey said grimly. "If only there were some way to prove it was he, not I."

"But where is the babe?" Lettice cried in distress.

"Mistress." Jack stood with his hands in the pockets of Philip's coat. "It seems to me that before we can think of anything else, we must think of these hangings."

"A mother's first thought must be for her child," Alf said, modestly ducking his head with its roughly cut brown hair so that the wall torch shone down upon it.

"Jack is right," Lettice decided, pushing away all intruding thoughts. "Though too much is happening too fast." She turned to address her husband. "Let us think clearly as we can. I suppose that even though you swore you were nowhere near Nurse Brown's cottage, Giles swore you were, and since you are twins. . . ."

"Another boyish trick," Geoffrey said with gallows humor.

"Fatal, unless we can prove you elsewhere," Lettice moaned.

"Giles bribed the magistrate, and my case was rushed so that I had no time to prepare and no lawyer to represent me, else I might have sent for James. Until now I thought all was hopeless. . . ."

Her lips trembled. "You must remember where you were that day!" she cried.

"Truthfully, my dear, I do not even know the date in question."

Lettice raised the bulletin. The date was clearly noted, for it had been a Sunday, and the writer made much of how the Sabbath had been profaned.

To think more clearly, Geoffrey leaned his dark head against as much of his shoulder as he could reach with his arms upraised by his shackles. A toothless man at his side began mumbling encouragement. "Go on, sir. Get out if you can. Don't let the hangman get you."

"The captain of my ship transported me as my brother," Geoffrey mused. "So his testimony would be no help. Besides, I spent weeks tracking down the poor boy who helped me escape. The man stealer who spirited him away would not speak for me. But on the exact day in question . . . I was. . . ."

Saliva dripped upon the old man's chin as he urged once more, "Go on, sir."

"I was . . . my God!" Geoffrey raised his head. "I was with Sir William."

"The governor!" Lettice cried. "Perhaps he will testify for you. Though he is in ill favor with the king just now."

"You must try, mistress." Alf, with his usual modesty, forgot his own dire circumstances.

"And you, Alf!" Lettice cried. "We must save you both. I am the one who can clear you. Oh, if only we had more time."

"There is not enough time for an appeal," Geoffrey said. "Our best chance is to take our evidence to James to see if he can obtain the king's pardon."

"The king has pardoned you once already as a rebel. But he added as a condition that you must not commit any other crime."

"But I have not," Geoffrey said. "We must chance that he believes me. Or not chance. The governor must help us prove it."

"Well, then," Lettice said resolutely, tucking back a stray lock of hair. "I will write a statement clearing Alf, then go to the governor. Then I will go to James. Oh, dear, that will take almost the whole day, and the hangings are set for this afternoon. If only someone else could go to James. . . ."

"It might be too late," Jack said, scratching his head. "I'm of a mind to gather our friends about and take a mob to Tyburn to delay the hangman's work." Lettice nodded

Alf took heart. "And if Master Geoffrey here and I spend a great time at our prayers with the ordinary of Newgate, it might delay the time when we set out. But they will want a bit of coin to let us pray long for our souls. Everything costs here."

"And I have nothing," Lettice mourned.

"I have still a bit from two gentlemen's wigs I snagged and sold just before I set out for Sir Philip's," Jack offered. "And there were one or two bits of silver in the pocket of his coat."

"I have a few coins left," Geoffrey said, "despite the expense here in prison."

"The keeper will surely want something for paper and ink. I must write out my statement immediately. But can I reach James when I must seek the governor first?" Lettice tried to keep her agitation from overwhelming her. There was too much to be done.

"Mistress," a voice came timidly. Gone were Nance's usual boisterous tones. "D'ye think such a grand gentleman would talk to me?"

"I'm sure he would," Lettice said with relief. "If you can reach him and I give you a letter. You may tell James that he can make the king's pardon conditional upon our proof that Geoffrey was not at Nurse Brown's cottage. As for Alf, I can vouch for him myself."

"And as for us here in Newgate," Alf said, "we will practice our final speeches and pleas to the Lord for forgiveness and make them long as we can. But if we are to be saved, mistress, you must get back before the speeches end."

Lettice swallowed and looked upon the husband she had not seen these many months and had thought cold and dead.

"We cannot think of failure," she said.

Once free of Newgate, Jack seized Lettice's and Nance's hands, and they all ran through the narrow crowded street toward the tavern where they had abandoned the horses.

By some miracle they were still in the inn yard, and the landlord was scratching his head and regarding them with puzzlement. Lettice, still in her man's clothes, sprang into one saddle while Jack helped Nance up.

"But I never bin on a horse!" Nance objected.

"You must hang on. There's the girl," Jack said.

"I'll do me best," she vowed.

"Good luck!" Lettice called after her.

"You too, mistress."

Lettice urged her horse to a gallop, for the landlord was looking at them strangely, and once more they risked being arrested as horse thieves. Hair streaming out behind her, she looked back once to see Jack, arm about the shoulder of a man who appeared to be their old friend, Tom O'Bedlam. Tom would aid them, sure. Several other figures were drawn toward them. One ragged man with a crutch straightened as he heard Jack's words. He then walked as strongly as Lettice herself. Lettice half smiled and gave Jack a wave. These rogues were proving the truest of friends.

Lettice handed her horse to a groom standing outside the house where Sir William was staying. For the first time she was aware of her unusual appearance. She drew her cloak more closely about her despite the warmth of the day in order to hide the travel-worn appearance of her man's clothes. A man's hat sat atop her woman's hair. As a somber servant opened the door, her courage left her for a moment.

"If you please," she said with tremulous voice. "Is the governor within?"

"He is very ill," the man answered.

"Oh, please," Lettice begged. "I must see him. It is a matter of life and death. Tell him that the sister-in-law of Squire Albright must see him."

At this the servant's eyebrows rose even higher, but he was too proper to put his questions into words.

A bad beginning, Lettice thought as she waited in a small receiving room with brocaded furniture and walls that would have awed her outlaw friends.

Noiselessly the dark-clad servant returned. "Sir William will only see you if you bring a message from the king. His doctors do not expect him to last long."

Lettice ducked her head and tugged at her lip with her teeth. She had no message. All she knew was that the king was gravely displeased with Sir William. But Geoffrey's life was at stake. "I have seen the king. And I do have a message." Not precisely a lie, but she could not meet the servant's eye. Disapprovingly, the servant nodded. What else, after all, could he do?

Lettice took off her plumed hat and shook her disordered hair about her shoulders. She prayed the governor would remember her. She swallowed nervously as she entered the sickroom. It was easy enough for Sir William to be intimidating when he was well. Nance would never have been able to speak to him. A doctor stood at Sir William's bedside. An old woman servant tidied up.

"You may speak to him only briefly," the doctor whispered, blowing stale breath into her pinched nostrils. "He does so wish to hear from His Majesty."

Lettice's face flamed with guilt as she approached Sir William's bed, clutching her cloak more tightly about her so he would not notice her strange attire.

Sir William's breathing was heavy, his color bad. Slowly he opened his pouchy eyes. Gone was much of his arrogance.

"My dear," he whispered hoarsely, reaching for her hand. "I do recognize you. What does my king say? Will he clear my name of the disgrace of the rebellion?"

"Sir William." Sorrowfully she bent closer to the old man upon his pillows. "I have seen the king. He sends no message. But I have come to you on a matter of life and death. My husband, Geoffrey Finch, is to be hanged."

The sick man's eyes clouded. "Finch," he sighed after a moment's silence. "I remember the man. One of a pair of twins, as I recall. The rebel brother. He tried to reach the king for me and failed."

"Yes, Sir William!" Lettice cried, her voice rising in the sickroom despite herself. "And now he lies accused of a crime his brother committed on the very day Geoffrey spent with you. Oh, if only you will testify on his behalf."

"My dear," the governor sighed. "I lie here gravely ill." He closed his eyes, and for a moment she feared he would never speak again. Then his faded eyes found hers once more. "I do not expect to survive for long." His breathing rasped so loudly that she had trouble hearing him. "I only pray the king's forgiveness before I go. For all else I care not. For years I have made other men's concerns my own. Now I must be alone with my soul and my God." He let go of her hand and rested it upon his coverlet. He looked gray and bloodless.

Lettice's heart sank. "Sir William, Geoffrey is to be hanged today. We must have a statement from you!" She paused, then desperation made her continue. "The king did speak of you. He said, 'That old fool has hanged more men in that naked country than I have done for the murder of my father.'" Then she stopped, wondering if her urgency had carried her too far. Bright sunshine streamed in through the chamber window. The day was much advanced.

"Mistress," the doctor objected. "You are cruel to dash the hopes of a man so weakened."

Ashamed, Lettice buried her face in her hands. But she heard the governor's words clearly, though they were very faint.

"When I was with the old king in pursuit of the Earl of Essex in '44 or '45, the king gave orders to seize the horses, goods and cattle of many who had declared against him. Yet when I have done the same to those who would disrupt his son's order in Virginia, the son turns his face against me. He blames me for the huge debt he incurred putting down the rebellion. I have, it seems, outlived my time and usefulness."

Lettice raised her head to look at him. "I have been cruel, Sir William. A good Christian lady would not have said what I did. Yet I beg you to understand the desperation that moves me. My husband will go to Tyburn this very day without the evidence for which we can gain a pardon. The king has complained at court that you have hanged too many. Can you not, while it is yet in your power, save this one man?"

Sir William gave a sigh that was almost a groan. "Bring me pen and paper," he instructed the doctor. To Lettice he added, "You must help steady my hand."

When Nance arrived at Whitehall where they told her Master James would likely be found, the very look of the place tied her tongue into knots so that her knees shook and she could scarce speak to the guards and officials about the place. Once inside, she stood in the passageway for some time before she could work up the courage to ask for James. Her beribboned bodice, which had seemed so fine upon the road, seemed sleazy and cheap compared to the fine cloth of the gentlemen's coats and the silks of the ladies in portraits upon the walls.

Master James, if he was all that important, must be a frightening man indeed. She smiled nervously, conscious of the spaces between her teeth.

"Here, now!" Master James's clerk cried. "Who said you could come in here?" With importance he arranged a pile of papers, fluttering his thin, knobby-knuckled hands. His skin was yellowish and opaque as though he seldom ventured out-of-doors. Nance was not used to such as he.

"It be a matter of life and death," Nance whispered.

"They all claim that," the clerk responded, plucking a bit of fluff off his dark coat sleeve.

Nance had all but turned away when she recalled that Alf and Geoffrey would be hanged if she failed in this errand.

"I got important papers for Master James," she said.

The clerk took them from her and laid them away under a pile on a table. Then he rested his starved-looking hand upon the pile. Nance noticed that his fingernails were dirtier than any rogue's.

"Very well. Now you may go," he said with contempt.

"But I need an answer!" Nance cried. "It be a hangin' matter."

He curled his lip. "Not the first hanging you've seen, I'll wager."

Nance's sun-darkened face flushed. "I say I cannot go without an answer!" she cried, stamping her foot.

"And I say Master James is very busy with His Majesty's business. Whatever concerns you can wait."

"It can't wait!" Nance insisted, her voice carrying as it did when she and Jack faced the crowds with their tale of shipwreck. "I must see Master James."

A pleasant gentleman's face, which was framed with brown cavalier locks, appeared about the corner of the inner door. "Here, now, Smythe," he said, rubbing a long finger alongside the side of his slightly crooked nose. "What's all this?"

"This, this creature," Smythe said, drawing himself up, "insists she must see you."

"Oh, if you be Master James, I must!" Nance cried. "Mistress Lettice has sent me on a matter of life and death."

"Indeed? Mistress Lettice would hardly say such a thing if it were not true."

His clerk shrank shamefacedly and looked down upon the floor. "That rogue has hid my papers under that pile," Nance said with outrage.

"Did you indeed, Smythe?" James asked, his large, brown eyes warm. "You must learn what is important and what is not."

Hastily Smythe dug them out again.

"Hmm," James mused as he read. "This is more trouble than I expected, even for Geoffrey. But Giles has exceeded himself this time. Smythe, take this message immediately to Will Chiffinch. Tell him this woman and I must see the king immediately—upon a matter of life or death."

"The King?" Nance uttered, ready to faint upon the black-and-white tiles of the floor.

"Chiffinch owes me a favor or two," James muttered as Smythe bounded away.

Lettice galloped almost to the foot of Holborn Hill before she abandoned her mount. Even were the horse not stolen, she would have had to leave it, for hundreds were thronging toward the gallows to witness the hangings. The condemned men must have left the prison by now. Pray God she was not too late. She made the most of her male attire so the rough crowd would think her a young gentleman instead of a lady.

Tyburn was a mere suburb of London, with open fields all about, but Lettice could see little of it as she pushed through the crowd. Church bells tolled constantly, adding to her feeling of fear and unease. The crush of well over a thousand people was so great that some gentlemen paid vendors to let them stand upon their carts for a better view. Lettice could barely see the three posts of the scaffold. Still bare, thank God.

The crowd swept her up, but after a time, though she pushed and struggled, she could make no headway in the crush. Waves of terror, which threatened to make her faint, swept over her. She had put all thought of failure away from her as she raced about her errand. Surely they could not have gotten this far only to fail!

The sturdy voice of Alf reached her. She could make out snatches of his plea now and then.

"I never did mask myself nor cover my face . . . nor disguise my voice with a pebble in my mouth . . . nor strike anybody with a stick . . . nor use a pistol. . . . Tis not my way," she heard him announce clearly with the dignity befitting his hanging clothes.

Then the crowd moved forward again, half stifling her. After a time she could hear Geoffrey's voice ring out as he spoke his final words. "Ah, this world has been sweet to me, given me the loveliest lady to wife!" he cried. Lettice felt tears sting her lids. Desperately she shoved her way closer. Roaring its approval of drama, the crowd pressed closer together toward the condemned men.

Now Alf began to pray, now Geoffrey, both in dead earnest. They must think the woman had failed them. Had they?

"Oh, no!" Lettice shrieked.

Then a voice shouted, "You cannot hang innocent men!" Plainly it was Jack. Several other rogues shouted in the same vein. Lettice was dragged along a few paces as the crowd suddenly surged forward. Fear turned her cold among the mass of sweating bodies. Her hat was swept off, and her hair hung down.

"Please!" she pleaded. "Let me through! It is my husband who will hang!"

A few people appreciated the poignancy of her appeal, and the made way. But soon that was was blocked again as the rest of the crowd rushed toward the gallows. Would she be held back by the very people trying to aid her?

"Mistress Lettice!" a voice screamed.

Lettice looked over to her right to see Nance in a tangled mass of Londoners, waving a paper and screaming desperately. They pushed toward each other.

"I have the king's pardon!" Nance screamed as the two women reached each other. Her words carried to those around them.

"The king's pardon!" some whispered in awe.

Tom O'Bedlam heard and straightened and flapped his arms. "The king's pardon!" he screamed.

Pleased by this added development to the day's events, the crowd pulled back. At last the women and Tom were able to make their way through. They were just in time to see Alf standing upon the cart in his beautiful white clothes with a noose about his neck. He raised his nosegay to breathe in the sweet smells of the earth just as the hangman drew the cart away. Alf, his face purpling, hung quite free by his neck.

And now the hangman was fixing the noose about Geoffrey's neck.

XX

"Cut him down, boys!" Jack shouted. "Storm the gallows!"

Someone leaped to do his bidding, but Alf, when they laid him on the ground, seemed lifeless. The hangman moved quickly toward Geoffrey, all the while keeping one eye on the rogues.

The two women screamed together. "Stop! Stop the hanging! The king has pardoned them!"

At this the hangman and the clergyman and the keeper of Newgate all looked up in surprise. Could it be some new trick? But no. Nance was waving her paper with the king's seal upon it. Red-faced, the authorities saw that the king did indeed mean to save the two, though it was apparently too late for one of them.

Lettice sprang to the cart to be near her husband while he struggled to lift the noose from about his neck with hands that had been deadened by shackles. As soon as he was freed, they fell into each other's arms for a long embrace. His body was warm and very solid, though somewhat wasted with all his trials. The hands that held her were raw from the shackles that had just been struck off. She felt as though she never wanted to take her arms from about him again.

The crowd cheered madly. They had never expected a show to equal this, though hangings were always theatrical events.

"Oh, darling," Lettice cried. "I hope we shall never have such adventures for the rest of our lives."

"I think I shall lock you safely in a room and never let you venture forth," he laughed. "Nor shall I."

Her face clouded. "Oh, if only the babe might be with us. How will we ever discover what has become of him?"

"We will, sweet," Geoffrey said. "But it is a pity we were too late for your friend, Alf. I've met few honest men who were better."

"Poor Alf!" Lettice cried, dropping down from the cart to the ground. "He did so want to look upon me as he died." She went to join Nance and Jack by the lifeless form while Geoffrey followed her. Lettice sank to her knees to press a kiss upon his lips.

There was a croak, a stirring, a fluttering of eyelids.

"Mistress Lettice." The hoarse words could barely be heard.

"By God, he's resurrected!" Jack cried.

"He's alive!" Lettice said with surprise.

The crowd pressed forward with this new development.

"Mistress Lettice," Alf managed to gasp out. "I've had my . . . hangin' in my white suit. . . ." He closed his eyes for a moment, then looked about at the citizens of London who were straining for a look at him. "What a great crowd, and all my friends. And the lady I love close by. I could die happy now, but it seems I shall live!"

They helped him to sit up while the crowd broke into murmurings that changed into a roaring cheer. "He's resurrected! He lives!" they screamed.

Jack and another man lifted the half-fainting Alf to their shoulders to carry off.

"No, Jack," Nance called. "The king has sent for us. We must go to the king himself."

" 'Twould be easier if he had sent some troops," Lettice grumbled. "My husband almost died. And how are we to get to Whitehall without any horses?"

"It seems, my sweet," Geoffrey said, placing an arm about her shoulder, "that we shall have to walk."

And walk they did, with the great crowd following them and cheering away. Few days at Tyburn had ever proved so entertaining. Shopkeepers on the way looked up with surprise and some fear of riot.

Footsore, the party arrived at Whitehall after dark with some of the crowd still behind them.

Smiling, James came out to greet them from the official buildings. "I cannot tell you how worried I have been," he said.

"Well, then, why did you not come with poor Nance and ask the king to send troops," Lettice said with some indignation.

"The king did not wish to appear to interfere unduly," he answered.

"His friends were forced to cut Alf down, and Geoffrey stood with the rope about his neck," she complained.

Geoffrey put his arm about his wife's shoulders to quiet her. "But it has ended well. Except that poor Alf can hardly stand nor speak."

In truth, Alf had not spoken a word since they had left Tyburn. But then Jack, great word spinner that he was, could talk enough for 20 others.

"And how can we go before the king dressed as we are?" Lettice demanded.

"He understands who and what you are and what you have suffered," James said with a smile on his dark and somewhat-horsy face.

"Does he really?" Lettice cried. "Can he understand our thoughts when Alf swung free at the end of a rope? Does he know what a wife thinks as she sees her husband with a rope about his neck?"

"Perhaps not," James admitted. "Still, he understood that his father suffered when he was killed. And the king barely escaped with his own life at the time. He, too, has suffered exile."

"I hadn't thought of that," she said, shamefaced.

"The king thinks of it often," James said. "That is why he rules with such care and seeks comfort in the arms of so many women."

"He was very kind to me this morning," Nance reminded them. "Though I was so crazed with worry I hardly knew which foot to pick up first to walk."

"And he has saved us," Lettice said. "So perhaps if you would allow us a little water to wash, we might, after all, go as we are before him."

"He is waiting for your story," James said.

"I think we must declare your brother an outlaw," the king judged when they were all before him.

"And so he is," Lettice said. "A worse rogue than any I have ever met."

"That will leave you heir," the monarch said to Geoffrey. "And I trust that you will prove a more loyal subject here than was the case in Virginia."

"You may have no doubts on that score, Your Majesty."

"And as for you, Mistress Finch." The king's eyes for a moment lost their look of cynicism and boredom. He gave a slight smile. "It seems that you have taken up strange ways—not to mention your dress and your companions."

"My breeches helped me to travel fast, sire," she said. "Else my husband would be hanged by now. And as for my companions, they have proved to be the most loyal of friends."

"So it seems," King Charles said. "And loyal, I trust, to their king."

"Oh, yes, sir," Jack and Nance said, dipping a knee.

"To be sure," Alf croaked.

The king's eyes glinted with amusement. Then his dark face turned serious. "But I fear that though they have escaped the hangman once, they may meet him again. Is that not so?"

Ashamed, the three rogues looked down upon the black-and-white checked floor.

"I thought as much," the king said. "In which case a fresh start in the colonies might be the answer for them."

"Oh, no!" Lettice cried, then flushed with confusion. "Your Majesty," she exclaimed, "I would not have them transported as felons nor bound as servants. We know well enough what suffering that can bring."

"Well then," the king replied. "Perhaps your husband, as compensation for his former rebellious ways, will pay their passage and give them something so they can set themselves up in a new life far from London and their old companions."

"If my parents will free some money to me," Geoffrey said.

"You are the heir," King Charles responded. "Let them make no mistake as to that. They have been too lenient with their elder son."

Geoffrey nodded his assent, but Lettice worried that the hard life in the colonies would prove too much for the peculiar skills of her new friends.

The twinkle was gone from Jack's eyes, and even his dark curls seem to settle gravely about his face. "I would like an honest life, sire. I worked hard as a boy. In the colonies I might marry Nance proper-like."

"But England will have lost a great storyteller," Lettice laughed.

"We shall survive this tragic loss through thoughts of the reformation of these rogues," the king said, "and hope they will speak of me to the poor men who rebelled against me in the colonies."

"We will, sire," Jack promised.

But Alf said nothing at all.

"You may go now." The king dismissed them with a nod. Turning to a liveried servant, he added, "See that they are refreshed. They have had, I understand, a difficult day."

James's servant lit the way through the dark London streets. The flickering torch cast wild shadows upon the legions of sleeping brick houses. Lettice leaned against her husband's shoulder only half listening as James and he talked quietly.

"I have never walked so many miles in a day," she said.

"We will have a quiet life from now on, I swear," Geoffrey said. "And live soberly like our friend James. You have been very good to us, James."

"You have provided a dash of excitement in my otherwise sober life," James laughed.

"Oh, if I only knew the babe was well," Lettice said. "Or if he is not alive, that he died without pain." The thought of her darling had taken much joy from her reunion with her husband.

"One more crime to lay at the door of Giles," Geoffrey said grimly. "But you are fortunate in your friends, Lettice. The rogues and vagabonds will search the countryside for the babe, and they will have a better chance than anyone of finding him."

"Once we have told your parents you are alive, I will go myself," Lettice vowed. Her eyes searched among the dark houses and narrow streets as though the babe might be hidden there. Suddenly she saw a glint that made her start.

"Geoffrey!" She grasped his arm. "Someone is following us."

The torch man swung about, raising his light high above

his head. The glow from his torch illuminated a familiar figure. Giles stepped forth. His hair was matted and dishieveled, and he had a growth of beard upon his usually clean-shaven face. In his hand he carried a drawn sword.

"I thought to see you hanged today," he said. "But I shall make sure that you are not free yet."

"Your sword, James!" Geoffrey cried, reaching toward his friend.

"You cannot," James answered, drawing his weapon. "You are too weakened from prison."

"Don't be a fool, James. You are no swordsman," Geoffrey insisted. When James hesitated, Geoffrey lunged forward to free the sword from his grasp. But it was true. His muscles responded slowly from the effects of his shackles. He swung about to meet his brother.

"Geoffrey," Lettice gasped in fear.

Giles, too, was somewhat weakened from the emotions of the day. Earlier he had drunk heavily, though his head was now quite clear. With his sword upraised, he ran toward his brother. A vicious backhand swing would have half severed Geoffrey's head, had he not blocked it. But Geoffrey was knocked off balance. He tripped and fell back upon the pavement. Before he could spring to his feet again, Giles was upon him. Lettice bit her lip to keep from screaming. Was she to lose him again so soon? But Geoffrey parried. Yet he seemed to be weakening, his movements slowing, until with a lucky thrust he struck Giles's sword hand. Giles started back with pain. His knuckles were oozing blood.

At last Geoffrey was able to spring from the cobbles and meet his brother face to face. Giles tossed his sword from his disabled right hand to his left so that he might fight on. It would be more equal now. And Giles's heart was more unprotected, since his arm would not angle across his body with his thrusts. He placed his right hand across his chest to present a less vulnerable target. Blood dripped down his shirt. Sensing his momentary advantage, Geoffrey gave him another cut upon the weakened right arm. But Giles lunged again, giving his brother a cut across the cheek, bloodying his face. Unable to bear more, Lettice screamed. And Geoffrey turned to glance back at her.

Giles saw his advantage. Running forward, he met Geoffrey head-on. Their swords locked, neither giving way. For a long moment their eyes met and each watched for the flicker that would announce the other's anticipated movement. Then Giles kicked out, tripping Geoffrey up. Again he fell. His body taut, Giles raised his sword. He aimed to split his brother's skull. Lettice screamed again.

Suddenly there was a swishing sound and a blaze of light as the servant threw the torch directly at Giles's face. As the torch guttered out harmlessly at Geoffrey's side, Giles fell forward with a cry of pain. He was impaled upon Geoffrey's sword.

"By God, I did not intend that," Geoffrey cried with shock. For a moment all was confusion, for they could not see. Then as a candle was lit in a nearby window and their eyes grew used to the absence of torchlight, they were able to see Giles moaning upon the ground and clutching the sword in his belly.

"Giles!" Geoffrey cried.

Blood-choked, Giles spoke no more. But a fresh torch revealed the dying eyes of a man who had always wanted to be first.

Geoffrey climbed down from a coach that James had borrowed for them. He stood looking up at the house for a moment before helping his wife down. Her face showed many emotions.

Finch's Fortune was not the largest of estates. Nor was the house of unusual size. But Lettice thought she would, if it were possible, happily spend the rest of her days here and never travel farther than the closest market town. All she needed was her husband—and her babe.

The house had been built shortly after the death of the good Queen Elizabeth. It had been modernized only after King Charles had regained his throne. It lay in a pleasant meadow by a riverbank, its brick exterior a ruddy spot among the fertile green. Pleasant arched doorways and many chimney pots promised warmth and hospitality within.

"Let us go inside and see what awaits us," Geoffrey said, grasping his wife's hand.

"They are in the marble dining room," a servant told them. But Geoffrey would not be announced.

His parents looked up as, hand in hand, the pair entered. Stamped leather covered the panels of the room. The

367

marble floor and chimney piece obviously gave the room its name. Geoffrey's parents were seated about a small table with turned legs. A strange woman was also seated there. She was Giles's wife.

"Geoffrey!" His mother sprang to her feet to embrace him. Her hands shook, and her voice quavered, revealing her frailty. "Is it truly you?"

"Is it Geoffrey, then?" Old Sir Giles querulously rubbed the white stubble upon his chin. "I thought it might be Giles." It was obvious that he was dazed and senile.

"Giles is no more, Mother," Geoffrey said. "The king declared him outlaw—and then we fought. I have buried him near London. His blood is on my hands."

"Oh, no, Geoffrey," Lettice objected, gathering her borrowed skirts about her. "He attacked you. The final wound was an accident. You cannot blame yourself."

His mother sat stonily, staring at them. "For a time I suspected that you were dead," she said, finally. "It was not given to me, it seems, to have two sons in health and happiness." Her aquiline features became even more drawn and pale, her lovely eyes sunk and dark.

A woman's harsh voice cut in. "He's dead?" Giles's wife cried. "Giles truly dead?" Then burying her face in her hands, she burst into forced and unnatural laughter.

"My dear Celia," Lady Finch said, patting the shoulder of her daughter-in-law's low-cut gown. "Do not grieve."

"Grieve?" Celia demanded. "Do you think I would grieve one hour for Giles's death? Ah, no, dear mother-in-law. I laugh with glee at the thought that I shall never look upon his face again, never know he goes from our cold bed to the embrace of that witch Isobel, never again will humiliate me. And I am free now, free to marry again and perhaps bear children if I am married to a man who does not waste his strength in adultery."

"Please, madame," Geoffrey said, thinking to save his mother some distress.

"Let her be, Geoffrey," Lady Finch said. "I always knew somehow that one of you would kill the other. And so I must resign myself to whatever God has willed. Perhaps this is why twins were given to me."

They remained silent for a moment while memories of much that was past swept the room. Then Geoffrey reached for Lettice's hand. "Mother . . . ," he began. "This is—"

"Mistress Clifford, now your wife," his mother finished as they looked at her in some astonishment. "But I believe I have a surprise for you." With her delicate white head, Lady Finch gestured imperiously to the serving man, who left his duties. He returned some moments later and threw wide the dining-room doors.

Molly stood there—and in her arms nestled the babe.

"Molly!" Lettice cried, near to fainting. "It cannot be!"

"You can thank Nurse Smith, mistress," Molly shrilled. She seemed more washed and brushed and tidy than usual. "Nurse Smith wept for two days when the child was taken from her. But then she traveled as well as she was able— her body being as frail as it be—all about the countryside, searching out all the old nurses and servants she knew, hoping one would have charge of little Geoffrey."

"And it seems that she was successful!" Lettice exclaimed. "Come, darling." She gathered the baby into her arms.

Her words wakened old Sir Giles from his stupor. He beamed a smile, revealing one or two missing teeth. "Well, Geoffrey. So you have got yourself a son! Well, well, my boy. Sit down. Sit down here beside me. And welcome home!"

Lettice rested, drowsy and warm in her husband's love, hid behind the bed curtains, smelling sweet lavender from the sheets. She drifted into pleasant sleep. Suddenly she was haunted by the image of Lady Isobel's sensuous mouth crying pain, while blood flowed from her throat.

Lettice awoke with a start, realizing that there was indeed something strange sliding about her throat. Turning with a jerk, she looked into Geoffrey's warm, brown eyes.

"I thought you would be pleased," he said.

Lettice raised a hand, fingers spread, to feel her neck. Then she smiled as she encountered the familiar feel of the Queen of Pamunkey's pearls, which she had given to Alf those many months before.

"Your rogue friends proved very good at seeking them out," he said. "I've been keeping them for you for some time. I wanted you to think they were gone forever."

"Oh, Geoffrey." Lettice leaned forward to press her lips on his.

But they were interrupted once more by a maid's knock on the door. "A letter, mistress," she announced as she stepped into the room. "And it's come from ever so far away." Then the neat little figure turned to build up the fire.

For a moment Lettice wished sadly that the little maid were Molly and could share this letter that she soon saw was from Virginia. Molly had gone back to Virginia some months ago, and Lettice missed her so.

"And how fare our friends in Virginny?" Geoffrey whispered close to her ear.

"Give me room, my love, and we shall see." Lettice propped herself on an elbow, then broke the seal and began to read eagerly.

"Dorothy says now she understands truly what has happened, and she wishes you to forgive her coldness," Lettice said, looking up.

"It is forgiven," Geoffrey answered with a smile.

"John makes an excellent overseer and should be free of bondage soon. Dorothy will grant them a small piece of land for their own."

"That should please them."

"And she says Molly is with child." Lettice lay the letter aside, a look of worry in her eyes. "Oh, dear, I do hope the child will have John's blond hair."

"I expect Robert will prove an indulgent godfather, whatever the case."

Lettice picked up the letter again. " 'Jack and Nance arrived last week and are proving better workers than I might have hoped.' " Then Lettice read silently for a while.

"Listen to this," she said. " 'You will not have heard of the peace. I journeyed alone, Charles being still not himself, to see it signed at Middle Plantation. It took place on May 29, the king's birthday and the day of his restoration. All the Indian kings and queens were there, many in savage costume, some in English dress. They declared their fealty to King Charles, and it was decreed that no Englishman shall settle nearer than three miles to any Indian town.

" 'There I met once again the Queen of Pamunkey, who

370

was given special honors and asked to be remembered to you.'

"Well," Lettice said, fingering her pearls. "All's well that ends well, it seems."

"Hmm," her husband replied as the maid silently closed the door behind her. "And now 'tis time to begin."

More Best-Selling Fiction from Pinnacle